A SENSE OF MISSION

Novels by Ann Gaylia O'Barr

ROMANCE. MYSTERY. INTERNATIONAL INTRIGUE.

* * *

Singing in Babylon

Quiet Deception

Searching for Home

Distant Thunder

A Sense of Mission

A SENSE OF MISSION

ANN GAYLIA O'BARR

Ann Gaylia O'Barr

OAKTARA

Waterford, Virginia

* * *

In appreciation of the teachers
who taught me to love books and to write stories
at Dan Mills Elementary School and Isaac Litton High School
in a great place to grow up:
the Inglewood neighborhood, Nashville, Tennessee.

A Sense of Mission

Published in the U.S. by:
OakTara Publishers, P.O. Box 8, Waterford, VA 20197
www.oaktara.com

Cover design by Yvonne Parks at www.pearcreative.ca
Cover images © thinkstockphotos.ca: Stack of Passports/Igor Poleschuk; Driftwood on Kalaloch Beach/Thomas Northcut; Romantic Style/Color of Time
Copyright © 2012 by Ann Gaylia O'Barr. All rights reserved.

"The opinions and characterizations in this book are those of the author, and do not necessarily represent official positions of the United States Government."

Scripture quotations are taken from the Revised Standard Version of the Bible, copyright © 1952 [2nd edition, 1971] by the Division of Christian Education of the National Council of the Churches of Christ in the United States of America. Used by permission. All rights reserved.

ISBN: 978-1-60290-331-9

A Sense of Mission is a work of fiction. References to real people, events, establishments, organizations, or locales are intended only to provide a sense of authenticity and are used fictitiously. All other characters, incidents, and dialogue are drawn from the author's imagination.

Printed in the U.S.A.

1

I fancy I still hear the call to prayer from the mosque beside the U.S. Embassy compound, though I'm a grown woman now. I remember when the haunting tones of the imam woke me one Thursday morning, the beginning of the Muslim weekend. I had turned nine years old several months before, in 1396 according to the Islamic calendar. We knew it as 1976, the year of our distant country's bicentennial.

The imam's voice wavered, then strengthened. I murmured a prayer to Jesus, as Mama suggested I do during each of the five calls to prayer each day. She said the Muslims' faithfulness to their prayers put us Christians to shame, but there wasn't any reason we couldn't pray to Jesus during those times.

I heard Mama and Daddy downstairs but not their words, just the hum of their voices. I dressed, wanting to finish before they knew I was awake. I slipped barefoot from my room down the carpeted steps and stopped in the hall to listen to them.

"I know, I know," Mama said. "We have to go back. But I hate Washington, D.C. It's so frantic."

I never wondered until later why my mother preferred living overseas to living in the States, why she seemed not to fit into American life, she who had grown up there, unlike me.

I smelled the vanilla from her French toast, and my stomach growled.

"We have to think about Kaitlin, too," Daddy said. "She hasn't lived in the States since she was a baby. She hardly knows her own country."

"You probably could have gotten the Damascus job."

"It's a good time to go back to the Department. Nobody's paying any attention to the Middle East right now. Too focused on China."

"The Middle East doesn't let anyone forget it for long."

A cup clinked on a saucer, and I imagined Daddy frowning at his coffee as he stirred it. "Maybe that's a good reason for leaving for a while."

A chair scraped, Mama's probably. "You know something, don't you?"

"Nothing I can give you details about. Only hit or miss intelligence about this shadowy group, small, but mouthing some pretty harsh rhetoric against westerners in general and Americans in particular. You know how these things sprout. Usually turns out to be nothing."

"Don't sugar-coat things for me, John. You never have."

Daddy probably held her hand and stared into her eyes, but after a minute, he said, "Any idea why Kaitlin hasn't joined us yet?"

I scooted into the breakfast nook and into my chair.

Daddy peered at me through his glasses. I think he knew I'd been listening.

"Kaitlin," Mama said, "will you please return to your room and run a brush through your hair? It looks like birds have been roosting in it."

Daddy called that one of her Alabama phrases.

"Why? It always just frizzes again," I said.

"Kaitlin."

I sighed and did as she said. My hair is still a dark fire color like hers, but her hair never frizzed. Her freckles didn't stand out like mine, either. Mostly they spread across her nose, where Daddy traced them sometimes with his finger.

They'd never discuss stuff about the people who hated Americans, now they knew I could hear. Sure enough, when I got back, Mama talked about the best places to live in Washington.

"Arlington has wonderful schools. And so much diversity. I really don't want to live in some way-out, stuffy suburb."

"Will it be close to a library?" I asked. The last time we were in the States on leave, Mama explained to me about American libraries. They had lots and lots of books—not like the little one at school—and people could check out whatever they wanted right then and go back and get more when they finished those.

"Arlington has a wonderful library system."

We always referred to the States as home, but I only remembered America from our short leave times. I couldn't wait to live there, with books and clean water and malls crammed with clothes and restaurants and toys. I couldn't understand why Mama always breathed a sigh of relief when we left.

"It'll be great not to wait for books to come in the pouch," I said. "We can buy peanut butter and chocolate chips whenever we want, can't we? And watch TV? And movies?"

Daddy brushed my hair with his hand. "Yes, Princess Kaitlin. All of that."

"Will we see the Angulos?" I still liked Teddy Angulo, though his family moved to Washington months before.

"Maybe."

"As soon as we're back," Mama said, "we need to invite Matilda to visit us. She's got to be lonely on that island without Ray."

I washed down French toast with orange juice so I could talk. "What island?"

"An island in Puget Sound, north of Seattle. Where she and Ray built the home where they planned to retire." She leaned back. "We were there once when you were little. Madrona Harbor, the place is called. It's lovely out there, but I'm not sure it's a good place for her all by herself."

Ray and Matilda served with us in Abu Dhabi. Daddy and Ray told stories about being together when they started their first class as Foreign Service officers with the State Department. I remembered when Ray died in Jordan the year before. Mama went to be with Matilda and help her take Ray's body back to the States. "I like Matilda. Maybe she could come live with us."

"She and Ray absolutely doted on you," Mama said. "You reminded them of their daughter."

I had a bite of toast on my fork, but I put it down. "She died, didn't she?"

"Before you were born. Of spinal meningitis. They were in the Congo and couldn't get her out in time."

I frowned. Children died sometimes. Even American children like me. "I could die, too, couldn't I?"

Mama and Daddy looked at each other, and Daddy pushed aside his plate and leaned on his arms over the table. "It's kind of scary the first time you think about that, isn't it?"

I nodded. "Is it okay to be scared? Even if I know all about Jesus and going to him in heaven? It's just that I don't want to go there right now."

"Of course it's all right. Part of growing up is admitting you're scared sometimes and going on anyway."

"You're not scared, are you?"

Daddy took off his glasses. He wore thick glasses almost all the time, and when he took them off, he looked like a boy. I could see why Mama loved him. "Even grownups are scared sometimes, Kaitlin. Every once in a while I wonder about bringing you and Mama to places like this. That perhaps it's not as safe as if I got a job back home and we all lived there."

"But you keep on with this job."

"Yes."

"Why?"

"Your mother and I have talked about this. People have to do what God calls them to do."

I finished my first slice of French toast, but not my questions. "So you do that even if you're scared? And God protects you?" It seemed to me that if you did what God wanted you to do, he had to protect you.

Daddy said, "Depends what you mean by protect. Being in the center of God's will is the safest place you can be for the inside part of you, the thing we call the soul. But Christians die physically like anybody else. And sometimes even are killed."

I traced powdered sugar with my fork. "I guess so."

"It's hard to understand sometimes. We'll talk more about it later if you want to. But the last of the French toast is going to waste if you don't eat it."

Mama got up and took her and Daddy's plates. "You need to finish soon, if we're going to make it out to the desert today for our picnic. We have some things to talk to you about."

Maybe they were going to let me have a kitten or a puppy when we got to the States. I stopped thinking about dying and the people who hated Americans.

* * *

Mama always woke us early for breakfast together during the work week, before we left the house, me to the American international school and my parents to the Embassy. Daddy worked in the political section, and she worked part-time in the consular section as kind of an assistant. She helped Americans who lived in the country where we were stationed, mostly businessmen and their families.

I needed time to clear the kitchen after breakfast. Mama was strict about making sure I did my chores. "I don't want you to be like a lot of Foreign Service children who think servants are their birthright, Kaitlin," she said more than once.

That first morning of the Muslim work week, Saturday, the phone rang before the alarm clock went off.

I got out of bed and went to the door, even though my parents wouldn't say anything really important over the telephone. I learned early that FSOs—that's our name for U.S. diplomats, short for Foreign Service officers —know things they can't talk about even with their families, only with other FSOs in secure sections of the Embassy.

"Got it," Daddy said. "But school's still on? Fine." The phone dinged when he put it down. "Emergency action meeting today," he told Mama.

"Think it's related to what we talked about the other day?"

"Probably."

Daddy didn't read the Arab language newspapers before breakfast. After we finished our oatmeal and dates, he cleared his throat and glanced at Mama before he turned to me. "Kaitlin, I think I'll walk you to catch the school bus today."

"Why, Daddy? I'm not some first grader."

"I wouldn't be surprised if some of the other parents are there, too."

He was right. Even Jeremy, a couple of years older than me, stood with his father.

Jeremy's dad, Mr. Hickman, headed the consular section where Mama worked. They were our good friends, and I liked Jeremy. Daddy asked if the consular section planned to send out a warden message.

Mr. Hickman nodded. "We've got one going through channels. Probably this afternoon." They didn't say what about, of course.

I held Daddy's hand then, even in front of the other kids. A warden message meant the American citizens living in the country where we were stationed needed to be warned about something.

When the bus came, our Embassy security officer drove his car in front of it, leading it, the first time he had done that.

Before I got on, I looked back at Daddy, and he smiled. I didn't understand why the smile made me sad, but I wished I could go back home and be with him and Mama.

I thought about pretending I felt sick. Mama would stay with me, and Daddy would come home for lunch.

Then Thérèse, my best friend, waved at me through the bus window. I felt better when I flopped beside her.

"Bonjour," she said.

"Bonjour. Comment va-tu?"

Thérèse's dad was the ambassador from Côte d'Ivoire. Thérèse spoke beautiful French, but only halting English, the language of the school. We practiced speaking the two languages to help each other. I took French while she took extra English.

Later in French class, I jerked up my head to examine the palm fronds outside the window. Did they sway? What made the cracking noise I thought I heard, like a slammed baseball in the distance?

Maybe I imagined the sound, but my body felt heavy, like it did before a sandstorm, before you see it but can feel it, the change in the air.

I turned back to my lesson.

Ave vous un chien? (Do you have a dog?)
Non, mais j'ai un chat. (No, but I have a cat.)

Pretty boring stuff. I scribbled the translations, then my mind took me off somewhere more exciting. A house in the States with lots of kids my age to play with. A cat for me. I moved my pencil once in a while so Madame Gautier wouldn't tell me to stop daydreaming and do my work. I even daydreamed when we had the drills, although I had to watch it. Sometimes Madame Gautier skipped around.

I jumped when the classroom door opened. The headmaster motioned for Madame Gautier to come out. Jeremy's dad stood with the headmaster. Mr. Hickman's tie hung loose, and he no longer wore his coat.

When they came back in, they stared at me.

I shivered, even before they took me into the hall and told me.

"No," I said, working to keep from trembling, because what they said must not be so. "Mama and Daddy are at work."

Mr. Hickman stooped level with me. "Kaitlin, I'm sorry. So sorry. Your father called. Something came up, he said. They'd be late coming in. They were there when the bomb—" He bit his lip before he continued. His face turned white, like the hottest coals in our desert fire. "When it happened."

I didn't cry, because crying would make it so.

Hussein, our driver, cried as he took us a roundabout way from school. The police studied our diplomatic plates and waved us through roadblocks. I tried to block out the wailing sirens.

Ave vous un chien?

Non, mais j'ai un chat.

When we get to the States, they'll give me a kitten.

To enter the Embassy grounds we had to pass our house on the outside edge.

Mr. Hickman pulled my face against his chest. "Kaitlin, please don't look at it. It will be worse if you do."

I did what he said and closed my eyes, but that didn't stop the smell of the explosion from burning my nose and souring my throat.

As we entered the Embassy grounds, my stomach heaved. Mr. Hickman asked Hussein to stop, then opened the door and stepped out with me. He stood with me as I threw up the oatmeal I'd eaten with my parents that morning. Wiping my face with his handkerchief, he folded it, and blotted his eyes with it. Back in the car, he took me on his lap and held me close all the way to the ambassador's house, where I stayed until Matilda came for me.

2

Nightmares still woke me, along with an awful sadness for something I couldn't name, but summer skipped along tolerably well, as Mama used to say. Then Matilda opened the letter. She spread it on the porch table and smoothed a page in the afternoon drowsiness. A woodpecker drummed on a dead tree, and the incoming tide shushed below the house.

"Oh, how wonderful," she said. "Ethan's coming to visit for a couple of weeks, he says, before he goes to university."

I stroked Oreo, purring on my lap, still a kitten but no longer the fat ball of fur Matilda had for me when we arrived in Madrona Harbor, back in the damp winter.

"Ethan?" The name scratched a memory that didn't come out all the way.

The days shortened now, with chilly mornings and evenings, and warned of fifth grade starting in a few weeks. An end to days racing around town with my best friend, Cindy, and digging up geoducks on the beach, and searching the library for the latest Nancy Drew book.

Best of all, Matilda waited for me whenever I came home. Just us. I didn't have to share her with anybody. Now some guy named Ethan threatened to upset everything in the last days of summer.

"Ethan's my nephew. My brother Joshua's child. You remember? Joshua and Eleanor were at the funeral."

Sure, the couple who sounded like Yankees, the way Mama said our ambassador at the Embassy talked. Joshua had been a Foreign Service officer like Daddy. He and Daddy and Ray entered the Foreign Service together, but now he worked for an American company in Hong Kong. He and Eleanor had flown in for the funeral, then left immediately afterward.

A Yankee accent flavored Matilda's words, too, but something softened them that I couldn't place.

She studied the letter, written in neatly formed words. "It'll be wonderful to see Ethan. He's always loved it here."

"Does he come very often?"

"Not so much now. He's older, made friends at that prep school Joshua put him in. Just before he and Eleanor went off to Thailand for Joshua to be ambassador." She frowned. "He resigned after that."

"Ethan used to come more?"

"Oh, yes, as a little boy on leave with Joshua and Eleanor. We tried to take leave at the same time. I guess you're too young to remember the last time you and your parents were here and Ethan came out, too, by himself." She stared at the water. "He was twelve, a little young to travel alone, I thought, but they raised him to be independent. Your parents and Ethan became close during that visit."

So even my parents had liked Ethan.

Over the next few days you'd have thought Matilda prepared for Jesus' second coming. While she cleaned and cooked, I spent a lot of time on the beach splashing rocks into Saratoga Passage below the house. That's the arm of Puget Sound that passes to the east of Simon Island.

In between splashes I stared at the old pier that jutted out, the one Matilda forbade me to climb on. So far I had obeyed.

I stepped toward it, then pulled back. I still acted uppity (one of Mama's words) and did things I knew my parents wouldn't like, though I no longer threw tantrums like in the first few weeks.

Suppose Matilda grew tired of me and sent me away to boarding school? I imagined Sarah Crewe in *The Little Princess* suffering in her attic room. After all, Matilda wasn't even kin to me. It wasn't fair Ethan had his mother and father and Matilda, too.

We drove in Matilda's old Cadillac to meet Ethan at SeaTac. I could have guessed who he was even if she hadn't run and grabbed him as soon as he stepped into the arrival area.

He looked a lot like his father but thinner and darker, like he'd been in the sun a lot. He stood taller than Joshua, who's pretty short. With his dark hair swept to the side, he reminded me of one of those cocky Bedouin Arabs I used to visit with Daddy. Unlike a Bedouin, he had eyes like I imagined Jesus' eyes, blue as the sky on a clear winter day, able to slice to your insides.

He grinned at Matilda and untangled himself but kept an arm around her shoulders for a minute. "I'm glad to see you, too, Matilda." He sounded stuck up, with that Yankee twang.

Matilda pulled me forward. "And this is Kaitlin. You remember her parents. Don't you think she looks like her mother?"

Ethan turned his gaze on me. "A little. Hello, Kaitlin." He didn't hug me or shake my hand. I might as well have been a smashed bug on the windshield.

When we drove up to the ferry, he took my place in the passenger seat next to Matilda. I sat in the back and listened to the two of them talk about people I didn't know. Ethan kept talking about somebody named Chopra.

After a while I played my pretend game, where I wrote the story different from the way it turned out. Mama and Daddy weren't here because the State Department assigned them somewhere they couldn't take me, but pretty soon they would come for me.

When we drove on the ferry and climbed the stairs to the passenger cabin, I had to leave off pretending, and I ached worse than ever.

Usually the ferry at night changes to a magical place. The engines chug, and the few passengers mostly whisper if they talk at all. You can't tell the black water from the islands. Tonight, though, I felt as lonely as the dark that tried to erase those tiny dots of light on the shore.

* * *

I spread homemade zucchini muffins with butter and local elderberry jam while Matilda scurried back and forth between the kitchen and the dining room for more breakfast dishes. I could've been invisible for all the attention she paid to me.

"I want you to eat," she said to Ethan. "You're even thinner than when I saw you last. Haven't you been eating properly?"

"Probably the hiking trips with some of the guys. Up in the Adirondacks. Couple of sailing trips off Maine, too. Chopra and I took his family on a big tour of Washington after they came over to see him graduate. I'm making the house there my headquarters now. The folks have never rented it out."

"I'm still not sure your father did right. He loved the Foreign Service, even if—"

Ethan leaned forward. "These eggs are great. I'll have another helping, please."

How come he didn't want to talk about Joshua?

Matilda heaped more scrambled eggs on his plate. "I got a letter from them. Said they had a good time at the graduation exercises, even if they were only over a few days from Hong Kong. I was disappointed they didn't have time to come out here."

"We did a short tour of the Berkshires before they went back. Checked on the old ancestral monstrosity. The renters seem to be taking care of it. I think they'd like to buy it." He shoveled in a mouthful of eggs, then sat back. "This place is so great to unwind in. I promise not to completely let myself go to seed, but if it's okay with you, Matilda, I don't think I'll even shave for a few days. Wear sloppy clothes and beach walk and read."

"Ethan, the place is yours. Do what you like." She turned to me. "If you're through, Kaitlin dear, why don't you begin clearing the kitchen while I gather a load of laundry?"

I guessed she wouldn't dare think of asking her precious nephew to help.

"I want to read," I said.

Ethan shifted his heaven-eyed gaze to me, and I changed my mind. "I'll help a little."

I scooted out and took my plate to the kitchen. I didn't want to go back where Ethan sat, so I rinsed some of the dirty pans and loaded them in the dishwasher.

After a while he came in with a stack of dishes and scraped them. "Well, Squirt, what are you doing today?"

"My name is Kaitlin, thank you, and I'm not a squirt. I'm almost ten."

I hated the half grin on his lips, the way grownups do when they're not taking you seriously.

"Okay, Miss Kaitlin, want to take a walk?"

"No, I'd rather read." I emphasized the "no" so he'd understand I didn't want anything to do with him.

He shrugged. "Suit yourself." He swept out like he owned the place.

I'd have run over to Cindy's, but she was camping in Idaho with her parents for a couple of days, so I brought my new Nancy Drew book to the porch to read on the glider.

Ethan sprawled there ahead of me, reading his own book. That wasn't the worst thing, though.

Oreo burrowed into Ethan's side, and Ethan stroked her neck the way she especially liked. You'd hardly know I fed and watered her. Oreo barely acknowledged me. She simply yawned, stretched, and snuggled closer to Ethan. The traitor.

Ethan looked up from turning a page. "Nice cat you've got here. I always wanted a dog or a cat, but the parents nixed it, said it was too much trouble with our traveling and moving so much." He went back to reading but kept petting Oreo, who sandpapered the air with her purring.

I stalked back into the living room to read. Honestly, if I weren't a Christian, I would have hated him for sure.

The next morning after breakfast, I raced out early to the glider. A few minutes later Ethan plopped beside me, sending it swaying so that I lost my place in the book. "Come on, Squirt. I'm glad you like to read, but you don't want to spend all your life that way."

"I told you, I'm not a squirt. I want to read."

"Okay, Mademoiselle Kaitlin, do me the honor, *si'l vous plait*, of accompanying me to the shores of our beloved Saratoga Passage."

I didn't smile. That would have been giving in too much, but I agreed to go with him.

After we hiked down the cliff path, we passed the old pier extending into the water, and I started to climb on it. Ethan caught my arm.

"Too rotten. Leave it alone."

"Is not. I want to climb out."

"I said 'no,' Kaitlin."

"Big deal." But I left the pier.

Then Ethan stopped, seeming to forget me as he studied a blue heron standing motionless a ways out in the water. On the Island we call them shikepokes. They're one of God's beautiful creatures, tall and graceful, as long as they stay silent, because they squawk.

I crept back to the pier. A minute after I crawled out on it, a shuddering groaned through it. I glanced back at Ethan turning from the shikepoke and clawed at a rope that twisted from one of the piers, but it broke. I tumbled, screaming, into the water as the wooden planks splintered into Saratoga Passage. Water poured into my mouth, nose, and lungs, and the cold filled every pore of my skin. I flailed with all my strength but didn't know how to swim.

Then Ethan's strong arms clutched and dragged me onto the barnacled-rock shore. The roughness digging into my knees told me I wasn't going to join my parents after all. For the first time since they died, I knew I wanted to live. Ethan stood me up and wrapped his sweatshirt around me like a strait jacket.

I coughed and gagged. Despite the cold, heat warmed my face, and I imagined my hair stood out the way a red feather duster might.

Ethan's first words peppered like blown grit. "I told you not to go out there, you pea-brained little dunce. What's wrong with you? You could have drowned." He measured out the words with that Yankee hardness, low and awful.

"I'm not pea-brained. Leave me alone."

"I will not leave you alone. You're nothing but a selfish brat." He grabbed my shoulder and hustled me toward the path that led up the cliff to the house.

"I'm not a brat." I swiveled within his hold and swung my leg to kick him, but his arms, lean and hard, held me away from him like a puppet master directing a marionette. My anger swelled with my helplessness. "I hate you."

"That's obvious."

Nobody had ever talked to me the way he did. He might as well have slapped me. I longed to run to my parents, wanted to hear my mother's soft words or feel my father's hug, but they were gone and never coming back. My legs gave way, and I crumpled to the path, leaving Ethan's shirt hanging in his hands.

The awfulness within me burst out like lava. Some hard scab that plugged my feelings softened, and my sadness, let loose, flowed out with my tears. I couldn't stop it.

Ethan scooped me onto his shoulder, covering me with the sweatshirt against the cold. "I'm sorry, Kaitlin. You didn't deserve that. I'm the pea-brained one. Hang on, and we'll go up."

I held on to his neck and felt his arms tighten around me as I sobbed. They were not the arms of my parents, but they comforted me.

"Ethan, what's wrong?" I turned my head and through my tears saw Matilda clomp down the stairs. I guess she thought I was dying, her second daughter to lose.

"She's okay," Ethan said. "Just fell into the drink. Can you get some dry clothes on her? I need to change, too."

I clung to him. He held my hands for a moment before prying them from his neck. "Kaitlin, it's all right. Go get some dry clothes. Then we'll talk if you want to. All right?"

I gasped through sobs. "Promise?"

"I promise."

His smile lightened me, and I climbed the stairs, my squishy clothes hanging on me as they trailed water.

Matilda soaked me in a tub of warm water until my teeth quit chattering and my tears no longer mingled with the bath.

After I dressed, I went into the kitchen where she stirred milk in a pan. "I'm sorry I climbed on the pier. You won't send me away, will you?"

She put her arms around me. "Kaitlin, what ideas you have. Maybe it's from reading so much. Of course I won't send you away. Never. Just promise me you'll do what I say from now on. All right?"

"I promise."

"We'll forget about this. Now, do you want lemonade or hot chocolate?"

"Hot chocolate, please."

Cradling the chocolate, I joined Ethan, who leaned over the porch table with his lemonade.

I sat for a while and sipped the hot chocolate, letting the liquid warm my hands through the cup. It warmed my insides after it went down. The cedars showered wood smells into the sunshine, and a wave rippled through the Passage below before Ethan spoke. "Kaitlin, I know what happened to your parents hurt you terribly."

Talking about my parents didn't bother him, because he looked right at me. I hadn't talked much about them with anybody except Matilda. Most everybody else averted their eyes whenever they were mentioned.

"You need to remember how much they loved you. They'd want you to go on with your life and make them proud of you."

I took another sip and thought about what he said. "I'd like to—to amount to something, like Mama used to say, but sometimes I hate school. It's boring, and the kids are so slow, and some of them think I'm weird. Even the teachers can't pronounce the places I tell them I've been. I'm not even sure they believe me." I stared at my cup. "It's such a stupid time."

"Yes," Ethan said, "some periods in life are like that. Stupid times. You use those times to think and prepare and plan for when you can do something to make life less stupid."

"You think it'll get less stupid some day?"

"It's what your father told me once, sitting right here on this porch with me."

"Daddy?"

Ethan scooted his glass around the table. "About the time I turned twelve my family lived a year in Washington for Dad's assignment at the Department, and I did something that angered him. He decided I needed toughening up. I was, he said, spoiled, and I needed to have it shaken out of me."

I imagined Ethan as a smart-aleck twelve-year-old, which wasn't hard. "So what'd he do?"

"He said he was yanking me out of my easy life and sending me to prep school in New England the next fall. Dad had been appointed to the Embassy in Bangkok for his next assignment. I really wanted to go, learn to speak Thai, and all that. He knew how much I looked forward to it."

My parents would never have been that mean to me. "You couldn't talk him out of it?"

He shook his head. "Even Mother couldn't change his mind. They've got something beautiful between them, I'll say that, and he'll jump through hoops for her. Not that time. I did talk him into letting me come out here by train that summer while Ray and Matilda were taking a month's leave."

"You didn't fly out?"

He shook his head. "When we traveled in Europe, I got used to trains. They give you a place to read and think. I felt miserable seeing the time ahead—years of it, I figured. Dad gave me to understand that the school he'd chosen wasn't the coddling type."

I called up my memory of Joshua from the funeral. Probably he'd be a strict father, not like mine. What had Ethan done to set him off? I didn't ask because I didn't want to embarrass him. After all, we were barely friends.

"At Union Station in Washington, D.C., waiting for the train, I picked up C.S. Lewis' autobiography, *Surprised by Joy*, and started reading it. Lewis' father also sent him off to school, and he was miserable. I could sure identify."

"We read the Narnia books," I said. "Mama, Daddy, and me. We read them weekends on picnics, our reading time."

His mouth tightened. Maybe Ethan's parents didn't have times like that with him.

"When I got to Chicago, I bought a couple more books by Lewis. I read them on the way to Seattle, all across the plains and the Rockies and the Cascades, drinking in that magnificent scenery and thinking about what I read. Away from everything. Finding out about myself and God and what my life was about."

I breathed in the quietness and waited. I felt like I'd just gotten over the flu. Weak but no longer aching.

"They were all on leave at the house together when I got here. Your parents and Ray and Matilda."

"Where was I?"

"Here, of course. You were two or three. Running around being spoiled rotten by four adults who thought you were the cutest thing in creation. Me, I thought you were a nuisance. Maybe I was jealous. Here you had this soft life with people who loved you while I looked forward to prep school boot camp. I wanted your father for my own. I fell in love with your mother, too, and that soft accent."

I studied the leftover foam in my hot chocolate cup and tried to imagine them, wishing I could remember the time, but I couldn't.

"Your father helped me make that leap of faith in God. 'It's a risk,' he told me, sitting with me on that porch step."

I shivered, a good shiver, almost seeing Daddy.

"We take the risk of believing or not believing. Staying on the fence isn't an option. Not deciding is not believing. I knew all about risk, of course. My father took risks—yours did, too— every time they sent in a cable advising Washington about a foreign policy. Your father drew me in with his talk of risk and challenge. So I made the leap. Right then. And it gave me a reason for going on."

If I squinted my eyes, I could almost keep the image. "Once Daddy told me we had to step out in faith sometimes. Do what we believed was right and act."

Ethan turned a sweet look on me, one I hadn't noticed before, or maybe he didn't show it much. "I'm glad you had those years with him and your mother. They've left something behind in both of us. You'd never know it, I guess, but their deaths shook me up." His face took on hardness. "I'd have come to the funeral, but I was in the middle of senior midterms. Dad told me I had to stay at school." He shifted. "Sorry I've been so hard on you."

"Oh, that's okay. I haven't acted all that great, either."

In a way, he'd lost his parents, too, when he went off to school, and I felt sorry for him. "Was your school really bad? Like in *Tom Brown's Schooldays?*"

He laughed. "No, Squirt. Nothing like that. Just strict. They put me with a boy named Chopra, from India, a Christian, would you believe, but lots more mature than me. He was scared, though, like me, about coming to the school. I had lived in India a couple of years while Dad served as consul general in Madras. Chopra couldn't believe the guy he roomed with actually knew about his country, had even lived there."

"Are you still friends?"

"Of course. He's off to college in Indiana. Purdue. I'm going to miss him." He looked down at his glass. "You know, I only met your father that once, but sometimes I try to be like him. He handled a political job like Dad, but—well, you could get close to him."

Not like Joshua, I guessed.

I hated that Ethan had to leave so soon.

3

Ethan only stayed a couple of weeks, but after that time, I could forget my parents for long stretches and not ache when I thought of them.

He said we should call each other cousins. "After all, Matilda's my aunt, and she treats you like her daughter."

I thought about that. I only had one mother, and Matilda never could quite take her place, but she loved me as though she were my mother.

"All right," I said.

We talked a lot. I could share with him in ways I couldn't with Matilda, even though I loved her.

We all went to church on Sunday. Until I came to the Island, I'd only been in a church a few times when we visited the States on leave. The places where we lived overseas didn't have many churches. Small groups of Christians, only grownups, mostly westerners and Filipinos, met in somebody's house, and they had to be careful not to offend the local citizens.

Mama and Daddy taught me about Jesus and told me Bible stories. They liked it when I asked questions.

On the Island, we had church school. The teacher never said we couldn't ask questions, but I was the only one who did.

"How come God didn't stop Herod from killing John the Baptist when John did what God wanted and told everybody the Messiah was coming?" I asked that morning during the lesson.

Mrs. Frelick said, "We can't always know God's reasons for things. His ways aren't our ways."

I smiled like she had answered my question, because I didn't want to embarrass her. I guessed I'd have to live with my questions for a while.

I sat between Ethan and Matilda during the service. After coming to the Island, I learned about sermons. I liked the singing better than the sermons and wished we could sing the whole service. Usually I daydreamed, once Brother Gunderson got going after the Bible passage.

I didn't this time.

He read some verses about forgiving your enemies. I tried to think about the roast beef we were having for Sunday dinner, but daydreaming didn't work like it usually did.

"You have heard that it was said, 'You shall love your neighbor and hate your enemy. But I say to you, Love your enemies and pray for those who persecute you…'"

The roast beef would smell like the roasting spices and herbs Matilda used, things like allspice and nutmeg, but now I only smelled the furniture wax on the hard pews.

"Just in case you didn't get that, let me read a passage from Romans. 'If your enemy is hungry, feed him; if he is thirsty, give him drink; for by so doing you will heap burning coals upon his head. Do not be overcome by evil, but overcome evil with good.'"

I shifted to watch the tourists going by outside the window, but that didn't help, either.

"Brothers and sisters, I'm telling you, if you nourish hatred in your heart even toward somebody who hates you, you are sinning. You are not following Jesus."

After we got home and settled for dinner, the roast beef didn't taste nearly as good as I expected. Nothing did.

"You feel okay, Kaitlin?" Matilda asked.

"Sure, fine."

"Why aren't you eating more?"

"I guess the pancakes at breakfast filled me up."

Ethan ate enough to make up for what I didn't.

Afterward, we wandered onto the porch. Ethan and I sat on the steps, Matilda on the glider. The Passage lapped beneath the bank, and the breeze from the north blew the heat out of the summer afternoon. Oreo divided time between Ethan and me until she wandered off into the woods.

Did Ethan question things like I did? I glanced at him once or twice, trying to frame my words, but I couldn't get them right in my mind.

He turned to me like he felt me watching him. "What's with you, Squirt? You squirmed in church like the seat was hot, you ate almost nothing of the great meal Matilda cooked, and you've been about to say something for the past half hour but not gotten it out. What gives?"

I blurted out, "I don't want to love my enemies. I don't want to stop hating the people who—you know." I got up and plopped by Matilda. Before I cried, I wanted her next to me. "I try not to, but sometimes I can't help wanting to know what Mama and Daddy thought when—"

I leaned against Matilda, and she hugged and rocked me while I sobbed.

"I know it hurts," she said. "But crying's normal. It bothered me all those months you never cried."

I guess I made up for lost time. My tears soaked her dress, but she didn't seem to mind. "Go on, darling. You have to."

I had bottled up my questions, but now they spewed out like a soda when you shook it. "I wonder, did they hug each other? When the bomb—" I swallowed. "When they knew. Or did they have time? Did they think of me? And—" After a lot of tears, I said, "And did they hurt much? Were they awfully scared?"

The glider shifted. Ethan surprised me when he pushed in on the other side of me.

I turned front ways between them and swiped my face. Ethan dug in his pocket and gave me a handkerchief. "Hasn't been used, I'm pretty sure."

"How can I forgive them after what they did to Mama and Daddy? Mama and Daddy weren't hurting them at all." I wiped more tears with Ethan's handkerchief. "It's not right, you know. How come God didn't protect them?"

"I don't know the answer," Ethan said, "but God didn't stop people from killing his own son, did he? Because he had a greater purpose in mind. And Jesus forgave those who killed him before he died."

I twisted the handkerchief. "Do you think my parents forgave the people who did this to them before they died?"

"I doubt they had time. I think they'd depend on you to forgive for them. Your father spent his life trying to reconcile people—bring them together, work for better relationships between our country and others."

"I don't want to forgive them. I'm not sure I can."

"Kaitlin, hate won't help. Hate only causes people to keep doing bad things to each other. The way to get back is to forgive and keep living the way your parents did. To carry out what they did."

"It's not fair, though. Horrible people do all this stuff and get forgiven."

"I didn't say we shouldn't stop them from doing things like this or not call them to account for what they've done. But if Jesus forgave, we're supposed to forgive, too."

"It's awful hard."

"It's the most natural thing in the world to hate people who do bad things to you. Most people hate those who do bad things to them. Christians—well, Christians are called to be different."

The glider moved when he shifted. "That's what Chopra said to me once when I had a lot of trouble with anger and hate. He was a Christian in India, you know, where Christians are a minority. He said it might be easier for him to understand he had to be different, but that all Christians should understand it."

"Meaning we have to forgive?"

A flicker lit his eyes. "We have to aim in that direction."

"It sure isn't the easiest thing in the world."

"No, it's not easy. We get all hung up sometimes about what we do or don't do, but I think things like forgiveness are harder than simply not doing certain things. Forgiveness, love, those things—they're the ones that make us different. Or should."

The wet on my face had crusted. I gave him back his handkerchief. "I'll think about it."

* * *

The day before Matilda and I drove Ethan to SeaTac to catch his plane, he and I hiked at Double View. Double View overlooks Useless Bay, so called because at very low tides, it completely empties into mud flats. Sand and driftwood and barnacled rocks cover the beach that you can walk except at the highest tides. Going away from a row of beach houses, you view the Kitsap Peninsula and the Olympics, and hiking back, you see the Cascades. On a sunny day the loveliness catches my breath.

We strolled a long time, jumping over rocks and logs, going past the cleft that divides the bluffs, and I found a sand dollar. After ambling back, we rested on a log.

"It's awful, your leaving," I said, "and I've got to start school in a week, too. Double awful."

"Is school such a pain?"

"Everybody there is like white flour bread."

"I'm sorry?"

"Mama used to make all kinds of bread. She told me once that the bread came out like people, all in different colors. Rye, white, whole wheat—whatever. Like people come in different colors and make life more interesting. But here everybody is white flour."

"That's because so many of them have Scandinavian or Dutch ancestors."

"I know. It's not bad. Cindy's a Swensen. But everybody's the same, not like it used to be." I traced a pattern with a stick. "Thérèse was my best friend at the other school. Her skin reminded me of dark chocolate." I finished tracing a star.

"You and Cindy are in the same grade, aren't you?"

"Sure, and Cindy's fine. She likes to read, like me, but Arla's in there, too."

"Who's Arla?"

"A first-class weirdo. She gets together with her jerky pals and makes fun of me. She calls me 'Dabby Kaitlin from Abby Dabby.'"

"Abby Dabby?"

I sighed. "Matilda gave the principal copies of my school records when she enrolled me. The principal got excited at the places where I'd gone to school, including Abu Dhabi, where I went to kindergarten. Then she had to go and tell the class when she introduced me about where I'd lived. She pronounced them all wrong, of course, and Arla thought it was so funny." I tossed away the stick. "We didn't have to worry about things like that in my other schools. Just about everybody had a funny name and came from a funny place."

"You ever think maybe your differentness is a gift from God?"

"I would never wish my differentness on my worst enemy. Except maybe Arla."

"Look, a lot of Americans don't know anything about the rest of the world. I bet half of them couldn't find Canada on a map. They're all wrapped up in the latest celebrity craze. But you and I, we're kind of a bridge. We can let God use us to call them to something deeper. Chopra did that for me."

"Me? Change somebody like Arla?"

"You're already changing Cindy aren't you? She talked to me when she came over the other day about looking up in an atlas all the places you told her you'd lived."

* * *

That night at supper, Ethan's last night, we had fresh salmon, which he likes a lot. I wasn't a bit jealous of the attention Matilda paid him.

"I can't believe your father is letting you go to Georgetown and not Yale. There's probably been a Coverwood at Yale every generation since it began."

"Took some doing. Dad got into one of his quiet rages when I said I wasn't going there. I would have knuckled under before. Not this time. Figured I could drop out and get a job flipping hamburgers if he wouldn't let me go."

"Ethan, I can't believe you'd actually consider that. You know your father loves you even if he's—a bit hard on you at times."

Ethan grinned but not a real grin. "He hides it well."

I put down my glass of milk. "How'd you get him to let you go to Georgetown? And where's Georgetown anyway?"

Now he did smile. "Georgetown University, Miss Kaitlin, is in Washington, the other Washington, our capital. Which we shall call D.C. to differentiate it from Washington State. Chopra came to my rescue as he so often has. He pointed out that Dad's a diplomat and values negotiation. So, Chopra said, why not negotiate with him, instead of fighting him?"

"I like that way much better," Matilda murmured.

"I marshaled my arguments like negotiating a peace deal between the United States and the Soviet Union. One, Georgetown's in the capital, close to the State Department I hope will employ me someday. Two, lots of retired Foreign Service officers teach on the faculty of the international affairs school there and have experience doing what I want to do. Three, several are Dad's friends, with lots of hands-on expertise. He's worked with some of them."

"And you won?" I said.

"After a bit of hard going back and forth. During which, you'll be glad to know, Matilda, I did not once lose my temper or show disrespect to my esteemed parent. Actually, it was kind of fun."

"You're going to be a Foreign Service officer?" I asked.

"Congratulations for figuring it out. Yes, Squirt, an FSO, provided I pass the exams for it."

I barely tasted the peach cobbler Matilda had baked.

An idea cleared my sadness like a dry cold front from the north cleared a damp south wind. If I had to forgive the people who killed my parents, I'd make up for their dying in another way. I'd finish what they couldn't, like Ethan had talked about. "I'm going to be a Foreign Service officer, too. I'll serve in the Middle East, like Daddy did."

Matilda drew in her breath. "Kaitlin, why don't you do a little breaking with tradition and stay home?"

I shook my head. "I want to do what Daddy did. I want to finish for him."

Ethan tilted his head toward me. "So you've decided, just like that?"

"You want to be an FSO. Why can't I? You think because I'm a girl I can't decide to be one like you? Well, I can. See if I don't."

"I never said you couldn't. Just keep your options open, that's all."

* * *

On the beach, a high tide can maroon you or send you scrambling up steep banks if you don't leave when it comes in. You have to obey it, like you have to do a lot of things you don't want, like we had to take Ethan to the airport.

An old feeling tugged and came alive in me again when we entered the

SeaTac terminal: airports, customs, passports, and new foreign places to explore. When would I ever travel again?

Ethan grinned at me before he turned to go through the gate. "Come on, Squirt. If you're going to be a Foreign Service officer, you have to learn to tell people good-bye."

"When are you coming back?"

"Not for a while. I'll be on the east coast getting used to the college grind. When I have vacations, I'll probably visit the parents in Hong Kong. I want to watch what's going on in that part of the world, with China opening up like it is." He put his hand on my shoulder. "I'll write you, though, okay?"

"Promise?"

"I promise."

* * *

I lay that night on my back, head resting on my clasped hands, listening to night sounds. An owl hooted. Oreo hopped from my bed to prowl the house. Evergreens and alders creaked in the breeze from the Passage.

Why was I not sad, with Ethan's leaving? Why, instead, a pulse of anticipation?

From the vantage point of decades, I now know that a teenager's awkward compassion imparted hope to a grieving child and with hope the first touch of healing.

Georgetown. I'd go to Georgetown like him. I'd take the Foreign Service exams and pass.

I waited only for Ethan to write. He gave me his promise, didn't he?

4

Hey, Squirt: How do you like fifth grade? How's Cindy doing?

And how's my cat, Oreo? Just kidding. I know Oreo is your cat. Thanks for sharing her with me.

Someday I hope Matilda will bring you to the other Washington, the D.C. one. I can show you around. Dad still has a lot of friends at the State Department, and I can probably get you in to see the historical stuff on the upper floors. Sometimes one of his friends is good enough to take me out to eat and tell me what's going on at the Department now. I miss the old life. Do you miss it, too, or have you become a confirmed Islander?

Georgetown is terrific. So different from prep school. I love my classes, and I'm making a lot of friends. We're already planning for the Foreign Service exam. Study hard so you'll be ready, too, when your time comes.

Thanks for the invite over the holidays, but I'm planning to go to Indiana and spend the time with Chopra.

Ethan

* * *

Dear Ethan:

The Swensens invited Matilda and me over for Christmas Day. I got lots of presents from Matilda—books, clothes, etc. Thanks for the new Nancy Drew book. I gave Matilda a necklace I got when Cindy's parents took us over to the mainland to shop.

Billy Marshall is in my class and acts like he might like me a little. He's cute and has the neatest curly blond hair.

I like the Island better now. I'm making more friends (except for Arla, who's still a major pain), but Cindy and I are best friends. I still don't quite fit in, though. I have to be careful about what I say or it sounds weird.

I know you said keep my options open, but I've decided. I want to be in the Foreign Service, for sure. I want to be a political officer like Daddy.

I'm studying hard. On my last report card, I made all A's.
Love, Kaitlin

* * *

Dear Kaitlin,

Sorry your elementary school doesn't teach languages. Not to worry. I'll send you some Arabic tapes to help you keep the Arabic you learned when you were growing up in the Middle East. I'll send you some books so you can begin reading it, too. Once you pass the exams and are accepted into the Foreign Service, you'll be on language probation until you qualify with a foreign language. You have to pass both speaking and reading tests, so you need to study for both if you're really serious about this thing.

I'm going out to Hong Kong for the summer, but plan to spend some time in Europe coming and going, meeting one of my friends from Georgetown.

I'll get the tapes and books to you before I go.
Ethan

* * *

Dear Ethan,

It's summer here, and you're traveling, so I don't know when you'll get this.

Matilda takes me to the mainland for swimming lessons. Don't worry, I'm not going to climb on any rotten piers, but in case the ferry should sink or something, I'll be able to swim.

Thanks for the tapes and books. I'm practicing speaking and listening to the Arabic. Matilda laughs at me and says God didn't mean for us to make some of those sounds.

I don't practice Arabic in front of anyone else, not even Cindy. It would make me seem really weird, and I'm already different enough.

I think I'm getting a crush on Ned Sutherland. His family just moved here, and they joined the church. We'll be in sixth grade together.

Oh, yes, Matilda found somebody who cuts naturally curly hair like mine. It still frizzes, but it doesn't matter as much because it's shorter.

Love, Kaitlin
P.S. Oreo had KITTENS!!!!

I rubbed the backs of the tiny creatures. Oreo wasn't just my pet anymore. She was a mother and brooded over her offspring, twitching her tail now and then, as she lay on a clean towel next to the fireplace. Her kittens mewed and stumbled and suckled her. She allowed us to lift them out of the box we provided for her and hold them.

A baby. Something about a baby.

The thought vanished like an object you think you see at the corner of your eye but isn't there when you turn toward it.

Matilda picked up one of the kittens and put it on her lap. It poked around before settling down. Mothers. Kittens. Children. Matilda had been a mother once. I glanced at the picture of the little girl with the tiny doll dishes next to the picture of Ray.

I had never talked with her about it, but I guess when you get to know people, you don't tiptoe around the bad things. "Do you miss your little girl a lot? And Ray? Like I miss Mama and Daddy?"

I had worried that I shouldn't remind Matilda about her daughter, but she didn't seem to mind my questions. Maybe she wanted somebody to talk to about her, like I did sometimes about my parents.

She stroked the kitten. "When Laura died, it was like our world ended. But of course it hadn't. I still had Ray to love and help him move beyond our loss. Then Ray died. We'd planned our home here—but now it wasn't going to be that way. Maybe, I thought, I'll just wait here to die."

I shivered, feeling her loss the way I had felt the loss of Mama and Daddy. "But it wasn't over."

"After I grieved a while and cried a lot, I began to see people who needed me. Older people. People who'd had strokes and couldn't get out. Younger women, even, who needed somebody to talk to."

"Then I came."

Matilda nodded. "As soon as I stepped out, you came. Like God had prepared me for this new calling. One I thought I've never have again, but—well, God surprises you sometimes. Ray used to say that. He started out as a teacher and ended up in the Foreign Service."

"How did you and Ray meet?"

"We met when he was in A-100 with Joshua. You know about A-100, don't you? The course for beginning Foreign Service officers? Joshua and Ray and your parents were all in it together. Joshua introduced me to Ray when my parents and I came down to visit Joshua."

"My mother was in A-100, too?"

"Certainly. She served a tour as an FSO before she married your father."

"I didn't know that. I thought she always worked part-time in the Embassy wherever we were just to have something to do."

Matilda put down the kitten, who wobbled toward Oreo and was rewarded by Oreo's licking tongue. "She was trained along with your father and Ray and Joshua."

I had to get used to this. Mama wasn't only Mama. What else didn't I know about her? I dredged bits from my nine years with her.

Servants. We didn't have a live-in servant like a lot of Foreign Service families in developing countries, where we could easily have afforded one. Mama didn't like having servants. Maria, the young woman from the Philippines who helped us a few hours a week, was Mama's friend, not a servant. I was polite to her like I was taught to be to all adults.

But, growing up, Mama had servants. How did I know that? How did I know my mother's upbringing was genteel Southern? And where was her family? How did she travel from such a childhood to a Foreign Service career in the 1960s, when U.S. diplomats included few Southerners and fewer women? Had she gone through some kind of hippie stage? A flower child? Why didn't she look forward to living in the States? Did she feel different, like me? An outsider?

"We have something to tell you."

I reached for one of Oreo's kittens and delighted in its trusting softness while I shook my head to blot out the sadness that threatened. I must not go there.

5

Matilda greeted me from the couch and handed me a letter from Ethan after I came in from school. I tossed my books to sit and tear open the envelope, still aware of irritation that he couldn't at least have visited us a few days during the summer. He hadn't even added a postscript to his mother's letter from Hong Kong saying he was with them.

Kaitlin:

Sorry I haven't written. Back into second year at Georgetown and glad to be back, though the summer was terrific. I talked with Dad about possibly choosing the Far East for a specialty like he did. Dad says China will massively figure into our foreign policy in the future, but so will the Middle East. I haven't made up my mind yet. I think I'd like a tour once in a while in Europe, too. Learned some interesting things about Eastern Europe when I came through Belgium on the way home. An old friend of Dad's is serving at the NATO headquarters in Brussels. He briefed me on the situation in Europe—nothing classified, of course, but eye-opening.

You know, don't you, that Poland, Romania, Latvia, and the other eastern European countries are part of the Soviet Union? They'd like to be free of the Soviets. You've probably never heard anything about "Prague Spring," back in the '60s. The Czechs wanted to loosen the Soviet hold but were put down by an invasion of the Soviet army. I have an idea we may see more action in that part of the world one of these days.

Glad you're practicing your Arabic. You are working on reading it, too, aren't you?

Ethan

I fingered the letter. "When did the Soviet Union begin?"

Matilda looked up from thumbing through the rest of the mail. "Oh, my. It's been a long time since I've studied history. Back during the First World War, I think. After the Russians overthrew the czar. Sometime after that, Joseph Stalin came in and killed a lot of Russians who didn't want communism. He ruled pretty ruthlessly until—I think he died back in the early '50s. Two or three others ruled, but I can't remember all the names. Brezhnev is prime minister now."

"We talk about him sometimes in current events at school. Why did we let the Soviets take over Eastern Europe?"

"I don't know all the reasons. I was only in elementary school. Europe was in such horrible shape after the war. We signed treaties and things. I guess we were tired of fighting and wanted to bring our troops home."

"But Eastern Europe doesn't want to be ruled by the Soviets, do they?"

She sighed. "Not at all. They want their own countries back. We formed NATO with some other countries to keep the Soviets out of the rest of Europe."

"But remember on TV the other night, some people were talking about how horrible it would be if we had a nuclear war? We might die of radiation or starve because we couldn't grow food."

"Darling, I'm not sure you should watch programs like that if they scare you so much."

"Honestly, Matilda, I have to keep up with current events if I'm going to be a Foreign Service officer, don't I? Anyway, it could happen, couldn't it?"

"It's not inevitable. Back when John F. Kennedy was president, the Soviets tried to bring missiles to Cuba on ships, but we found out and confronted them. We thought it might be the beginning of World War III, but it wasn't. They worked something out, and the Soviet ships turned around and went back."

"Suppose we don't catch them next time until it's too late?"

"I wish Joshua were here for you to talk to. He said something once about how much stronger economically the NATO countries are than the Soviet ones. Maybe it will all be decided peaceably. Don't be so pessimistic."

I reread Ethan's letter a couple of times. "Do you think Ethan and Joshua love each other?" I asked.

"What started you thinking about that?"

"Ethan says he talked with Joshua about his career. First time I've heard him talk about his dad like they were friends."

Matilda put down the mail. "Coverwoods have always pushed their sons pretty hard, and Joshua was no exception with Ethan. Of course, Eleanor used to spoil him a little bit. She had a couple of miscarriages, and Ethan was their only child. It gave him a loveable, impish side, even if you don't see it much anymore. Of course, sometimes I think she neglected him, putting so much energy into advancing Joshua's career."

"Eleanor's from New England, too, isn't she?"

Matilda laughed. "My, yes, with blue blood going back to the founding of Boston. Her mother was sick for years when Eleanor was a child, though. I think she developed a deeper, caring side that you wouldn't expect from somebody with her background. We grew up together, and Eleanor and I were like sisters. Joshua's been in love with her since adolescence."

"Ethan said Joshua didn't like it that he was so spoiled and that's the reason he sent him to that school."

"Joshua was assigned back to the Department, going places, when Ethan turned eleven or so. They put him in some elite private day school in the D.C. area. He was full of himself in those days. I thought Joshua reined him in a bit too tightly. Ethan certainly pushed the limits, though, not in a bad or mean way—far from it—merely mischievous, trying to see what he could get away with. I suppose it was inevitable that he would go too far someday."

"What'd he do that made Joshua so mad?"

"Ethan and some friends put Limburger cheese on the school radiators. I understand it made the place smell like a malfunctioning sewage plant. They had to close the school a couple of days to get the smell out."

I laughed, imagining Ethan doing something like that, and Matilda grinned, too. "Of course it was funny, a boyish prank. But Joshua exploded. He should have grounded Ethan or something of the sort. Instead he sent him to that boarding school, knowing how much Ethan looked forward to living overseas again." Matilda's smile vanished. "Ethan worshiped his father when he was little. After Joshua sent him away like that, it broke something in the relationship. They respect each other, but I'm not sure about love."

* * *

Dear Ethan,

Guess what? I started feeling sorry for Arla after I found out her father gets drunk a lot. He treats Arla, her brothers and sisters, and even her mother awful. Sometimes neighbors have to call the police when they fight.

She's got problems with learning things, too. She's a couple of years older than the rest of us. I feel sorry for her for that, too, because I think learning new things is so much fun.

I can see why she acts the way she does, and I'm not bothered by her now. It's hard to be bothered by somebody you feel sorry for. I guess when she saw it didn't get a rise out me, teasing me wasn't fun anymore, because she stopped.

We actually speak to each other now. Not that we're bosom buddies or anything like that.

Love, Kaitlin

* * *

I gave Matilda the nickname of "Tildy" one day after I entered seventh grade. It slipped out like she'd become my older sister. "Do you mind if I call you that?"

"Not at all. It's what Ray called me. Joshua used to call me that, too, when I was little. Once in a while he slips and still does."

We lighted the oil lamps and put wood on the fire, because the power was out in the first windstorm of the fall. Shadows and flickers from the fire chased around us, and the cedar sweetness from one of the logs spiced the air.

"Tell me about you and Ray and my parents. What happened after Joshua introduced you to Ray?"

"Ray and I started writing. He asked me to marry him after he received his first assignment. Joshua had been engaged for a couple of years to Eleanor, so we had a double wedding before we all left on assignments to the far corners of the world." She got up to rummage in a cabinet and bring out photographs. "Your father and mother were in the wedding, of course."

I bit my lip as I stared at my parents, young, unmarried. I felt like a shard of glass had gone through me. It needled me, told me I had lost something else that awful day besides my parents. Each time I reached for it, it floated away, like an apple does in a tub of water when you try to grab it with your teeth and never can, in those games we played at the county fair.

I studied the others. "Joshua looks almost like I remember Ethan. Of course it's been so long since I've seen Ethan I may be making it up. It would be nice if he could see his way to visit the Island once in a while. And to think, when I first saw him, I wanted him to go away and never come back."

Matilda laughed. "You certainly let him know he wasn't welcome."

"Do you think he's a lot like Joshua inside?"

"In some ways. Ethan might have had an easier time if he'd been a girl. Or had brothers to share Coverwood expectations for him. Father treated Joshua much differently than me. I could get almost anything I wanted out of him. If it weren't for my mother, I'd have been hopeless, I'm sure."

"But girls ought to be expected to do things, too."

"Yes, of course, nowadays. Times have changed."

"I'm going to be as good a Foreign Service officer as any Coverwood son."

* * *

The shortened autumn day played out, and I sprawled over a pillow in front of the fire and an oil lamp with my social studies book, intending to work on assignments the teacher had given us. She gave assignments a week ahead for those days we were stuck at home with power outages.

I flipped through a section on the end of segregation in the South. "You know, Tildy, Mama never let me be waited on by the people who worked for us. She seemed to have some kind of horror of it."

Matilda raised her head from the *Island Record* she was reading on the couch under another lamp. "Your mother had strong views about some things."

"But I know she grew up with black servants. She said once she didn't even know how to make a bed, much less cook and clean, until she moved to Washington to join the Foreign Service. She was determined I wasn't ever going to be in that position. I was griping about having to do chores."

Matilda smiled. "I remember her talking about learning to cook and clean at the same time she was taking language courses and country studies. I can understand why she wouldn't want you to have to learn that way."

"My mother must have changed an awful lot from being a child in Alabama in the 1940s."

"We came back to that over the years, your parents, and Ray and I, as we got to the point of deciding if our religion was skin deep or a part of us we took with us. I think your mother is the one who led us to the point of real commitment. She had the most changing to do, so it cost her more."

I moved to sit with my back to the couch. So this was my mother, Victoria Morgan Sadler. I knew her only for the first nine years of my life, denied mature knowledge of her except from the memories of others.

Perhaps I would always yearn for her, picking up bits of her, never able to put her picture completely together. "How did she decide to join the Foreign Service?"

"As I remember, your mother's father was killed in the Second World War. Later her mother married somebody else. I don't know all the reasons, but your mother went to her grandparents to live until she went off to college. She was an unusual woman, your mother. Interested in the wider world, current events, and so on. Maybe it had to do with her father dying in Europe. I don't know. At any rate, she was one of the few women in the A-100 class where she met your father."

"When did they fall in love?"

"They may have fallen for each other the first day. I wasn't there, of course, but Ray told me later how besotted they were for each other. Your mother wouldn't marry right off, though."

"Why not?"

"She didn't want to resign. Said she wanted at least one tour as a Foreign Service officer. So they waited a few years to marry."

"Why would she have to resign?"

"Didn't you know? At that time female Foreign Service officers had to resign if they married. Even to another Foreign Service officer. Not now, of course."

"I can't believe it. That's awful."

"Well, that's the way it was."

I shook my head. "It's medieval."

"Like I said, times change. Some things are better and some things worse."

"If Mama hadn't had to resign, she might have become an ambassador or at least in charge of consular sections instead of just working as a part-time assistant. I'll certainly never give up my career like she had to do."

Matilda's gaze flickered toward the family pictures on the mantel, then to me. "Kaitlin, darling, like Ethan told you once, please keep your options open. You never know what God will call you to."

"I know what he's calling me to."

Matilda despised arguments, but her glance back at the pictures told me she didn't like what I'd said.

6

One afternoon, at the beginning of my eighth-grade year, I picked up the mail on my way home from school and glanced through it. Stuck between the *Island Record* and *Good Housekeeping* was a letter from Joshua and Eleanor, according to the return address, but the street and city were unfamiliar. Some place called Tiburon, California.

When Matilda saw the letter, she stopped cutting up a chicken for supper, washed her hands, and opened it. A check fluttered out. She caught it, gasped, then read the letter. "Joshua's finally sold our Coverwood home in Connecticut . He told me he was going to, if I didn't have any objections. Of course I didn't. The Island's where I want to spend the rest of my days. I didn't think he'd really carry it through, though."

She looked at the check again. "He's sent me half the profit. I had no idea they could get this much for the old house." She ran her hands over the kitchen counter. "I wanted to remodel the kitchen. This will certainly pay for it, with lots left over. We'll buy you a whole set of new clothes before you head to high school next year."

Oreo swished around my legs until I rubbed her neck while Matilda shook her head as though she still couldn't believe the check's figures.

She studied the note with the check. "The house and the whole Coverwood legacy meant more to Joshua than to me. I was sure he'd want to pass on everything to Ethan."

"Did they move to California from Hong Kong?"

She read the letter again. "I'm so excited it's hard to concentrate. No, he's still got his job, but they closed on a house in northern California. Easier to reach on their vacations from Hong Kong, Joshua says. Wonderful. They'll surely stop by here instead of going through Europe when they come over to see Ethan."

* * *

Right before the huge storms of late fall rocked the Island, Matilda got her wish. Joshua and Eleanor stopped by on their way from California before flying to D.C. to see Ethan. I hadn't seen them since my parents' funeral.

I tried to unscramble my thinking toward them. On the one hand, I didn't like the picture of them that Ethan drew, at least of his father—harsh, not like mine. But I remembered them from the funeral, too. I had liked them as well as I had liked anyone then. Eleanor had put her hand on my shoulder and said, "Your parents were among the best people I ever knew, Kaitlin. You have so much to be proud of."

I watched her now after we got past the greetings and hugs and settled in the living room before the fireplace warmth. Who did she remind me of?

Ethan, of course, even if he looked like his father.

And Joshua? I had gotten the idea that Ethan's father didn't have emotions, but now I remembered the way he wiped at his eyes during the funeral and then averted them, as though embarrassed. Maybe he had feelings, but he didn't want people to notice. In a way, that was more painful than not having them. I tried to hide my feelings, too, right after my parents were killed, but it hurt less after I was able to cry about them.

Joshua seemed a shorter edition of Ethan with gray hair and a lined face and a mustache on his upper lip as clipped as he was. He carried a compact slenderness like his son. Throughout the visit, he gravitated to Eleanor any time he entered a room where she was and once in a while held her hand. Why did they say he didn't show his feelings?

Slightly taller than Joshua, Eleanor spoke in cultured accents, but whenever we talked, I got the idea she listened carefully to everything I said. Maybe as the wife of a diplomat in high positions, she'd learned to draw people out, but when she asked me questions, I answered without thinking about it.

"He loves school," Eleanor said to Matilda about Ethan, and I noted the pride in her voice. "He's planning to begin the Foreign Service exams next year."

"Has he considered anything else?" Matilda asked.

"Not that he's ever told me. He loved growing up overseas. He always picked up the language within a few weeks and ran around the streets making friends with the local children. Sometimes I think he was more at home with them than he was with the children of our American colleagues."

Matilda nodded. "I have to confess I worried a bit about his adjustment after such a different kind of childhood, but he's landed on his feet quite nicely."

"I'll be forever thankful the school put him with Chopra," Eleanor said.

Joshua didn't contribute to the conversation, but I got to know him better after he drove the two of us over to Double View, and we hiked on the beach where I walked with his son a few years earlier. I think he enjoyed our time, and he seemed to like me.

As Matilda said, Coverwood men are softer with their womenfolk. And, I guess, being Ethan's adopted "cousin," I was one of Joshua's womenfolk.

"Will Ethan choose South Asia and the Far East like you?" I asked.

He walked silently for several minutes, then smiled at me. His smile transformed him, erasing his austerity. "I think he's trying to decide whether China or the Middle East will occupy the U.S. foreign policy community the most over the next few decades. I told him to pick the one he's drawn to, that it's a toss-up which one will be the most important to us."

"I'm going to pick the Middle East and be a political officer like my father."

His smile vanished, and he studied me before speaking as we tracked over the sand. "I hope before you decide for sure about making a career out of the Foreign Service that you give it more thought."

"Oh, I have. I've already decided. I'm not going to change."

I thought his look for me held affection. "You and Ethan. You two Foreign Service brats. I suppose it's hopeless."

When Joshua and I entered the house, Matilda jumped up and asked if we wanted something hot to drink.

"Tea," Joshua and I said at almost the same time.

Matilda scurried to the kitchen and put the kettle to boil. I had the feeling she and Eleanor had been talking about something and broke off the conversation as soon as they heard us at the door. Eleanor sat in the middle of the couch, and Joshua joined her.

"Come tell me about yourself and what you've been doing," Eleanor said to me, patting the couch cushion on the empty side. "Matilda tells me how well you do in school."

I sat beside her and crossed my legs. "School's pretty easy, but sometimes it's boring. I'll be glad when I go to high school next year. They let you choose some of your classes then."

"What do you like best?"

"English. Writing things. Geography, too."

"Studying other countries?"

"Sure. How they're alike and how they're different."

"You like to analyze."

I blinked. "I guess so. Yes. Of course, I'm planning to be a Foreign Service officer like Ethan, so I have to take the right subjects and study hard."

She didn't change expression, merely nodded.

"When you see Ethan, would you tell him I'm still using the Arabic tapes?" I didn't say anything about my neglect of reading Arabic.

She reached out and straightened the collar of my shirt. "I'll tell him when I see him next week."

I decided Ethan was lucky to have her for a mother.

That evening after supper, Joshua threw more logs on the fire against the chill. I figured it was time to find out what was going on with him.

"Why did you leave the Foreign Service? Everybody talks about how much you loved it."

The three adults looked at me like I was an alien from *Star Wars*.

"It was rather a painful time," Eleanor said, a gentle rebuke.

Joshua's face softened. "It's all right, Elly. No reason we can't talk about it with you, Kaitlin. After all, you're one of us, and besides, you stubbornly persist in wanting to be an FSO." He stretched his legs toward the fire. "The short answer is that I disagreed, in the strongest terms, with our continuing buildup of forces in Viet Nam. I opposed our policy there from the beginning."

"They fired you for that?"

"They didn't fire me. I resigned. Not right away, but after I understood I would never serve again in a policy position. I was Under Secretary for Political Affairs. When they saw I was not going to change my position, they sent me off to Thailand as ambassador. Got me out of the way."

"Because you wanted something different from what they did?"

"I didn't resign because my views weren't accepted. Coming into policy discussions, you know you're going to be overruled sometimes. It's part of the job. I resigned because of—things that were said about me by those who disagreed."

The fire hissed in the silence.

Eleanor said, "If you're going to tell her the story, Josh, you have to tell her all of it." When her husband shrugged, Eleanor continued, and even her graciousness didn't cover her defensiveness, like Oreo had for her kittens. "One of his friends—up until that moment—began saying Joshua was soft on communism, that he was, in essence, betraying his country because he hadn't supported our policy in Viet Nam."

Joshua took his wife's hand. "To disagree with another's opinion is one thing; to be so insecure that you must attack the character of the person with whom you disagree—well, I decided I wanted no more of it. When they made that final attack on me, I quit."

He halted again, and Eleanor said, "Joshua had given years of service to his country. To have his integrity questioned—it hurt all three of us."

All three of us. I thought of Ethan, off in boarding school he didn't want to attend, hearing his father maligned, watching the end of his father's career.

What would my father have done in a situation like that? Or my mother?

"Weren't we fighting communism?" I asked.

Joshua sat up as though impatient. "Of course we were fighting communism, as we should. It's the place we chose to fight it that I disagreed with. I said Viet Nam would distract us from our main task—dealing with China—and take too many of our resources."

I stared at flames consuming fir logs. "I guess it's not always a clear choice, is it?"

"No. It's our job to study the situation, advise in the best way we know, then let our leaders choose as they see fit. Sometimes, though, you take a risk when you advocate an unpopular position. Sure you want to join the Foreign Service?"

I thought of my father again. "I'm sure. I'll take my chances."

Joshua laughed. I think he liked my answer. Eleanor smiled at me, but Matilda shook her head.

* * *

Ethan:

Sorry I haven't written in a while, but then you haven't been all that great at writing, either. I'm super glad you passed the Foreign Service exams. What happens now?

I can't believe it's almost summer. When school starts in the fall, Cindy and I'll be entering high school. We can't wait.

You know what? Arla and I are friends now. Well, sort of.

It happened like this: I stayed late at school to meet with my science project group. Just before I went home, I went into the restroom and there was Arla, sobbing and looking all blotchy.

At first, she wouldn't tell me what was wrong, but I guess she was desperate, so finally she told me.

She was afraid she was pregnant. I couldn't believe it. She's only fifteen. Apparently, she's been making out with a guy I've barely heard of who dropped out of school and is working on his father's farm.

I kept myself from acting surprised or shocked or anything because I knew that wouldn't help. I asked what her family thought about it. She said they didn't know and if she really was pregnant, her father would kill her. I think she meant it.

I told her she should go to my church pastor, that he knew about a place where she could go and have her baby and be taken care of. I said I'd go with her to the pastor if she wanted me to.

You know, she looked so startled, like nobody had ever listened to her before or done anything for her. She said she might do what I suggested if it turned out she was really pregnant. At least if her boyfriend wasn't ready to marry yet.

It turned out she wasn't pregnant, although Matilda thinks maybe she really was but lost the baby because she's so young.

Arla and I have talked a few times since. I told her I thought it wasn't that smart a thing to go all the way with a guy you weren't married to, but she said it was hard not to because she didn't want to lose him. Anyway, he knows ways to prevent pregnancy, she says, and they'll be careful from now on. Yeah, I'll bet. He's just using her, and it makes me mad, but I can't get her to see it. I guess she wants to be loved so badly.

I've kept her secret, of course. I didn't even tell Cindy, but I did tell Matilda, who won't tell anybody. I needed somebody to talk to about all these things.

Matilda is great. She doesn't go into lecture mode or anything. We just talk. She says she knows it's harder these days for young women than it was for her because the way we live now encourages a different lifestyle.

I remembered what you said a long time ago, that physical sins were easier to avoid than hating your enemies, but I guess all of it's hard sometimes.

Anyway, like I told Matilda, boys don't pay much attention to me. I'm too weird. Except sometimes for telling me their problems, like what can they do when they like somebody who doesn't like them?

I've taken up too much time. We have end-of-the-year tests.

Love, Kaitlin

Ethan hadn't written in a while, but he answered this letter within a week or two.

Kaitlin:

I can't believe you're growing up like this and facing all these issues. I tease you a lot, but believe me, I'm glad you have a head on your shoulders. I'm especially glad you understand that some guys do use a girl's desire to be loved to have their way with them.

Please, please, keep that understanding, so the first time some jerk tries to make you do things you know you shouldn't, you'll tell him to soak his head in the sand.

Glad you've got Matilda. She's an angel in human guise. Keep sharing with her.

And don't worry about your so-called weirdness. You have a more serious nature than most your age. That's why people confide in you. I suspect you're not much of a party animal but a great one to share with after the party's over. And an awful lot of life is after the party.

Ethan

I fingered Ethan's letter. We weren't writing as much as we used to, and I missed sharing things I couldn't with anybody else. A part of me stayed submerged, rarely shown, even to Cindy, as though I still had an imaginary friend from my preschool years and knew better than to admit it.

Sometimes when I talked with the kids at church, that part of me slipped out. Like the time somebody talked about the Wailing Wall in Jerusalem. Before I thought, I mentioned that I'd seen it with my parents.

My friends said things like, "You've seen it? Really seen it?"

They seemed to think it was cool, but I felt embarrassed, different. Something in me belonged elsewhere. My years overseas marked me, and I couldn't erase them no matter how hard I tried.

Cindy and I began trips to the mainland to buy clothes for the big jump to high school. When we talked of plans after high school, I never wavered in wanting to be a Foreign Service officer, but Cindy changed several times before we began high school.

"You're really going to live in all those places overseas?" she asked.

"Sure. I'm going to go to Georgetown University and study foreign policy. Then I'm going to be a Foreign Service officer."

"Maybe I'll be a flight attendant and fly over to see you sometimes."

The older Islanders had worked at diverse occupations to make a living like farming, logging, and fishing. Now they added newer jobs: real estate, insurance, and construction. Cindy's father set up a successful real estate office. As her family became richer and college became a possibility, she veered toward teaching.

We discussed marriage, as did all our girl friends.

"Any man I marry has to be an FSO, too," I said. "Or at least not mind my going off on assignments."

"What about when you have children?"

"Well, if he's not in the Foreign Service, he'll have a job he can do anywhere." I searched for that kind of vocation. "Maybe he'll be an artist and can stay home and take care of the children."

"That rules out all the boys we know," Cindy said.

* * *

Summer tourists outnumbered Islanders when I picked up the mail one afternoon and spotted the envelope with Joshua and Eleanor's California address. The quality of the envelope indicated an invitation.

"What in the world?" Matilda said. "Ethan's already graduated from Georgetown. I sent the gift last spring."

She tore open the envelope and stared at the card. "Of all things."

"What, Tildy?"

"Ethan. He's getting married. Labor Day weekend. In California." She unfolded a note with the invitation. "Eleanor says the young woman is from there, California, I mean, and her father's in Congress. A representative from the San José area." She frowned. "Yes, I recognize her father's name. She and Ethan met two months ago and fell madly in love, according to Eleanor."

After a minute when I must have stared at her, I shifted my gaze toward Saratoga Passage. This would take some getting used to.

7

Ethan's fiancée was a California goddess, and I adored her. She and Ethan had met at a government reception in the nation's capital. Didi was everything I wasn't but wished I were.

Her hair hung in silken, beach-white strands with not a tangle, certainly not a frizz, to be seen. Her eyes appeared colored by the ocean she swam in. Her skin, despite the amount of time she must spend in the sun, was flawless. Not a hint of the freckles that made me feel like Huck Finn poling down the Mississippi.

Didi had a tolerant California manner that welcomed you, whoever you were, and that contrasted with my Island-learned caution.

"Kaitlin? What a beautiful name. Irish, isn't it? Goes with your hair. I love it."

I don't think Ethan recognized me when he first saw me. I suppose my short curls changed my appearance from the wild-haired child he remembered.

He blinked and didn't say anything for a full minute, so unlike the Ethan I remembered. When a grin spread across his dark features, he became the friend I knew.

"Kaitlin? Your hair's that flaming red, so I guess you're the same person I once pulled from Saratoga Passage."

I pretended to be angry with him. "Really, Ethan, do you have to remind me of that?"

Later he took a few moments to stroll with me after the rehearsal dinner. "Come on, Kaitlin. I haven't seen you in forever. Walk with me and fill me in on your life. Letters can't substitute for the real thing."

"Which you haven't done much of lately. You owe me for several."

"Guilty as charged, Mademoiselle Kaitlin."

We rambled over the manicured grass of the elegant country club, the scent of cut vegetation surrounding us.

"You're not Squirt anymore, are you? You're a delightful young lady who'll soon break the hearts of all the boys on Simon Island."

"Fat chance. You sound like a diplomat."

"I am a diplomat. Finished with A-100, sworn in to protect and defend the *Constitution,* and have my first assignment. Didi and I are headed for Peshawar after the honeymoon and a few more weeks of training."

"Peshawar?"

"Assignment as a typical first tour visa officer. They liked the fact that I'd lived in south Asia before and speak a little Urdu and a bit of Pashto."

Peshawar is in Pakistan's northwest frontier, not far from the fabled Khyber Pass. I'd never been there, but I had an idea what it was like and wasn't sure how the daughter of a congressional representative would take to it. Especially since Ethan was beginning, like all FSOs on their first or second tour, as a lowly visa officer, interviewing masses of would-be visitors to the States.

Did Didi know what the career of a Foreign Service officer included? Hardship posts? On call 24/7? Constant packing up, unpacking, packing again for the next post? "What does Didi think of going to Pakistan to live?"

"Oh, she thinks Peshawar's going to be exciting, like the great game Kipling's Kim played, or maybe like British Victorians living in India's Raj. She'll get used to how it really is."

I hoped so.

"How's your Arabic coming?" Ethan asked.

"I think I speak it pretty well. At least I can understand all the tapes without looking at the book and answer all the questions in the dialog."

"Do you read it?"

I sighed. "Not yet."

"Kaitlin, I told you, you've got to read it, too."

"Oh, come on, Ethan. Lay off. We've only got a little bit of time."

"Wish we had more." He sounded like he meant it. "What about Billy whatever–his–name–was? The one with the curly blond hair."

"I got over Billy a long time ago. And Ned, too. I like Sander Oakley now. We worked together on a science project. I think maybe he likes me, too, a little."

"I bet he does, if he's got any sense at all."

* * *

The wedding party included Chopra, Ethan's close friend from prep school days. He took Matilda and me out to lunch one day before the wedding.

"So did Ethan ask you to take care of us?" I inquired over our meal. I liked his cheerfulness.

"He may have hinted at something like that. He didn't have to hint more than once, though."

Matilda said, "Chopra, you're a diplomat yourself."

He inclined his dark head. "Thank you, Ms. Matilda, but perhaps I would prefer to have a good bedside manner, since I will enter medical school next month to become a doctor."

We stayed with Joshua and Eleanor in the guest apartment of their Marin County house, north of San Francisco. Wall hangings, vases, and paintings decorated the rooms, evidence of their past lives in South Asia and the Far East. I touched a rough tapestry, and the memory of my overseas childhood stirred me.

* * *

I hadn't been to a lot of weddings in my life, but I was pretty sure this one was the fanciest I'd see in a long time. Didi's bridesmaids floated out in sherbet colors. The groomsmen wore tuxedos with shirts and ties matching the bridesmaid colors.

Joshua was Ethan's best man, which surprised me. I would have expected him to pick Chopra. How much alike those two Coverwoods seemed, both of them trim and hard, draped in New England crustiness that contrasted with Didi and her California entourage.

Ethan turned as Didi began her triumphal entry. I doubted he had ever demonstrated so publically his feelings as when he watched her march down the aisle toward him.

Pronounced man and wife in due course, the couple kissed, and Ethan escorted his new bride down the aisle, with his gaze nowhere except on her face. She was a couple of inches taller than he was, not that it mattered.

After the reception, the photographers—several—snapped last pictures as the star-blessed couple entered the limousine for their trip to the airport and their honeymoon in Mexico. I knew I must be mistaken in my last glimpse of them, although the pictures seemed to capture it, too, when I looked at them later. Didi was excited, that's all, and probably photographed poorly. She wasn't really flashing an acquisitive gloat that said she had caught her trophy husband.

* * *

That night a bad dream troubled me. I hadn't had one in a year or more. It wasn't a nightmare exactly, not the howling kind I used to have, merely a reminder of my fragility. And the one memory that always slipped away with the other wisps when I awoke.

The next morning, though, shimmered in sunshine and the lethargy that follows the end of frantic activity.

We all found our way at about the same time to the sunny breakfast table overlooking San Francisco Bay and the Golden Gate in the distance. Water sparkled, more brittle than in the Passage. The tang of fresh fruit newly cut overlaid the air.

Even Joshua appeared to relax and lose the normal wariness that guarded his words. He speared a truncated triangle of California melon. "Glad that's over with. Work will seem a breeze after that whirlwind. At least Hong Kong is a long way from our cheerful in-law politician and all his cronies. Have to watch it. I almost said outlaw."

"Josh, dear," Eleanor said, "do remember he's our son's father-in-law."

He put down his fork to wrap his hand around hers. "Don't remind me yet that we will share the grandchildren. Maybe Ethan and Didi won't have children for a while."

"Josh, really."

"Will they visit you in Hong Kong from Pakistan?" I asked.

"Perhaps," Eleanor answered. She fiddled with her napkin before she placed it on her lap and reached for a pitcher of fresh grape juice.

Joshua said, "At least with only one child, we won't have to go through that again. Unless, of course—"

Eleanor laid a hand on his arm.

"Just kidding, Elly. I hope they'll be very happy." He coughed and turned my way. "Kaitlin, what do you say to a drive through the Napa Valley? I can show you Jack London's old house. You know, the author who wrote *The Call of the Wild*. Perhaps they don't read that anymore in school."

He seemed to enjoy talking to me. Perhaps he found me easier to talk to than Eleanor or Matilda at the moment.

Later, as we crisscrossed northern California vineyard country, burnt brown, I asked, "Will you ever live in New England again?"

"I don't think so. The winters are too cold for us now after living in warmer climates for so many years. Ethan didn't want the old home place. That's why we sold it." He stared through the windshield. "Of course, he doesn't care much for Marin County, either. Maybe he'll make Washington his home—D.C., I mean. A lot of FSOs do that. Eleanor and I gave Ethan our house there as a wedding present. We only go there once in a while to see friends."

In school that year, we had read *The Man Without a Country*. Philip Nolan, the protagonist of the story, renounces the United States and is sentenced to live on a ship, forbidden ever again to hear of his country. A bit of Nolan's agony touched me as I watched Joshua, a man who once held high political office in the State Department. All lost now.

His gaze fastened on something beyond the windshield, and, I thought, beyond those times. "I wonder where our grandchildren will be raised."

I tried to imagine Didi as a mother, raising children in places like Peshawar.

"We Coverwoods have been ship captains, farmers, ministers, university professors, missionaries—now we've dwindled to Ethan. I wonder if I've done for him what I needed to do to teach him to be a good father. Maybe he doesn't even want children."

"You don't know?"

"We never talked about things like that. Mostly about careers. What you have to do to get ahead."

That would help Ethan as he began his first Foreign Service job, but I wasn't sure it would help him with Didi.

8

"I'm pregnant," Arla whispered, in between our ninth-grade classes at the high school. "I'm sure this time."

I stared at her over my locker door, finally said, "Do you want me to help you find a place to have the baby like we talked about before?"

Arla shook her head. "James and me are going to run off to the mainland and live together 'til we're old enough to get married without our parents' say. Leave here. Right after school today."

"Then what will you do?"

"James has landed a job over there in a car wash. After the baby comes, I'll get a job, too."

"But who'll take care of the baby?" I didn't figure between them they'd have enough money for child care.

Her smile showed her crooked teeth. "After the baby's come and Dad's had some time to get used to it, I'll get him to let my sister come over."

The warning bell clanged for classes.

She tossed her stringy hair. "Look, thanks for letting me talk to you all these times and not letting out what I've said. But I knew I could trust you, and it's easy to talk to you. I'm sorry I was ever mean to you. Maybe I'll see you sometime and show you the baby. Bye now."

The hall was clearing, and she darted off before I could answer.

After school, I raced to the front door, telling Cindy I'd be at the bus in a minute, that I had to see somebody before they got away.

I glimpsed Arla getting into an ancient Ford pickup with a busted back window stretched across with plastic wrap. For the first time, I saw James, as he turned to greet Arla. His hair was a rustier red than mine, and his complexion appeared perpetually pink, the way fair skinned people look when they work outside a lot. I guess he got that way working on his father's farm. I wondered how he would like being tied down to a car washing job.

Arla slammed the door, and the pickup shuddered away, belching smoke out the tailpipe.

I haven't seen Arla since then. As life churned on, I stopped thinking about her so much. But her broken-toothed grin flitted across my mind when I prayed for her once in a while. I wondered if I could have helped her more.

Listening seemed about the only thing I'd done. In fact, listening seemed about the only thing I could do to help anybody. I felt pretty useless.

"It doesn't seem fair, me having so much in the way of love, and her having so little," I told Matilda that evening.

Matilda quit cutting apples for applesauce and turned to me where I sat on the kitchen stool peeling them for her to cut. The air held the aroma of cinnamon she sprinkled on the batches, and the kitchen windows steamed against the cold front blowing in. "Nobody should feel guilty for having a family that loves them," she said. "I'm sorry as I can be that Arla didn't have that. I think that's why she got into trouble with James Guthrie."

She peered over her glasses at me. I hadn't noticed until now how gray her hair was growing. My stomach crimped. "You know, if you're getting tired, I can finish this for you."

The squeezing disappeared when she smiled at me. "I'm fine. You worry too much, you know that?"

I picked up another apple. "Arla's not the only one who got pregnant without being married. It's happened a couple of times before in the past year or so. Senior girls, though, older than Arla. One of them left school and went over to relatives on the mainland, so everybody said. The other one got married, although the gossip was that the boy she married wasn't the father."

Matilda had a way of saying nothing that pulled more out of me. She did it now, just went back to cutting apples while I talked.

"Some kids at school say it doesn't matter anyway about going to bed together before you're married. Or even getting married at all. Because of the pill, you don't have to worry about getting pregnant now."

"Well, the pill didn't stop Arla and the other girls from getting pregnant, did it?"

I thought a minute. "I guess they didn't use it. I mean, you have to think about it ahead of time."

Matilda started the next batch of applesauce to cooking before she spoke again. "Seems to me people don't think much; they just go for what they happen to want at the time. No matter the consequences." She sighed. "So many of us older folks waste time talking about how it's not like it used to be and all that. We have to live in the now. I want to be here for you, to help you live in a world that's so changed from the one of my childhood. To help you choose differently from what screams in your face from TV and magazines."

"Well, I'm already different. A little more won't hurt, I guess."

I peeled another apple, discovered a worm in it, and cut it out while I talked. "I guess Arla's family has taught her to be the way she is. Not think ahead and things like that. Her dad has a couple of DUI convictions. Guess he doesn't bother to think ahead about what might happen if he killed some innocent person in an accident. How can you help people like Arla if her family's taught her that way?"

"Sometimes people outside the family can reach them. Teachers, for example. Cindy's planning to be a teacher, isn't she?"

"She's pretty well set on it."

I remembered the fourth-grade teacher who seated me next to Cindy when I first got to the Island. I think she knew Cindy would befriend me. Such a small act, but it contributed to my healing.

And me? I was going to be a Foreign Service officer. How was that going to help people like Arla?

I cut another worm out of an apple.

* * *

During my second year in high school, I became concerned about Matilda.

Joshua and Eleanor flew over from Hong Kong on business that fall and drove up to see us a couple of days. We didn't talk so much serious stuff, but shared over cribbage and Parcheesi and dominoes. We laughed while we concocted the meals, a combination of Matilda's down-home cooking and Eleanor's more exotic fare. Joshua and I helped. He even whipped up a curried chicken dish one evening.

When they left in their rental car, I looked down the driveway after them despite the wind that spiraled around the evergreens. Happiness brushed over me, like it hadn't in years. I thanked God for the family he'd allowed me.

Matilda turned and called back, "Come on. It's too cold. Let's go in and stoke the fire."

Inside, she stirred the logs in the fireplace and reached to pick up a fir branch, cut small for easy handling. She stopped, put her hand on her chest, then moved backwards to sit on one of the chairs.

"Tildy?" The warmth from Joshua and Eleanor's visit disappeared in the squeezing of my own chest.

When Matilda looked at me and smiled, my heart stopped pounding, but the fear of tragedy's nearness hovered over me. I had let my guard down and forgot how near it was. Always.

Matilda's next words soothed, pushed it back. "You look as pale as I felt there for a moment."

"What happened? Are you all right?"

"Just what they call a heart palpitation. I get them from time to time. You know, when I bend over, straighten up too quickly. That sort of thing."

"Why don't you see a doctor?"

"Oh, I'll mention it on my next checkup."

* * *

Oreo disappeared. We searched and called, but she never came back. Stories circulated about the increasing population of coyotes on the Island. They killed cats, it was rumored. I tried not to think of what might have been my pet's last moments.

Pets. Parents. Anybody you loved.

They got taken off. You never even got to tell them good-bye.

I didn't cry, wouldn't let myself. What good did crying do?

After a few weeks, Matilda suggested we get another cat.

"I don't want another one."

The nightmare returned about my parents, but I forced myself not to cry out for Matilda. From now on, I'd handle my fears by myself.

* * *

Joshua and Eleanor returned the next spring. They intended a week with us before they drove slowly across country, a relaxed vacation ending with a visit to old friends in D.C.

"We've never really seen that much of our country, you know," Joshua said. "Always so busy overseas, quick trips home."

An unusually warm afternoon for early April drew us to drowse in bird song on the porch. The island across Saratoga Passage greened with the first promise of alders peeping among the darker evergreens.

Joshua leaned forward from the porch glider, where he sat next to Eleanor. "Tildy, why don't you and Kaitlin come with us? Didn't I hear you talk about her having spring holidays next week? We'd fly you both back here."

I turned from the steps where I was sitting. "Please, Tildy, could we?" A longing to travel spilled over me, like my parents and I had once enjoyed.

Matilda glanced toward me from her chair. "Why don't I think about it this week? Maybe Kaitlin could go with you. I'm a little tired for doing that right now, but it would be exciting for her."

I jumped up. "Wait 'til I tell Cindy."

The other three laughed. "A done deal, I think," Eleanor said.

But that night, I wasn't so sure I wanted to leave Matilda. I had watched over her, helped as much as I could with meals and chores. Her perennial tiredness worried me.

I didn't say anything to Cindy the next day at school about the possible trip. Maybe I wouldn't go if I couldn't persuade Matilda to come.

I forced myself to concentrate on an algebra test. Somebody knocked on the door, and the class turned toward it in one movement as it opened.

The principal motioned for our teacher.

Maybe this was what they called hyperventilating. Like I was dizzy and almost couldn't breathe. This is the way they had told me about my parents.

I stumbled into the hallway when the teacher returned and beckoned to me. To join Eleanor, standing with the principal.

9

"Darling," Eleanor said after we drove onto the ferry for the trip to the mainland, "I'm sorry we scared you so. I'm sure Matilda will be fine. She said she felt dizzy, that's all. Joshua called her doctor, then took her over to one of the medical centers in Seattle for tests. She might have to take medication, but I'm sure it's nothing that can't be controlled. I thought we'd all like to be with her, that's all."

I sat in the car, not bounding up the steps, as the ferry vibrated and moved toward the mainland and the wind from an approaching cold front blasted the decks. I clenched my hands like I clenched my feelings so nothing would show. I knew what would happen. I wouldn't cry, just accept it.

People you loved died. God took them away. You could never trust a good time.

In the waiting room of the hospital, we sat in plastic chairs beside tacky tables covered with thumb-worn magazines. I wrinkled my nose against the antiseptic odor and sat between Eleanor and Joshua, for once separating them.

I didn't care that they glanced at me with worried frowns. I didn't try to make them feel better. Nothing mattered anymore.

Then Matilda walked through the door from the examining room, striding like she always did. Not a doctor to tell us she was dying. My tears broke. I wept. Hysterically. I couldn't play the adult anymore.

When Matilda and Eleanor's hugs didn't placate me, Joshua turned me to face him. "Kaitlin, you're upsetting Matilda."

It wasn't an observation. It was an order to stop. My breath caught a few times before I lapsed into snuffles. I hadn't known a father in a long time, but I guess that's what he was to me now. Ethan may have spurned Joshua's authority, but I welcomed it.

When I rode back with Eleanor, I actually dozed, feeling like a rubber band held taut but now loosened. When we entered the house, Joshua rose from the couch in the living room where he sat with Matilda.

"Kaitlin, why don't we take a walk on the beach?"

I followed him down the bluff path, basking in the comfort of someone telling me what to do next. We dodged logs that spring storms piled like a giant playing pick-up-sticks. The changed weather blew a spring-fresh wind from the north that chilled, but its bite calmed me. Joshua appeared oblivious to it.

We stopped before a log blocking our path, and I rubbed my foot at barnacles on a rock. "Okay, so Matilda didn't die like I was afraid she would. This time."

Joshua pushed his hands into his pockets. "Yes, of course, we all die, but the doctor assured us her condition's not serious. She'll take the medication he prescribed and live normally. What she has is not unusual, and it can be controlled." He turned toward me. "Is it because of your parents that you always expect bad news?"

His soft tone didn't fool me. He expected an answer. I rubbed my foot as though the barnacles must be ground to powder. "Because. Because good times don't last. Ever."

"True. Neither do bad times."

I formed words around an idea blossoming in my mind. "It's like—you know—those pictures you see of hungry children. Or anybody suffering when we have such good lives."

"Yes?"

"Like some—monster—some weird creature from *Lord of the Rings* or something. Standing at this door that's cracked half open. He's staring at me while I'm feasting at a banquet."

"Waiting to grab you."

I stopped smashing the barnacles. "Something like that."

"You're a Christian, aren't you?"

"Sure." I didn't know if Joshua was or not because he never talked about religion.

He nodded. "Believe it or not, I am, too, even if I don't practice it as exuberantly as Matilda."

He seemed to enjoy our sparring. I studied him while he talked.

"Think about this: Was Jesus right to enjoy the feasting and the fellowship with friends? The Bible says he was called a wine bibber and a glutton. Even allowing for his enemies' jealousy, sounds to me as though he enjoyed a good time. Think of all the funny stories he told, like the one about the man who goes around with a plank in his eye trying to get a speck out of his brother's. Was his enjoyment wrong?"

I kicked away the rock. "Of course it wasn't wrong."

"And that was with his knowledge that all his earthly good times were going to end in his crucifixion."

"But he knew he'd be resurrected."

"Perhaps he knew that, if he did his father's will, he'd be resurrected. But an awful time of testing his love for his father lay ahead. Yet he had enough faith to enjoy the good times."

"You think it takes faith to enjoy good times?"

His smile turned thoughtful. "You know, I think it does. At least for those who've gone through times of suffering like you have."

Joy poked through my sadness like the blue peeked around scurrying clouds overhead. I exploded with thoughts that had simmered inside for a long time.

"You know, Matilda's great at listening to me when I talk about school problems and things like that. But I can't talk to her about these kinds of things. It would upset her. She thinks I'm too serious and worry too much."

"You have a gift."

"I do?"

"A gift of perception and empathy. Besides that, you're a questioner. My sister, whom I love dearly, is not a questioner. She has other gifts. We each work out our own salvation."

He actually knew the Bible? Verses like that?

Joshua wasn't a touchy-feely person, to understate the obvious, but he rested his hand on my shoulder to lead me back.

"You've suffered, too," I said on our way up the path. "Do you enjoy the good times?"

He turned that half smile on me. "I'm beginning to."

* * *

I told them I'd rather not travel right then, and even Matilda seemed content with my decision.

"Someday," she promised, "we will travel. The medicine's already making me feel better."

After Joshua and Eleanor left, I sat with her in front of the fire and thought about how much Matilda had suffered. Yet she was one of the happiest people I knew.

"For a brother and sister you and Joshua aren't a bit alike. You're all gentle and open. He's standoffish until you get to know him. Then he's kind, but it takes a while."

She smiled. "Joshua and I are only half brother and sister, though I don't think about it very often, and I don't think he does either."

"No kidding?"

"Joshua's mother died when he was about three. I understand she was a wifely paragon in the Coverwood tradition. A couple of years after that, Joshua's father—mine, too, eventually—had a car accident. Fortunately, he recovered, but he spent a few days convalescing in the hospital. He fell in love with his Irish-American nurse."

"Your mother?"

Matilda nodded. "I never really liked Father's family, except for Joshua. They made me feel inferior, but Joshua was unfailingly kind to me, and I loved him. He loved my mother, too. She was the nurturing type."

Matilda laughed when I said, "So that's where you get it from."

"A bit different from the other Coverwoods, for sure."

"So maybe your mother helped Joshua be a little softer than his father."

She nodded. "Joshua's a lot like him, but, yes, I like to think he got his soft streak from my mother."

"Even though they're not related by blood?"

"It's the nurturing that matters."

I rolled a piece of kindling wood between my hands. "Maybe Ethan got a little more nurturing from Eleanor."

"Oh, I think so. The soft streak widened a bit with her mothering."

"I miss him, you know that? Ethan, I mean."

She studied me. "Yes, I know you do. Well, God has his ways."

I couldn't tell what she was thinking.

10

We saw Ethan and Didi once during that time, the summer before I turned sixteen. When they were on home leave between assignments, they visited us, then flew to their families in California.

I came down to breakfast the first morning of their visit, surprised to see Ethan there before me, sipping coffee with Matilda. I had expected jet lag to keep him and Didi in bed until noon.

"Aren't you sleeping in?"

He seemed tired, more tired than could be explained by the long trip. Dark circles outlined his eyes. "Morning, Kaitlin. No, couldn't sleep. You know how jet lag is. I'll probably be nodding off before noon."

Matilda looked at him the way she looked at me when something worried her. "Why don't you stay longer, at least a week? You know you rest well here, and you look exhausted."

He stared into his cup. "I would love that. Can't, though. Mother and Dad are only back for a week."

"Does Didi miss her parents when she's overseas?" Matilda asked.

I bit into toast. Interesting how she phrased that question.

Ethan pushed leftover eggs around on the plate. "As a matter of fact, she does miss them. In fact, she's going to stay with them while I head to Yemen."

I stopped eating. "Yemen? You're going to Yemen? After Pakistan? I bet you could have gotten something better than Yemen after a hardship tour like Peshawar."

His expression resembled the one after he'd pulled me from Saratoga Passage. "Of course I could, but I wanted the position in Yemen, okay? It's a lot more challenging, a lot better chance for something besides meaningless junior officer work." He chopped his words, like he'd made the argument before.

I shrugged, but Matilda asked, "You're going unaccompanied the whole two years?"

Ethan poked the congealed eggs. "It's better this way. Didi misses—things from the States. Yemen would be even worse than Pakistan for her. I'll get to see her on leave. I get an extra R and R, of course."

He sounded like the extra leave made it all okay.

We didn't see much of them the few days they were there. Mostly they went shopping on the mainland in their rental car.

"Real stores. A shopping mall. I don't think I'll ever get enough of them," Didi said after returning the first evening.

Ethan stared out the window and stroked his chin. He wasn't letting his beard grow this time.

He hadn't once called me Squirt, either. And I missed our funning.

* * *

"Guess what?" Cindy announced one day toward the summer after our junior year in high school. "Daddy said we have enough money for me to go all four years to college. He can't believe the way people are building houses and the prices they're willing to pay."

For anybody in real estate or construction on the Island, as was Mr. Swensen, the times were golden. Matilda had shaken her head at the assessment when the tax bill for her house arrived. "Do you realize this house is worth ten times what Ray and I paid for it?"

"You wouldn't want to go east to school, would you?" I asked Cindy. "Like Georgetown? In the other Washington?" I described it to her.

Cindy shook her head. "Mom and Dad would never let me go to some school like that. Really, I don't think I'd like to."

"Are you planning to come back to the Island to teach?"

"If I can find a position."

I sighed. Sometimes I envied Cindy and her secure Island calling.

Neither of us dated a lot. I didn't have much choice since boys rarely asked me out, though they often sought me to talk about problems, such as how to make Cindy like them.

She was Scandinavian beautiful with her fair hair and no freckles, but her opinion of most Island boys our age was that they were dorks. "I guess I'll have to leave the Island to find somebody. And chances are he'll want to live in Seattle or somewhere like that." Unlike me, she wanted to stay on the Island close to her family.

Matilda settled the four years of college for me.

"Kaitlin, I know you want to enter the Foreign Service like your parents, and I'm reconciled to that. However, I want your first time away from home to be a little closer, please. For now, would you, for both our sakes, attend college close by? With Cindy maybe?"

"But Georgetown's in Washington, D.C. They have a whole school for international studies. A lot of the professors are retired FSOs."

She put her hand on top of mine on the table where we were eating. "All right. If you really want to go, I'll help you with it."

"The money from Mama and Daddy isn't enough?"

"I put everything you inherited from them in a trust fund for your education. There's enough for four years at a state school in Washington State and probably a master's after that, if you decide you want one." She studied my face. "Of course, if you've got your heart set on Georgetown, I can help you. I've still got some money from the old house sale."

Shame flooded me. I had ignored Georgetown's cost. "No. Of course not. You're probably right. I'd just be homesick at Georgetown. It's better to go off somewhere close with Cindy."

Matilda squeezed my hand. "I'd feel much better about it. I'd rather you take your leaving home by stages. I do hope it won't damage your career and that I'm not being selfish."

I wasn't beyond manipulating those I loved. "Well, do you suppose we could visit Ethan and Didi now and then in D.C.? Now that he'll be assigned at the State Department his next tour?"

The worried look left her face, like I'd offered perfect penance for her guilt at pushing me away from Georgetown.

"Why, yes, that's a wonderful idea. What say we visit them next summer, as soon as they're back?"

Finally I'd get to travel again, at least to D.C. I'd still have to finish high school and spend four years at college before I could join the Foreign Service. Provided I passed the exams for it. Without going to a school like Georgetown.

* * *

On an early June day over a year later, I ran to the porch after Cindy dropped me off. She'd driven a bunch of us over to the mainland to eat and shop, proud of her new Ford Escort, her high school graduation present. Matilda sat on the porch, a letter in her hand, and I dropped next to her on the glider.

"Enjoy the day?" she asked, but her eyes didn't focus on me.

"Something wrong?"

"Well, Ethan's coming for a couple of weeks."

"A couple of weeks? How'd he talk Didi into doing that?" I assumed, since he'd been away from Didi most of the past two years, he'd want to spend every minute alone with her and that Didi would want him to.

"He's coming by himself."

"I don't understand."

"They're divorcing. He and Didi. I think he's coming here to—start getting over it."

* * *

For the first few days Ethan was with us, he looked like a man who, tossed in the ocean, discovers he can't swim. Perhaps I looked that way after I understood my parents weren't coming back, the time I found I literally couldn't swim.

He said little, just ate a bite or two at mealtimes, spoke only enough words to acknowledge our presence, then went for long walks. He didn't ask me to go along.

One day I decided he'd had enough alone time, like he'd decided for me when I was nine. I found him sitting on a flattened log on the beach, shuffling his sneakered feet in the sand and peering at the marks like they were some kind of secret code he needed to decipher.

He raised his head but didn't say anything when I sat beside him, just went back to staring at the sand.

I got right to the point. "Can't you and Didi make up? Now that you're back in the States? She'd probably like living in D.C. After all, her dad's still in Congress, and she's lived there before."

He cleared his throat like he had to get used to talking again. "Maybe she might have liked that if I'd done it another time—before now. If I'd stayed with her. But, you see, now she wants to marry somebody else."

How could she want to marry somebody else? This must be how a mother felt when her child was maligned.

"Couldn't she try living with you for a little bit, now that you're back in the States? Before she decides for sure about the other man?"

When he turned to me, his eyes sucked pain from within. "Thanks for the suggestion, but she's already living with him. An old flame from high school, into directing movies, so she said."

Was this the first time in his life he'd failed at something?

I pulled up my knees on the log to tighten my arms around them. The smell of beached seaweed floated from the sand. We sat in the stillness of late afternoon until I said, "It's a stupid time, I guess, isn't it?"

A glimmer of the old Ethan flickered in his eyes. "I guess it is. And what did I so glibly tell you that time?"

"You said to use it to plan for when things won't be so stupid."

"So, Mademoiselle Kaitlin, how shall we plan? You'll have to help me, because I don't feel in the least like planning anything. I feel like going to bed and never getting up. Or maybe walking forever on the beaches of Simon Island." Obviously, he needed something else to think about.

"Maybe you could help me with Matilda. She feels pretty down about my leaving to go to college."

He nodded. "Matilda likes to mother everybody. A talent in increasingly short supply today, it seems to me. And as far as she's concerned, you're as much her child as if you were born to her."

"I know. It's why I didn't choose Georgetown. Well, that and how much money it would cost. I want Matilda to have enough money to enjoy old age."

The expression he returned to me conferred adult status, as though he hadn't realized it before.

"I hope I'll still have a shot at getting into the Foreign Service," I said, "even though I won't be going to Georgetown. It's like planning a military career and turning down West Point."

"Kaitlin, all kinds of people become FSOs. My A-100 class included a former rodeo rider, a bartender, and a single mother of two. None of them went to Georgetown. You have to believe God's got a plan for you no matter what happens."

A sudden spasm, pain, I'm sure, contorted his face before he turned away. I squeezed his arm. 'I'm sorry for the way it's turned out."

"Thanks. Thanks for helping me through a stupid time."

"Well, you helped me once."

We watched the tide turn.

"Have to go up soon," Ethan said.

"Yes."

But we stayed a while longer.

"Matilda's kind of a second mother to you, too, isn't she?" I asked.

"I stayed here a week or so most summers when I was a kid and Ray and Matilda were on leave. Back when Mother and Dad were off in Washington furthering Dad's career. Too bad she and Ray lost their daughter. I think Matilda's been trying to make up for it ever since."

"You know what? You're like Matilda and your mother in some ways. You're not just your father. You've got this sensitive streak in you that comes out sometimes."

"Am I supposed to like that? I always thought of Dad as the ideal FSO. And he was pretty successful at it, too, except for that last little bit."

"But was he successful at being your father?"

I caught him midstream with that one. He took a minute to respond. "Not as successful as your father was, I guess."

My father. That last time I saw him smile. I started crying before I could stop myself. I stamped my foot in the sand. "Great. I wanted to make you feel better. Now look at me. I can't do anything right."

He hugged me but laughed at the same time. "Sorry, Squirt. Life all of a sudden got to you. It's fine. You're funny when you get mad, that's all."

I laughed with him and wiped my eyes. I didn't understand the closeness of weeping and laughter, but it seemed to help Ethan, so it was okay.

*　*　*

"I'm glad you're going to school around here," Ethan said before he left. "It's better you aren't going alone over to the east coast."

"What do you mean? Women my age go off to college. I don't have to be pampered because I'm female."

"Don't get your back up. I just think you need a little more growing-up time."

"Ethan Coverwood, even if you pulled me out of the water once when I did something stupid doesn't mean I can't think for myself now. For somebody who's always calculating the odds, you can be pretty dumb at times."

"Really?"

His grin evaporated my anger. He could always get around me with that grin.

Matilda agreed we'd travel to D.C. during the summer to visit Ethan, to the city I'd last seen when I left it with my parents on their final overseas posting.

The morning after Ethan left, my waking lingered between dream and consciousness. "Mama?" I kept my eyes shut to retain the image, but like a butterfly when you approach it, the image floated away.

I punched the pillow in longing and anger. Somewhere was the remembering I both wanted and feared.

11

Toward the end of July, Ethan hugged Matilda and me at National after our plane landed. "Welcome to the city built on the swampland of the tidewater Potomac. The weather's a bit different from the Island, isn't it?"

"Stifling," Matilda said, "but worth enduring to see you again."

"Thank you, Matilda. So, Squirt, you finally got on an airplane again, didn't you?"

"How long are you going to persist in that juvenile nickname?"

"As long as it gets a rise out of you, I expect."

I forgot my faux irritation when he took us to his new Camaro. "Wow. Cool."

"Thought you'd be impressed." He stowed our luggage, and we took off and meshed with traffic on a highway that passed the Pentagon before exiting to local streets.

Arlington, a suburb of D.C. across the river in Virginia, melded a sky-scrapered landscape with clusters of quiet neighborhoods. The fifty-year-old enlarged bungalow to which Ethan brought us blended with other well-kept homes and emerald green pocket yards.

We entered through the kitchen, and I smelled fresh cleaning.

"I contracted with a household cleaning service to spruce it up twice a month. Your time here is too short to worry about scrubbing bathrooms."

"How many do you have?" I asked.

"Three and a half. Plus five bedrooms. And the other usual rooms. Formal living and dining room. Remodeled kitchen with a den and eating area, including a fireplace. Too big for me alone, of course, but it's nice for entertaining. Which is what Mother and Dad did a lot of."

We examined the rooms one by one. "The furniture in each room matches," I said. "Even better than what's in Cindy's house."

Ethan followed us around. "I probably couldn't afford to buy stuff like this today. Nice of Mother and Dad to leave it here for me."

Matilda examined the curtains. "It's a little dark. The draperies and all."

"The décor you mean? You want to change it? I'll spring for new curtains, couch pillows, area rugs, that sort of thing. What about some new prints?

With lots of color?"

During the next month Matilda and Ethan and I transformed his Arlington house. The furniture stayed, of course, the much polished cherry and oak dining and bedroom suites that Eleanor and Joshua had chosen years earlier when Joshua was an important figure in the State Department.

Like children with a new plaything, we replaced the drapes and curtains and linens with bright fabrics from the colors of the rainbow. We tore out the den's faded wall-to-wall carpeting and refinished the beautiful oak flooring and added area rugs to go with the curtains. We tossed bean bags and cushions on the floor and brought in vibrant prints.

"I don't know why I'm spending so much energy on a house not my own," Matilda said.

I turned from straightening a Renoir print on the wall, the one of the girl with the watering can. "Sure you do. D.C.'s part of our life now. You want us to have a home here, too."

I sobered, reminded of the long haul until I could take the test for the Foreign Service exam with no assurance that I would pass it.

* * *

I didn't have many remembrances of Washington from my childhood, only of long corridors in the State Department, where my parents and I had shuffled between bureaucratic offices before assignments abroad. The Department handled the shipment of our household effects, and arranged our airline tickets, and took our applications for diplomatic passports and visas. I remembered the medical offices where Mama or Daddy held me and encouraged me to be brave while I suffered through the interminable series of shots required for our overseas postings.

I had a vague memory of the "C" Street entrance to the Department, the lobby overhung by flags of the nations with whom the United States has diplomatic relations. News reporters assigned to the Department broadcast from here, before wars or other diplomatic crises. Names of Foreign Service officers line the walls, names of officers who died on duty.

"Over here," Ethan said. On one of the walls, midway up, were the names of my parents. He put his arm over my shoulders while I fumbled for a tissue.

We talked after he led me to the main cafeteria through corridors crowded with employees, their necks hung with badges showing their security clearances. I checked my visitor's badge that the receptionist had given me after Ethan met me at the front desk.

When we found an empty table and settled to our meal, I said, "I'll remember every time I enter that lobby. I won't mention it much. But it'll always be with me."

"You've talked a lot about carrying on what they didn't finish."

"Isn't that what you're doing for your father?"

"You think so? I think it's mostly for me. I can't think of anything else I'd rather do. Imagine having a job that doesn't change every couple of years or so."

I put sugar in my iced tea. "Do you ever talk now with your father about what happened to him?"

"No. You've probably talked with him about it more than I have."

"You were away in school, but you knew what happened?"

He rolled his eyes. "Of course. Some of the other students were Foreign Service brats, too, including the son of one of the guys who practically accused Dad of betraying his country. He was a couple of years ahead of me."

"He got on your case?"

"So much that we finally had a terrific fight. We were trying to kill each other, I guess. We fought so hard we didn't see the headmaster, who hauled us into his office. I figured I'd be expelled. I tried to think how I'd explain it to Dad without going into the real reason."

I put down my tea after sipping it. "Why couldn't you tell him the real reason?"

"I told you. We don't talk about things like that. I didn't want to embarrass him, remind him of it. Anyway, I didn't have to. The headmaster bawled us out, then said things that hit home. I always respected him after that."

"What things?"

"He said, 'I thought you were the sons of diplomats. Is this the way diplomats settle their differences? By fighting? How are you going to handle negotiations between two nations who hate each other if you can't even handle your own differences?'"

Ethan leaned back. "It stopped us cold. We both owned we'd been foolish. The other guy apologized to me, and I accepted his apology. He graduated later on, and that was the end of that. Except I still think a lot about what the headmaster said."

"Your mom knows something about how hard it was on you."

Ethan focused on his plate. "In the middle of all that was going on with Dad, she came up to see me. I was still bunged up from the fight, and I had to tell her what happened. For a minute I thought she was going to make a scene over me or pull me out of school or something, but she was a trooper. Said she was proud of me even if she didn't think fighting was the way to handle it. When I asked her not to tell Dad, she promised not to."

"You know what? Maybe your father picked the wrong school for you, but I think he wanted to spare you the humiliation of coming back from Thailand under the cloud of all those accusations after he resigned. I think he cares a great deal for you."

"He certainly never let me in on the secret. I got a concussion in a kid's soccer game when I was seven. The first thing he said after I regained consciousness was, 'Really, Ethan, you could have avoided that if you'd been more alert.'"

His face softened. "Your father put his arm on my shoulders the first day we sat together on Matilda's porch. It was like it was okay to—feel things. I don't ever remember my father hugging me. He stood off on the mountaintop like Zeus. I tried, but I could never please him."

I leaned over my plate. "Sometimes I'd like to strangle both of you. Get real, Ethan. You love him, and he loves you."

"I'll have to think about that one."

* * *

After Cindy and I went off to Bellingham to college and roomed together, Matilda returned to D.C. to be with Ethan a few months each year while he was posted there. She renewed her security clearance with the State Department that she'd had overseas with Ray and filled vacant office manager positions in the Department from time to time.

I think she wanted to be there for Ethan when he came home to an empty house in the evenings, or maybe she was establishing herself for both her children—for we were her children, as Ethan had said—in case I became an FSO as well.

After my sophomore year in college, I traveled with Matilda again to D.C. Ethan, now a mid-level political officer, had finished his Washington tour and was in language training before he headed for his next assignment in West Germany.

"Why not back to the Middle East?" I asked

"I just got promoted. Good time to do an out of region tour...for fun. Anyway, I want to be in Europe when things break."

"What things?"

"The new Russian premier, Mikhail Gorbachev, is bent on reforming the

Soviet Union. Western Europe has beaten the Soviet Union in the economic sphere. They're much more prosperous, and the Soviets can't keep that fact from their citizens anymore. Communication technology's making the Iron Curtain a big joke. It's more like a gauze veil."

I caught his anticipation. Something was going to happen in Europe in the next couple of years, and he wanted to be there for it. Meanwhile I, of course, had to suffer through the last two years of college. And who knew if I'd pass the exams for the Foreign Service even when I took them?

I didn't take into consideration how love can challenge a young woman to look at options she's never considered before.

12

I announced to Ethan by mail the day Michael entered my life.

Dear Ethan,

I think I've found him! A guy I'm interested in who's actually interested in me! I met him at this Habitat for Humanity weekend build. His name's Michael Donati. He's a senior, from Spokane, studying law and justice, and he's going on to law school when he graduates. He wants to work for a law firm for a while after he gets his law degree, then go into advocacy work for things like affordable housing.

I think he likes me, too. He's not serious about anybody else.

He's started taking me to his church, a really big one, with a bunch of youth programs. Lots of college students, and we discuss things and have fun.

Michael reminded me a little of Ethan, hair the same color but wavy, and his eyes matched his hair. Those eyes thrilled me with their scrutiny after he took me to Ivar's for clam chowder when we finished that first day at the Habitat for Humanity site.

The camaraderie we developed working together contrasted with the drippy autumn day, hastened by the warmth and seafood aromas of the restaurant that steamed up the windows.

We bandied the usual get-acquainted questions about our home towns and our majors. I mentioned Matilda several times, and he drew his brows together. "Matilda? You call your mother 'Matilda'?"

I explained that Matilda became my guardian after the deaths of my parents.

"Both of them? That must have been hard on you. Was it an accident?"

I could have said, as I usually do, yes, it was an accident, and left it there. I avoid telling my story if I possibly can, because I hate the awkwardness as people fumble for what to say, usually ending with something like "how awful." Then I have to find a way to steer the conversation to something else.

Michael, however, drew me out. When I finished, he asked, "Have you resolved it yet, or does it hang there?"

"Sometimes I think I've dealt with it, but something will remind me of it, and I'm not so sure. It's like it waits for a really good time to—to haunt me. Spoil the good time."

Why was I telling him this?

Michael nodded. Then, surrounded by other diners caught in the bubble of their own conversations, he told me about his older brother, killed in Viet Nam. "Unlike you, though, a friend was with him when he died, and told us what he said about his love for us. I'm sorry you didn't have that."

I nodded, grateful he understood.

* * *

I didn't hear from Ethan for a while. As I learned later, he was in the midst of tracking the first hints of revolutionary changes in East Germany, a world away from my pursuits.

His first letter after I wrote him about Michael, when it finally arrived, disappointed me.

> Squirt:
> So glad you've found your supposed one and only. Do take it easy and don't do anything you'd regret later. For example: Are you planning to give up your Foreign Service career?
> My job gets more exciting all the time. Some real ferment going on over here in this country divided by the Berlin Wall. More next time I see you.
> Ethan

Supposed one and only? Really, did he have to be sarcastic? His use of "Squirt" did not sit well, seeming an insult rather than the usual affectionate reminder of our relationship, so I didn't answer his letter right away. Then I got another one from him.

> Kaitlin:
> So are you engaged yet? You must be busy since you haven't answered my last letter. Seriously, I wish you well, however it works out. Remember, I made my own mistake in the matrimonial department, so I have good reason for cautioning you to go slow.
> I've made contacts in several churches over here, who've fed me information from the other side of the Wall. Can't tell you

much, except to hint at the involvement of churches in the changes that are beginning. I hope that will keep things peaceful.

I'm planning on taking leave during the holidays and flying over to SeaTac and the Island. Mother and Dad are coming in from Hong Kong. I understand from Matilda that they plan on coming up and all of us celebrating Christmas and the New Year at her place.

Ethan

Guilt bothered me for not writing him, good friend that he was. He sounded like the holidays were becoming more important to him. He hadn't paid much attention to them before and never seemed concerned about where he spent them.

I fired an answer the next day, saying I was looking forward to seeing him and to give me flight times as soon as he had them. Then I returned to my new life.

Michael was in the college/career class in his church, and they were a friendly bunch who made me feel at home. For the first time in my life I got to know the suburban side of America.

The Island life I knew after coming to the States wasn't like life in the average American suburb of the 1970s and 1980s. I don't mean it was Eden, but life moved more slowly on the sparsely populated bit of land.

By the time I left to go to college, the Island was changing, more tourists and retired folk coming in, but it remained somewhat isolated. The social classes were less segregated. Some of us were poor, some better off, and a few of us were rich, but we knew each other by name and watched movies together at our single theater in the middle of Madrona Harbor and dug for clams next to each other on the beach.

In Michael's suburban church I joined in the contemporary hymn sings and the Bible and book study discussion groups. His friends accepted me and seemed to enjoy the different light I could throw on issues. As we talked and explored, some of my own ideas jelled. I will be forever grateful for this religious niche during those times.

While I was explaining that Muslims couldn't see how the all-powerful God would allow himself to be killed, I understood Jesus' death as I'd never understood it before. I struggled to place my parents' death in the context of love and sacrifice.

"It had to do with love," I said, as much to myself as to the others. "To help us, he had to give up his power and allow himself to be killed. For us. In a way, he chose a more powerful way—voluntarily giving out of love."

To relinquish power when you had it? That took a courageous love. That was it. Love that vanquished darkness.

I wrote Ethan about it over Thanksgiving on the Island, my last letter before I would see him.

> My mother and father suffered when they shouldn't have, a little bit like Jesus. They were serving their country, working for better relationships between our country and others. Yet, they weren't rewarded; they died because of what they were doing.
>
> I understand it better now. This life, really, isn't all there is. We go where we're called. We accept whatever happens to us because we know it's only temporary. Mama and Daddy loved me; I'll always have that. It helps to believe, finally, that God loved them, too, and that they go on living, no matter what happened to them here.

Some of the ideas that fermented during that time made their way into my one extracurricular activity, a weekly column I wrote for the campus newspaper, titled "The World at Large."

Ethan had said he and I were able to see the world through a different set of eyes, and we could use our experiences to help others see beyond the latest fad. Writing helped me believe I was doing that.

I discussed changes the new Soviet premier, Mikhail Gorbachev, was pushing in the Soviet Union and what those changes might mean for U.S./Soviet relations. In another column, I asked what might be the consequences of our continued dependence on foreign oil.

The column developed a following, and Michael read it every week and tried to comment on it. I say "tried," because I think entering my world required as much effort on his part as my entering his.

13

I met Ethan at SeaTac a few days before Christmas, driving down in the Sunbird Matilda had given me for my twentieth birthday. The car was used but in good condition, and I loved it.

"Ethan? Over here," I called when I saw him coming through the international arrivals gate. His boyish grin flip-flopped my heart. How I missed him—more than a friend he had become, more like a beloved brother.

He looked the same as ever, still too thin.

"Lo, 'Cuz," he said after a quick hug. "So where's Michael?"

"Home in Spokane with his folks, of course. Did you expect him to be here?"

His smile was as broad as the Cheshire cat's. "Guess I did. But that's okay."

On the trip to the ferry and the voyage to the Island, he intrigued me with tales about his job. I'd planned to tell him all about Michael and couldn't believe we landed on the Island with my hardly mentioning him. In fact, the only time I thought much about Michael was when he phoned me on Christmas Day.

Joshua and Eleanor had come up a couple of days before Christmas. Presents opened and exclaimed over, we were playing one of our new games, Trivial Pursuit, in the late afternoon when Michael called.

Ethan picked up the phone. "You wanted to speak to whom? Oh, sure, and this is—? Sure. Okay. Here she is." He pointed the receiver toward me, his face as blank as a newly washed whiteboard. "It's Michael for you."

I left him holding the receiver. "Michael? Oh, wonderful. Would you put it up when I take the call upstairs? It's quieter up there." I raced up the steps.

Michael sounded curious. "Who was that answering the phone?"

"Oh, that was Ethan. You know, my almost cousin."

"Oh, yes, the one you talk about so much."

We spent fifteen minutes or so, sharing about our Christmases and how much we were enjoying each other's gifts. He had given me a sweater before I left, and I'd given him a book on the history of subsidized housing in the U.S.

By the time I got downstairs, the Trivial Pursuit game had broken up. "Ethan said he wanted to take a walk, get some fresh air," Matilda said. She seemed preoccupied. Joshua and Eleanor had taken up books.

"Oh, good. I'll join him." I grabbed a jacket.

I caught up with Ethan close to where the old pier used to be. He was staring at what was left of it—three wooden timbers in a row, sticking up out of the Passage.

He turned to me. "Michael okay?"

"Oh, sure, he's fine. Wow, it's already getting dark. I can't get used to how short the days are in December. Look how brilliant the stars are tonight. I think I'm Island homesick. Maybe I won't go back to college."

"Well, don't."

"Silly. I'll be all right when I'm there. Anyway, I'm looking forward to my classes next term. When do you think I should take the exam?" I meant the Foreign Service exam of course.

"Next year. Fall of your senior year."

"What if I flunk it?"

"Then you start grad school and keep taking the exam until you pass. I think you'll pass on the first go, written and oral both, but it'll still take months before you get on the list and they finally offer you a slot. You know how it is."

One of the jokes among applicants for the Foreign Service was that, when the Department finally got all the processing done and asked you to join, you were too old to meet the age requirements.

Ethan said, "So you're still planning to be an FSO?"

"Of course."

"What if you marry Michael?"

"Ethan, really, we're not even engaged."

"Do you want to be engaged?"

"Would you stop pushing me about it?"

"Sorry. I'm cold. Let's go back up."

* * *

I wasn't prepared for the post holiday blues. Usually, I looked forward to getting back into the swing of things after the holidays. Ethan and I said goodbye at SeaTac. We hugged, and he went through the gate, not looking back. Then the loneliness hit me.

After Michael met me at school and took me to get something to eat, my spirits improved.

"I didn't realize how much I'd miss you," he said.

"I've missed you, too." Right after I said it, I wondered if it were true, but I didn't wonder for long after he kissed me before letting me off at the dorm.

In social terms, I rode a high that year. I belonged to the American dream. Cindy and I went everywhere with Les, Cindy's fiancé, and Michael.

"Can you believe," Cindy had said to me after her first date with Les, a few months before, "that I had to come off Island to meet an Island boy I could fall in love with?"

Les had been ahead of us in school, and he went to another church, so we hadn't known him that well until the three of us attended a couple of retreats for campus Christians.

Les was going for a master's degree in business before he took over his father's custom cabinet shop on the Island. He took two years on that master's degree. I suspected he did that to remain in school with Cindy. I mean, does it require a graduate degree to run a cabinet shop? His was an old Island family like Cindy's, and his father had made a killing off custom kitchens for new Island homeowners.

After I started going with Michael, the guys hit it off, and we went somewhere every weekend. We hiked on Mount Baker, took the ferry to Vancouver Island for a proper British tea, and cruised in a boat on the Sound to watch the return of the gray whales. Our area is a courting couple's dream. Nature outdoes itself in the provision of romantic backdrops.

The last evening before summer, Michael took me to a fancy Italian restaurant. With his hand in mine, he told me how much he thought of me, how he wanted me to decide over the summer about being his wife.

"I have to be honest with you. It may not be easy being the wife of a guy working against social injustice. It's only fair to suggest it'll be easier if you're part of the fight, too. That's why I'm not pulling out a ring now. I want you to think about it this summer."

I knew I could have him now, get him to go that evening to a jeweler's and get me a ring, and I was tempted. He loved me. I knew that. What held me back? What caused me to accept his idea that we not see each other over the summer?

When I'm confused, I tend to acquiesce. So I agreed with Michael for a summer of silence between us.

I didn't see Ethan that summer. His letters told me how busy he was. He took a week to visit his parents in Hong Kong but otherwise stayed on the job. He worked in the office of the U.S. ambassador to West Germany, and his assignment changed and lengthened. I understood he was dealing with what we call in the trade "substantive issues." They would be on the front pages of newspapers before the year was out, but the only hint was the thawing of relations between President Reagan and Russian Prime Minister Gorbachev.

I thought about what Ethan had said that evening on the Island. What if I decided to marry Michael? Could I still be an FSO? No, of course not, not if we wanted to have children. At least I didn't think so. But weren't two career families the norm now? Not like with my mother.

I could join Michael in his passion, working for the disadvantaged, surely an apt career for a Christian.

A sense of alienation nagged me, but it was obvious with our first kiss of the fall that Michael had missed me. I had missed him, too, hadn't I?

"So what's your decision?" he asked.

It was easy to make a decision snuggled in his arms. I hedged, though. "I want to take the Foreign Service exam first, just to see what I can do." I remembered my mother, giving up her career to marry my father.

"And if you pass?"

"I won't pass. Most people don't."

If I didn't pass, I wouldn't have to make a decision. It would be God's answer. Simple. No sweat on my part.

I comforted myself with that. So comforted was I that I relaxed for the exam, given all over the country, including Seattle, like I was taking a weekly literature test on Shakespeare. I experienced one of those rare moments when everything seems easy and you are made for the time.

"Oh, yes," I told Michael, "it was fun, but I don't expect to pass. And that'll be that."

Matilda and I celebrated Christmas with Joshua and Eleanor in their California home. I told them I was prepared to find out I had failed the exam. Matilda and Eleanor looked relieved. Joshua smiled. "You never know."

I had begun the winter term when Matilda called me at school.

"Tildy? Anything wrong?"

"You got a letter from the State Department. What do you want me to do with it?"

I breathed deeply to counteract the blood rushing to my head. "Open it, please."

The phone thumped, and I winced at the sounds of ripping paper. Did I want it or not? I was torn like the envelope into disparate desires.

Matilda read the words that announced the next stage of my life. "I am most pleased to inform you that you have passed the Foreign Service Written Examination...."

14

Michael held my hand over the table at Ivar's. "I think you should go with it. We can work something out."

I wasn't sure we could "work something out" if I decided to go for the Foreign Service. How would we manage long separations, pregnancies, children?

I opted for uncertainty instead of a final decision. I had only passed the written test, not the oral one. "I'll just try out the oral exams to see what they're like. The chances are I won't pass."

"That's what you said last time."

A couple of months later I took the orals with four other terrified young people. I had to buy a power suit for it. At that time, I had no professional clothes at all, only the Pacific Northwest uniform of jeans and sweats, and a few skirts and blouses I seldom wore.

Among other ordeals, I had to explain, in a face-to-face interview with one of the examiners, what ideas I had on helping third world nations out of their debt. Economics doesn't qualify as my big interest, but, as the instructions said, the examiners are more interested in your poise and bearing than in how you answer the questions.

I passed the orals.

* * *

I looked at Michael's face. "All right, so I've found out what I can do. It's meaningless. I'd rather marry you. When are you going to offer me a ring?"

Michael's mouth twisted. "Not now. You've just found out. I don't want you throwing away your chance at the career you've always wanted without thinking about it. Okay?"

He led me to the dorm from our walk around campus.

I tried to share Michael's world. I hammered and worked to be of use on the house builds. I worked slowly because I've never been good with my hands, and I had to make myself do it.

I went to meetings with Michael and pretended the enthusiasm that those gifted, called people exuded.

All the time, I felt as if I were a left-handed Christian in a world of the religiously right-handed.

Why was I out of kilter? We were doing things for the poor, making the world a more equal place for them. If anything were a God-given task, surely this was. Why did it not give me joy? Something must be wrong with me. The same thing, perhaps, that made me less than an eternally joyful Christian,

I captured my qualms in a letter to Ethan and asked:

How important is what the Foreign Service does in relation to helping poor people? Isn't building houses for them a more Christian occupation than attending Embassy receptions?

About two weeks later, I received his response.

Didn't answer for a few days, Kaitlin, as I had to cap my anger before responding. You know very well that your parents' main work was not attending Embassy receptions. They encouraged other nations to support our foreign policy, reported on what was happening in those nations so our leaders could better understand them, helped American citizens in trouble, and interviewed people who wanted to come to the U.S.

Believe me, my twelve-and fourteen-hour days now rarely include Embassy receptions. Fantastic events are unrolling over here. I can't go into detail, but they have a potential to give us a real chance for a more just world. What we will do with the chance, I can't say, but many of us are hoping we can soon begin beating our swords into plowshares.

If the whole thing happens without bloodshed, it will be a miracle, but I dare hope for that. Without revealing more than I should, I can say that I've had contact with a lot of Christians, on both sides of the Berlin Wall, all of whom are praying and working for that miracle.

Of course, what we are doing isn't more important than building houses for the poor. It's not a contest. We need Christians in both places. We don't have enough in either one, in my opinion.

What you need to do is decide what you're called to. Maybe you should reevaluate your attachment to the Foreign Service. It's okay to change if you feel so led. Your attachment may be wrapped up in your feelings about your parents and not about your calling. I know, though, that, like Esther, you and I have come to this world today for such a time as this. Answer like Esther and pursue whatever your prayers and your aptitudes and God-given circumstances lead you to pursue.

Be prepared, though. Changes bubble below the surface of our world like molten earth heaving once again beneath a long dormant volcano, as Mount St. Helens surprised the world a few years ago with its sudden eruption.

Ethan

I kept the letter open on my desk for the next several days and mulled over it. "Father," I prayed, "why do I make it so hard? Why can't I figure it out?"

Why did Christians have this thing about calling, anyway?

One Sunday, the minister preached a sermon about God calling Moses. "Almost an old man now," he said. "Life over, a failure, a murderer living in the desert. But God wasn't through with Moses. In fact, God was just starting."

Moses, called as an old married man. Jeremiah, called as a young prophet. Jesus born, not in Herod's palace, but in a manger. Later, Jesus coming out of Nazareth to begin his ministry, though, as one of his disciples said, nothing good was supposed to come out of Nazareth.

"Don't put God in a box," the minister said.

I'd gotten in the habit of putting our God callings in a box. No, I'd made it a contest. Things like being a nurse or a teacher were better than being a mechanic or a Foreign Service officer.

I talked with Cindy. She was in the throes of true love with Les, and consequently with God and the whole world.

"I never dreamed God could work things out like this," she said when we discussed callings.

"Like how?"

"Well, you know, I've always wanted to go back to the Island and teach, but I wanted to be married, too. I didn't think I wanted to marry any of the boys on the Island, and how many men we meet here would want to live there? I didn't even think about Les until now. God surprises you."

God surprises you. That's what Matilda had said. Imagine Christianity coming out of a little backwater like the Judean province of the Roman Empire. The disciples asked how a rich man could be saved. Jesus said with God all things are possible. Don't box up God.

Like Ethan wrote, the important thing was to find my calling, whatever it was.

Michael picked me up one Saturday evening, and we drove to his church. Interesting that during all this time, I persisted in thinking of that church as "his" church.

The church is open most days and evenings with its many programs. We went to the tiny chapel and sat in a holy moment and prayed.

Before he let me out at the dorm, I said, "I don't want to give you up."

He tightened his arm around me and kissed me. "We'll take God's answer when it comes."

* * *

One gray February day, I was late meeting Michael for lunch.

"What kept you?" he asked.

"I got stuck watching the news."

"What's happening?"

"You know, the Soviets are leaving Afghanistan. They've been trying ever since Jimmy Carter was president to turn it into another Soviet republic, and they're finally giving up."

Michael shook his head. "You're such a news hound. I don't see why anyone gets hung up on some country we don't care anything about. Maybe my brother would still be alive if we hadn't gotten involved in Viet Nam."

I poured ketchup on my fries. "You're not the only one who thinks we shouldn't have gone into Viet Nam."

"But we did anyway."

"Maybe we wouldn't have if more Americans had known about the place in the beginning, how it had been a colony of the French, who suffered a massive defeat there before we took it on."

"I think we've got things at home to worry about. Who cares about Afghanistan?"

I sighed. "Michael—"

"Look, surely you're not going to tell me we're going into Afghanistan like we did in Viet Nam. Now that the Soviets are gone, why do we have to be concerned about the place?"

I ate a couple fries before I answered. "I'm not talking about military intervention. I'm talking about something to prevent that. What happens in the vacuum created when the Soviets leave? The Afghans actually had a functioning nation at one time. Then the Afghan king got overthrown in a coup in the seventies, and the place fell apart. Eventually, the Soviets took advantage of the situation."

"But why's it our problem now?"

"Because when countries fall apart, if some kind of stability isn't found, bad guys come in and take over. It's always a potential problem when a country doesn't have a stable government. The bad guys can cause a lot of grief for others. For Americans, if they don't happen to like us."

I thought of Ethan and the work of our Embassy in Germany to encourage a peaceful solution to the conflict there. *"If the whole thing happens without bloodshed, it will be a miracle, but I dare hope for that."*

"Well," Michael said, "missionaries have worked on improving societies for years, things like agriculture, with the people they bring the gospel to."

"Of course, what we are doing isn't more important than building houses for the poor. It's not a contest. We need Christians in both places. We don't have enough in either one, in my opinion."

I echoed Ethan. "We don't have enough Christians working in any of these places, like my cousin does or like you want to do or in missions, either. American Christians give so little money and attention to missions, whether it's saving souls or saving bodies, that it's ridiculous. All the time we're singing 'Send the Light, the Blessed Gospel Light' we're not using our money to send the light. We're using it on houses and cars and gasoline and clothes and fast food and entertainment like all the other Americans."

I stopped because his face looked like I'd hit him.

"I can tell you feel strongly about it," he said.

I ached to make up for almost losing it. With Michael, of all people. "Oh, Michael, I'm sorry. It's just that the Soviet Union's becoming weaker and our country will have so much power in the world. I'm not sure we're paying enough attention to what goes on outside of this country to use it wisely. But you're different. You're called. You don't live like the average Christian."

He exhaled as though I'd given him permission to breathe. "Thank you."

Only I was going to have to decide between two paths of service.

* * *

That evening Ethan made his first ever telephone call to me at school.

"'Lo, Squirt. Following the story?"

"You bet. What's going to happen now that the Soviets are giving up on Afghanistan?"

"Well, if we're smart, we'll work on stabilizing the country before fanatics with some kind of ax to grind take over. Without the Soviets to hate, they're going to flounder and be fair game if we don't."

"I wish we could talk about this stuff more often."

"So much is happening over here, too, that I wish I could tell you about."

"Maybe someday we'll be assigned to the same place."

The telephone connection hissed while I waited for Ethan to continue. I thought about what I'd said. The words had issued automatically. In that instant, I decided.

"Probably see you sometime this summer," he said at last. "Have a good evening. I have to hit the sack. Too many late hours. Bye, 'Cuz."

After listening to the news, I lay in bed and wished I were somewhere closer to things—in the Middle East or even in Germany with Ethan.

I cried because of my love for Michael, a wonderful Christian concerned about biblical justice, but his calling was here; mine was elsewhere.

* * *

Michael, kind soul that he was, did not require that I "break up" with him. He pronounced his benediction on our relationship before spring vacation. "You've helped me see things about the world I never would have, Kaitlin. I hope I've helped you as much."

I said before I choked, "You have. God bless."

I went home to heal. And help Cindy prepare for her wedding.

15

"You look so good in green," Cindy said. "I think that'll be the color for the bridesmaids."

We had spent the first day of our two-week spring holiday planning the coming June wedding. I put down a swatch of material. "It's your wedding. Pick out the color you really want. You don't have to feel sorry for me."

"It's just that—"

"Look, don't tiptoe around my feelings. I know you thought we'd have a double wedding, but you don't have to feel sorry for me. Really, it's for the best. Sure, it hurts, but, you know what? I feel relieved, too. That means it was the right thing to do."

"Michael's such a nice guy."

"Very nice. He'll make some young woman a wonderful husband."

"But not you?"

"Not me."

I admit, though, I stopped what I was doing every time the phone rang the first several days at home, unable to quench hope it might be Michael. He didn't call, of course; our parting was permanent. I gave myself up to the abandonment of my short life as a domestic American woman.

When the phone rang toward the end of my first week, I didn't even look up from my book until I heard Matilda's exclamations. "Ethan, really? You're where? Certainly, it's fine. Wonderful, in fact. You know you're free to drop in any time, even all the way from Germany."

By the time Matilda hung up the receiver, I had flung aside my book and pushed next to her elbow. "Ethan, here?"

"At SeaTac. Said the ambassador's taking a couple of weeks off, so he decided to come out here while he had the chance."

I hadn't noticed the greening of the alders that year until I took the trip to the airport. The sunset burnished the sky over the Olympics with rusts and mauves. I drove with the window down so I could feel the wind and smell new growth.

Ethan sagged with exhaustion. I didn't mind when he dozed on the way to the ferry. We walked on the outside deck on the way over because he said he needed the air. I don't remember what we said. Maybe we said nothing, just enjoyed the hushed twilight together.

Matilda, of course, had whipped up a feast, which Ethan consumed like a starved explorer returned from the wilds.

"Ate hardly anything on the way over," he said between bites. "Just couldn't take the airplane food this time. Sat in the aisle of the middle section next to a family. Two small boys kept fighting each other, when they weren't squeezing past me to go to the bathroom, so I didn't sleep all that much, either. It's a refuge here, you know that, Matilda?"

When his head nodded into the carrot cake, Matilda ordered him to bed. "And don't come down for at least twelve hours, understand?"

He rose and staggered toward the stairs. "Yes ma'am."

I think it was more like fourteen when he appeared on the porch next day where I was searching for gray whales in the Passage.

I acknowledged his presence as he flopped beside me, clean-shaven and smelling of soap. "Well, you look like you might live. I wasn't sure last night."

He pointed. "Look, there's one."

I squinted. There it was, tail in the air. We heard the smack even up here as the gray whale hit the water and disappeared. Others circled out of the water's ripples. We watched them surface, blow, disappear again, before we called Matilda to enjoy the show with us.

She served us lunch out there, or, I suppose, brunch would be more precise. By the time we finished, the whales had moved up the Passage.

Ethan suggested a walk into town by way of the beach. "Looks like the tide's way out."

"I'm game."

We took our time on the beach, studying the erosion caused by winter storms. I found a broken balloon that had blown in from someplace. I stretched it out and read *Happy Birthday, Sean* and wondered where Sean was and how old he was.

Once below town, we hiked up the hill and into Sam's Place for ice cream and sat outside on the porch to lick our cones.

Ethan chomped into a vanilla scoop. Ethan prefers vanilla or, if he's feeling particularly wild, chocolate. "So what's Michael doing these days?"

I studied my mound of peach-raspberry. "Getting ready to graduate, I imagine. Planning for law school. We split."

He lowered his cone. "I'm sorry."

"It's okay. We parted as friends, thankful for each other. It's not a stupid time."

He licked his cone where it was dripping, then lowered it again. "A growing time, maybe?"

"That's it."

We didn't say much after that, but I felt the first tickling of joy as we returned home the faster way by the road.

We could hear the TV before we entered the house. Matilda sometimes checked the noon news, but she usually turned it off after that.

She barely glanced at us as we came in. "Have you ever heard of Tiananmen Square in Beijing?"

"No." I said.

"Sure," Ethan said. He advanced toward the TV as though mesmerized.

Then I saw it, the beginning of the famous, abortive Chinese student rebellion of 1989 against the ruling Chinese communist party.

Ethan sucked in his breath. "Those poor guys. I wonder what Dad's thinking."

For the rest of my spring break, the TV filled our lives, eclipsing even the gray whales. Through the camera's images, we joined thousands of Chinese students as they rallied in Tiananmen Square for democracy. Chaos spread across China until the government opted for a hard line and crushed the movement, killing thousands.

The epitome of the rebellion was the tiny figure of a man in front of a terrible, gigantic tank as he dared the tank to roll over him. Years later, I saw that picture in the office of an FSO who was in Asia at the time.

Joshua and Eleanor called to let us know they were okay; then Ethan and Joshua talked for a while. When they hung up, Ethan kept his hand on the receiver for a minute. "I know he wishes he was at the Department in the middle of it."

Amazingly, he soon was. After I returned to school, the Department tapped Joshua for a temporary assignment on a study group dealing with the Tiananmen aftermath. He took leave from his job, and he and Eleanor left for Washington.

Ethan lingered on the Island as I prepared to return for my last term before my graduation. We discussed my plans until I heard from the State Department.

"If I don't hear by summer, I'll have to decide whether to get a job or go for a master's."

"Listen, things are happening. Not just in Asia. Europe, too. You'll be entering the Department at a watershed time. Trust me. Go ahead and apply for graduate courses while you're waiting, though."

So I did, though impatient now with school. I managed to concentrate enough to graduate with honors for my undergraduate degree. Matilda gleamed from a front-row seat as I walked across the stage and received my diploma.

"Your parents would be so proud," she said after the ceremony.

"They'd be proud of you. You're the one who's put up with me all these years."

"Put up with you? I couldn't imagine life without you."

I turned so she couldn't see the moisture in my eyes and was glad when I drove us both back to the Island.

"Events," Ethan had said, would soon stun us all. At the moment I wasn't sure. I felt wrung out like a used lemon, wondering if life had passed me by.

16

Cindy and Les married in June. I was maid of honor (wearing a green satin sheath) and saw them off on their honeymoon, then studied the courses I planned to take at the University of Washington in the fall. The State Department remained a frustration, unable to tell me when I might be called up.

Staring at the three months of summer ahead, listless, lost, I wondered what I would do with myself.

Matilda solved that problem. "Why don't we stay with Joshua and Eleanor awhile in Arlington? They'd love to have us."

I'd almost forgotten about Joshua's temporary job at the State Department. They were staying in Ethan's house, of course. I danced around Matilda. "You're an absolute genius."

On the flight to D.C., I wondered what Ethan's parents thought about the changes in the house's decor.

This time Joshua and Eleanor met us at the airport.

"We changed the colors a little bit," I said on the ride to the house.

"Well," Eleanor said, "Joshua was a little stunned at first, but he likes them now." She squeezed her husband's arm. "Don't you, dear?"

"It's Ethan's house. I don't care if he wants to make the place look like a Van Gogh painting. Besides, it gives us an interesting conversation piece when we have people over."

If I had ever toyed with the idea of doing something else with my life other than the Foreign Service, the idea vanished as I watched Joshua come to life.

Eleanor, too. Perhaps she had liked the Foreign Service as much as her husband. Maybe it wasn't only simple submission. If she'd ever wanted to be an FSO, though, I reminded myself, she wouldn't have been allowed to be an FSO and married to Joshua at the same time, not in the early days.

Joshua even made the op-ed page of *The Washington Post.*

> Kudos to the State Department for inviting Ambassador Josh Coverwood to become part of the group that's reviewing our policy in South Asia and the Far East. Coverwood, one of the leading experts on

the region, resigned under a cloud several years ago because of his outspoken views on our involvement in Viet Nam. Apparently all is forgiven, and we congratulate the Ambassador on placing duty to his country ahead of any bitterness he might feel.

Coverwood's expertise is badly needed. He served previously as director of Intelligence and Research and later Under Secretary for Political Affairs as well as U.S. ambassador to several South Asian countries.

Of course, his bitterness may have been alleviated somewhat by vindication of his views. Too bad he wasn't listened to before. Hopefully he will be now.

Eleanor read the piece to us over breakfast. Joshua hardly stirred, except to growl, "They got one of the bureaus wrong. It was Policy Planning, not Intelligence and Research."

We had visitors to dinner, and I listened to tidbits of diplomatic life, as I had listened to them in my parents' house. I was baited, reeled in, and hooked.

* * *

In early September Matilda and I returned to the Island, and I commuted to the University of Washington in Seattle for my master's degree in international studies. After that, I would have to get a job.

That fall the world changed.

From our peaceful island, as we stacked wood for winter, cooked apples into applesauce, and noted the sun rising ever further south, we watched the slow liberation movement that swept across Eastern Europe. We held our breath, for at first it looked to end as tragically as had Tiananmen Square.

It did not. The prayed-for change materialized. The Berlin Wall fell without bloodshed. For good or for ill, Eastern Europe began meshing with the West.

Ethan worked in the middle of it. He was there when East Berliners dashed across the Wall and danced, when they broke down the Wall with hammers. His notes to us, when he stole time to write, caught a sober mood underneath the exuberance.

Matilda, Kaitlin:

A hurried note to you both. What's happening here, every day, is the most fantastic experience I've ever been involved in. The old Iron

Curtain is being demolished, peacefully, after all these years of fear of nuclear war, going to the brink at least once.

Yet, here we are, thanks be to God. How often do two nations, at each other's throats for so long, begin to settle differences without resorting to all-out war?

I have to remind myself the hard part is just beginning. So often with moments of political euphoria, even before the bonfires cool, the celebration becomes buried beneath realism: economic problems, corruption, and natural disasters. How will we deal with them? Will we turn our backs and isolate ourselves, fall into a materialism that will consume us?

But, hey, let's enjoy the celebration while it lasts.

Yes, let's enjoy the banquet while we have it.

The celebration continued awhile longer. As summer passed into fall, Matilda and I watched more of the world as we knew it come unglued: Poland, Czechoslovakia, Hungary, Romania. Cheering crowds announced the demise of Eastern European communism.

Everyone listened. In the car going to and from school, I traveled like a zombie, radio blaring. On the ferry, commuters sat in cars, listening, oblivious for once to nature's panorama.

One afternoon I accelerated the Sunbird up the hill from the ferry, the crackling newscasts vying for my attention. When I reached the house, I raced inside, lest I miss a single electronic minute.

"Oh, come and watch. I can't believe it. I never thought I'd see history like this," Matilda said, not even glancing at me as I joined her on the couch.

I wanted to be there. How I wanted to be there. I had passed all the exams and sent in every bureaucratic form and received my security clearance. When would I be able to join this brave, challenging world?

Outside, the wind whispered through the firs. The breeze through the windows blew cool with the promise of fall, as it had for untold years on this Island.

Sometimes now, awakened at night in an alien setting, my mind drifts to that clearing, ringed with firs and cedars, my memory hazed with beach hikes, verdant trees, rhododendron, and slapping waves from the Sound.

That night my mind was on none of those.

* * *

Joshua and Eleanor came out to the Island on their way back to Hong Kong after Joshua's stint with the Tiananmen group. He stepped with a vibrancy he hadn't had before.

"That job in Hong Kong's going to seem pretty tame after this," Joshua said. "I made contacts in Washington. Looking into some other possibilities. China's going to be very important to us in the years ahead."

The revolutions in Eastern Europe rolled on, and the four of us ate hurried meals between watching the TV.

We sat one evening munching chicken-salad sandwiches when Eleanor laid hers on her plate. "I can't believe it's finally ending. For over forty years, we've fought the Cold War. All the fears about a nuclear holocaust—"

"It's a tribute to both sides," Joshua said, "that the Soviet Union and the U.S. never really exploded at each other."

We stopped eating as Joshua mused aloud. "Part of it's the information age. It's become impossible to have a true Iron Curtain. You can't keep out information, even in a police state. Look at cassette tapes, not to mention radio waves. And the new fax machines. We get documents instantly copied to us even in Hong Kong."

Matilda shook her head. "I wish Ray had lived to see it. It's a new age. I don't think many people realize it. We've been frozen for years by the Cold War."

"It's over," her brother said. "Or going to be. We've won. What in the world will we do with it, I wonder?"

And if the stupid State Department would ever call me up, I could be part of doing something with the opportunity my country had been given.

17

I got through to Ethan's office at the Embassy on my fourth try.

As soon as he said, "Political section, Coverwood speaking," I yelled into the phone, "I got it, Ethan, I got it! The State Department just called. They want me in two weeks for the next A-100 class. The family's going to have another diplomat."

"Congratulations."

"Is that all you can say? Over a year since I passed the stupid exams and now they want me to drop everything in an instant."

"Welcome to employment with your friendly U.S. State Department."

A phone rang within hearing distance of Ethan's office. A woman answered in English, then switched to German.

"We're a bit busy over here. In case you've forgotten, the Berlin Wall toppled a few months ago and the Soviet Union looks to follow."

"You promised to bring me a piece of it."

"A piece of what, the Soviet Union?"

"Very funny. The Wall, silly."

"Not to worry. I personally hammered off a choice piece for you. Even has graffiti."

"I wish I were there. What's it like?"

"The Wall? I would have thought you'd seen pictures by now."

"Really, Ethan. East Germany."

"Gray. Bland. Boring. Like in the Narnia book where it's always winter and never Christmas. It'll change, though. The two parts of Germany are going to unite and we'll soon have West Germany's poorer cousin caught up in the normal Western consumer madness."

"Why are you always so cynical?"

"Because I'm a diplomat. As you soon will be. For us, the hardest part's just beginning. After the euphoria for the end of Soviet communism wears off, we'll deal with realism: desperate poverty, conflicting goals, greed, and all the debris of Cold War confrontation that litters the globe."

He must have remembered my own propensity for gloom in the midst of celebration. "Sorry, Kaitlin. I'm raining on your day of success. I'll have plenty of leave and a few weeks of training for my new assignment while you're in

D.C. We'll do up the town. As well as one can do up the nation's capital. Northern charm and southern efficiency, as John F. Kennedy once said."

"What are they giving you before you go out?"

"Some management courses. Consultations, of course, with the Near East Bureau. Some time with the European Bureau before I switch because of everything that's happened here. Really glad to be heading back to the Middle East, though. It's always interesting there. I expect some changes since that part of the world no longer has atheistic communism to hate. Interesting to see who the more fanatic types pick as their enemy now."

"Maybe I can find a position in Riyadh with you for my first assignment. Political, hopefully. Just think, you'd be my boss."

"You don't want that. I've a corridor reputation as a hard taskmaster. You're a junior officer and most likely to find a consular position. Listen, why don't you negotiate with the Department like a true diplomat? They can put you in a later group so you can finish your master's."

I shook my head as though he could see my negation. "I've waited too long for this. I've only got one class, with my advisor, and he likes me. He'll probably let me complete the requirements with another paper, come back on leave sometime and defend my thesis. Okay if I make your house my headquarters when I come to D.C.?"

"You'd better. Get Matilda to come with you. It's a huge house for one person."

"I'm old enough to take care of myself now. I'm no longer nine years—"

"Cut a guy a little slack, Kaitlin. I know you're a big girl now, but the house is a bit lonely for one person."

As it had been for him after his divorce. "Sorry. Didn't mean to bite you."

"I was thinking of selling it and getting a condo, but if you're going to be back and forth from overseas to D.C., I'll keep it. We can both use it, have Matilda in, too."

"What if your parents come back to Washington?" I knew Joshua was putting out feelers, bored now with his business job in Hong Kong.

"They want a townhouse in the District if anything comes of his job hunting. Hey, they're signaling me that my appointment's waiting. Give Matilda my love. And I really am proud of you, 'Cuz. You know that."

I stood with my hand on the receiver as I stared into the jungle-hued lushness of spring on the Island, the big rhodies fluffing in the breeze.

Matilda rushed in. "How's Ethan?"

She had, of course, listened in the kitchen to every word I said and wanted to know his part of it.

"He's fine. Busy, as always. Passes his love to you."

"Did he say when he might make it out here?"

"I think he'd like for both of us to live in his house while I'm in training. How about it? You filled a couple of temp positions at the Department when Ethan was there before. Your security clearance is probably still valid."

She pushed a strand of hair from her forehead, mostly gray hair now. "Washington is so frantic after the Island."

"Come on, Tildy. Ethan and I are both going to be there off and on during our careers."

"Yes. I should get used to it again, I guess. But don't ask me to go abroad with you."

"Of course not."

Would I always live with this guilt for not taking her dreams for mine? After all she'd done for me? Deal with her dread every time I went overseas? She'd brought home the bodies of a daughter, a husband, and two friends from overseas postings.

"I'd like to tell Cindy. She'll be home from school now."

I didn't drive over. I needed to temper my excitement to manageable levels, so I raced the short distance into Madrona Harbor, passed the movie theater, then ran up the street across from City Hall and the library and the post office.

I slowed on the Baker Point Road hill until I came to Ferris Lane and the small former summer cabins where young couples just starting out could still afford a house, at least if they had help from their old Island families, as did Cindy and Les.

Cindy had just arrived, had the key in her hand for the door. We never used to lock our doors, but we do now.

"What is it, Kaitlin? It's not—Michael didn't call or something?"

Bless her, she still had dreams about that. Like Matilda.

I shook my head. "No, the State Department called."

After I told her, I couldn't resist saying, "Now, see, if I hadn't broken up with Michael, I'd be in a quandary about whether to accept the appointment. I was right."

She led us into the living room, permeated by the smell of fresh paint. "You could have worked something out."

"No. Not if we wanted children. I'd have had to give up my career just like my mother did. It wouldn't have been fair to either of us to have a marriage with us living continents apart."

Cindy shrugged, newly-married and in love with Les, as he was with her.

I flung off a speck of envy.

"Why don't you have supper with us? Les is working late on cabinets for the new Totem development, so we'll have plenty of time to talk. And I don't have any papers to grade."

"No supper. Matilda'll be wanting me back. But let's talk before you start cooking." I refrained from asking if Les ever cooked or helped with the house.

Cindy tossed her purse and papers on the sturdy maple table Les had built. Their house was cabin-small, but an old-growth cedar in the front yard sweetened the air, and the Saratoga Passage was within walking distance.

We set on the pillowed couch. Cindy's less than enthusiastic response dampened my excitement.

"You're not going to forget us when you become an ambassador, are you?" she asked.

"Fat chance. I'll be a lowly junior officer for a while, interviewing mobs of foreigners who want to visit the U.S. Or stay here illegally. It'll be my job to figure out which."

"I think I'd rather teach."

"It's only for one tour. I really want to be coned as a reporting officer, political like Ethan and like my father was."

"Coned? It sounds like some kind of operation. A lobotomy or something like that."

I giggled. "All FSOs have a cone. It's another word for the function they carry out. Political, economic, consular, administrative, information affairs—things like that."

"You said once your mother worked with overseas American citizens. Helped them with problems if they got in trouble. Like if they got sick. Or put in jail. I think if I were going to be a Foreign Service officer, I'd rather do that. Sounds sort of like what Jesus told us to do."

"My mother was trained to be a consular officer, but she had to resign when she married Daddy. They let her work part-time as kind of a clerk in the consular section. I still get burned up when I think about that, but, no, the stupid rule then said women FSOs had to resign if they got married."

"Not now, though?"

"It changed about the time—well, anyway, no, nothing like that now."

Cindy reached out to touch my arm. "I'm going to miss you oodles. It's hard for me to imagine my best friend not being here. Remember the day Ms. Dalgathy introduced you to our fourth-grade class?"

"Sure. I felt like a circus freak. I don't know what I'd have done if Ms. Dalgathy hadn't sat me at your table."

"Well, she did, and I think it was God taking care of both us. We needed each other."

"I never would have made it without you and Matilda. And Ethan. I don't know what I'm going to do without you to lift me up. I get so depressed sometimes, for no reason I can see."

Such admission would have bothered Matilda, but Cindy accepted me as I was. "The flip-side is that it's made you special. People can talk to you, tell you things they'd never tell anybody else. They know you'll take them seriously. You don't ever seem embarrassed or want to push them off."

I hugged her. "Cindy, you're great. You know that? No wonder you're such a wonderful teacher."

I meandered home, taking the long way past the middle school that used to house eight elementary grades, where Cindy and I had met. Then the church, added to over the years. I sat for a while on the concrete steps and took in the overhanging scarlet rhodies. That holy sanctuary seemed a safe place to face down the hungry wraith who stared at me though the half open door at every banquet of my life, waiting.

My calling had come to me but pure enjoyment eluded me. It meant guilt for causing Matilda pain. It meant I could no longer hop over to Cindy's sure acceptance of me.

Going on meant pain. I understood that now. I would never be fully whole.

But Jesus didn't come to heal the fit. He came for those broken ones like me.

* * *

Tangy scents of lemon icebox pie sent my stomach into spasms when I opened the door at home. Matilda had fixed mushroom pork chops, too. She ministered through food and mothering and actually appeared to enjoy such things. I'd learned to cook because she insisted my mother would want me to know how, but my heart wasn't in it, and my dishes never had the pizzazz of Matilda's cooking. Her food teased, then satisfied; mine kept you alive.

"What are you going to do about your degree?" Matilda asked over supper.

"I'll go down tomorrow and let them know what's happening. I'm almost finished with my thesis. I'll come back and defend it on leave sometime. Maybe before I go overseas."

Matilda put her hands in her lap. "I don't want you throwing away your education. Your mother would be so proud of you."

"I'll hardly be throwing it away. I'll be using it." I scowled at my plate. "I'll never let marriage interfere with my career, believe me."

I looked away from her eyes when she said, "That's why you and Michael broke up, isn't it?"

"I guess I disappointed everybody."

"You don't have to snap at me."

I looked back at her, surprised. She smiled, and my irritation vanished. My love for her, seldom acknowledged, crept on me like a bittersweet ache.

"Tildy, you do know how much I appreciate you taking care of me all these years, don't you? Especially when you didn't give up on me when I was so unruly and hated everybody. I'm not even blood kin to you."

"Friendship can be stronger than kinship."

"Yes," I said and looked away for a moment to allow space. I stood. "I think I'll go for a walk on the beach before the sun goes down."

I picked my way down the bluff trail to the beach, watching the shine of the sun's western rays reflect eastward and bathe the Cascades.

Where would my parents have retired? Somewhere with a university, perhaps, so my cerebral father could teach. My gentle, learned father and my passionate, Southern-touched mother. What a pair. Their giving to Matilda and to Ethan had come back to me after they died. Who would I pass all this love to?

18

I described my first day in A-100 to Ethan in a letter that night as a cross between processing in for the military and the scary first day at a new school. We filled out forms and received a ton of handouts to read. Then we began our learning experience by formally introducing each other to the rest of the assembled class. Of the forty-nine of us, I was one of the three youngest members. It was scary, exhilarating, and heady, especially when we were sworn in as new officers.

The next day I dropped the letter into a box just off the Rosslyn metro before walking to my second day's classes. I had awakened early that morning, eager for the day. Now it was a full hour before class. I wandered into the first-floor coffee shop, bought a bottle of orange juice, and searched for a place to sit among the crowded breakfast-seekers. Squeezing through a narrow aisle to the only available seat, I felt myself brush something and heard the something smack to the floor behind me. When I turned, I saw a man a few years older than me retrieve his paperback.

I recognized him. He was the one whose grave manner appeared to overcome the nervousness the rest of us exhibited when we had to introduce each other.

"Sorry," I apologized.

"My fault. I was reading too far into the aisle."

I flopped into the seat, which happened to be on the other side of him. "I think you're in the class, aren't you? The A-100? I just can't remember your name."

He turned to face me, reluctantly I thought. Perhaps he was enjoying his early morning read.

"Anson Andrews. You're name's Kaitlin, and you're from Washington State, right?"

"Oh, yes, you're from Portland. You were a family life counselor before you joined."

Again I sensed his reluctance and searched for words to fill the blank space. I glanced at his book. "You're reading *Life Together*? I read that not too long ago. After reading a biography of Bonhoeffer my cousin gave me."

He seemed less reluctant now. "What did you think of it?"

"I think I enjoyed most the chapter on ministry. He wrote something, if I remember, about our having to be willing to be interrupted by God. That our schedule isn't necessarily our own."

"You mean, maybe, that, for a lot of us, our lives were interrupted by coming here? Judging by the introductions yesterday, only a few people, the younger ones, I'd say, had gone to school with the goal specifically of being a Foreign Service officer. Like you."

"Right, but how old are you?"

"Twenty-nine." A haunting aura hung about him, reminding me of Ethan after his divorce. He was aloof, as though still sore from hurt and not wanting to be touched.

"You were interrupted? You had a counseling career you had to give up?"

He set the book by his unfinished cinnamon roll and laughed, but the laugh was not one of a young man. "Actually, I am—was—a minister. I'm fleeing the ministry, a Jonah, you see. I wasn't exactly lying when I said I was a counselor, since I did do plenty of counseling. Unfortunately, I couldn't counsel myself or my wife, who divorced me. Over another man."

He faced me, and I read the fear. "Please, don't tell anyone else. I haven't the vaguest idea why I'm telling you all this. And so early in the morning, too. You caught me off guard, I guess. Or maybe it's your sympathetic face." He sounded younger.

"Don't worry. People are always telling me things, and I never spread around what they don't want me to. And I have a confession, too. I'm a Foreign Service brat, but don't tell anyone."

"Foreign Service brat? You mean your parents were officers? Why on earth wouldn't you want people to know? What's wrong with that?"

"Well, what's wrong with being a minister?"

This time his laughter sparkled. "Okay. I deserved that. Why are we both wanting to hide things from our past?"

I popped the lid of my orange juice bottle. "In my case I don't want to be thought different, that I've got an edge or something." I didn't add, *Plus sooner or later I'd have to tell everybody what happened to my parents.* Instead I said, "What about you?"

He sobered, shied away, came back. Perhaps he found I wasn't so threatening and that we shared a kindred feeling of not belonging.

As I drank my orange juice, he asked, "Are you at all religious? I mean, have you ever had anything to do with a church? In this case, a Protestant one."

"Obviously not Catholic, since you were married. I'm a Christian. Will that do for being religious? Okay, you were a minister, you divorced, you left the ministry, now you've fallen into the arms of the Foreign Service on rebound instead of another marriage. Something like that?"

He flashed a delightful grin. "I like the way you put things. My whole life, you see, was going to be dedicated to the ministry. I won't go in to how it all fell apart. You're the first person I've ever gotten this far with since it happened except my mom and dad. And even they—

"Anyway, people have this thing about ministers—you know how they're usually portrayed in movies and books. Like they're all out in left field. I could deal with it when I was practicing—I could prove otherwise, or thought so. But now—well, I'm afraid if people know, they'll think a former minister couldn't possibly perform in this profession. A failed minister at that."

His laugh became brittle, like an old man's. "I'd, you know, felt 'the call.' I'd been so close to God—at least I thought I was. I thought he'd touched me with this mission. In college."

After a pause, he said, "I thought he led me to Stacy. We married just after college. She worked while I went to seminary. We were partners. We didn't have much money, but we had a good time. It seemed to me then that we grew so much together, too" He stopped and turned away.

I said, "Bonhoeffer was a minister. Some people thought he was a failure, too, during his lifetime. Today even non-religious people admire him."

He looked at the book, then at his watch. "I don't think we want to be late on our second day of A-100, do we? Promise we can continue this conversation again, though. Maybe over the weekend, when we have more time?"

I stood with him. "Maybe we could look for a church. I don't have one here."

He grimaced as we headed toward the elevator. "You know, I haven't been in a church since it happened. Couldn't bear it. I'll think about it. Maybe just visit. I don't want to be involved."

We left it at that.

* * *

The A-100 course is a crash introduction to the Foreign Service. For nine weeks, we studied everything from composing cables to managing employees (foreign and American,), from oral presentations to interactions with other U.S. government agencies.

Toward the middle of the course, we began spending time with our career development officers, who were in charge of assigning us to our first tour of duty. We called them CDOs.

The climax to A-100 is bidding on and receiving that first assignment. As the days passed, our impatience grew to finish classes and head out, though some of us would take six months or more of language study and other training after A-100.

After the first sessions, we began informally meeting after classes and on weekends, sometimes in class-wide groupings, sometimes in smaller circles based on the natural blossoming of friendships.

Anson and I often lunched together, usually joined by Natalie El Hinn and Mike Graham, who, with me, were the youngest members of the A-100 class. I was less pleased when Betsy Abrams joined us. Betsy was older, closer to Anson's age.

I suppose the sensing of a rival is hard-wired into the female brain.

* * *

Matilda arrived to fill a temporary vacancy in the Department, then Ethan a few days later, finished with his tour in Germany. Matilda said on our first evening together at the small breakfast table, "It's like I've been given a family again."

She was soon gifted with a larger family. My lunch group from A-100 adopted the Arlington house for weekend gatherings. The others lived in tiny, sterile apartments, and I could understand the attraction of Ethan's comfortable home, polished by years of diplomatic coming and going.

Anson came first, then Betsy, spoiled, rich, and arrogant, because of Anson, of course. To be honest, even through my jealousy, I sensed a loneliness about her, a need to be with all of us, not just Anson.

Natalie, the daughter of Christian Palestinian immigrants to America, drifted in, then Mike, who confessed to me at one point that he came because of Natalie, which I had already figured out.

Ethan was temporarily assigned to the European Bureau as a result of his work on German reunification, but he was slated to head to Riyadh in the fall.

We plied Ethan with questions by virtue of his experience. He and Anson hit it off especially well, being nearer the same age and sharing the pain of divorce. Betsy flirted with all the men but especially with Anson.

I didn't think Betsy suited him at all.

19

One Saturday evening, when only the three of us shared homemade chicken pot pies, Matilda suggested we visit a church.

Ethan frowned. "I tried a few of them around here when I was at the Department before. I'm not too impressed. It's not like overseas where I was blessed by those little groups of Christians we used to pull together, especially in Muslim countries."

"Regardless, I'm going to find a church tomorrow morning. You two can stay home if you want to."

Of course we went with her. We chose one within walking distance of the house, but toward the commercial district, nestled among new high rises. Ethan wore a suit and tie, and Matilda and I wore dresses.

We walked past yuppies in jeans and flip-flops heading for restaurant brunches with the Sunday *Washington Post* under their arms.

The church, surrounded by thousands of apartments of a rapidly developing northern Virginia, wasn't even half full. We listened to an excellent musical presentation and a mediocre sermon. By mutual agreement, we hurried out as soon as the service ended, none of us wanting to be accosted by greeters.

We headed to a nearby Greek restaurant and took a table in the back to avoid standing out in our good clothes.

"So?" Ethan said, after we had ordered.

Matilda sighed and unfolded her napkin.

I said, "It's amazing. All these high rises around. Lots more people, probably, than when the church was in the middle of a suburb, but the church seems to be dying."

Matilda moved to one side to allow the server to fill her water glass. "I guess they're doing their best to meet the needs of a changing neighborhood. Did you see the signs for two other groups that meet in the church? One Spanish, I think, not sure about the other."

"Vietnamese," said Ethan. "But one group seems almost totally absent, even though it's probably the largest one in the neighborhood."

"You mean the middle-class professionals enjoying a leisurely Sunday morning in their apartments and condos?" I asked.

"Right. How come Christians can't seem to reach this group?"

I shrugged. "Look at the building. It fit fine with the architecture of the single-family suburb. Now it reminds me of those European cathedrals—kind of a dinosaur as far as relevance to the way people live today."

"But why isn't it relevant anymore?" Ethan asked. "That's why the people don't come now—the church doesn't seem relevant to them. For the most part, they aren't atheists or hostile to the church. They're just indifferent to it. How did our exciting story become irrelevant to so many?"

After the server brought our food, we concentrated on eating until Matilda said, "Well, people are busy these days—"

Ethan interrupted. "You think they weren't busy during the days of the early Christians? They worked more hours than we do now. Besides, it could be dangerous to ally yourself with Christians. What gives today? I felt closer to God in prep school when Chopra and I and a couple of others met in our rooms to check out what the Bible said to us. Or in Yemen, for that matter, with the little group there."

"So why aren't people drawn now?" I asked.

"Well, why were people drawn then?"

I considered. "They came because they found meaning. Something gave them meaning. Enough meaning to risk their lives in some cases."

"Did you find meaning today?"

"The music was beautiful. Inspirational. But I can listen to inspiring music at home. The rest of the service? No go. My mind kept wandering. Maybe that's my fault. Maybe I didn't prepare myself or something."

"So how did the early church folks prepare themselves?"

I sighed. "It's like we're living in a past that doesn't exist anymore. I want something that dares me to live in this age."

Ethan's eyes challenged me. "Christ isn't tame, is he? He doesn't wait in a box for us to open it on Sunday mornings. If you find where that Christ is, let me know. It'll be scary, but I want that."

* * *

"You know anybody in the Refugee Bureau?" I asked Ethan one evening at home. "I've got to do a report on it for class. I've got an appointment with one of the directors, Joe Harlan."

"I've seen his name. I think we were in something together at FSI. Area studies maybe."

* * *

A week later, I walked down 23rd from the Foggy Bottom metro station. The breeze under a sparkling sky refreshed, whipping off the Potomac. I looked down one of the cross streets to the Kennedy Center, still not believing I was here, doing what I was doing. Planes flew over, landing and taking off from National. Excitement tingled through me. Someday, before too much longer, God willing, I would head out to my assignment on one of those planes, my first time out of the U.S. since I left it with my parents, except for a few day trips to Canada.

I walked through the "D" Street entrance and managed to insert my ID card correctly through the turn-style slot for entrance. The first time I'd done this, I couldn't make it work, and a grinning guard had to help me.

Finding my way to the Refugee Bureau proved more difficult. The floor was correct; the corridor seemed nonexistent. Finally, I gave up and asked someone. To get to Corridor Five, you had to dogleg through Corridor Four. I found the bureau's main office and approached the receptionist with my request.

She dialed the director for Near Eastern and European Refugee Affairs, Joseph F. Harlan, Jr., while I thumbed through a new issue of *The Economist* from the coffee table. The director arrived unhurriedly and looked to be about forty, no excess weight but more stolid than many male Department types. His pale brown hair was thinning at the temples.

After pleasantries, he led me to his crowded office. Rather than the usual framed family portrait or two, a collage graced his back desk of what appeared to be family members in various activities. He noticed my glance.

"That's my family—my wife and my two teenagers. Trey's finishing up his first year at Purdue. Robin Ann—Annie we call her—still has one more year in high school."

"Did they like living abroad?" I had done my homework and consulted the "stud" book of the Department. Harlan had served in a number of posts abroad, mainly in the Middle East.

"We all did. Hated to come back to Washington, quite frankly." He looked away for a moment, but when he spoke, his voice was natural. "My wife, Robin, developed cancer while we were in Riyadh. So we curtailed and returned here. Thankfully, the chemo appeared to work, and she's in remission. I'll probably make another Washington bid just to be safe before we head out again."

He smiled. "This job's more interesting than I had expected. The only job

I'd had in Washington before was a North Africa desk job. Anything dealing with that part of the world is always interesting, but I rarely was able to spend time with the family. This one's a pleasant surprise. Some travel, but most weekends I'm home. No middle-of-the-night calls. And the work is fascinating if a bit sobering."

"I would imagine the problems seem insoluble at times."

He was off and running. Some statistics, more anecdotes. He visited refugee camps, talked to camp directors, as well as government officials, sometimes conferring with other agencies like the United Nations High Commissioner for Refugees. He dealt with administrative matters and budget allocations.

When Harlan paused, he handed me copies of some of his reports, and his passion shone through the standard bureaucratic language.

"I hope these help you a bit. But you said you wanted me to talk to your class? It's been a long time since I was in A-100. I don't even remember if we had anything about refugees then."

After we made arrangements, I glanced at the picture of his family before I left. Joe Harlan reminded me of my own father—not his looks, but his concern. If I married an FSO, I'd want him to be like my father or Joe Harlan or—maybe Anson?

I mused as the shuttle carried me back to class, over the Potomac and past the park on Roosevelt Island. Okay, so I had a crush on Anson. Maybe I'd have a chance with him if Betsy would leave him alone. Why didn't she go after somebody in her own league?

Something moved in the marsh below the bridge and, in the brief instant before we passed, I saw a snake wiggling out of the water. Here, in practically downtown Arlington.

Not a good omen, I thought.

20

"Aren't most refugees, at least in the Middle East, religious refugees? What hope can we possibly have for settling the problems that cause these refugees? Haven't they been at each others' throats for thousands of years?"

The question from Leona Tingstad pleased me. Leona was a George Washington University graduate who spoke three languages fluently and sported the no-nonsense intensity of one already on the way to State Department legend. If Joe Harlan's presentation had touched her, he had succeeded in presenting the human face of the Department.

He nodded. "Certainly, conflicts have been waged in the Middle East for millennia, but you could say the same thing about Europe. Remember the DPs—Displaced Persons—following the Second World War? Yet, Western Europe hasn't had any wars since then, almost half a century. Unheard of. Reconciliation, peacemaking, challenging the status quo, even calculated risk taking—that's part of our job as diplomats. For our jobs, you have to be eternal optimists."

Later I walked Joe to the elevators, famously slow in this building. I asked a polite question to fill space while we waited: "Do you really have any hope for the situation in the Middle East?"

"I told you, we have to be eternal optimists. The Middle East is special, though. For me, it's where history began."

I couldn't resist challenging him. "But isn't that ignoring the Orient, Asia, all the other civilizations?"

"Sure, it's a valid criticism. You're right in pointing out that other parts of the world reached a high state of culture when Europeans were still in the Stone Age. Like it or not, though, the three monotheistic religions—Judaism, Christianity, and Islam—have influenced the East more than the East has influenced the West."

"Even China?"

"China has succumbed to communism. Think about it. Communism, Marxism if you will, is really a corruption of the Abrahamic view of history. Interesting when you realize that Karl Marx was the grandson of a Jewish rabbi. With China's switch to communism, I'd say a majority of the world's people today hold to an Abrahamic persuasion."

The elevator came, but we ignored it. "You said history began in the Middle East?"

"I'm not talking about civilization per se, or intelligence. I mean the beginning of value systems of the West and much of the world today. Regardless of how poorly we follow those values sometimes."

I hesitated before daring to ask: "Do you go to some sort of—ah—religious gathering?"

"Yes," he answered. "I belong to a group of radicals. We actually believe the claims of Christ should be taken seriously." He grinned. "I'm sorry. I should have just answered your question. I'm making fun of the fact that we so tiptoe around anything religious today."

"No problem. So what church do you go to?"

"My family and I worship with a group that meets in the Laurel Street Church in Falls Church, Virginia. It's an odd little collection of Christians as diverse as any group I've ever been in on this side of the Atlantic. More like groups I was in overseas. Care to join us sometime?"

The elevator bell dinged, but we again ignored it.

"Actually," I said, "we've been looking for a church. Is yours anywhere near a Metro station? Although on Sunday morning, maybe we'd take the car."

"It's a few blocks from the Metro. We don't meet on Sundays. We begin around five on Saturday afternoons. We have a worship service followed by a meal and a study group. The meal's provided by the church, and it costs a whole dollar."

"Why on Saturdays?"

"A lot of us get called in on weekends, but seldom on Saturday nights. Plus, a lot of our singles, especially our foreign singles, like having it then. It helps some of them cope with the loneliness of a Saturday night when you don't have family."

"I might bring Ethan and Matilda, too."

"By all means, bring your family. Ethan is your husband?"

"No, my cousin. Ethan Coverwood. He's Foreign Service, too, in Washington right now."

Joe pulled his brows together. "Ethan Coverwood? He's Ambassador Coverwood's son, isn't he? We were together in one of the country studies. Your cousin, you said?"

"Yes, his aunt is my guardian. We've been looking for a church."

* * *

Matilda waxed brightly enthusiastic, once I assured her it wasn't a New Age kind of thing. "It sounds just like what you and Ethan are looking for."

"I suppose we can try it." Ethan didn't sound hopeful. "Think we should invite Anson along?"

"But what if it's awful? He'll never enter a church again. Let's wait until we go once or twice and see if it's something he'd like."

So we went, and the next Monday morning I practically danced to class and cornered Anson during a break. "It's great. You've got to go with us."

"Yeah, sure." His tone dripped sarcasm. "I've tried a couple places since we've been here, but the churches are just too tame. I don't mean to brag, but my church was alive. These churches seem to be on their last legs."

"Not this one. It's like the early Christians—"

"Now it's like the early Christians, is it? With Peter preaching and Roman soldiers knocking at the portal?"

"No, but the community, I mean. It's a community of Christians who've made a commitment."

I could tell he was interested even if he didn't want to be. "What was the sermon about?"

"Well, it wasn't so much a sermon as an opening of Scriptures, see. We're seated around a long table, together—"

"So now we've got the Last Supper motif."

"I told you, it's a community. Don—that's the teacher; he's one of the pastors—opened the Bible and started talking to us. Sometimes they have music, Robin and Joe said. Somebody plays on a guitar, or sometimes on a piano, or they just sing or somebody sings a solo. That's what they did this time."

"I see. Whenever somebody feels like it."

"Don plans the services. He's a deep, intelligent guy. Plus the people—some Foreign Service families, an Iranian/American woman—she teaches, I think—a guy from the Hungarian Embassy—these people have been around."

"So what'd this Don preach on?"

"I don't know if *preach* is the right word. He talked, but he asked questions. He spoke about two ways of walking and seeing. We're all born naturally. In order to see truly, we have to be born spiritually."

"So? I've preached on that theme myself."

"And did very well, I'm sure. But did you have input from your congregation—did they share how difficult it is, in this day and time, to believe in the supernatural, walking 'in the Spirit' and all that, without feeling like freaks?"

"So you have all this searching of Scriptures and sharing. Then you eat. So?"

"Yes, but it's a continuation of the service. We're still discussing what 'walking in the Spirit' means if you're a secretary in the Department of Agriculture, or like Joe, a director in the Refugee Bureau of the State Department, or whatever."

"Okay, okay. I'll try it. Promise you'll get off my back after that?"

"I promise."

We were sharing pizza the next Friday evening—Matilda, Ethan, and I and the usual crew. I told them what Ethan, Matilda, Anson, and I planned to do the next evening. "It's a Christian group that meets in this church in Falls Church. It's different from any I've ever been in."

Falls Church was one in a string of northern Virginia suburban towns across the Potomac from the capital, but Natalie thought it was funny."A Falls Church church," she said, "that meets on Saturday nights? Cool. Different. Count me in." I'd never been sure whether her family's Christian commitment was to their culture or something deeper.

Mike looked over his pizza. "Saturday night? What a time. I was going to suggest a movie. How come they have it on Saturday night?"

"Something to do with that time of week being a lonely time for some people. Plus, they're all usually free then. Some of them work or get called in on weekends, but not usually Saturday night."

Mike said he'd wait and see how the rest of us liked it. Betsy said it didn't seem like her kind of thing. That was fine with me.

Ethan stretched a section of pizza until it broke, then put it on his plate. "I've got to go in tomorrow, but I'll try to be back by late afternoon."

"You went in last weekend, too. Does it have anything to do with Saddam's threatening noises?" I asked.

Everybody turned to Ethan, because he was consulting with the Near East Bureau before heading to Riyadh. A few stories about problems between Kuwait and Iraq had surfaced in the news. Our assignment bid list was due to us the next Friday, and Mike, Natalie, and I had discussed bidding on posts in the Near East region. We took note of anybody working odd hours in that particular bureau.

Even though we all had top secret clearances, Ethan wouldn't let any classified information slip, nor did we expect it. New officers that we were, we had been drilled on that. Besides the proper clearance, one had to have a "need to know."

"We're just keeping a close eye on things." Ethan seemed to measure his words. "Of course, Saddam does this every once in a while."

I wasn't fooled. Ethan had slipped into his reassuring mode, but I knew his furtive look away from us proved he was worried.

* * *

"What's going on?" I asked Ethan after he returned home on Saturday afternoon.

"What makes you think something's going on?"

"You've been staring out the window ever since you came in."

"So I'm not allowed to stare out the window?"

I flounced toward the stairs. "You'd better get ready. We don't have much time."

The three of us met Anson and Natalie at the Rosslyn station. The train was about two-thirds full, and we scrambled for seats. I ended up sitting next to a teenager listening to music through earphones and in front of Natalie and Matilda. I think Natalie missed her close family and enjoyed Matilda's mothering.

Anson and Ethan sat in front of me. I checked on their conversation while pretending to study an advertisement above the window extolling a new development in the far suburbs, out in the foothills of the Blue Ridge.

The two men discussed Anson's chance of getting a post in Latin America. He already spoke Spanish and wanted to specialize in Spanish speaking posts.

My mind wandered until I heard Anson mention Stacy, the name of his former wife.

"For the first time, you know, I'm able to think of her without this stabbing pain. For a while, I still felt married to her, even though the divorce came through a couple of years ago."

"Takes a while, doesn't it?" Ethan said.

"I'm a definite introvert," Anson continued, "but, hey, I've run introversion into the ground. My little pad at Dupont Circle is giving me the stir crazies. When I was a pastor, I loved studying for sermon preparation, but I enjoyed the ministering side of it, too. Sure, meeting my people's needs exhausted me sometimes, but withdrawal doesn't have that much meaning if I don't have something to withdraw from."

"You don't know yet which cone you're going to be in, do you?"

"No, they changed the rules with this class. We'll be coned later."

"I was thinking you might make a good consular officer. I should think you'd like it if you enjoy working with people."

Joe Harlan and his family met us at the station. Anson and Natalie remembered Joe from the presentation. Trey and Robin Anne, Joe's children, appeared to slide through life with unself-conscious grace, unusual for teenagers, a sense of belonging to the scene and time they're in, something like Matilda, I guess, except for their youth. After a while, you forgot age differences with them.

Would I have been that way if my parents hadn't died?

I watched Robin Anne's effect on Anson and wanted to laugh. He looked like he'd suddenly awakened from a dream, then caught himself. *Foolish,* I could imagine him thinking, *to be attracted to a girl still in high school.* Good. He was starting to escape his exile. I hoped to be there when he threw off the rest of his chains.

Our introduction to the gathering took place in the large hall outside the meeting room. After entering the room and sitting at the long table, Joe explained before we went in, all remained silent until Don began the service.

Once inside, I sat beside Anson and caught his glance at Joe's wife, Robin. I wondered if he, surely more practiced than I in dealing with the sick, had noticed her pallor, seen also the tenderness with which Joe Harlan seated her.

Perhaps our empathy tuned us to the spirit we felt in that place, for we surely felt the moving. Precious times before, Anson told me later, he had been with a knot of believers when God had chosen to attend also.

"I knew what the stirring meant," he said, "though I preferred not to. I'm not sure I wanted to know God is still here, that he loves me. I preferred to hate him, you see, to think he had turned his back on me. To think that he still loved me, Anson Andrews? Wasn't sure I wanted the risk of love again."

I knew from the tears he wiped away that he could not deny the force in that room.

Anson and Natalie joined Ethan and me at the Arlington house for a couple of hours afterward.

"Plenty of food in the refrigerator, if you want it," Matilda said. "I had a wonderful time, but I have to go to bed. Can't stay up like you youngsters."

"It was different," Natalie said. "Different from anything I've ever been to. My family and I worship pretty often, and sometimes I've felt things but not like this."

Ethan leaned forward over the chips and dip on the kitchen table. "When we were eating, I felt like this must be what the early Christians felt. I even caught myself thinking we shouldn't attract too much attention—like when a group of us worshiped in Pakistan—because we wanted to avoid the notice of those hostile to us."

"It's an intentional community," Anson said. "Everybody's there because of a desire to be in that community."

Ethan turned to him. "That's it. A passionate desire. Nothing tame. Even in the children's stories, the Narnia books, Aslan isn't a tame lion."

I watched the two of them, Ethan and Anson, alike in an eager intensity, but different, too. Anson seemed to express every emotion with eyes, mouth, turn of his head. He would never make a political officer.

Ethan leaned forward, expressing a more controlled faith, but white hot if he trusted you enough to share it with you. I did hope he found a woman who would love him.

I thought about that. She'd have to be good friends with me, of course.

21

I picked at the chicken cacciatore Matilda had prepared for supper.

"Look, Kaitlin," Ethan said, "You worry too much. It's going to be all right, no matter where you go, okay? If you really want to go to the Middle East, you'll eventually get there. Africa and the Middle East are bid less than any other region."

Matilda sighed. "Both of you. You're crazy. As soon as you're out of here, I'm going back to the Island."

I glared at Ethan. "I bet you were on pins and needles, too, before your assignment lists were handed out."

"Who me? Cool as ice I was."

"Yeah, I'll bet."

He spooned Matilda's berry cobbler onto his plate. "I'll come hold your hand wherever you are, Squirt. You're worth it, I guess."

I kicked at his leg under the table, but he avoided my foot.

* * *

Anson, Natalie, Mike, Betsy, and I ate a quick lunch the next day. We were almost mute, until Natalie spoke about a conversation she had with her career development officer.

"She said the CDOs have the final choice in the junior officer assignments. After that, mid-level and beyond, it's the geographic bureaus."

"After that, you're on your own is the way I understand it," Anson said. "You have to lobby for the jobs you want. The junior level CDOs help you find at least one assignment that you really want. Their word's the law. Get a hardship assignment the first time around, and you're almost guaranteed a plusher one the second. But once you're tenured, you have to sell yourself."

I recalled verbatim the words from one of the booklets introducing the Foreign Service when I first applied.

In all fairness...potential candidates must be aware of the discipline and sacrifices the career demands....The competition...does not abate appreciably throughout the career.

But it was what I wanted, wasn't it?

* * *

Excitement in the A-100 auditorium permeated the noisier than usual buzz of voices. The coordinator walked to the front with the class's three CDOs, and the buzz evaporated into hushed silence.

"Well, this is it. We have the bid list. You've already met your CDOs. We'll hand out the copies, you take about five minutes to glance at the list, then you can ask whatever questions you want of the CDOs. After that, you spend the next few days deciding what posts you want to bid on."

The pieces of paper might have been gold doubloons, for the barely concealed greed of the class in snatching them.

Scanning the list, I added my indrawn breath to the soft exclamations around me. I looked at the *R* cities. No Riyadh. I checked for the two Saudi consulates. No Dhahran, but Jeddah was there. It was a consular position, though. Well, I had to do consular at least one of my junior officer tours. Maybe it would be best to get it out of the way on the first tour.

Some of the cities were well known: London, Paris, Moscow. Some were fabled in history: Baghdad, Bombay. Some I'd never heard of: Bujumbura, Yaunde. Mostly the posts conjured up exotic thrills: Belgrade, Islamabad, Libreville, Sanà, Wellington.

Did I want to limit myself to the Middle East for first choices?

Ethan and I could travel around, maybe, if I got a European post. I had to bid on at least ten posts in at least three regions, so I could try for some of the European ones. Or Asian.

"So, what's your first choice?" Betsy asked when the class had gathered at one of the Rosslyn watering holes while we studied the list together.

"Probably Jeddah, or maybe Baghdad."

"So you're serious about the Middle East? NEA posts?"

"I'll bid as many posts there as I can. Africa and Europe for my other two regions, probably. But I've got to really study it."

Anson sat across from Betsy and me and examined the list. "Wish I could bid all Latin America. Let's see, Canada's still considered part of European. They haven't put it with Western Hemisphere yet."

"You know, I'm really not into Europe," Betsy said. "I was in London for my junior year abroad and traveled all over. But definitely not NEA—not sure I could hack the way women are treated in the Middle East. Most of the posts I want are subcontinent or Asia." She glanced at Anson. "Maybe I'll bid a few Western Hemisphere posts. Mexico City, Tijuana, maybe."

"So what's your first choice?" I asked Betsy.

"Oh, Hong Kong, definitely."

Good, I thought. *Hong Kong and Latin America are about as far from each other as you can get.*

Betsy ran a hand through her lustrous hair, no doubt expertly coiffed by an expensive hairdresser. "Although I wouldn't mind Beijing. I'd have to take language training for that one, of course. Having Chinese under my belt could be a career advantage, though. I'd be sure of staying in that part of the world forever if I wanted."

Forever sounded fine to me.

* * *

"Where's Ethan?" I asked as soon as I sped into the house and into the kitchen that evening.

Matilda looked up from stirring a pot. "He's not home. Called and said not to wait supper. He's working late."

"Oh, great," I said. "Wouldn't you know."

Later Ethan yawned over his late supper after I joined him at the table with my list. He protested my pestering him. "You've got the weekend. Tomorrow we'll go over them. I promise."

* * *

By late the next morning, I had divided them by regions: Western Hemisphere, Africa, Asia, the Near East, Europe, and one from the Pacific, New Zealand. I looked again. New Zealand? Maybe.

"Three bids have to be hardship posts," I said to Ethan, when he groped his way to the table for a late breakfast." And we have to spread our bids between three geographic areas, too. Of course, hardship posts pay more."

"It's a game," Ethan said. "Just don't throw away a bid. Only bid on the ones you want or at least could endure. One guy in my A-100 bid on London as a throw-away, figuring he'd never get it, because it would be so heavily bid. Ended up going there when he really wanted Moscow."

* * *

The flags were lined up on the front table, and I inhaled anticipation like a small child before Christmas. I was only half conscious of the preliminaries, coming to reality when the names were read off and the flags handed out.

Athens: "Bonnie Sanders." Loud applause: we all knew Athens was her first choice.

Baghdad: "Mike Graham." I clapped like I didn't mind that I had lost my top choice. Okay, so no archeological ruins dating from the beginning of western civilization.

Belgrade: "Samuel Peterson."

Bogatá: "Anson Andrews." That was his top choice. It was an adults' only post because of the terrorism threat, which suited him since he had no family. Yet.

Natalie got Damascus, one of her top choices.

Finally, Hong Kong: "Betsy Abrams." Loud applause, whistles. Betsy had done everything but sell herself into slavery to convince the CDOs that this post should be hers.

Jeddah: "Kaitlin Sadler." I dashed forward to pick up the green Saudi flag, unable to control my grin.

I squealed when I met Ethan, who waited for me after class. "I got it, Ethan. Jeddah, I mean. It'll be a lot easier to visit than Baghdad, won't it?"

He hugged me. "Just be glad you didn't get somewhere in South America. That would have been hard to arrange."

We joined my classmates for a celebratory gathering at a Rosslyn grill. Natalie, Mike, and I formed a subgroup, christening ourselves the "sandbox lot." Natalie spoke fluent Arabic, but Mike would have a full six months of Arabic. I was down for a fast course in Arabic.

I guess the CDOs believed me when I assured them I spoke Arabic, even though I hadn't yet chosen to test in it. I hadn't practiced reading it like I should have but figured I knew it well enough to pass the exam with a few more weeks of study.

Anyway, I was off language probation, having tested above the required level in French, which I'd learned as a child in a couple of the international schools. Two years of French in high school had refreshed my ability to speak and read it well.

On the other hand, I may have been the only one to bid on Jeddah. I knew none of the women bid on it, because they didn't like Saudi Arabia's ban on women drivers.

Once again, we perused our tattered assignment sheets. Mike's tour didn't begin until next spring. Natalie's began this fall and mine in early December. We all had to take Near East area studies, as well as a security seminar and the consular course, since our positions were consular.

"I'm going to push for a political job my second tour," I said.

Mike looked up from his assignment list. "I don't see how they'll manage to give you enough Arabic for this job in the time you've got left. Your job's language-designated, though."

Natalie looked at me, but I shrugged and remained silent. So did Ethan. Wrapped in a haze of excitement, I couldn't be bothered with details now. I'd never shared with any except the Falls Church group that I was more than an Island transplant to the big city.

I sidled over to talk to Anson and Betsy, huddled together. Since neither needed language study, their tours began in the fall. At least they were going to be a long way from each other. Also from me. Perhaps I should have considered bidding on Latin American posts.

Anson turned to me. "Betsy's coming with us tomorrow night. Isn't that great?"

"It sure is." I tightened my hold around my Coke. Now I knew how the prophet Jonah felt, called to preach to the inhabitants of Nineveh, whom he loathed.

* * *

The next morning I pushed around a fresh cheese biscuit on my plate when Ethan ambled in and helped himself to cereal and the biscuits. Matilda had already eaten and gone up to dress.

He poured coffee and sat down. "What's wrong with you this morning? Excitement worn off?"

"Nothing."

"Come on. Give."

I sighed. "How do you make somebody fall in love with you?"

He appeared to digest the question along with his food for several minutes, then laid down his spoon. "Anson?"

"Do I show it that much?"

"No, I just know you."

He must have remembered his divorce because the blue in his eyes darkened. Then he smiled. "Anson would be good for you. I hope it works out. In answer to your question, I'm not the one to ask how you make somebody fall in love with you. My record in that department's a bit lousy."

On the train going to Falls Church that night, Ethan hung back when we boarded. I think he was trying to avoid sitting by Anson so I might have the chance. As it happened, Anson sat in a seat facing the aisle, but Betsy beat me to the seat beside him. I grabbed a place on the seat angled across from them with Ethan sitting beside me. The others scattered to find empty seats toward the other end of the car. Mike had decided to go, I guess because Natalie announced she was going as often as she could before she left for Syria.

I have always thought Betsy liked me even then and that she had no inkling of my jealousy. I felt guilty and waxed and waned in sympathy for her, for the sadness she carried around. At the same time I wanted to snarl at her to leave Anson alone, that she wasn't good for him. He was deeply spiritual; she wasn't. If she got her claws in him, she'd lead him astray, I just knew.

Her next words vindicated me.

"I think the only time I've been in church is for weddings and funerals. I mean, I know this church thing helps some people, but really, this idea about worshiping a crazy Jewish rabbi and saying he was resurrected is on a par with the Hindus believing that the world rests on the back of an elephant."

"So the resurrection bothers you?" Anson asked. He must have kicked into preacher mode.

"It doesn't bother me; I just don't pay any attention to it. A lot of primitive people believe in some god coming to them, being resurrected after dying for them, that kind of thing."

I did feel like Jonah now. He must have felt this way when he finally preached and hoped the Ninevites wouldn't listen to him. "You know, Tolkien turned that idea upside down."

"Tolkien? J.R.R.? The *Lord of the Rings* guy?"

"He said Jesus was the myth become reality. We've always had the myth because we're waiting for God to come to us."

Betsy's face softened. "I suppose it puts a different spin on things."

I don't remember the order of our comments after that, but I actually enjoyed the give and take of our discussion the rest of the trip. Ethan got in his thing about risk. Anson talked about forgiveness. For me, it had to do with redemption, the need for it, the need for sacrifice, as I suppose it always will.

I knew the meaning of bitter sweetness that evening, as I watched Betsy begin a spiritual journey that amazed her. Anson ministered to her with what I suspected were pastoral instincts he could not suppress. His attitude toward her, though, was charged with a tenderness different from the way he ministered to Mike, who renewed a commitment made in his childhood.

So this was community, I thought, not just a ritual, that drew in Betsy and Mike. Like the way Christianity began in those early churches. My musings overcame my prickly jealousy at Anson and Betsy's interaction.

On the way home, Ethan got me alone with him on a seat away from the others. "It's all right, Kaitlin. It'll work out. Okay?"

I dabbed away a few tears, and he put his arm on my shoulder until I could control myself. I sniffed. "I'm happy for Betsy, of course. It's just—I think I know how this is going to end."

"Or begin."

"I wonder if God is mad at me for being sad about how Anson and Betsy are going to suit each other now."

"You remember the story of the two sons and which one did the will of their father?"

I sat up and thought for a minute. "Oh—where one of them said he'd do what his father wanted but never did it and the other who said he wouldn't do it, but changed his mind and did it?"

"Which did Jesus say did the father's will?"

"The one who acted, of course."

"It's the actions that count. You did a wonderful thing, starting Betsy thinking like you did, even if you didn't want to."

"Really?"

"Really, Squirt."

I rarely characterize Ethan as happy-go-lucky, but that night you would have thought he was the life of the party. Joyous about Betsy and Mike, I guessed.

We returned to the Arlington house and talked, literally half the night, except for Matilda, who said she had to go to bed so she could get up and cook breakfast for us. She suggested the others stay the night and found toothbrushes for everybody from airline travel kits stashed in a hall closet. Anson and Mike took the guest room. When I finally got to bed, I crept in beside Matilda so Natalie and Betsy could use the twins in my room.

We had quite a breakfast the next morning, or rather brunch. Kind of like Easter morning.

* * *

Dear Cindy:

I'm going to Jeddah!!! It's in Saudi Arabia by the Red Sea. It's a merchant town, been there for centuries. Legend has it that Eve is buried there.

Ethan will be in Riyadh and can visit when he has time, although I don't want to impose on him, as he'll be very busy with his job as a political officer.

I've been reading all I can find out about it. We have two more weeks of orientation. Then we scatter to specialized training. I have a week for a security seminar and consultation time with the Arabian desk, as well as consular people, and some others. I'm going to be a consular officer, by the way: I will actually have titles, two of them: "Third Secretary" and "Vice Consul." They told us, but I can't remember why I have two.

Then I take eight weeks of "fast" Arabic. That's supposed to bring me up to speed, considering that I already can speak it. Then I have over a month of consular training. In Jeddah, I'll be interviewing people who want to visit the States. As I think I told you, that's one of the things a consular officer does.

Absolutely ecstatic, Kaitlin

I just wished I had a political or economic assignment, a reporting job like my father and like Ethan. The number of women and men in my class approached equal proportions, but more women still were found in the consular function than in the reporting jobs. The fact that my mother may have enjoyed consular work did not occur to me. I wanted to excel in what had been a man's sphere, like she never had the opportunity to do.

22

We entered the final days of A-100. I went to bed late one night and slept delightfully until the phone rang. And rang again. I pulled the pillow over my head. Someone would catch it. Ethan, most likely. Probably a wrong number, although once last week, the State desk officer for Saudi Arabia had called Ethan about midnight, and he had driven in to the Department for a couple of hours.

I must have gone back to sleep under my pillow. Somebody was shaking me out of my slumber. I felt fresh air as the pillow was pulled off.

"Kaitlin, wake up."

I jerked upright. "Ethan? What is it? What's wrong?"

Something was wrong, of course. Sudden interruptions to sleep and life are caused by something going wrong.

"It's Kuwait. Saddam Hussein has attacked Kuwait."

I grabbed my robe, and we joined Matilda in front of the TV. We watched meetings at the United Nations and then a report from the State Department, the reporter framed by flags at the "C" Street entrance.

Matilda grabbed my hand. "You foolish children. You're both going to be there." She meant Saudi Arabia, of course, just below Kuwait.

"I wish I were there now."

Ethan grinned at me. He was dressed and had been standing and watching the TV, but now he went to Matilda and hugged her.

"Yes, your foolish family." He started toward the door. "I'm going in. Don't expect me back for a while."

I jumped up. "I want to go in with you. Can't I?"

"Wait 'til later when they'll be starting a task force. They'll be searching for warm bodies to fill it, and they'll be happy to have you. Just think of all the American oil workers and their families in Kuwait and Saudi Arabia. Saddam's going to take over Kuwait and its oil fields while everybody's still in a state of shock most likely, then head straight for the Saudi fields over the border."

Ethan did not come home that night.

The next day the sandox lot clustered between breaks. Mike had received unwelcome news. The Embassy in Baghdad, he said, would be drawing down. His CDO couldn't tell him yet where he'd be reassigned.

"I'm not a happy camper," he moaned.

I didn't want to make Mike feel bad, but I said, "I wish I could skip Arabic. I think I'll take the test and see if I can test high enough to get out of it so they'll send me sooner."

We kept the TV on at home and stayed up late, finding it hard to do anything else. *So much for peace,* I thought, as I watched this first confrontation in the post-Cold War world, limed in living color on CNN.

> "The Department of State announced today that Secretary James Baker will travel to the Middle East, with a major stop in Jeddah, Saudi Arabia, to confer with Saudi government officials. It's no secret the U.S. hopes to send troops to that country to stop the Iraqi advance before it reaches the oil fields located in eastern Saudi Arabia, just below Kuwait.
>
> "Meanwhile, diplomatic efforts continued in the U.N. to pass a resolution condemning Iraqi aggression against Kuwait and calling for a coalition force to oust the invaders.
>
> "The U.S. Embassy in Kuwait says all American employees at the Embassy are safe and have food and water to last indefinitely."

I sought to grasp the implications for my life, what I was doing, how I was involved in these events. One of our A-100 instructors had a friend at the besieged U.S. Embassy in Kuwait. Shortly, I'd leave for a country mentioned in each hour's newscasts. I thought briefly of Michael and thanked God I hadn't married him. Think what I would have missed.

Ethan came home late Friday evening, then returned to the Department early Saturday morning. About three in the afternoon, he swept in. "I'm going out early. They need me now. I'm packing this weekend and leaving next week as soon as they can get my visa."

I failed miserably in hiding my envy.

* * *

I gripped the phone. "Cindy? I'm so glad you called. It's been ages. How are you and Les?"

"Better than you, I expect. I can't believe you're going to this place. I never even heard of it before, and now we're going to fight a war over there. Surely you're not still going."

"Of course I am. The Iraqis haven't invaded Saudi Arabia." To myself, I added *not yet.* "Even if the Iraqis do cross the border, Jeddah's on the far western side. I just wish I were going to Dharhan in the Eastern Province—excuse me, the northeastern corner—below Kuwait. Now that would be exciting."

"Exciting? You've lost me. Being in a war zone is something you want?"

"I'll finally be doing something worthwhile. You know, going where the action is."

"Well, whatever you say. The whole church is praying for you."

Tears threatened. I managed to stammer, "Thanks."

"Don't forget the Island now."

"As if I ever could."

* * *

"Nobody takes me to the airport," Ethan said. "We'll say our good-byes right here. I want it that way. Got it?"

Ethan had become positively arbitrary during his years in the Foreign Service. Whomever he orders around, though, does what he says. Matilda crossed her arms but agreed. Maybe I wouldn't have Matilda see me off at the airport, either, when my time came. Maybe it would be easier that way.

"I can't get out of class anyway," I said, so he wouldn't think I was giving in to him.

The night before he left, I told him to be careful.

"I'm always careful, Squirt," he said, "but you haven't traveled abroad since you went with your parents. I hope you know enough to be careful yourself."

For a moment, his eyes went softer than I'd ever seen before, but I played our game of pretending to be mad that he still called me "Squirt."

* * *

Matilda and I met the others in the usual place, the Rosslyn station, for the Saturday evening trek to Falls Church.

"Ethan get off okay?" Anson asked.

I nodded and tried to think of other things.

Thankfully, Mike changed the subject by announcing that he had been reassigned to Qatar. "Same time frame. Six months of Arabic and all that."

His cheerful manner indicated that his main worry had been whether he would remain in the same region as Natalie.

The talk drifted to the Kuwait task force where I had taken a shift the night before, taking calls from American citizens wanting to know about relatives in Kuwait and Saudi Arabia.

A sense of foreboding sobered the Falls Church group that night. Many of us had jobs directly affected by what was going on in Kuwait or had friends who did. Don allowed us a few minutes to share our concerns.

Joe's wife, Robin, spoke first. "It's our friends in Riyadh and Dhahran that we left over there. I keep thinking of them, wondering what happens if the Iraqis push into Saudi Arabia. I'm picturing all the emergency action meetings, the alerts, what they're telling the children. The officers will be working around the clock, analyzing, preparing for VIP visits, serving on control committees, answering inquiries from nervous Americans. The telephone in the consular section will be ringing off the hook. "

And, I thought, *Ethan already is in the middle of it. What is he doing even as we remember him and the others over there?*

After the meeting, Robin headed over to Matilda and me and the other four as we grouped to walk to the Metro. "You're finishing A-100 this week, right?"

We nodded.

"Joe and I would love to have all of you out next Sunday to our vacation place in Maryland, on the coast. Sort of a sending off party for those of you leaving in the next few weeks."

Robin said they had a van and could pick us up if everybody made it to the Arlington house.

* * *

Our "graduation" from A-100 was anticlimactic, probably because the events in the Gulf had already shoved our spirits into the next phase of our lives.

The speaker, our class sponsor, an assistant secretary in the Department, told us how much she envied us, entering the diplomatic stage at such an exciting time in world affairs. "How I wish I were in your place. You'll take assignments all over this rapidly changing world. You'll represent the one remaining superpower. Yet, go with humility as well as pride. You will face tests you have not yet dreamed of, surprises, frustrating and even dangerous situations. You'll have to make crucial decisions with limited knowledge. People's lives will depend on you. You must learn how to get along in the small communities to which you are assigned. You will need to learn how to support and be supported by these small communities of your colleagues while working insane, sleepless hours on issues that affect the globe."

And so Anson and Betsy, Mike and Natalie and I, and the rest of us swore to protect and defend the *Constitution of the United States* as had countless A-100 classes before us. My parents, Ray, Joshua, and Ethan had taken the same oath in peacetime and wartime, in prosperity and recession, in times of hope and times of despair.

I looked at Matilda once—once was all I could do or I'd start weeping as she was.

Only I did wish Ethan were here.

23

"This week, the Saudi Arabian government announced it will allow American and allied troops to use bases for dealing with the Iraqi threat. Our guests today will discuss how long before—"

I switched off the television set. "Break it up, guys. The Harlans are here."

We crowded into the van's two middle seats. The Harlans' children, Trey and Robin Ann, were squeezed into the back cargo space, laughing at something one of them said.

Joe apologized for the big car. "Maybe we wouldn't be in the latest crisis if it weren't for these things and the gas they use."

"We got it when we were in Saudi Arabia to be safer on the roads over there," Robin said, "but we're thinking about trading it in for a smaller car now. We'd feel less guilty, I think, driving over as often as we do to the Eastern Shore. It's good to be able to get away, though."

I knew from our conversation the night before that Joe had been tapped for an internal group on the Iraqi crisis and had gone in several hours on Saturday for meetings.

Anson said he was considering volunteering for a weekend shift on the task force. "Until I start consultations for pack out. Can't believe we're this close. Can you, Bet?"

So he had a nickname for her.

I still remember that day by an ocean, not the cold one of Puget Sound, but an ocean nevertheless. The world, it seemed, stopped to allow simple pleasures: conversation, good food, walks by the shore, slow serenity.

After lunch on the patio, I helped Robin stack the dishwasher and used the opportunity to ask her about Saudi Arabia. "Did you wear one of those black abiyahs over your clothes?"

"No, I never did. Some do. I dressed conservatively, skirt almost to my ankles. Once in a while, a passing religious type would say something. I ignored it."

"What about Christian groups? Did you find one?"

We had finished loading the dishwasher, and Robin led me over to the chairs at the breakfast table. "Christians worship in small groups, carefully. So long as you're just Westerners and do it quietly, the authorities usually let you alone. You'll find places, in a home on one of the compounds, probably. We invited a group to our house. Since we're diplomats, we felt we'd be safer. It was one way we could serve." She brushed a stray lock from her forehead. Her ebony hair, lustrous and full, had come back, I guessed, from the chemotherapy she'd taken.

"I always thought our secretive house worship gave an early Christian flavor to the worship. In a way, I miss it. You knew everyone with you took their Christian commitment seriously. The group at Falls Church is the closest we've found to it." She studied me. "You talked once about your parents. How do you feel now about your assignment? Especially with what's going on?"

I made sure Matilda wasn't around. Looking through the glass patio doors, I spotted her talking to Joe. "I'm surprised I'm feeling a little scared in between the excitement. I mean, I've wanted this all of my life, and I still want it, but at the same time I'm afraid."

"That's a good understanding of it. We're handed lots of different assignments. Callings, if you like. Some of them we ask for. Some of them we don't. Some we're ready for and some we have to accept and grow into."

I mused on what she'd said. Different callings. It dawned on me how her words might have come out of her own experience."Your cancer? It's been a kind of assignment?"

Robin nodded. "I think it's probably my last. Of course we all have this last assignment eventually. In a sense, we're preparing for it all our lives."

I thought of my parents. "You've accepted it?"

"It's like you saying sometimes you're scared, but most of the time you're excited. I think I'm like that. I went through a period of anger, then denial, then began to feel called and satisfied. Sure, I'd like the journey to last longer. I think about my family, especially Joe. But, as I step out in faith, I feel joy because it's what I'm called to now. You start out scared, carrying a paltry grain of mustard seed faith, keep going, and end up with a blossoming trust."

I became aware of Joe's presence only when he stood behind Robin and put his hands on her shoulders. She leaned into those hands. I left them for their moment together and walked toward the beach, brushed by envy, sorrow, and hope.

* * *

The tide was out, and I turned to the figure strolling toward me.

"Betsy? You're looking joyful this morning." I felt no envy of this friend, only the happiness flowing from her.

We sat on an upturned stone, and Betsy gazed toward the ocean horizon.

"Just think: I'm off to Hong Kong in a matter of weeks." She got up and whirled like a delighted child. She seemed years younger. "God is so good to me."

Yes, I thought. *She's lovely, in this honeymoon of her faith.* In that moment I accepted whatever happened between her and Anson. I loved her through a sad kind of joy. "You and Anson will be pretty far apart."

She sat again. "We're thinking of buying fax machines for both of us. Faxes are so amazing. You put the fax in the machine, and the other person receives it instantly."

"Sounds like something Matilda and Ethan and I could use."

We sat for a while before Betsy spoke. "I don't guess I ever told you about Dwight, did I?"

"You said the other night in the group that you lived with a boy during your senior year in college. Was that Dwight?"

She nodded. "Living together was really my idea, because I had an awful crush on him. I thought it was love and all that. He was glad enough to go along. I mean, most of the students lived with a boy or girl friend sometime during college. It was sort of a rite of passage, something everybody did."

Would I have been tempted to live with Michael if he had asked me? How much of my staying out of trouble was the grace of God in sending the right people into my life?

Arla. Poor Arla. Please, God, send people into Arla's life, even now, wherever she is.

"The only trouble was," Betsy said, "when we reached the end of our senior year, I was even more hooked on him, but he didn't feel that way about me. He was going to Stanford for graduate study; I was headed for George Washington University. That was fine with him. He didn't even suggest we write. He just said, 'It's been great. Wish you well.'" She choked.

I squeezed her hand. "I'm sorry, Betsy."

"Thanks. I'm okay about it now. I'd gotten hooked up because of this desperate need I have for someone to care for me. Now I know it's there, and I have hopes that God and I can deal with it better.

"But I didn't know if I was going make it through that summer before graduate school. I spent it with my dad and stepmother on Nantucket Island. My stepmother wanted me to see a therapist and get some pills. I wouldn't do it. I knew if I got into therapy, I'd have to mention it when I applied for the Foreign Service. I thought about attempting suicide, but if I failed, they'd put me away somewhere. As an undergraduate, I'd decided on a diplomatic career, and I didn't want anything like that on my record. Maybe that goal kept me going."

She pressed my hand before removing hers and leaning back, bracing herself on the rock with her arms. "You know, you and Anson are the first people I've met who've been kind, and seemed to care for me."

Dear God, I prayed, *forgive me for the feelings I used to have for her.*

"I guess God was taking care of me. I don't know any other reason for where I am now." She hopped up. "Let's walk a bit. The ocean's so lovely and peaceful."

We ambled awhile, dipped our feet in the ocean, and squashed the sand between our toes. After we found our way back to the patio where the rest had gathered, I wasn't surprised when Betsy slipped into a chair by Anson and they shared smiles. Good thing Betsy hadn't needed a language for Hong Kong. She would have a better chance of training in Spanish when she applied next time for a South American post. I hoped they bought good quality fax machines, because they were going to be sending lots of faxes to each other in the next two years.

I remember the feeling of sharing between us in the next hour before we left rather than what we said. I do remember Robin's words before we left. "How exciting. To be a Christian in this day."

I caught the wistfulness in her voice.

24

A legend made the rounds about a new officer who resigned immediately after going through the security seminar. I admit the sessions were sobering.

One of the diplomats who had been a hostage during the Iranian crisis back in the 1970s talked to us about his experiences. "Boredom was the main problem. An inner life to draw on in times like that is helpful."

I pictured myself meditating as contemplatives did during the Middle Ages. It sounded like I would have plenty of time to pray, and prayer might keep my mind off being tied up. Probably today's captors wouldn't let me sing like Paul and Silas did in their jail, though.

A diplomat who had survived an airliner hijacking narrated his ordeal. We were told that a hostage's chance of survival increases with each day he or she isn't killed.

We also discussed situations one might meet in everyday life. Since then, the first thing I do when staying in a hotel is count the number of doors between my room and the nearest exit. Crawling on your knees when the corridor is full of smoke, you need to know how many doors to pass before the exit. Plus, after the seminar, I always wore my seat belt. Traffic accidents on dangerous roads in developing countries kill more Foreign Service officers than anything else, they said.

The thought of Ethan traveling around Saudi Arabia's highways depressed me. He called one Saturday morning.

"Ethan, it's so good to hear you. How's the traffic over there?"

"Traffic? I call for the first time after leaving, and that's all you can think to ask?"

"We just talked about traffic accidents in the security seminar."

"I think I'm more worried about scud missiles."

"Oh, dear."

"Sure you're cut out for this life?"

"I wouldn't trade places for all Midas' gold."

"Yeah, me, too. I love what I'm doing. You have to promise me, though, Squirt, that you won't take foolish chances."

"How about both of us agree that neither of us takes foolish chances?"

"Deal. Let me speak to Matilda. I don't have a lot of time. This is a work day for us. Of course, all our days are pretty much that at the moment."

He gave Matilda his home phone and an office number where we could reach him if we needed to.

* * *

Dear Cindy,

Can't believe how busy I am getting ready to leave. So glad teaching remains exciting. I can't wait to see the new cabinets Les has made for your kitchen. How handy having a cabinet-maker husband.

I hope to see you over Thanksgiving before I ship out. Matilda and I will close up the Arlington house after I pack out. I can take a few days' leave, so we plan a quick trip out there. Matilda says she'd rather tell me good-bye from the Island. I'll come back and stay in a hotel until I leave.

My Arab exam is tomorrow. I'm hoping to do well and go out to Jeddah early. My CDO said they're short-handed and could use me today, as far as that goes. I have to make a 2 in both speaking and reading Arabic to pass. A 5 is native speaker level.

Love, Kaitlin

* * *

"Ethan," I sobbed, "I flunked it."

"Flunked what?" Ethan's voice sounded thick coming over the telephone. I realized that in my haste I had calculated the time wrong. "Did I wake you?"

"What did you flunk?"

"I won't be able to come out there early. I only got a 1 in reading."

I guess he was trying to figure out what I was talking about. Finally he said, "I assume you mean your Arabic language exam. What did you get in speaking?"

"Oh, that—a 3. It doesn't help. I can't average them together to make a 2. I have to have at least a 2 in both."

"Yes, Kaitlin, I know that, but that's still very good for the first time. You didn't flunk it. You just have to take it again at the end of your six weeks. If you'll read the Arabic newspapers regularly like I told you to do, you'll be fine. What's the problem?"

"The war's starting, and I won't be there."

"Don't be absurd. To fight a war, we have to have troops here. Troops do not suddenly appear; they have to be transported. That's going to take a lot longer than your Arabic training."

"You're sure I'll be there when the war starts?"

"I'm sure. Now can I go back to sleep?"

"Oh. Okay. Sorry I woke you."

When I hung up, I felt better. Ethan was probably my best friend. I hoped he got back to sleep.

I felt cheered enough to write a letter to the Jeddah consul general, which is what they call the FSO in charge of a consulate, as well as to the administrative officer. They told us in A-100 that we should write a courtesy note to the chief officer before we arrive at post and also to the administrative person to let them know when we'll be arriving.

> Dear Consul General Margaret McPherson:
> I look forward to serving under you in Jeddah and working with the Consulate staff.
> Prior to joining the Foreign Service, I received my degree in political science, then took graduate courses at the University of Washington. My home is in Madrona Harbor, Washington. I am single. I consider the opportunity to serve with the Foreign Service as both a trust and an exciting adventure.
> I will let your Administrative Officer know my travel plans and arrival time as soon as they are firm.
> If I can be of service, do not hesitate to contact me.
> Sincerely,
> Kaitlin Sadler

I did not mention I was a Foreign Service brat.

* * *

TMFOUR

SUBJECT: TMFOUR PERSONNEL ACTION AND TRAVEL AUTH FOR SADLER, KAITLIN VICTORIA...

WASHINGTON, D.C. TO JEDDAH...ETA 12/90...TOUR 2 YRS (1 R & R)

THIRD SECRETARY AND VICE CONSUL...

I compared my orders with those of the sandbox lot before the two-week Near East area studies began. We traded what we believed to be useful information about when and how to do what in the long list of preparatory items.

"Take your passport to the passport office early. I know somebody who had to wait extra because her passport didn't come back in time."

"I heard they lost somebody's passport; assigned to Somalia, I think."

Mike was as excited about his assignment to Qatar as he had been about going to Baghdad. "I had my mouth all set for it, had read up on it and all that—but, hey, Qatar's kind of exciting, too. I've been reading the post reports. It's on the Gulf, too, where all the action is these days."

We had one more gathering at the house after area studies before Natalie left. I would miss Natalie for more reasons than one. She had helped me as I struggled to improve my reading skills in Arabic. Betsy would depart soon after.

"I'm really going to miss you, Betsy," I said. "I've already missed you not being with us in area studies. Mike and Natalie and I might be able to get together once in a while, but when will I see you after you go to Hong Kong?"

"We'll have to make it happen—life after A-100," Mike said. "We're a community, remember?"

Nice talk, but I knew we'd never be this close again.

"If you're going to be a Foreign Service officer, Squirt, you have to get used to telling people good-bye."

"Fine, but I don't have to like that part of it," I retorted to my imaginary Ethan.

I'm still called to this life, aren't I?

25

Dear Ethan,

    We saw Natalie off and then Anson. Betsy's next. Then me!!!! Mike is in for the long haul, with his six months of Arabic.

    The Arabic newspapers are easier to understand. Here's hoping my exam goes okay this time.

    I bet you're awfully busy there. Lots of activity at the Department, too. I'm taking a shift on the task force once a week, one of the graveyard shifts, but lots of lights on everywhere in the Department no matter how late it is.

    Consultations with allies, I guess, as the buildup in the Gulf rolls on, and the bigwigs travel to Europe and the Middle East to cement relationships or whatever.

    Of course, trouble doesn't stop in the rest of the world, just because most people's attention is riveted on the Gulf. Did you know we may get another task force, this one for Somalia? Probably you know the U.S. Embassy there in Mogadishu is practically under siege as Somalia falls apart.

    Love, Kaitlin

I was taking a turn on the task force when a desk officer called the op center's attention to a cable from U.S. Embassy Mogadishu, capital of the African country of Somalia. He thought it signaled a developing trouble spot to place on the front burner.

A few nights later an op center watch officer bringing cables to the task force said they would be putting out a call for people to begin a second task force, this one on Somalia.

Senior officers on the force took time to drop bits of advice my way. That night, one of them turned to me. "You'll find, Kaitlin, that watching the world is like watching a tennis game with more than one ball—with several balls. Hard to keep focused on them all. Our job is to warn the Seventh Floor about balls coming from nowhere before they arrive. Don't let them learn about some disaster from the evening news."

Senior State Department officials have offices on the Seventh Floor in a controlled section of the building. You had to know the cipher combination to get in, but one of the op center FSOs took me there once when he was delivering a paper. The passages made me think of a somber manor house with family portraits focusing the weight of history on the inhabitants. In this case, portraits of all the former Secretaries of State stared at me from the walls.

I read the nameplate of the office where we were taking the paper before we entered from the carpeted hallway. *Under Secretary for Political Affairs.*

Joshua Coverwood had reigned from that office once.

* * *

Dear Ethan,

I passed, I passed!!!!!

A 3+in speaking and, can you believe, a 2+ in reading? So I'm on. I've sent my arrival information to post, but you said you're in Jeddah a lot these days. When you're down there, please find me as soon as possible. I can't wait to see you.

Of course, I've got to go through the stupid consular course before I can pack out.

After that, Matilda and I are heading to the Island for Thanksgiving. It'll just be the two of us. You probably already know that your parents plan on coming home for Christmas and having Matilda down there. Maybe they'll commiserate together about their two errant children who insist on going to the far corners of the globe in the midst of war. And right before Christmas, too!

Matilda doesn't say much anymore about my going, but I'm afraid she worries about me. She worries about you, too, of course, but she seems to think I'm especially vulnerable or something.

Love, Kaitlin

* * *

Matilda and Kaitlin:

A quick note. Congrats to you, Kaitlin, for passing the Arabic exam. Hardly worthy of note, though, since I knew you would.

To say we're busy is an understatement. Lots of planning, meetings, consultations, VIP visits.

Thanks for your update on the Harlans. I've had several trips to Dhahran, and I'm supervising a young officer there, Patrick Holtzman, who's been a big help. Top-notch officer; he'll do well in the Service. He knew Joe Harlan before Joe and Robin had to leave Saudi Arabia. He asked that I give them his regards and would appreciate any further news on Robin. Can you pass this along?

I knew Mogadishu was going down the tubes. We are, as the saying goes, living in interesting times.

Love, Ethan

* * *

Ethan called once more that last month before I was to leave. I think he was in a place of doubt, maybe, and needed to talk. We discussed the changing times.

"Whoever thought we'd ever see the day when Russia and the U.S. would work on the same side?" I said. "Russia's actually sent a warship to the Gulf with the other allies."

Ethan's cynicism flavored his voice. "I'm not sure we know how to deal with the new Russia. I hope we don't lose this window of opportunity."

"What window of opportunity?"

"The one opened by all this wild hope caused by the end of the Cold War. In places like Russia, people's expectations are tremendous. But they haven't the faintest idea how a democracy works. And then we have countries like Somalia. Somalia's a failed state, and I'm afraid we're going to see more of them. It's going to be worse if we squander this time now."

* * *

Dear Cindy,

I'm into the last round of training: the consular course. I've told you, I think, that my first assignment is a consular one. That means I do things like interview people who want visas to visit the United States. I'll also be learning about the process for immigration, which is different than for the visit visas.

Our instructor told us to trust our instincts and not be afraid to refuse a person if they're not qualified.

I'm not sure I'll get used to refusing people, but it has to be done.

The third "leg" of consular work is working with American citizens. I may have to back up the ACS (American Citizens Service) officer at post.

Must study for our test on the ACS material.

Love, Kaitlin

* * *

"The White House announced today that the President will visit U.S. troops in Saudi Arabia over Thanksgiving. He'll use the opportunity to meet personally with the Saudi government in Jeddah. Since a Gulf War appears almost certain now, no one doubts that a possible date for its beginning will be on the agenda. Troops are still pouring in. We cut to our military analyst…

"The largest troop movement since World War II is taking place at this moment…"

I left Matilda staring at the TV, her coffee growing cold in the cup on the table beside her chair.

The house echoed with my steps. The movers had come for my small assortment of household effects, HHE we called it, and we had prepared the house to be closed up until one of us needed it. A company that specialized in such operations would oversee lawn care and perform regular inside maintenance checks. Our suitcases were packed for the trip to the Island for Thanksgiving.

Mike and I met one last time at the Department cafeteria between the flurry of last minute appointments for me.

"Got a letter from Natalie." Mike's eyes went vacant, overshadowed by a silly smile. "She said she missed me."

"Cheer up. You'll only be a country or so away from her before you know it."

"Am I glad we both bid Near East. It's worth learning Arabic."

"I'm looking forward to trying it out in Jeddah."

"I'm envious," Mike said. "The war'll for sure be over before I get out there. Don't you wish you were in Jeddah for the President's visit?"

"I bet Ethan's busy out of his mind. VIP visits are an awful lot of work for the posts, he says."

"Especially one by the President, I should think. Still, it'd be fun to be part of a presidential visit your first time out."

"What are you doing over the holidays?"

"I'm staying here and swatting the books."

"Surely you're not planning to study Thanksgiving Day."

"The Harlans invited me up to Maryland with them."

After we hugged and parted, I rushed to pick up my airline tickets from travel. I crossed the hall to the employee lounge and studied them, evidence of my first time flying out of the U.S. since I left with my parents.

I pressed my hand over the stiff folder that held the tickets. My father used to hand them to my mother for safekeeping, along with our passports. She wore a leather pouch around her neck, created for travel documents.

My father pulled the two travel totes. We held what we might need en route: books, of course, and coloring books for me, snacks. Somewhere in the course of the trip one of them would pull out a surprise for me. Once it was a set of little figures to play with. The last time out, my father produced a code wheel for making the kinds of codes in which letters are substituted for each other: E becomes T and so on. Fascinated, I made and coded messages for hours on the way to post.

I rose to walk to the Metro and the last night in the Arlington house for who knew how long.

26

Cindy and Les met us at SeaTac. We talked of friends: who had stayed on the Island, who had left, and who had returned. New people continued to build houses.

"You won't believe the changes," Cindy said. "You know where the gas station was? They're building an inn."

"Place is becoming a tourist town." Les sounded like the old Islander that he was. "Next thing you know, we'll have a shopping mall, like down in Seattle."

I stood on the deck of the ferry going over, searching the landscape of the approaching Island, noting bare alder trees among darker evergreens and a recent housing development carved on a hill above the ferry landing.

The ferry swayed in the choppy water as clouds scudded overhead before a late fall weather front creeping in from the Pacific. I inhaled it, the smell of a land not quite tamed, and disbelieved that next week airplanes would sweep me to a rocky desert in less than twenty-four hours.

We prepared the Thanksgiving meal at the Swensens', men and women separating under the old rules. Matilda, Cindy, and I gabbed and worked with Ms. Swensen and Cindy's sister-in-law, Trix, to produce the traditional dishes.

Mr. Swensen, Les, and Bill, Cindy's brother, watched Bill and Trix's toddler daughter in the family room. Every once in a while, I paused from cutting vegetables for the salad or filling the glasses with ice to overhear bits of TV news, in between the Macy's Thanksgiving Day parade.

Matilda and I slipped in to see a breaking news report on the President's visit to Saudi Arabia. The report included a few clips of Jeddah, mostly of the palace where the President was staying. Then the scene changed to the President seated in a room with Saudi officials.

"There's Ethan," Matilda murmured, so softly that I was the only one to hear. By the time I focused on the people around the President, the camera had returned to an outside shot of the palace.

The TV reverted to the parade, and Mr. Swensen muted the channel.

The usual Thanksgiving storm blew in while we ate, but the power stayed on. Matilda and I left the Swensens later that day with enough leftovers to produce another feast.

It's funny how you know certain things won't happen and understand why they can't, yet allow yourself to be disappointed when they don't. I knew Ethan had to scramble for time to catch even a minute of rest because of the presidential visit, yet I was let down when he didn't call us that weekend.

I left the Island on Saturday afternoon to fly back. Matilda and I agreed it would be best if we said good-bye at the house. After I left, she said, she was going to visit homebound members of the church.

"Do you plan to take any assignments at the Department?" I asked.

"Not for a while. I'm going to clean house from top to bottom, pray for you and Ethan, and get back to Island life."

Saturday slipped in with sunshine and more warmth than normal for this time of year, one of those anomalies that happen once in a while in our usual gray season. Cindy drove me to the airport and talked about her teaching. "It's funny. I look forward to Monday, can you believe. Getting back with my students again."

"I need your cheerfulness. Do you know how guilty I feel for leaving Matilda?"

"I'll stop by on my way home. Surely you know we'll take care of her." She waited until she passed a slow truck on I-5 before glancing at me. "Listen, Kaitlin, take care of yourself, will you? Even though I wouldn't do what you're doing for a whole set of new furniture for our house, I think it's right for you. I'm proud of you for following your goals like you have."

I hung on her words for most of the flight to D.C. to press back the sadness.

27

Dear Matilda,

    I know we talked last night, but I wanted this letter to reach you after I've already arrived in Jeddah. I wanted you to know that I love you so much and also how much I appreciate you taking me in and not giving up on me when I was an obstinate orphan.

    I didn't go by the Arlington house; figured I would cry if I did. Don't know why, as I'm expecting it to be a gathering place for a lot of us as we go and come.

    Like I told you last night, the Harlans will take me to the airport.

    Oh, the most important thing: Ethan called right after I talked to you. He'll be in Jeddah for meetings the day I arrive. He plans to meet me with the expediter at the airport. He's already arranged with my sponsor for that and will take me to my house and everything. Isn't that great?

    You have the Consulate address. I'll write you as soon as I arrive. I don't know yet if the phone in my house will be working. Maybe Ethan can arrange something, but don't worry if you don't hear from me right off.

    I love you, and thanks for indulging me in doing what I believe I'm supposed to do.

    Love, love, love, Kaitlin

* * *

I spent the last hour going through checklists until the Harlans picked me up.

    Before we left, Robin checked me out again. "You're sure you've got a pair of sunglasses? You'll need them over there."

    "They're right here."

    "Passport, tickets, money, credit cards?"

    "In my travel jacket." I had dispensed with a purse. Better to keep my valuables close to my body and not have to worry about leaving my purse somewhere.

    I hugged Robin, then Joe at the entrance to the boarding area, so very glad Ethan would be waiting for me in Jeddah. Suppose I didn't have him?

I turned from the Harlans and did not look back.

The roller coaster of my life moved through the short plane hop to heady, exciting New York City. My schedule before departure called for consultations with officials of the U.S. Immigration and Naturalization Service, the INS. Taxis carried me downtown and back to supper in the airport hotel restaurant the first day. Twin to the excitement was an air of unreality. Perhaps I was dreaming and would wake up.

Those who set up the meetings between new officers and INS officials hoped newbies like me would connect the visas I gave overseas with the work of the officials at the port of entry, in this case, New York City.

On the first day of my consultations, the immigration officer allowed me to listen in on her interview with a Haitian couple applying for asylum in the U.S. The couple had entered on a visitor's visa and overstayed. The couple had been granted permission for temporary residence and to hold a job while their appeal was considered.

The immigration official asked for papers the couple was supposed to present.

The young man turned to a section of a notebook and pulled out a packet, neatly organized within dividers.

"He is always organized," his wife said in perfect but lilting English.

The official examined the packet. "I'll need to keep these. You have copies?"

"Yes, ma'am," the man said.

"Says you have a job as a nurse's aide in—" The official examined the papers. "The Living Oak Hospice, Brooklyn. That true?"

"Yes, ma'am."

"How's the job there?"

I don't know how the man could seem so relaxed. I'd have been terrified.

"It is sad, sometimes, when we know the people are there to die. But we take care of them; they do not suffer much pain. I like it when the family comes by and they talk about good times together. It happens a lot, though not always. Those who do not have family, we try to listen to them when we have time. It is so little, but they act as though it is very much."

After the couple left, I asked the official if they would be granted asylum.

"Most likely. They have a little boy, born here, so he's a U.S. citizen. The wife's parents are already here, legal permanent residents, run a cleaning service. The husband was a teacher back in Haiti. He claims to have gotten in trouble with the Duvalier regime because he opposed it, says he would be in trouble if he were sent back. No way, we can verify that, and of course people in his situation sometimes lie through their teeth. My gut feeling, though, is, he's a decent sort who wouldn't have approved of things there. That's all you have to go on sometimes, your gut feeling."

I thought about what she said as I strolled through the teeming streets toward the World Trade Center to catch a taxi. Gut feelings. People's lives depended on your instincts. How would I do, making those kinds of decisions?

Once at the trade center, I stretched my neck while I gawked at the twin towers, then hailed a taxi, not even glancing back. The taxi transported me through a humanity-packed antithesis of my Island community while the driver talked about a murder in the neighborhood close to the airport. I strained to make sense of his—Brooklyn? Bronx?—accent.

"Yeah, can you believe, all for a coat the poor guy was wearing? One of those fancy leather jackets, the cops said."

We entered through the security gates to the hotel, neatly bubbled-wrapped from the neighborhood of the cab driver's story.

The fast-forward film in my head stopped for the briefest of times while I watched the immigration agents at work in the airport on my second day. They pulled aside a Guatemalan woman for "secondary" questioning. Her visa was suspicious. She had no return ticket. She could not answer questions posed to her by a Spanish speaking agent. Verdict: She would be denied entry to this country and sent back on the next flight to Guatemala.

Food was brought to the woman, but she refused to eat. The world of elegant restaurants and taxi rides and exciting airplane flights faded, replaced by the vision of one poor woman, desperate for any chance to leave her poverty. *Welcome, Kaitlin, to the real world, the one you've chosen—or the one chosen for you.*

After my final night in the hotel, I joined a pilot on the van to the airport. At least, I supposed he was a pilot, judging by his airline uniform.

"What airline?" the van driver asked.

I answered, "Pan Am" and marveled that I was doing this. I don't think I've ever been so excited in my life, and it had been a long time since so much fear had swaddled me.

I thought of the last time I left the U.S. with my parents, indeed the last time for them. What had they thought? Had they had any premonitions?

I wished Ethan were with me. Well, God willing, I would see him soon.

Why did the darkness of this evening, suffused in urban glow, seem darker than an Island night with no light except what might shine from the sky?

What was Matilda doing? Was she thinking of me?

Why did we have to take off so late? Inexperienced as I was, I learned later that many international flights across the Atlantic from the U.S. take off in the evening, landing in Europe early the following morning so business people could begin the day there. After a few of those trips "across the pond," I mourned the loss of Atlantic crossings by ship that allowed a traveler to adjust to the time change before arriving.

The driver took out my luggage, and I knew enough to tip him. I made myself stop and put away my money, check once more for my new diplomatic passport and my ticket. Then I pulled my two stuffed suitcases behind me into the airport.

Departures: Pan American. Stand in line. Gradually creep to the counter. Then it was my turn, and I laid my passport and ticket before the agent.

"Smoking or non-smoking?"

"Uh—non-smoking please."

"Window or aisle?"

"Umm. Window, please."

Finally it was over. I had my boarding pass. What a relief to be rid of the suitcases. Two hours until flight time.

I headed through the immigration check. We had been encouraged in the security seminar to pass through immigration as soon as possible. "No airport bombings have happened on the other side of the security check in," the presenter said.

It seemed a mile to the gate, perhaps because I went in the wrong direction for several minutes before realizing it. I found the proper section, sat down, and thought about my list of a half-dozen things to do before and during the flight: file my nails, read a book, work on a crossword puzzle, go over my checklist. I had no inclination to do any of them. Exhaustion slammed into me like a freight train, even overtaking the rumbling in my stomach from the fumes of a taco someone was consuming next to me. Packing out, shots, visas, orders...

I jerked myself from deep drifting. The announcer was calling the flight.

When my row was called, I followed the queue down the long passage, into the airplane to the row listed on my boarding pass. Trying not to stack up the people behind me, I managed to stow my overstuffed tote and slide to the correct seat, by the window. After a bit of maneuvering, I settled with a book in the small space, arranging bulges in my travel jacket to allow more comfort.

There I sat, but the book I pulled out remained unopened on my lap. A man, in appearance from the Indian subcontinent, sat by the aisle. The seat between us remained empty. I listened to deadened pre-flight noises, peculiar to airplanes before departure, and dozed again.

Announcements woke me, and the plane shuddered to life. The plane backed out, taxied, and lumbered toward the take-off queue. I was frightened, almost to trembling. I breathed, *Father, I'm scared, but I'm yours.*

The plane accelerated down the runway, took off and gained altitude, humming and vibrating like a giant insect. I fancied I saw the lighted Statue of Liberty in the far distance. Exhilaration pushed aside fear, pummeled it. I wouldn't change places with anyone else in the world, no matter what waited on the other side of tomorrow.

28

Ethan greeted me after Anwar, the expediter, shepherded me through immigration and customs on the Wednesday afternoon of my arrival in Jeddah. Per Ethan's instruction, I chose a flight that landed before the Muslim weekend of Thursday and Friday so I'd have time to rest from jet lag.

Ethan held his slight build as though he struggled not to droop. His face looked taut until he caught sight of me behind two Saudi men, then he grinned and advanced as close he could to the end of the roped-off arrival section. I almost hugged him when I reached him before I remembered we were in Saudi Arabia, where public affection between men and women is frowned upon.

He took the cart on which Anwar had placed my suitcases and turned to the expediter. "Anwar, thanks so much. I can handle it from here. Take off for a little rest while you can."

I thanked the expediter, too, in Arabic. I couldn't resist showing off my hard-won language skills. He humored me by responding in the same language and said how happy he was to have madame among them and hoped I would enjoy my life here. "You are fortunate to have the son of your father's brother to help you."

So Ethan was using the old "cousin" routine. Did he think I needed protection?

"Exhausted?" Ethan asked.

"Running on empty. Thanks for being here."

I gasped as we stepped out of the terminal into a gigantic sauna. "I thought I was prepared, but the heat is unbelievable."

"Sure you're—"

"Don't start that. Yes, I'm cut out for the Foreign Service. I just have to acclimate."

I examined the van where he led me as he piled my suitcases in the back. "This isn't yours, is it? You didn't drive all the way from Riyadh?"

He shook his head. "Mine is a Jeep, and, no, it's in Riyadh. I borrowed a van from one of the Jeddah officers so we could do without a Consulate driver. Everybody's exhausted these days. So many visitors, and Jeddah doesn't have the staff like Riyadh."

For my first foray into the Saudi kingdom, I had dressed conservatively as Robin had suggested. Even if I could have found one, I decided not to wear an abiyah. A navy skirt reached to my calf, and the sleeves of my full, dark blouse covered my arms to the wrists. After hours of travel, they looked like I'd been in a wrestling match.

Ethan hit the AC button as soon as he started the car, and I shivered when the frigid air connected with my sweaty skin. While we sped from the airport down a super highway, I examined the arid, rock-studded landscape. A vague sense of familiarity stirred me. My parents seemed close; I could almost remember what they looked like now, without a picture.

"Matilda saw you on TV," I said.

He grunted. "Glad it's over with." As we passed dusty highway buildings, he said, "I'm staying on the compound in temporary housing, a literal stone's throw from where you'll be. It's a form of shuttle diplomacy. All these VIPs—State, Treasury, Defense, congressional, you name it, not to mention the President— come to Jeddah because the king's here. I've sort of set up shop on the compound since I have to come down so often."

"I bet the President's visit topped everything."

"Tell me about it. We're still moving like zombies from working 24/7. It went off well, though."

We entered the city, and he pointed to the water. "See the fountain spouting up from the Red Sea? Anytime the king's here, the fountain is on."

"Joe Harlan told me the king likes Jeddah better than Riyadh."

"No matter how much new construction they build, Riyadh remains this austere desert city. Jeddah's got the waterfront and the excitement of a merchant town. When the king comes here, the government essentially follows him. We keep the airplane seats warm traveling back and forth between Riyadh and Jeddah. Would have been so much simpler if the Saudis had just kept the capital here."

We reached Jeddah, sprouting from the flat landscape. Saudi men strode in white thobes and gutra head coverings; the women walked demurely in their black abiayahs and veils. South Asian men wore Western laboring clothes and an occasional turban. Office workers, many of them from India or the Philippines, dressed in slacks and light shirts.

"There's your home for the next two years." Ethan pointed to a walled, down-at-the-heels compound on the other side of the street. A median separated us. "No doubt it was in better shape when it was the Embassy."

Jeddah, I had learned, was the capital of Saudi Arabia until several years before, when the Saudi monarchs modernized their ancestral home, Riyadh, and turned it into the capital, complete with a diplomatic quarter for embassies. I found Jeddah's chaotic atmosphere more appealing than the upscale Riyadh. As one of my area studies instructors said, "Jeddah, having seen everything over the centuries, sports a more tolerant air."

We passed the Consulate compound, turned at an intersection, and headed back into it before stopping for the security check. Ethan and the guards exchanged greetings in what I decided was Urdu, not Arabic, as the guards performed a cursory check under the car with mirrors attached to long handles. All the men appeared to be Pakistani.

The American flag topped a pole in a grassy area in front of the main building. Emotion rippled through like the wind through the flag. Ethan watched me, and I almost choked again at the smile he favored me with.

My house—my own house—nestled under gnarled desert trees. It was worn and unpretentious, but spacious: two bedrooms, a small den and kitchen, and large living and dining rooms, plus a laundry room. Recently, I understand, they've changed the Consulate beyond anything I'd recognize, after a terrorist group broke into the compound and killed employees before the attackers were stopped. I grew to love the old, threadbare place.

Another consular officer, Susan, who was to be my sponsor, lived on the compound along with the consul general and a few other Americans. Most officers, including the head of the consular section, lived in modern townhouses and apartments around Jeddah, but it was handy for Susan and me to live on the compound, available to dash into the office at odd hours to handle emergencies.

Ethan headed toward one of the bedrooms with the suitcases. "This is the larger one, so I assume you'll want it for yours."

I danced through the house. "It's fabulous. I didn't expect to have so much room."

He positioned the suitcases for opening, then checked the kitchen. "Looks like Susan got in a beginning supply of food for you, and the water distiller works okay. I'll take you out tomorrow for more groceries. We'll meet Susan, too."

"What kind of person is she? Her letter was nice but kind of short."

"Be glad she wrote at all considering she's handling the district's American citizens. Fielding calls from scared Americans, setting up telephone trees, visiting the Emirate to plead for exit visas. I'm not surprised she took the time to write, though. She's an older lady, caring type. Reminds me a little of Matilda."

"What's my boss like?" I hadn't corresponded with her, but Susan had mentioned her name, Christine Armbruster, head of the consular section.

"Christine's part of a tandem couple. Her husband's an econ officer in Cario, and she's over there for a long weekend taking a breather."

"So what's wrong with her?"

"What do you mean what's wrong with her?"

"It's the way you haven't answered my question."

He sighed. "It's uncanny, you practically knowing how I breathe. Nothing's wrong with Christine. She's the type you'll appreciate having had as a boss once you finish your first tour."

"Meaning I won't appreciate her while she's my boss."

"My take on her is that she expects the best from the people who work for her."

"Like you do."

"Okay, like I do. I've been with her in meetings. She's efficient, brutally direct sometimes, but the kind you want on your side in a crisis. Take advantage of her. She can teach you a lot of things."

"I can't wait."

He headed to the door. "I need to look at cables in the chancery and check one last time with the CG before I hop back to Riyadh tomorrow evening. Take my advice and shower off the travel grime and crawl in bed. Get a handle on jet lag before they start running you on Saturday. I've left you the phone number for my quarters if you need me; otherwise I'll come over tomorrow morning about nine."

I unpacked a few things and took a shower in tepid water that issued from the cold faucet. The Consulate grounds drowsed in quiet. As soon as I lay in bed, I conked out, rousing for the evening call to prayer, then falling under again.

* * *

The next morning Ethan woke me with his knocking.

"I can't believe it's nine already," I mumbled after I let him in.

"Better adjust to this time zone before Saturday."

I yawned. "Got to remember. Today's Thursday, the beginning of the weekend. Which is good. I don't think I could manage going to work today." I thought of the new things that would greet me on Saturday.

I followed Ethan into the kitchen, where he opened a cupboard door. "If you think it's confusing to remember that the work week starts on Saturday here, wait until your first time home when you have to relearn the days there.

I haven't had breakfast. Good, there's granola. And those sweet toaster things. Instant coffee."

I wandered back to the bedroom and dressed, listening to him pulling out various items and thumping them on the small table in the den just off the kitchen.

"You know what?" I said when I sat down across from him, "I must have left my toothpaste in the hotel in New York. I can't find it."

"We'll get some at the store. Make a list before we go. I told Susan we'd stop by first about 1000." He pronounced it "ten hundred."

"Do you always use military time over here?"

"Most people do. Twenty-four-hour time's more sensible."

"Wonderful. I have to get used to the week being all messed up and a different time system as well."

"They do the month and day the opposite in dates, too. Sure you're cut out for this kind of life?"

I stuck out my tongue at him.

An hour later we walked over to Susan's house past palm trees and nondescript buildings. The chancery, where the main Consulate offices were, spread itself in wings and annexes behind the American flag. Ethan pointed out a sandy golf course back of the Consulate grounds.

"It looks like one large sand trap," I said.

"I think they keep the tee-off places groomed. See the enclosed place over there?

I studied the tall, blank fencing.

"You'll get a key to it. That's the swimming pool."

"Really? A pool half a block from my house? I'm liking this place better all the time."

"And what's nice is that you can swim year round. The Embassy pool in Riyadh even has coolers because the water gets too hot in summer without them."

He led me the rest of the way to Susan's house, a twin to my own, except it had a patio area in the back. A middle-aged woman, approaching overweight status but not quite there, stopped watering flowers and greeted us as we approached. She put down the watering can and apologized for the flowers.

"I haven't had time to water them much lately. Kaitlin, so very glad to see you. Let's sit down and chat."

She did remind me of Matilda. I wondered if she had ever been married.

Ethan said, "Susan'll take you around to all the Consulate sections and handle your processing on Saturday. I'm heading back to Riyadh this evening. You're on your own after that."

I wondered if he had stayed an extra day because I was coming in. He was bound to have loads of work waiting for him in Riyadh.

After we exchanged the usual pleasantries about my trip, Susan said, "I'm having the consular section and a few others over tomorrow evening to meet you. Just a simple buffet about six in the evening."

"Wonderful. How thoughtful of you."

"The staff is anxious to meet their new boss. Per normal, we've been short-staffed. Used to, the tours overlapped, and we had time for training. Not anymore. Your predecessor finished her tour a couple of months ago, and Christine's been handling her own job as section head and your job, too, with a little help from me. Of course, the war footing increases our work. I'm afraid you're going to have to learn on the job."

After we left, Ethan said, "She's a good manager, but everybody's doing more than one job right now. More and more officers have sent their families out while they can, so we don't have spouses to take up slack. You'll be expected to help with the warden system. They've been updating the telephone tree, trying to cover every American with a warden. Good you're living on the compound."

"So I can work more?"

"Oh, you're going to earn your salary, but you can't drive, you know. It's easier for you to live here and not worry about calling a driver in the middle of the night and that sort of thing."

"Stupid, not being able to drive just because I'm a woman."

"Be glad, what with the crazy drivers. Speaking of which, why don't I drive you over for a meal at the restaurant in Saudia City? After that, I'll take you by Safeway for replenishing your larder."

"Saudia City?"

"Where the foreigners live who work for Saudi Arabian airlines. I can get us in on the van's diplomatic plates and my iqama." He used the word for the identity card we had to carry.

He was right about the Jeddah drivers. The one rule seemed to be to drive as fast as you could, ignoring all other rules. I thought we were going to crash into one driver who insisted, without any signal, on veering suddenly across four lanes, including in front of us, then slowing for a right turn.

I grabbed the dash as Ethan braked. "I'm beginning to see why they warned us that more FSOs die of traffic accidents than anything else."

"My Saudi friends who travel to the States tell me they can't believe the way Americans obey traffic rules. Do remember a lot of the drivers aren't Saudis. They're third-country nationals and may never have driven a car until they got here."

"I read the reports. A large percentage of our visa applicants aren't Saudis. Our refusal rate's pretty high for them."

Ethan turned at an entrance into a large, walled compound and showed his iqama, The guard waved us through. Inside the huge complex of private houses, townhouses, and apartment buildings, most residents walked around in Western dress, though a few women wore abiyahs.

"Some of the employees now are Muslims, Pakistanis, for example, but Saudis aren't allowed to live here. It's an attempt to segregate the workers, who used to be almost all Western and non-Muslim, from the general population."

"Avoid contamination from the foreigners?"

"Something like that. Of course, in this part of the world, different ethnic and religious groups have lived for centuries in their own enclaves. I think the rationale is that it's better at keeping the peace between them, plus gives them a chance to set up some of their own cultural norms within the enclave."

The Saudia City restaurant fare reminded me of stateside diners. "I think I'll have the eggplant parmigiana. My appetite's finally recovered from an overdose of airline food."

After I had satisfied the first pangs of hunger, I said, "It's hard for me to get used to all this segregation of the population."

As soon as I said that, I realized segregation had been part of American life, too. "Sorry. How could I forget the ugly racial segregation of my mother's time?"

Ethan swallowed before he spoke. "And don't we still practice economic segregation to a great extent? The segregation over here is more for perceived religious reasons. To keep the faith pure."

"I'll have to think about it."

"Take Europe. We're all rejoicing over the demise of the Soviet Union, but with all its wrongs, at least it kept the lid on ethnic and religious conflict."

"Surely, you're not in favor of the hegemonic Soviet Union?"

"Of course not, but I have to admit dictators are handy for keeping down internal conflict."

"Sure, with secret police and torture."

"I didn't say I sanctioned any of that. I'm only pointing to how difficult it is to handle freedom, especially when it's thrust on you suddenly. Do remember, the Western world developed freedom over centuries."

I stopped with a bite of eggplant on my fork. "I guess we have to learn to get along."

"What button are you going to push to make it happen?"

I shrugged and finished my meal. Sometimes Ethan's cynicism grated.

* * *

The grocery was standard Safeway, but I was glad to customize the basic foods already in my kitchen.

After we reached the house, Ethan paused in the foyer. "I'm going over to the chancery and see what cables have come in, then catch a little shuteye before the driver picks me up for yet another airport run. Listen, Kaitlin, promise me you'll be careful, okay?"

"Be careful? I'm surrounded by a compound wall, the gate has guards, and a Marine is on duty twenty-four hours a day in the chancery. I'm safer than I would be at the house in Arlington."

"All the same, be aware of your surroundings when you're out and about. Do remember not everybody likes us."

With those cheery words, he left.

* * *

I slept heavily but woke earlier than I'd intended the next morning, Friday. I lazed in bed and listened to the early prayer call. After I gave up on sleep, I spent the day unpacking, making the house my own. Ethan would have arrived in Riyadh, but I didn't call him. He'd spent enough time on me.

I organized and reorganized for the next day's work, reading every page of the Consulate orientation package left for me in the living room. The solitude after the long trip from the States, welcomed at first, passed into loneliness. I was glad to go to Susan's for the Friday evening gathering.

* * *

I struggled to remember the names of the locally hired staff, the Foreign Service Nationals, FSNs, they were called then, who would be working under my direction in the nonimmigrant visa unit.

"You're Lavali, from India, right?" The young woman in a sari, her sleek hair partially wrapped in a colorful head scarf, smiled. "Perfect."

I turned to the slender young man with dark, curly hair, wearing

Western slacks and shirt. "And you're Farid, from Lebanon?" Farid's smile signaled approval.

I nodded to a young man with oriental features, also in Western clothes. "Ramelon, you're Indonesian." Ramelon inclined his head.

"We look forward to working with you," Lavali said, who seemed to be the group's spokesperson.

We chatted while I realized that these three, all of them older than I was, with years of experience in consular work, would be supervised by me. I was grateful for the management course sandwiched into A-100 orientation but decided the course had given me only a vague idea of how to be a boss.

I met others as we mingled with finger food on our plates: the three FSNs from Susan's American citizens services unit, and a few American officers, including Lynne Bauman-Redding and her husband, Charles Redding. They had been here almost two years and had extended for another year. They were the couple who lent Ethan the van.

"Didn't know," Lynne said, "that the war would start up right after we agreed to stay another year. It's fine, though, never dull here." She was the political-economic officer, and Charles the administrative officer at post.

A lanky young man in jeans and blazer was introduced to me as Jeff, the junior political officer who helped with visa interviewing a few hours in the mornings. "You can't believe how ecstatic we are to see you. Place has been a mob scene since your predecessor left."

He introduced his wife, Eileen, a short brunette with a pixie haircut who looked about my age and was starting to show her pregnancy. "I'm glad you got here before I have to go back to the States for the baby. I'm leaving a little early while I can get out."

I hid my relief when she said Jeff wouldn't be able to join her until after the baby was born and she was ready to return. "Of course, who knows when that will be, with everything going on."

That night at home, I studied the list of employees in the welcome package and strived to put names with faces. How well could I, barely twenty-three, manage this job? Could I interview, sometimes hundreds of people a day, and weed out the fraudulent visa seekers from the legitimate ones? Handle employees and reports and cables and all the rest?

I slept fitfully and woke in the night, unable to go back to sleep until I finally rose at the early mosque call.

29

I sat with my spine tight against the satin fabric of the winged chair in the consul general's office. Across from me on a similarly upholstered couch, the CG, Margaret McPherson, spouted the polite questions any condescending superior asks her new employee in a first encounter. A maple table with neat stacks of the *New York Times*, the *Washington Post*, and *The Economist* separated us. The table was polished recently. I could smell the lemon polish.

"So you and Ethan are cousins."

"Yes, ma'am."

"I think highly of Ethan. Capable like his father, the ambassador. He'll go far."

"Yes, ma'am." Did she expect my work to approach Ethan's rarified heights?

"He told me you're from the Puget Sound area. Have you ever traveled abroad?"

"I—er—spent time in the Middle East with my family when I was a child. My parents died when I was young, though, and I went to live with my—uh—aunt, Ethan's aunt, too, of course, in the Seattle area."

"How tragic, your parents dying. What did they do?"

I sighed. "They were Foreign Service officers."

It all came out, of course, and I wasn't sure it was a good thing, having the CG poke into my memories. Would she harbor anxieties about how my childhood trauma might affect my ability to handle myself in the midst of wartime stress? I hoped she wouldn't tell Susan or Christine.

I don't think she did, but it wouldn't have altered my relationship with either of them, though for vastly different reasons.

* * *

Christine returned Monday, the third day of my first work week. I came to work early each day to catch up on tasks that threatened to grow exponentially like one of those man eating plants in horror movies.

I was answering a letter from a U.S. congressman who demanded to know why someone had refused a visit visa for the brother of a constituent of his.

My computer screen indicated a gaping blank square, as I had only typed the addresses and salutation. I wanted to type:

Because, dumb-dumb, the applicant has no job, is about to be kicked out of Saudi Arabia, and knows well he can't find a job back in war-torn Somalia. It doesn't take a rocket scientist to know he plans to stay illegally with his brother and drive a taxi like him and never return to his home.

A cultured voice knocked me from my reverie.
"Hello. You must be Kaitlin, our new officer."
I jumped, turned, and knew this was Christine. She was a feminine—very feminine—version of Ethan, raven-haired, dressed like a model, and with ice blue eyes that could drill a hole in the compound wall.

I tried to stand but couldn't. I looked down at my long skirt, caught under the wheel of my chair. "Sorry," I said, remembering to add, "won't you come in and sit down?" I moved the chair to disentangle the skirt. The skirt, I saw, wasn't just under the wheel but wrapped around it. Heat warmed my face as I stooped and worked to free the fabric.

"Stay still a minute," she said, her voice infected with disdain. "You're only making it worse."

The ease with which she deftly undid the tangle of fabric and pulled me to my feet reminded me of Ethan's sparse efficiency.

Her lips turned in what I supposed was her version of a smile before she said, "Why don't you come back with me to my office?"

I followed her, feeling like an elementary student summoned by the principal.

Christine's office was even tidier than the CG's. A single folder lay on her desk. Glancing at it, I determined the subject: *Sadler, Kaitlin V.*

Unlike Margaret McPherson, Christine sat behind her desk. Our conversation never touched on personal matters. We began with a crash course on efficient visa operations.

"A visa officer must practice a certain ruthlessness."

"Ruthlessness," I echoed.

"You cannot handle the large numbers of people wanting to go the U.S., some for legitimate reasons, some for illegitimate, without ruthlessly working through the applications. Some can be dealt with quickly. Do so. You do not have to interview those who obviously are qualified. Simply approve and give to the FSNs to process."

"I understand."

"Likewise, to those who obviously are unqualified, grant a few seconds to refuse them and call for the next applicant."

"A few seconds."

"For those borderline applicants, interview them quickly and decide. And as you gain experience, less of them should appear borderline cases."

I said nothing, but I thought about the young Philippine woman my first day who said she wanted to visit the grave of her father in the U.S. She wasn't able to be with him in his dying, she said, because the American officer had refused her a visa last year. I knew her story was as likely to be untrue as true and that according to the law, I should refuse her.

A single young woman in Saudi Arabia who had already left her home country had few reasons to leave the U.S. once there. Most likely she had relatives, maybe even a fiancé. She could find a good job, even if she were illegal, plus a lot more freedom than this strict Muslim land allowed a woman who probably professed the Christian faith. I couldn't think of a single reason she would return.

Christine's narrowed eyes drew me back, as though she had seen my stumbling interview of the woman. "If you're in doubt, don't give."

I had refused the young woman, after taking more time than my new boss would have liked, and felt as guilty as if I had killed the applicant, knowing I had dashed her hopes for a better life.

I cleared my throat. "Sometimes it's hard to refuse people without feeling—" I searched for a substitute for "bad" or "guilty" and finally let the sentence hang.

Christine's eyes narrowed further, and I regretted the words, as though I'd confessed to letting a mass murderer go free because his mother begged me to.

"You cannot allow yourself those kinds of feelings. They will slow you down. You must be ruthless."

And so it went. I don't think I made a good impression.

30

I doubted just about everything in those first days of visa interviewing: my sanity, my intelligence, and my choice of the Foreign Service.

The nonimmigrant visa process sounds simple enough. At that time, in the early 1990s, foreigners who applied to visit, study, or otherwise engage in legitimate, temporary activities in the States filled out paper visa applications. After an FSN checked the form for completion, an American consular officer did what is officially called adjudicating the application. Adjudication simply means judging the merits of the application against U.S. laws regulating the issuance of temporary—otherwise called nonimmigrant—visas. You, the officer must decide whether the applicant is eligible.

The law requires the U.S. officer to refuse visas for many reasons. The law forbids issuance to known terrorists, criminals, and those guilty of genocide. Visas may not be issued to anyone the officer has reason to believe may become a public charge for U.S. taxpayers.

The reason for the majority of visa refusals is because the applicant, in the opinion of the visa officer, doesn't have good reasons to leave the U.S. The officer is required to refuse any applicant who can't document strong reasons for return to a country other than the U.S. after the temporary stay. In other words, does the applicant intend to visit or does he or she plan to live there?

The burden of proof is on the applicant, since officers hardly have time to investigate several hundred applicants a day, even if they were able to, in a country not their own.

"You mean I'm presumed guilty until proven innocent?" the rare applicant with an understanding of the U.S. judicial process might ask.

"You're not in a court of law," I'd answer, either with grace or a snarl, depending how many hours I'd been standing at the visa interview window.

Unfortunately, the world is teeming with desperate people who wish to flee to any stable country. Many of them queue before U.S. consular officers each day with the hope of convincing the officer to give them that temporary visa, taking a chance they'll never have to leave the promised land once there.

I knew the facts. What I didn't know was how the reality of these desperate people would cut into every compassionate value my upbringing had taught me.

Since I often had to adjudicate hundreds of applications in a day, it was physically impossible to interview all applicants. Like all issuance posts, I passed applicants I was confident were qualified, instructing issuance without interviews, to save precious time.

I interviewed those I wasn't sure about while examining the documents he or she presented. I had to decide in a matter of minutes, because lines stack up with what seems the speed of light before visa windows. I could issue the visa, refuse the visa, or ask the applicant to bring in more information. We were encouraged to make decisions based on what we had, not ask for more information, since a second interview chews up valuable time.

"Also," one of my instructors in the consular course said, "anything you ask for, they'll get for you. Whether it's actually genuine or not is something else."

I had little problem with quick decisions. However I agonized over saying no to certain applicants, even when I knew the applicant was unqualified.

I felt time breathing down my neck even as I interviewed, because the interview was only part of the process. We needed to finish the interviewing in the morning for the rest of the work. The FSNs entered the data into the system and after other checks, stamped the visas into the passports of accepted applicants. They entered the refusals into the system as well. The system at that time, though automated, was antiquated and labor intensive.

In the last task of the process, I sat down with hundreds of visa'd passports and checked them against the application forms. The deadline for us was four o'clock in the afternoon, when successful applicants returned for their passports.

I also squeezed in the preparation of answers to letters from U.S. congressional members about refused applicants (usually because a U.S. residing relative or friend of the applicant requested information about the refusal), wrote reports required by the Department, tallied visas to make sure they were accounted for, counted money paid for visas to certify it was correct, attended meetings, and answered phone calls from other U.S. residing relatives upset because their brother/nephew/sister was refused a visa.

No matter what I was doing, even interviewing, Lavali or Farid or Ramelon often appeared at my elbow, murmuring, "Ms. Kaitlin, "I'm so sorry, but the caller insists she must speak to an American about the case of her cousin. Here, I've pulled the application."

The FSNs could answer the calls from the U.S. at least as well if not better than I could, but many callers became angry if they couldn't talk to an

American about a case. I think they assumed we sat in comfortable offices and drank tea as we interviewed a couple of applicants an hour. They seemed to have no idea how few Americans were around.

The FSNs would scramble to find one application from hundreds so I could look at my scrawled notes on the form and struggle to remember anything about this person from the hundreds I had interviewed.

Susan supervised my first several hours of stumbling visa interviews before she left for a jail visit to an American citizen. After that, I began the first of many days facing the huge line of visa applicants that every Foreign Service officer knows at some point in his or her career.

I would never have made it without the FSNs. A newly minted consular officer learns one thing right away if they're smart. The FSNs know everything, and you know nothing. They've got institutional memory and you have only a few weeks of book knowledge. Treat them well, and they will sacrifice themselves to make you look good. Treat them ill, and they won't overtly rebel but will do only the minimum necessary to get by, and you'll trip on your own arrogance.

Most of Jeddah's problems at that time were not with Saudis but with third-country nationals, those many workers who had flocked to the kingdom for jobs created in the wake of the oil boom. Many were desperate for a better life in the States and pretended to be going for a temporary visit but harbored the intention of staying in the States and working legally or illegally.

I rushed to scribble some words on the paper application form, and make what can only be called a snap decision, the only kind possible under the circumstances, then hand back the applicant's documents. If we refused them, we gave them a form refusal letter and stamped the dreaded refusal notice in the back of the passport before handing it back.

Sometimes they argued when I stamped the refusal. They knew they were losers if they applied at another Western consulate or embassy with that U.S. refusal stamp in the back.

More than once, one of the FSNs saved me from handing back the application form with the other documents, the form on which I had scrawled my cryptic notes: *here 2 mos, thinks Dsnywrld in Denver, 2 trips in yr, etc.*

In my exhaustion, I sometimes was tempted to hate the mass of applicants, beggars to whom I must seem a stand-in for God. As a Christian I fought that temptation as well as the one to treat the FSNs as my hired servants instead of my colleagues.

My mother's training came in handy, and I remembered my father's admonition as though he had just spoken it.

"Kaitlin, you are no better than anybody else, okay? Just because you pay another person's salary or have them under your command is no reason to treat them any differently than you would a respected friend. I can't encourage democracy or represent my country if I don't treat people decently. Remember that."

To my credit, I at least tried to do that, and my staff responded.

When I forgot the qualifications for exchange students, Lavali was there with the appropriate reference in the consular section of the *Foreign Affairs Manual*.

Many of the applicants spoke English well enough to be interviewed in that language. Most of the others spoke Arabic. Though my Arabic usually was adequate for those interviews, one of the FSNs magically appeared if I needed help with difficult words or phrases. Ramelon translated with Indonesian applicants, often maids to wealthy Saudis.

Farid performed the pre-interview, to insure that each applicant had correctly filled out the form. This task was not as easy as it sounds. Although the application was in Arabic as well as English, some applicants, from Asia, for example, could not read or write either language.

The culture did not favor precision. I became familiar with the Middle Eastern shrug indicating this was the best one could do. Why were the rules so important, anyway? If I liked them and Allah willed, I would give them the visa. That the decision could be based on law and not on the whim of the officer seemed so quaint as to be unbelievable to many of the applicants.

The staff gave me hints. "This person," Ramelon might say to me, "his documents say he works for the ministry, but the paper is not like it should be for that."

Or, "Her Saudi visa expires in a month, though she says she is coming back."

They encouraged me when I felt overwhelmed. "You'll soon be so familiar with the passports, you'll only have to glance at them to know what is important," Lavali said.

No one but myself, however, could overcome the hurdle of civility that I had been taught all my life. What I must do warred with my training as a Christian. To be a good officer, you must develop a certain callousness, akin to the callousness of a medical professional who, in order to function, must care for patients without becoming too involved emotionally.

My inability to develop this callousness earned me the first reprimand from Christine.

31

Christine wandered through the consular section from time to time and listened to my halting refusals of obviously unqualified visa applicants.

One day I returned to my office in the middle of an interview to take a phone call. When I had finished, I saw her at the door. She sat down in the chair in front of my desk. I have to admit she seemed, for her, sympathetic.

"Kaitlin, sometimes new officers tend to be rude to applicants. Then I have to listen to complaints that the only representative of the United States most foreigners will see is discourteous."

I wondered what was coming.

"Believe me, I don't have to worry about that with you. Quite frankly, you're not ruthless enough. You take too long to refuse applicants."

I rolled a pencil on the desk. "It's hard to get them to leave sometimes."

"Might I suggest that you practice being firmer?"

I tried to be firmer. I think I made inching progress toward it, but Jeff still saw twice as many applicants as I did, and the burden fell on him for having to take more than his share, though he was nice about it. He was only part-time, and he left at noon.

I had to finish the rest of the applicants and sometimes was still interviewing at two in the afternoon, ignoring the hunger that rumbled my stomach. That meant the FSNs had to wait to enter the applicant names in the computer. Then I had to check the applications and passports while I tried to grab a bite of the sandwich I'd brought from home. The hour approached six or seven in the evening by the time I finished with applications, visa tabulations, reports, cables, and unending paper work.

I knew I had to do something when Christine told me a second time, without smiling, that I must do a better job of refusing applicants.

I tried, I really did, but a family with handicapped children almost did me in, and the interview took far longer than it should have. They were from Mauritania, a poor country. The father was a laborer; they had no reason to return to Saudi Arabia. He could find illegal work in the States and be far better off. They showed the children to me. They were seriously handicapped, the little one, about three, not able to sit up.

I was a Christian; I was supposed to help people, but I couldn't help them. If I gave them a visa, they would go to the States, stay there, and their children would be a tremendous burden on the American taxpayer. Not only was I forbidden by law to grant a visit visa to one who obviously had no reason to return, but I was forbidden to issue visas to anyone who would become a public charge.

I had to refuse them, but they must have sensed my sympathy and my pity. In my guilt, I let them argue with me far too long while other applicants waited. When I finally snapped at them and sent them on their way, I almost cried. I couldn't, though. I had too many applicants to interview.

That evening, exhausted, I pulled out leftovers for a late supper when the doorbell rang. After checking the peephole, I swung wide the door like flinging wide the gate for the king of glory. "Ethan, come in."

"I'm down for a couple of days with the ambassador. Business with the royals. You have anything to eat?"

I got him a plate so he could help himself to food, such as it was.

After munching without complaint on a piece of days-old, soggy fried chicken, he said, "You've got visa line exhaustion written all over you."

"I'm going to flunk out of the Foreign Service. I take too long to refuse people."

"You're a soft touch. That's not bad when you're comforting some American citizen over the death of a family member, but it doesn't work on the visa line."

The next day he came in while I was interviewing applicants. I was refusing an applicant for a student visa, which I hated to do. The man was applying to study English in the U.S.

Many people apply to study English in the United States. Some apply for legitimate reasons, and some apply as an excuse to enter the States and stay illegally. They take advantage of the fact that one needs few qualifications to study English, unlike, say, math, for which the visa officer would expect qualifications in the mathematics field, perhaps a high school transcript with good grades in math. (Assuming the officer believes the transcript is authentic, but bogus documents are another story.)

I was speaking to the man in Arabic, explaining over and over that I was sorry, but I couldn't give him a visa. I felt someone move up beside me.

Ethan stood there. He spoke to me in English. "Are you planning to give this man a visa?"

"Of course not. He has no reason to come back."

Ethan turned to the man and said in his perfect Arabic, "Sir, I am sorry, but you are not eligible for a visa to the United States. Here are your papers and a letter explaining our refusal."

The man took the papers but began, "Why am I—"

"Sir, you are not eligible." Ethan's tone was not friendly.

The man sighed and left. Immediately.

Ethan turned to me. "If you're going to refuse a person, refuse them. Don't prolong their agony. When you keep explaining it to them, they think you're bargaining with them, that they've still got hope. It's cruel. Just refuse them."

"But don't you feel sorry for them?"

"Doesn't matter if I feel sorry for them. If they're not eligible under U.S. law, if they can't show they have good reason to return, I have to refuse them. It's cruel to go into unnecessary explanation."

Looking at it from that standpoint, that it's kinder to refuse quickly, I found I could breathe deeply and refuse applicants with fewer qualms, accept the callousness necessary for the job. Sometimes I remembered in my prayers a few of the refused applicants.

I looked around one day when I had finished my applicants before Jeff had finished at noon, for once. Christina stood there, nodded, and returned to her office.

The consular section hummed that afternoon. I'm sure the FSNs enjoyed my victory as much as I did.

Life shortly became more serious for all of us.

32

I remember precisely when the allied forces begin bombing Iraq. Susan woke me with a phone call an hour or two after I'd gone to bed on that January night.

"The air war's started. Nothing you need to do yet. But be aware. We're restricted to the compound until further notice. We'll be working out grocery visits. The visa unit will be closed to the public tomorrow."

I lay back in bed and listened to the drone of B-52 bombers as they began missions to Iraq. Those ominous vibrations we would hear each night for the remainder of the war. A few weeks before, I had gone with other Consulate staff to visit a U.S. aircraft carrier that had paid a visit to Jeddah on its way to the war zone. No doubt the carrier was in the Persian/Arabian Gulf by now, its young pilots preparing for deadly missions.

The Saudi national guard stationed armed soldiers in jeeps in various places, including at the Consulate entrance. I went with the CG's office manager on one of the allowed visits to the grocery. As we passed soldiers with guns trained on the highway, I reminded myself of what Ethan had told me before he left, standing in my hallway.

"No way the Iraqis are going to get all the way across the Arabian Peninsula to Jeddah. Not even close enough to send scud missiles. No worry on that score. Just watch when you're out and about. Okay, Kaitlin?" He made me promise to stay alert before he hugged me and left.

The Iraqis sent scuds down on Dhahran, though, and a few as far as Riyadh. I prayed for Ethan and hoped the Patriot missiles the U.S. had stationed in Saudi Arabia would take out the scuds before they took lives. For the most part, the Patriots worked, but not always.

* * *

Ethan called from time to time, and we dealt in staccato conversations.

"Okay, Squirt?"

"Sure, just busy. The scud wasn't near the Embassy, was it?"

"No, we're fine. It's Dhahran who's getting it."

He didn't tell me until later that he made several trips to Dhahran, hunkering down during the attacks. I could tell from his voice that he was enjoying himself, finding one of those moments of purpose and certainty of calling.

One night Christine's phone call pulled me from exhausted sleep. "I'm with Susan in the consular section. You need to come in and help us with the calls."

Dizziness threatened when I raised up suddenly from bed. "Calls?"

"You didn't hear the air raid sirens when they went off an hour ago?"

"Scuds?" I didn't know my heart could thump this loudly.

"No," she snapped. "False alarm, of course. But I think we've got every American in Jeddah in a panic and calling us. Something else, too. Just get here."

After throwing on the slacks and shirt I kept handy for such times, I raced to the consular section. Dappled shadows thrown from the Consulate's spotlights on the trees and Consulate wall transformed shapes and shifted their forms. Traffic that never seemed to stop hummed from the streets around the compound as I punched in numbers on the cipher lock and entered.

Susan finished a phone conversation and hung up the receiver as I came in. Christine talked into hers. "No. We have confirmation that the sirens went off accidentally. No, I'm sure it's not a trick. We've conferred with our military, and they assure us they detect no enemy activity anywhere on this side of the Arabian Peninsula."

Susan took me into my office away from hearing distance of the phone. "We're sure the sirens were set off accidentally. However, an unrelated incident's a bit more disturbing. Seems that late last evening an unknown assailant or assailants shot into a military bus returning U.S. soldiers after a visit to a shopping mall. No one injured, fortunately, just a lot of broken glass flying around from the shots."

"Any calls on that?"

"No. Hasn't made the rounds yet. I've sent in separate warden messages about the two incidents to the Department for approval." She checked her watch. "Evening there, of course, so it may take awhile to run down the principals for clearance."

We received approval and telephoned the messages to the wardens the next morning. In reading the cable traffic afterwards, I found no indication that anyone ever found out who fired the shots into the bus or why.

Ethan called the next day while I was at work, which he had never done before. We did not discuss the incident openly, of course.

"You'll be careful like I asked you to, won't you?"

"Of course, Ethan, but I don't understand why the—why the incident happened. We're so popular right now."

"*Right now* is the operative phrase. Popularity is quite fickle, you know, and should never be depended on. We're never liked by everybody. Just remember that."

A short time into the ground war, it became obvious that Iraqi opposition was melting. Saddam's elite republican guard vanished, to fight another day, abandoning the Iraqi grunt soldiers to their fate, some of them buried alive in their bunkers as the victorious allies poured over them in tanks. Those who survived surrendered in long lines reaching to the horizon.

Why, I asked myself, did the powerless so often suffer for the sins of the powerful?

Ethan called again. "I'm in Taif."

Taif is the resort town in the mountain range east of Jeddah. The Saudis allowed the Kuwaiti government in exile to headquarter there. Our recently appointed ambassador to Kuwait had settled in Taif to work with them as they prepared to return to Kuwait when hostilities ended.

I said, "So why aren't you minding the store in Riyadh? Scuds run you out?"

I was joking. The scuds no longer attacked, only a part of history now.

"Seems they've tapped me for a coming trip to Kuwait," Ethan said.

"You're going in with the ambassador?"

"That's right. Help set up shop there after the war. It's temporary, of course. I'll return to Riyadh after a few weeks. And I've probably said more than I should over this phone."

"Could I go with you? Couldn't you find a place for me?"

"Afraid not, Squirt. Who would they replace you with? You're a consular officer, not some expendable political officer like me."

The war ended, and we celebrated, euphoric. A few like Ethan understood the opportunity handed our country and hoped we would seize it.

I fought envy when I saw pictures of the return to the reclaimed U.S. Embassy in Kuwait.

There he was, Ethan, I mean, at the side of the ambassador as the ambassador entered and raised the American flag. Ethan, lean and controlled as always, had turned his head to watch it unfurl in the breeze.

There was Patrick Holtzman, too, the junior political officer from Dharhran. How had he, a junior officer, finagled a spot in that group? I suspect Ethan, serious mentor that he was, had found a way for him. Patrick, younger than Ethan, had allowed himself a half smile, but they were much alike, these two. No one would accuse them of giving away anything by their physical manner.

So there we were, the victorious liberators. That first spring, work started in earnest after the hiatus, and we struggled to catch up with the visa load, let loose with a vengeance, but for a short while we basked in the afterglow of the war. We Americans were popular, and people greeted us everywhere we went, sometimes waving little American flags.

On Memorial Day weekend, we had a flag ceremony by the pool for the American staff members, and I wasn't the only one who wiped away tears after the Pledge of Allegiance.

It was a heady time to be an American, but as I exulted with the others, the certainty nagged me that everything is temporary, especially victory.

33

Ramadan arrived, the holy month of fasting for Muslims. By law in Saudi Arabia, no one is allowed to eat or drink during the day in public. Out of deference to my Muslim FSNs, I did not eat at my desk but skipped lunch or dashed to my house or the snack bar for a quick meal.

After the sun goes down, the feasting begins. The season is a little like Lent during the day and New Year's Eve at night. Stores stay open until dawn.

Jeff and I staggered under the increased applicant load, some of it caused by backlog, some of it by growing popularity of visits to the United States. During the summer, the load increased to heights unseen, as it was increasing at U.S. posts all over the world. America was "the indispensable nation," seemingly invulnerable. Everybody wanted to go there.

Margaret McPherson finished her tour and was replaced by George Lannigan, an affable but competent Arab hand, as they call FSOs who specialize in the Middle East. Unlike Margaret, he visited all the sections, not just the political one, and held regular meetings. He sympathized with Jeff and me as we slogged through hundreds of applicants each day.

One Sunday he invited the American consular officers for an informal lunch at his house. We closed to the public each Sunday to allow us to catch up with paper work.

"Unfortunately, I don't think it's going to get any better," George said. "I ask that you be polite, but other than that, run the lines through as quickly as you can. I get calls every day about refused applicants, but I'm rarely going to second-guess you about your refusals. Call them like you see them, and I'll support you almost every time."

He leaned over his plate. "Everybody acts like we've won the Middle East forever, but it isn't so. We kicked up some conflict in this country by coming in with our troops. Some feel humiliated because they see themselves as having to depend on a western, non-Muslim power to defend them."

Jeff put down his napkin. "We're getting reports. Not much yet, but an undercurrent by some of the more zealous. Just what you said. How come we're depending on a decadent, infidel nation for our Saudi defense? That sort of thing. A few of the mullahs are into it."

"What concerns me," George said, "about the heavy visa loads you folks are handling is that I'm afraid bad guys may slip through because we don't have the time to scrutinize as we should. Two officers for hundreds of applicants every single day during the summer doesn't cut it."

"Kaitlin checks them all, of course," Christine said. She glanced at me, and I nodded. I was beginning to appreciate her competence. She continued, "I understand all kinds of changes are underway in visa technology. Eventually we'll have systems that'll automatically lock issuance until the applicant's name has been examined and any flags manually resolved by an officer."

"The sooner the better." George paused and looked us over. "That said, I don't want you consular officers burning out. I want to see leave requests after the peak of the summer crunch. Understand?"

Christine nodded. "Every officer under me will put in for leave during the fall and winter. I'll pitch in to take up the slack."

She had already taken a window in the visa section a time or two after we reopened and were swamped. She was a joy to watch as she worked through a stack of passports and applications in half the time it took me, even with my increased speed.

With the war over, the VIPs began coming, cabinet Secretaries of Defense and Treasury and our own Secretary of State, James Baker, as well as numerous congressional delegations. They stayed in a hotel close to the king's Jeddah palace. The Saudi government had taken over the hotel to house visiting dignitaries and their staffs and attendant hangers on, like members of the press, if the dignitary was important enough. We had a control room there and could eat our meals in the huge dining room.

I helped man the room at night (given my daytime duties), and at first it was fun. The buffet in the dining room was like what you'd find in a fancy resort. I got to see the VIPs up close and could tell myself that I was part of historic events.

After the umpteenth visit with carefully orchestrated motorcade, the excitement of being part of history paled. I yearned for a night in my quiet house eating a baked potato and spooning soup.

When Ethan finished his Kuwaiti stint, he came down for the VIP visits, once bringing Patrick with him. I had control room duty one evening while they were there, and we ate together, choosing from the mammoth buffet. It was my sixth or seventh time to eat at the hotel, and I think it's the first time in my life I passed up chocolate mousse. In fact, I passed up dessert entirely.

The only physical similarities between the two men were the carbon coloring of their hair and the sparse flesh on their bones, but Patrick's hair curled, and where Ethan was merely lean, Patrick looked like a medieval monk on perpetual fast. His height topped Ethan's by several inches.

Ethan guided the conversation, asking Patrick what he thought about this meeting or that Saudi official, skirting the possibly classified, peppering their discussion with enough coded terms that an eavesdropper would gain little. No small talk. I could see that Ethan expected substantive answers.

His father, I thought. *He's like Joshua now. No coddling. No nonsense. Serving under Ethan would indeed be like serving under Christine.* Yet Patrick seemed to thrive on it, some common intensity bonding them.

Food appeared an afterthought, something you handled with as much enthusiasm as brushing your teeth. No wonder they never gained weight.

A worker clearing tables neared us, and they halted shop talk.

"Do you have family?" I asked Patrick.

His smile twisted. "My wife was evacuated to the States during the war." His tone did not invite further probing.

I remembered he knew the Harlans, and I asked him if he'd heard that Robin Harlan's last checkup had revealed the return of cancer.

He shifted his face away from me toward his plate. "Sorry to hear that. I'll try to get a letter off to them." He toyed with his napkin. "Joe and I used to talk a lot." Then, as though he was embarrassed to show that he suffered human emotion, he began talking to Ethan about a cable he needed to write.

* * *

A few weeks later Ethan came alone to help with another VIP visit. Secretary of Defense or Treasury or maybe a congressional. I can't remember. They blur.

He took the following weekend off, "Just to loaf, find out who I am," he told me. I had stopped by his temporary quarters on my walk home from work Wednesday evening. He got up from the couch where we were sitting, paced to the window, and stared out toward the compound wall.

"So what's bugging you?" I asked.

"Running out of steam lately."

"What else?"

He came back but sat in the chair across from me. "You don't give up, do you?"

"Let it out, 'Cuz."

He settled back, stretched his legs, and stared at his feet. "I'm having a bit of a disagreement with our masters back in the Department."

"Over what?"

"I'm very afraid that someday our dependence on this part of the world will get us into real trouble. We've dodged the bullet on this one, but it's not the end of the story. Not by a long shot."

"You mean our dependence on oil?"

"We don't realize how vulnerable that dependency is making us."

"Another oil embargo, you mean, like back when the Islamists took over Iran? We survived. The embargo went away."

"That's the problem," he said. "It doesn't go away, not the threat of it. We adjust to higher prices, like the old example of a frog sitting in a pan of water, adjusting to higher temperatures, not realizing he's slowly cooking to death. We seem to think oil is an entitlement, like Social Security. It isn't. We don't have as much control over oil supplies as we think."

"And the Department disagrees with you?"

"Some do. They say the oil-producing nations will always need to sell oil because it's their main revenue source. So, their reasoning goes, if they stage an embargo, it can't last that long. They have to come to terms with us."

"And you think?"

"I'm not so concerned about an embargo. I tend to agree with their reasoning on that. What bothers me is that we're not always going to call the shots. Other nations are going to come on line with huge needs for oil. China. India. Do remember I spent much of my childhood in Asia."

I was getting the picture. "So other nations might buy more oil than we do and end up with more influence?"

"Yes, but it's more than that. Look, as long as we buy lots of oil over here, we pay lots of dollars for that oil—the petrodollars. Look at how much of our money ends up in the coffers of oil-producing states. We transfer huge amounts of our wealth to nations, some of whom have unstable governments, vulnerable to coups by bad guys who hate us. Like what happened in Iran."

"So you're saying we'd be spending all this money for oil but have less influence than we're used to?"

"Ever think what might happen if China develops more economic clout than us? Suppose they become more influential than we are? China will not belabor the oil-producing nations with human rights reports like we do, and do you think the Chinese have the slightest interest in encouraging democracy over here? Remember how they bulldozed the Chinese democracy movement in Tiananmen Square?"

"Oh," I said. "So economic clout is as important as military clout?"

"Let's just say a good economy makes possible many things, including a sufficient military."

"But whether that's good or bad depends on how military power is used."

"Precisely. For several centuries now, first British, then American power was tops."

"We've still had horrible wars, concentration camps, the atomic bomb."

"Do you think a world ordered by the Nazis or the Soviet Union would have been better?"

I shuddered. "Of course not."

He sat up and looked at me. "Most Americans pay not the slightest bit of attention to what diplomats do unless there's a crisis. A crisis that might have been averted if our country had paid attention to the rest of the world before it happened."

He paced the room and spat out his words. "We think we're so popular, have just won this war, are all powerful. We think we can go back to ignoring the world. We Americans seem to think we're always going to be popular, that everybody over here, all around the world, for that matter, adores us. I love my country, but it vexes me at times."

"You think we need change now?"

"It's so hard to be realistic in the political world of Washington. They pay their diplomats to be here and find out what's going on, then ignore their findings."

"Like your father."

"It's always there, you know. It increases the tension between going with the flow or telling it like I believe it to be."

"If it costs so much, why do you keep on doing what you're doing? You've got a good education, training. You could find a job less risky that makes more money."

"I can't not do it. I'm called to it. For now, anyway."

I turned over his words. Was I called to this life? Or simply choosing the career to assuage the grief over my parents' deaths?

He stopped, glanced my way. "Sorry, Kaitlin. You don't need a Cassandra like me around. Let's talk about something else."

He sought me out Thursday afternoon in the consular section, where I took advantage of the weekend to catch up on paperwork.

"Come on, drop it," he said. "I'll drive us to some beach, we'll walk awhile, then take in a restaurant."

We found a beach frequented by Westerners a little way out of Jeddah and strolled, silent mostly, but for me, cares slipped away.

Over a meal in the Saudia City restaurant, Ethan said, "Like to try a religious service tomorrow?"

Some of the Consulate employees attended services in homes. Susan did, with Lynne and Charles Redding, I knew, and they'd invited me, but so far I hadn't taken them up on it. I usually caught up on work on Thursdays, and I enjoyed loafing on the one day left of the weekend, Friday.

Like Ethan, though, I was beginning to lose steam. "Sure, why not?"

I relaxed into the spirit of God the next morning, like coming home.

The text was Matthew 27, all about Jesus' trial before Pilate and the powerful of Jerusalem. They thought they had power. They didn't know they were judging the son of God himself. He who held all power chose to relinquish that power for the sake of saving those he loved. *This,* I thought, *is the heart of the good news.*

I found a message for me, too.

I talked about it with Ethan after we prepared a package of macaroni and cheese and a quick salad in my house before he headed back to Riyadh. "I'm one of the rich and powerful, see. I'm the American judge before whom all these people come to plead for visas. But maybe some of these small, insignificant people aren't that way in God's sight."

"So?"

"So I need to be more humble about it. I mean, I've still got to refuse people, like always, but I don't have to do it like I'm the great emir and these are peasants."

Ethan finished eating and stretched. "Not sure you're cut out for the visa section, but I enjoy the way you see things. You're also easy to be around. When are you planning to take leave?"

"You know how it is in a visa section in the summer. Next fall, maybe."

"Kaitlin, you can't get into the I-am-indispensable rut."

"Well, I can't take leave in the summer."

"Granted, but will you please plan to take some over the holidays in December? We both need it. We might even take a long weekend in Europe sometime before then. After Labor Day maybe."

"That would be fun. Paris?"

"Don't see why not. I think I'll go out to Hong Kong and see the folks in August."

"You want to talk with your dad about your differences with the Department, don't you?"

"I do want to talk to Dad. I'm getting an ornery reputation."

"The oil thing?"

"That and other things, too."

"What things?"

He laughed. "I'm this tight-lipped diplomat until you light into me. Good thing you're on our side. You're hard to resist."

"You're not answering the question."

"Okay, I took a contrary position on the countries that didn't support us in the Gulf War."

"And?"

"Some folks, including our Saudi allies, want to take a hard position toward them. I say they had good reasons for what they did. Like a significant percentage of their people didn't want their leaders to support the Americans. Or support the Saudis, either, who are perceived as arrogant. At any rate, I argue that we're victors and victors can afford to be generous. Like we were after World War II. We helped our enemies recover rather than going for reparations and revenge. It made friends and allies of them."

"Sounds like forgiveness to me."

He flashed me that lovingly exasperated look. "Maybe. But if I'm not careful, I'm going to garner the same reputation Dad had for too much independence, not being a team player. And look what happened to him. I think I can finally talk to him about it."

"You're starting to own your father again, aren't you? Failures and all."

His eyes searched mine. "You know me inside out. Or do you?"

I caught something for a moment, like a star that shoots across the sky, glimpsed as it vanishes. Then his gaze left me to wonder what it was.

* * *

I talked with Ethan the next time he was in Jeddah about what George Lannigan, the CG, had said. "Is it going like to be like Iran, a sudden coup by fundamentalists or something?" I mentally reviewed what those former hostages had said about survival.

We were sitting on the couch, and Ethan took my hand and squeezed it. Then he looked at our hands twined together, released his own, and put it on his lap.

"Squirt, you worry too much. This is not Iran. The royal family's a lot more involved with their subjects than the Shah of Iran ever was. It's one reason democracy's a hard sell over here. A lot of Saudis wouldn't want democracy if you gave it to them with a thousand rivers of water. They associate democracy with decadence."

"Sayyid Qutb," I said.

He peered at me. "You know about him?"

"Sure. The Muslim some call the father of Islamic fundamentalism, executed by the Egyptians a few decades ago, right? I wrote a paper about him for one of my classes. He linked us and Israel and even the Russians in a hatred of Islam. That's about all I remember."

Ethan said, "He used the term *Hubal* for America. That term is the name of a stone idol that pre-Islamic Arabs used to worship in Mecca. When Mohammed took Mecca, he cleansed it of the idols. *Hubal* came to mean a term for idolatry, for that which would corrupt Islam. They see us today as *Hubal,* meaning our corrupt American culture."

"So what happens?"

"Prepare to be hated. We have to live with it. Be forewarned."

After he returned to Riyadh I pondered the courage that pushed Ethan to express contrary opinions. I didn't think I would ever presume confidence enough to do to something other than what I'd been told, but I was wrong.

My temper got the best of me.

34

Susan took off some days off to travel to Egypt and take one of those cruises down the Nile. Christine handled most of Susan's work, but she had to visit an American in jail on a drunk-driving charge one afternoon, and I handled the routine ACS cases that came in, mostly passport renewals and notarization of documents.

Before leaving, Christine said, "A Mr. Al Khail may come in. Child-custody case. I talked to him on the phone, trying to set up a time to talk about letting his former wife, an American citizen, visit their little girl. He got into an angry snit when I mentioned my desire for the mother to visit. He vows it will never happen. The only thing I could get him to promise was to come by and talk to me about it, but he wouldn't set a time. Said he'd come when he felt like it. Anyway, if he shows up, ask him to wait until I come back. If he leaves, don't make him angrier by trying to hold him. Don't try to deal with it yourself."

"No problem," I said. It sounded like a case I wouldn't want to entangle myself with even for an extra R and R. What did I know about such things?

She left the folder for *Al Khail, Nafisah*, on the desk. "Look at it and get an idea of some of the cases we're dealing with over here."

I read the notes.

> Ms. Norbert alleges no abuse by her former husband, Munir Al Khail, but stated she could no longer stand living in Saudi Arabia and wanted a divorce and to return to the U.S. She wanted to take Nafisah, the only offspring of the marriage, with her. Her husband allowed the divorce but said the daughter could not go to the United States. She would stay with her father, as Islamic law decrees. Says he wants no further contact between mother and child. The mother, he claims, has admitted to having affairs with other men before they were married, and said he was sure she would revert to her former ways once back in the U.S. She has since remarried.

Fortunately, the day passed quietly, customers few and far between. I often compare the American citizens services unit with running a store. I'm the clerk in charge of an array of services: passports, notary duties, reports of the birth of an American child abroad, and so on.

That is, it was quiet until Mr. Al Khail chose to appear.

I was signing new passports when Fatah crept up. "We have the Mr. Al Khail. He is quite angry that Ms. Christine is not available. He demands to see an American."

Arrogant Saudis. I leaped up. "Well, I can be angry, too."

Fatah stepped out of my way, her brows tightened in a frown.

Mr. Al Khail was in the waiting room, his white thobe billowing out with each stride and his gutra edging back like the sombrero of a cocky cowboy. He halted when he saw me, and I glared at him through the interview window.

"I understand you insist on seeing an American. Well, I am the American you demanded to see, like an arrogant little boy." I completely forgot what Christine said, did not even consider that my anger might push back to zero any progress she had made in the case.

He charged to the window and drew himself up as though to show me he was taller than any little boy. "You, madam, are the arrogant one. You are a typical American, thinking to boss us around. You think we are savages, unable to raise our children properly. Well, I will decide what is proper for my precious Nafisah."

I opened my mouth to respond in kind, then closed it. Could it be possible that this man loved his daughter? "Nafisah? What a lovely name. I don't think I've heard it before."

He blinked. "It means 'precious gem.' I thought when she was born that she looked like a little jewel."

We stared at each other. The softness in his eyes resembled melting chocolate. I took a chance and smiled. He inclined his head. He was staring straight at me, so he wasn't a religious type who avoided even casual contact with a woman.

I took another chance. "Mr. Al Khail, do you suppose we might talk a minute? Perhaps I could persuade you not to feel so badly toward us. If you wanted me to, I could come out in the waiting room, and we could talk without this glass between us." I would have preferred my office, but I didn't think he would accept meeting me on my turf.

He hesitated, then responded, "I suppose. But do not think to bewitch me into allowing Nafisah to be corrupted by her mother."

"No, of course not."

I unhitched the door to the waiting room, walked to a table placed for clients to fill out forms, then put two chairs to face each other on opposite sides of the table. I sat down, gesturing my hand to the other chair. "Please."

He sat on the edge of the seat, back upright, resembling a kindly dog beset by wolves.

We passed though what might be described as confidence-building measures: What he did for a living (government employee), where Nafisah went to school (a private English school), what courses she liked in school (reading and art). I stayed away from the subject of his former wife.

He unbent a little and asked if my family was with me. He had studied several years in the U.S., where he'd met Nafisah's mother, and was bound to know that American women, single and married, often worked, but no doubt he held to the typical Saudi belief that any woman needed family close by.

"My guardian's nephew is in Riyadh and comes often."

He nodded. "You said 'guardian.' Your parents are not living?" Obviously, he had been in the West enough to know that I would not consider it improper for him to inquire about my family.

"They died when I was nine years old."

"Ah, I am so sorry. To lose them so young. I am blessed still to have my parents. Yours died together? An accident perhaps?"

"They were killed in the bombing of a U.S. Embassy." I named the nearby country.

Mr. Al Khail sucked in his breath. "You have returned to a Muslim country, despite that?"

"Yes. My parents believed they were doing good things for relationships between the United States and the countries over here. I want to continue what they did."

He stared at me. "You do not hate us?"

"No. It was a few, very bad people, not the whole country. And I have forgiven even the ones who did it."

"Ah. It is best that way, if you can do it."

He bowed his head, then raised it. "You understand I do not hate Nafisah's mother. I found after the marriage that she—had kept things from me. I, too, must work on forgiveness of her, like you have forgiven. That is best. However, I do not want Nafisah to be like her in the way of—I want her to have a happy marriage, with no man, ever, except her husband."

"I understand. If I ever marry and have a daughter, I also will want that for her. As I desire it for myself."

We sat for a moment. Should I broach the subject? I plunged. "Mr. Al Khail, as one who early lost my mother as well as my father, I can say how much I have wanted to know my mother. My parents loved each other. Still, even if they had not done so, I think I would always want to have some kind of relationship with my mother, to know her."

I knew he wasn't going to be angry when he said, "I never want Nafisah to go to the United States. I do not mean to be rude, but I do not want your country to influence her in any way. I have been there. Please believe me; I worry about the immorality there."

"I understand. But what about her mother visiting her over here? In whatever safe place you choose?"

He shifted. "Her stepmother loves her. You had a guardian. Was she not kind to you?"

"My guardian, Matilda, is the kindest woman in the world. We love each other very much. I still miss my mother and wish to know her. I cannot, of course. It's something I will never have. But Nafisah could."

Mr. Al Khail rubbed the table with his fingers.

At that moment, Christine entered. I had visions of being drummed out of the Foreign Service, with Christine reading her scathing evaluation of me as they ripped off my State Department security badge.

She would not, of course, light into me in the presence of Mr. Al Khail.

He rose and walked to her. He actually shook her hand. Thankfully, he wasn't the sort of Saudi male who avoided shaking hands with a woman. If he wasn't angry, maybe I could talk myself out of anything but a bare mention of it in my evaluation report. Maybe in the section where the rater has to note something the officer needs to improve: *Sometimes overly helpful. Needs to tone down her impulse to butt in. Needs to contemplate before acting.*

Mr. Al Khail pulled another chair to the table. "Please, we can talk perhaps."

I noted that even Christine couldn't hide a slight raising of the eyebrows. "Why, yes, of course, if you wish."

We sat. I determined to say nothing unless directly addressed.

Actually, I wasn't needed. Mr. Al Khail suggested that Nafisah's mother might visit. "I will pay for her to come. If it goes well, perhaps she could come several times a year."

When they finished, Christine walked with him from the waiting room. An American parent came in with questions about a report of birth for his child. I left him with the FSNs to answer his questions and fled back to the NIV unit and my office.

The hour was late, and Lavali and the others had left when Christine strode in and sat down before my desk. I searched for something to say and finally asked, "How did the jail visit go?"

"It took awhile for me to make him understand that we couldn't spring him from jail just because he's an American citizen. After that, it went okay, but he's still thinking about writing his congressional representative. I offered him paper for writing the letter and said I would mail it for him. That calmed him down. I think I'll let you visit him next time; then you can write the visit cable."

"Sure."

"Since it appears you have sound instincts in dealing with people."

"I didn't mean to get involved with Mr. Al Khail, but he did ask—"

She waved her hand. "It's fine, Kaitlin. You took a risk, and it worked out. It doesn't always end like this, though. Sometimes these cases will break your heart."

* * *

The Egyptian couple smiled, the picture of normality, in front of my visa window. According to their passports, they had made two previous trips to the States, one a year ago, the other two years ago. According to normal practice I should not only give them another visa, I should give them a multiple entry for the maximum length allowed. The theory was that if they had left the States before, chances were they fit the category of legitimate travelers and had no interest in staying illegally in the States. Applying each year for a visa took the consular officer's time as well as theirs.

The waiting room was packed with eager applicants still to be seen. Why was I struggling with a decision to grant them another visa?

"Do you have relatives in the States?" They had not marked any immediate family on the form, but they were not required to list more distant relatives.

Why did the man's smile irritate me? "No one."

No one? So why did they go every year? The man's salary for a Saudi accounting firm was adequate but would be stretched by a trip every year to the States, especially if they had to pay for lodging.

"Where did you go last year to the States?"

"Last year we went to Disney World. This year we want to see San Francisco."

"Why San Francisco?"

"We have heard that it is beautiful."

I sighed. My questions were eliciting useless information. "Excuse me a moment."

I hopped off my stool. I hated to take the time, and I hated to run to Christine, but I could not stop the gut feeling that this was a bad case, even though any reason for it escaped me.

Christine looked up from reading cables. "Yes, Kaitlin?"

I felt stupid. "There's a—I mean, I don't feel right about this case."

"Right?"

I wished I hadn't come. "Oh, nothing. It's okay. The couple's been to the U.S. and come back. I should just issue." I thought of the lines stacking up while I was in Christine's office. "Sorry. I shouldn't have bothered you." I turned to go.

"Kaitlin."

"Yes?"

"Obviously something is worrying you about this case. We all identify patterns, and that's as it should be as we gain experience. Knowing the patterns, like previous visas, good job, and so on, help us work more quickly and efficiently. Do not use them as your only guides, however. If you've got an instinct, an intuition, listen to it."

"All right. Thanks." I left.

Dear God, please help me decide right about this case. Why did I feel it was important?

I hopped on my stool, thinking I was going to issue. The man's teeth showed through his smile. Then he licked his lips.

"I'm sorry," I said. "I can't issue." I stamped his and his wife's passport with the refusal stamp as quickly as I could.

"No!" he exploded. I thought he was coming through the window at me. Jeff looked up from his interview, and Lavali crept beside me.

He shook his fist at me. "We have plans. We have tickets. You cannot do this to me."

I forced myself to look at him instead of running from the window. I was doing my job; no reason for me to feel guilty. "Where are your tickets?"

His eyes gleamed. "You want tickets? I will get tickets."

I regretted my words. He would get tickets and insist more vehemently that I issue.

"No. I do not want to see tickets. I have decided that you are not eligible for a visa." I handed him the passports, papers, and the visa refusal letter.

I was glad the glass window was between us. He spit on it before grabbing the documents and his wife and stalking out.

"My, my," Christine said, behind me. "He must have a lot riding on that trip. One wonders if he was setting up a business there or lining up a job."

She left, and I called the next applicant, able to will my hands not to shake because I knew Christine agreed with my decision.

*　*　*

Days later Christine called me to her office. "I received a call this morning from my contact at the Emir's office."

"Yes?"

"They've arrested an Egyptian. Normally they wouldn't involve us in a domestic case, of course. In confiscating the man's passport, though, they noticed he had previous visas to the States but recently had been refused here. Tawfiq asked politely if I could tell him why we refused the Egyptian. They were concerned, he said, that the man might be given a visa at some future time. I said, just as politely, that visa files were confidential documents of the U.S government, but that I don't think he had to worry about our giving a future visa to the man in question."

"The Egyptian? The one I refused?"

"Indeed."

"Why was he arrested?"

Christine smiled. "Tawfiq wouldn't tell me exactly, but from his broad hints, I gather they suspect clandestine activity with an undesirable group."

"You mean—terrorists?"

"That would be my guess. I'm sending a cable to the Department requesting that a more serious flag be put on him than mere refusal of a visa."

I went cold.

"I have, of course, talked to our interests at another level. I made copies of all the information we have on the case and passed it to them."

I put my hands on my cheeks. "Christine, suppose I had issued?"

"Hopefully the Saudis would have arrested him before he left. Although I imagine he and his wife would've left immediately after you gave them visas."

I shivered. "There's no guarantee it'll happen that way all the time, is there?"

"No. No guarantee. We do the best we can." Her gaze probed me. "Kaitlin, don't ever cut out that inner voice. Instinct, intuition, whatever you call it."

35

The VIP visits slowed, and Ethan came down on a Tuesday before the weekend and said he was taking off a few days to rest.

"So many things going on. Supposed to be the summer hiatus, but we've got two junior officers already on board. I'll need to break them in."

"New?"

"One of them's on his first tour, a guy with a deer-in-the-headlights look. The other's a young woman who just finished her first tour in Rome, Allison Crandall. She's going to be great, I think."

"Is she—er—are they married?"

"Both single."

We lazed in my living room that evening, me on the couch and Ethan sprawled across pillows on the floor.

We shared a letter from the Falls Church group and supplemented it with letters to me from Betsy and Natalie and one to Ethan from Anson.

Natalie said she and Mike had seen each other frequently.

"Reading between the lines," Ethan said, "I bet they announce their engagement before long. Poor guy."

"Ethan, honestly. You men."

"At least Mike and Natalie get to see each other a lot. But can you believe this." He read from Anson's letter.

> Betsy and I have decided that London is a wonderful destination more or less halfway between our posts. I've just gotten back from our first rendezvous there. Took me almost as much travel time to get there as we had together, but it's worth it.
>
> The long-distance commute is hard on us both, but the leaving is worse. We're already looking at posts for our next bids. Definitely, we're going to bid on the same posts.

Ethan shook his head. "Can't believe how bad they've got it. They should marry before they bid. If they're a tandem couple, they'll be more likely to get the same post." He used the designation for two FSOs married to each other.

"You serious about anybody?" I asked.

"I don't have time."

"Are you going to be serious about somebody, someday?"

"Why this sudden interest in my love life?"

"You can't stay single forever."

"Who says I can't?"

When I didn't answer, he said, "So, are you serious about anybody?"

"I haven't been serious about anybody since Anson."

"You over him now?"

"Pretty much. Guess it had seemed perfect, him being an FSO and all."

Ethan rolled on his back and stared at the ceiling.

I switched to another subject, the one FSOs always talk about. "Have you put in your bids yet?"

He shifted his gaze from the ceiling and sat up. "I've made the list. Just have to decide what my top bid's going to be."

"What can't you decide?"

"I can't decide between two of them. One's back at the Department. There's a great job opening up in Policy Planning."

I was glad he was looking away, else he couldn't have missed the way I closed my eyes like I'd been hit. I was a one-tour junior officer. I shouldn't bid on Washington tours until I'd completed two abroad.

I opened my eyes and struggled to keep back the moisture that threatened to film them. *Forget it. You know you and Ethan can't always serve close together.* "What's the other one you want?

"Casablanca. I've served two tours in Arabian Peninsula countries. North Africa would be a change but keep me in the Near East bureau. The chief political position is opening up there."

Hope warmed me. "Casablanca? Humphrey Bogart? The Casbah? The French Resistance?"

He turned to me and rolled his eyes. "Come on, Squirt, the French aren't there anymore or anywhere else in North Africa. Morocco gained independence in the mid-'50s, Algeria a few years later after the Algerians won their war for independence." He sobered. "What a bloody thing that was. Terrorism. Torture. Murder of innocent civilians. Somebody estimated that one out of ten Algerians died before it was all over. The French had a bloody exit from North Africa."

I remembered it from school. "The falling French empire. Vietnam. Then Algeria."

"The French didn't know what they were up against, all that native desire for independence."

Nor, I thought, *remembering Joshua, did we Americans when we went into Vietnam after the French gave it up.*

"I could get the list of post positions tomorrow," I said. "We could look at Morocco. Maybe I could bid on it, too. That is, if you don't mind my following you around like this."

Ethan's eyes flashed from steel blue to softness. "Squirt, you can follow me around all you want. You certainly need somebody to keep an eye on you."

I picked up a pillow from the floor and socked him over the head with it. He grabbed another one, and we batted each other around the living room until he kneeled and held up his arms in mock supplication. "Mercy."

The next day I got the films of microfiche that had the information about posts and positions and how long the tours were. Nowadays, you can get all this on the computer, of course, but then the information was sent to posts on microfiche.

After the FSNs left and I cleared up the essential jobs before the weekend, Ethan and I turned on the microfiche reader and studied the Morocco positions.

I shook my head. "No junior officer reporting positions coming vacant when I'm bidding." I looked at Algeria, the next country over. "A junior economic officer position. That'd be great. Political would be better, but at least it's a reporting position. The timing's good, too. I already know French and Arabic."

Ethan examined the fiche. "Don't be so impulsive. Sure, you could probably get it. They'll help you with a non-consular position for your second assignment. But you need to check out other places when the bid list comes out." He looked up and squeezed my shoulder, giving it a mild shake before releasing it. "You have this tendency to go off half-cocked without examining the whole picture."

"As opposed to you, who picks everything apart before you decide anything."

"Thanks. I intend to pick apart the bid list and give you a list of possible positions I think would be good for your career. What about Europe?"

"I want Middle East."

"Kaitlin, you have to bid on more than one region. You know that."

"Fine, but they have to be close to the Middle East, and I want my top choice to be Algeria."

"Stubborn."

* * *

Ethan came to Jeddah after his trip to Hong Kong in August, even before he returned to his job.

"Mother and Dad send you their love," Ethan said. "They're looking forward to seeing us on the Island for Christmas."

We wandered around the sandy golf course next to the Consulate one evening, and I kicked at a rock. "So what'd Joshua say about your differences with the Department?"

The last prayer call from the mosques hovered over us. When the last sound floated into oblivion, he said, "It's the first time we've ever talked about his problems with the Department. Why he resigned and all that."

"Is he sorry he did what he did?"

"I don't think he's sorry he took a stand. I think he's sorry he handled it like he did."

"Oh?"

Ethan touched my arm to halt us. He put his hands in his pockets and turned his face toward the gritty wall between us and the outside world.

"He's changed, you know that? He's not so hard now. Well, he's getting older, I guess. A few more years and we might even be friends."

"No kidding." I regretted the sarcasm that infected my words, but Ethan didn't seem to notice.

"Dad suggested I write a dissent cable. He said if I put words into reasoned arguments and kept at it, I might be respected as a gadfly and even listened to. He said, though, there aren't any guarantees. We call them like we see them and let it go."

Several years before, the Department had set up the dissent cable channel. Any officer who disagreed with official policy of the Department or to directions it was choosing could disagree by formally using the dissent channel. The idea was that dissent, rightly used, was good, that different viewpoints needed to be aired.

"So are you going to do that? Send in a dissent cable?"

"Probably."

* * *

Before Ethan left, we decided on a long weekend trip to Paris after Labor Day. "Something to tide us over until Christmas," he said.

After Ethan returned to Riyadh, I lost myself in the last of the summer visa crunch. I told Susan I was envious of her. "Your summer load goes down while mine goes up."

"Americans tend to go out of the country during the summer like everybody else. Which reminds me, I'm taking a week's leave to meet a friend in Rome for several days in a couple of weeks. Christine's handling my section, of course. She may need you to pinch hit, like before."

"Two weeks from now? I'm duty officer that week. I'm already dreading it."

"Come on, you'll do fine. You've learned oodles since you've been here. Anyway, Christine will be around if you have a real problem."

Jeff handed me the duty officer briefcase the day before we went into the weekend like he was getting rid of a colicky baby. The manual inside was supposed to guide the DO, most of whom weren't consular officers, through any emergency known to humankind. It also included the radio we used to communicate in those days.

"Pretty quiet week," Jeff said. "Hope it's that way for you."

I wished he hadn't said that. It couldn't stay quiet for two weeks in a row.

36

I dreaded the weekend as duty officer. Other officers would be off, maybe hard to reach, but Christine was the only one I needed if an emergency overwhelmed me. I would almost rather call in the consul general, but if I got in a real pinch, I'd force myself to call on her.

On Wednesday afternoon I closed up, exhausted and ready for the weekend, duty officer or no. Christine came in. "Thought I'd let you know. Charlie's flying over from Cairo for a couple of days. He just called. I can't believe he actually remembered our anniversary. Try to take care of any Amcit emergencies by yourself if you can. We may be out a lot, a trip to Taif tomorrow, that sort of thing."

I even smiled when I said, "Sure, no problem. Have a good weekend."

A few of the women spouses planned a night out and invited me to go with them. The driver deposited us at the restaurant and drove off. My beeper went off.

I stayed outside to call Post One on my radio. I never felt comfortable with the thing, but I was able to reach the Marine on duty.

"Lady is here, American," his brusque voice told me. "Says her husband kicked her out of the house. I think you'd better come in."

My stomach reminded me that I'd only gulped down some noodle soup for lunch. I smelled the Lebanese food, sighed, and asked the Marine to send back the driver.

The woman waited outside the Embassy guard booth and looked worried. I didn't blame her. She cuddled a screaming baby.

"She wants to be fed," the woman said.

I got the key to the visa unit from the Marine and led her over. I had to use the key as well as work the door combination lock while trying to calm the woman. "It'll be okay. We'll be private in my office, and you can feed the baby and use the bathroom." I was glad to see the diaper bag the woman had slung over her shoulder. She unwrapped her head scarf. A bright red mark adorned her cheek.

I drew up a chair for her. She sat down after taking off her abiyah, undid her blouse, and began feeding the baby. The baby's sucking sounds filled the room.

"What a beautiful little girl," I said. She was a frail thing with tiny button earrings that pierced her delicate ears.

The woman's smile erased some of her worried look. "Thank you. Her name's Aisha. I have a son, too, but my husband only let me keep Aisha when he threw me out."

Because otherwise the husband had no way of feeding the baby, of course.

"My name's Kaitlin. And yours?"

"Tessa."

She seemed young to already have two children. Almond eyes peered from an oval face topped by hair the color of honey.

"Your husband is Saudi?"

"Yes. Achmad. We got into a quarrel because I wanted to take a trip to see my mother in Detroit. He promised me we could go this summer, but now he says he doesn't have the money. He says all I do is remind him that we don't have money."

"What does your husband do?"

She grimaced. "He works for his father. They don't like me, his family. I don't like them, either."

Her story, as she told me, was typical. She and Achmad had met at a party when he was studying in the U.S. She had dropped out of high school to marry him in a Detroit mosque, Achmad no doubt fascinated by Tessa's youthful good looks.

"My mother was glad. He told her he had lots of money and would take good care of me."

"And now?"

Tessa shrugged. "We don't even have money for a driver. I have to wait for Achmad to take me everywhere. We live with his family and have this one small room to ourselves. It's not even as large as my room in my mother's apartment."

"Do they mistreat you physically?"

"No. Only, Achmad hit me tonight. First time he's ever done that."

I sighed, afraid such mistreatment would worsen. "What are your plans, Tessa?"

"I'm not sure I want to stay with Achmad. Especially if he's going to hit me like tonight." She rubbed her cheek. "I thought I loved him, but—well, I'd like to take my kids and see my mother and decide. Can't you make him let us? I'm an American. I ought to be able to see my mother if I want to."

She pulled Aisha away from her breast and fastened her blouse. The little girl, now gently sleeping and more delicate than ever, puckered her rosebud mouth. What a precious little thing. I felt as helpless as she and wanted very much to telephone Christine.

I called up everything I could remember from my consular course back in Washington and what I had gleaned from my few hours filling in for Susan. The case involving Nafisah Al Khail appeared simple beside this one.

"Tessa," I said, "the problem is that both you and your children must have an exit visa to leave Saudi Arabia."

Her eyes widened. "I can't leave when I want to? I'm American."

I nodded. "We can talk to the Saudi government and usually they can handle an exit visa for you, though they may have to persuade the husband to allow you to leave. You're not Saudi; you're American, as you have said. The problem is with your children."

"What do you mean? I can't leave them. I don't want to leave them."

"Of course you don't. I understand that. The problem is that the Saudis consider them Saudi citizens because their father is Saudi."

"But I'm their mother, and I'm American."

"I know, and in the U.S. they're considered American citizens. To us, they're Americans. But they're in Saudi Arabia, and to the Saudis they're Saudis, not Americans."

"But that's not fair. I thought you could get me and the children out. Get Achmad to hand over my little boy."

I searched her face, trying to let her know that I felt for her, that I wasn't merely some bureaucrat spouting a bunch of laws. "I can tell you love your children an awful lot."

She wiped her eyes with the hand not holding Aisha. "I do love them. You should see my son. He's the cutest little boy." She began to sob.

I couldn't help it. I put my arms around her and the baby. "I'm so sorry." *Don't lose control, or you'll never be able to help her.* I let go and leaned back.

She watched me as I steadied myself. She seemed to toughen. "It's pretty bad, isn't it? I've gotten myself in a pickle of a mess, haven't I?"

I swallowed. It's okay to be sympathetic, but you're no good to them if you fall apart. "Tessa, you have to make a decision. You're in Saudi Arabia, and those are the rules that apply here. The father has the authority over the children's lives. You have to decide how you're going to deal with it."

I told her what Susan had taught me. "Sometimes if the woman is a Muslim, the court allows very young children to stay with her if she lives close to the father, but there's no guarantee, and it would probably take money for a lawyer if Achmad doesn't want it to happen. He would have to pay for a separate establishment for you. Again, you're at the mercy of the courts here."

"I never became a Muslim. Achmad wanted me to, but—well, I'm not much for religion. You're saying I can leave, but the children can't?"

"As I said, we can probably persuade the Saudi government to give you an exit visa. It would depend on Achmad as to whether you were given another visa to come back."

In the silence, I watched her imbibe the harsh reality and take on a look years older than her age. Then her face relaxed. "Achmad's not such a bad husband."

I knew she was weighing the odds.

"I have ways of—of making him want me. Maybe if I stay with him and—forget about going to the States right now, just raise my children? Later I might get him to take us all to the States. At least after the children are older…"

I figured the decision would be with her for a long time: when would she consider her children old enough to leave them, if it came to that?

"Tessa, do you think Achmad might be willing to pay for your mother to come visit you? Maybe when he has more money?"

Her eyes brightened. "He might. He and my mother actually hit it off pretty well. I can play the good wife for a while and suggest it later, after we're okay again."

"Do you know any other American women here?"

"I don't get out except with Achmad."

"Maybe after you're doing okay, he'd let you attend some functions for American women. We have those every once in a while at the Consulate. Are you registered with us?"

She shook her head.

"You need to register with us—"

I picked up the ringing phone. The Marine said a man, Achmad something, was at the gate, looking for his wife. Should he tell him she was here? I turned to Tessa. "It's your husband. Do you want him to know you're with us? You're an American citizen. We won't tell him if you don't want us to."

She smiled, as though she'd found a weapon to give her confidence. "Tell him I'm here. He'll have to wait for a little bit, though. I've got to register with the Consulate."

After I passed the message and hung up, Tessa said, "I want to register. I want Achmad to know that you know who I am."

I registered the young wife and her two children, although I didn't have the passports. I told Tessa we'd eventually need to see the passports, figuring it would give her an excuse to return, if she could convince Achmad it was important. While we were doing that, the guard rang to tell us that Achmad was waiting for his wife at the entrance.

"Let me bring him in," I suggested, "and talk to him—not in a confrontational way, but to get acquainted. Maybe if he sees we're friendly, he'll be more likely to let you come talk to us from time to time."

Tessa nodded. I took her to the Marine station in the chancery while I went to show in Achmad. I didn't expect him to look so young and wondered if he'd stayed in the U.S. long enough to graduate from whatever college he was attending. He seemed a bit awed when the guard let him in to walk with me to the chancery, past the lighted American flag.

"It is like the States here." After a pause while he studied the flag, he said, "I hope Tessa did not tell you bad things about me."

"She said you had been a good husband, and she wanted to be your wife. She didn't like it when you hit her, though."

He recoiled. "I should not have done that." He slowed. "I do not like not having money to give her what she wants. When I make more money, we will all go to the States and see her mother. I like her mother. I want to show her that I am taking care of her daughter."

"Of course. Perhaps in the meantime, you could find enough money to bring the mother over here from time to time."

"That is an idea. I will think about it."

Men and women do not show affection publicly in Saudi Arabia. Nevertheless, Achmad, with his American schooling and within the U.S. Consulate, allowed himself to kiss her gently on the cheek when they met. Then he took the baby and turned to me.

"She is lovely, isn't she? She looks like her mother, don't you think?"

"I certainly do."

I breathed a sigh of relief as well as a prayer for the young family when they left. Then I returned to the consular section to write a report for Christine while the incident was fresh in my mind.

The next Saturday, Christine passed my office and looked in a minute before we opened the visa interview windows. "I've read your report. You handled the case very well. It will go in your evaluation. You're going to make a good consular officer."

I didn't tell her I planned on being a political officer.

37

I viewed with suspicion the young Palestinian woman in front of my visa window, hardened enough now to thrust aside my pity for her. "Why do you want to visit the United States?"

"Tourism."

"Yes, but you are a young lady, barely seventeen years old. You mean to tell me your family is going to let you stay by yourself in a hotel for a week?"

She shrugged. "I want to see Disney World."

Of course she was hiding something. Few families in this part of the world would allow a daughter her age to go alone to a strange country and stay in a hotel there. What about those cables lately about trafficking in women? We'd never had a problem with it here in an organized sense. The country was stable with no ethnic violence or revolutionary changes. Never with Palestinians. No, probably a young man in the States to whom she was betrothed. Or a brother with a job who would take care of her. Who knew?

"I'm sorry. I must refuse you the visa. I think you mean to stay in the U.S."

"Only tourism," she protested angrily as I stamped her passport and handed it back with the form refusal letter. I smiled and said, "Thank you," sure that I had done right and able to quickly refuse on these long days when the visa line seemed endless, even if I never could enjoy spoiling another's happiness.

Her type of anger usually meant the evil consul had just spoiled a dream, but not the dream of a tourist trip.

I played the possibilities over in my mind as I took other applicants. Trafficking. Illegal relatives in the U.S. A fiancé. An illegal job.

Days later I happened to glance at old visa issuances that Hassan was shredding. We weren't supposed to keep the paper issuances longer than a year. Now, of course, everything is on the computer.

Hassan often would glance at the issuances before he shredded them. He picked one up and passed it to me. "This one. The last two names. I think—the young Palestinian woman—do you remember from last week?"

I nodded and examined the application. Children in Middle Eastern countries carry, usually, some kind of what we would consider a family name for the last name, plus a middle name that is always the name of the father. Thus, even females may have Mohamed or Achmad as their middle name.

I squinted at it, then walked to the recent refusals, stacked by date. I finally found it, the application for the Palestinian woman I'd refused a few days ago. The last two names matched on both applications, as did the address. The birth date was about right. A brother, given a visa a year ago. He'd stayed, of course, and found illegal work. Or perhaps he'd married an American citizen and been granted legal status. Now he wanted his sister to come over. Perhaps he'd found illegal work for her, too. Or maybe a friend to marry her.

That night I warmed up leftovers in the microwave and munched them over an issue of the *International Herald Tribune*. I read an article about the U.S. Embassy and other posts in China opening up after a wave of violent demonstrations against them. The riots had been caused by some perceived injury that the Chinese felt U.S. foreign policy had perpetrated against them. However, "visa services were not yet being restored." That explained why the authorities were now eagerly cooperating to stop the violence. Shutting down visas to the U.S. remains one of the more potent weapons Americans can wield.

That young woman and her brother? The U.S. still represented a place where one could come and have a chance to make a better life. You might be dirt over here, but you had the freedom to try in the U.S. Not necessarily to succeed, but to try. And if you failed, you tried some other way.

I didn't blame the brother and sister for trying. Of course, if you gave visas to all the nice, hard-working people in the world who'd been given a bum deal in life, the U.S. would soon be trying to absorb half the world's population.

But couldn't I do something other than just refuse these people?

* * *

A few days later I was in the chancery checking classified cables and saw the ambassador down from Riyadh in the hall talking with the CG. When Ethan called a couple days later, I said, "Noticed you weren't with the ambassador this time."

"He was just making a routine visit. Didn't need me and let me off so I could drive with Allison over to a conference in Bahrain for junior political officers from the Arabian Peninsula. I chaired one of the meetings."

I stopped myself from saying, "Just Allison?" and changed it to, "The other officer didn't go? What's his name? Wendell?"

"Sure. Both of them went, but Wendell drove up by himself so he could take several days off to stay extra there. Not as restricted as here, you know."

So I'd heard. Bahrain, a tiny island emirate in the Gulf, was linked to Saudi Arabia by a causeway. Christian churches were allowed there. Women could drive. Expatriates and Saudis alike flocked there to shop and enjoy the resort hotels.

After we rang off, I pictured Ethan and Allison together lolling on the beach.

* * *

I stared down at the visa application in front of me. I had been staring at it for some time, thinking of getting away, sleeping all I wanted, reading books....

I forced myself to concentrate. Djamel Mustapha, an Algerian, was a young man of twenty-three, unmarried. He worked, according to the application, as a commercial attaché. Questioning revealed that he sold business supplies in someone else's store. He made the monthly equivalent of about 250 U.S. dollars. He was staying at a motel in Elizabeth, New Jersey, for one week at a cost of about eighty U.S. dollars a night.

Mr. Mustapha was dressed in a suit and appeared eager but nervous.

"Hello," I said in French, guessing he would prefer it to Arabic, "what do you hope to see in Elizabeth, New Jersey?"

"Yes, I want to see the United States."

"How long have you had your current job?"

He thought. "Two years. I want to see your great country."

"Where are you going in the United States?"

"I want to stay in a hotel."

"Yes, but who are you visiting while there?"

Some more thought. "New York?"

"Why have you chosen New York?"

Again, after thought. "It is my dream to see the capital of your country."

"And when you dream of seeing the capital of the United States, what do you dream of?"

This appeared a real stumper. Finally he said, "Disney World."

"Hmmm, Mr. Mustapha, I'm really sorry, but we cannot grant you a visa."

Two hours later, having worked through the current lineup of mostly earnest young men dreaming of going to the U.S., I found myself dreaming, too, of going anywhere away from Jeddah.

Christine rescued me. She wanted me to gain experience in the Riyadh consular section. "You need to see what it's like in a bigger post. I want you to spend a week up there."

I think she knew I needed a break from the constant grind. I would interview in Riyadh as in Jeddah but leave behind my responsibilities for managing a section. Christine would pinch hit for me for the week I was gone.

The Consulate communications center asked me to bring back the diplomatic pouch on my return to Jeddah from Riyadh. I would fly up but come back in the van carrying the pouch, saving a communications officer a trip. All the diplomatic mail for the Saudi posts came into Riyadh, and an officer had to accompany the Jeddah portion by land.

I couldn't believe Riyadh's modern facilities. True, the small townhouse where I stayed wasn't as comfortable as my time-beaten little house, but I enjoyed getting away and seeing Ethan in his own habitat.

His digs, about the size of my house but made of a concrete type material, flowed around an open courtyard that he shared with another family. We usually ate at least one meal a day together, as I actually was able to take lunch in the modern dining room of the Embassy, not like my hurried trips to Jeddah's ancient snack bar.

The sojourn in Riyadh melded into a blissful interlude until I attended a poolside party the night before I returned to Jeddah with the pouch. I met Allison in person. Still single, with beautiful mahogany hair. No frizz. No freckles either.

It dawned on me what a good catch Ethan was. The logical part of me knew that, of course, but that evening the fact registered like a kick to my intestinal regions.

"Kaitlin, I'm so glad to meet you. Ethan's cousin. How nice." I figured she was sizing me up, wondering if Ethan and I were distant enough cousins for me to be a threat to her plans. "I understand you aren't really cousins. It's sort of a friendship thing." How had she wormed that out of Ethan?

"No," I said, "but we're very close."

She smiled at Ethan like Delilah simpering at Samson. "Ethan, you're planning to go on the day trip to the red hills next weekend, aren't you?"

"You know I wouldn't miss it."

Why did he seem so enthusiastic? For the hike or Allison's company?

Her reminder of the trip was, I figured, a hint that even though Ethan and I might be close friends, she had the advantage of being closer geographically. Was there something electric between them? I sipped my Coke while they swapped talk about the hike and how much fun the last one had been.

The next day on the trip back to Riyadh by van, I had time to gather my thoughts. Mohand, the driver, was a personable young Pakistani, deferential but not obsequious. We made pleasant small talk from time to time, but I had hours to think, as the moonlike landscape rolled by, the heat of the reflected sun on hardscrabble rocks barely kept at bay by the van's air conditioning.

Did I expect Ethan to remain single forever, my confidante and comrade for the rest of our lives?

Of course not. The divorce might have rendered him gunshy of an attachment for a while, but not forever. Some woman eventually would come along. What about Allison? She was Foreign Service, not a spoiled debutante like Didi.

Why the unease when I had adjusted so well to the idea of his marrying Didi? Probably because I was twenty-four now and knew Ethan's friendship filled a lonely part of me that nothing else could.

What was I to him? Convenient friend to talk to? How long would that last once we were separated by continents and oceans?

38

Jeddah constricted me after that. I seemed to meet more men on the visa line who wouldn't look at me because I was a woman. They talked to me while their eyes sidled to the side, as though they had a deformity.

"I feel like a pariah," I told Ethan when he was down next. "And it's not as much fun to go out, either. More of the men are harassing us, telling us we should have our heads covered."

"The religious conservatives are pushing it now," he said. "They were reigned in because of the war. Now they're making up for lost time. Don't stress over it, Squirt. In a couple of weeks, we'll take our Paris break. Then before you know it, it'll be the holidays, and you'll be on the downside when you come back."

I avoided hugging or touching him now and fought to secure my feelings for him in an iron-willed box, so I wouldn't have to deal with them. Did Ethan sense my yearning? He no longer sat beside me on the couch in my house, seeming to prefer sitting across from me or on the floor. Or perhaps my tension, often expressed as irritation or even anger, led him to set a distance.

I almost spat at the mutawwa, the religious policeman who stopped Ethan and me in Baroom Center, one of the shopping malls, one evening. Ethan had borrowed an SUV from Jeff for the weekend and driven us over.

"You are married to the woman?" the mutawwa had the gall to ask.

I guess Ethan could tell how furious I was. "No, sir," he said, before I could respond. "We are not married. I am, however, her guardian. Her father is dead, and she has no brothers. I am the nephew of her father. She works for the U.S. Consulate, and I work in your country also, so I can protect her."

I wanted to sock Ethan as well as the mutawwa.

The man looked at our identity cards and let us go, perhaps influenced by our diplomatic status. We marched immediately to the car, although Ethan had to pull me along at one point when I tried to stop and vent my fury on him.

"Did you have to act so subservient?" I said as he drove us to the Consulate.

"Really, Kaitlin, what does it matter?"

"That's a typical male response. I'm a grown woman and quite able to take care of myself. Do you know how demeaning that little incident was to me?"

"If you're going to be a Foreign Service officer, you have to accept the fact that other cultures are different."

"You are the outside of obtuse. Just once, do you think you could leave off lecturing me?"

I jumped out of the car when we got to the house. "Don't bother coming in." I slammed the door. I heard the SUV purr away. Once inside, I cried.

* * *

The next day, Friday, the last day of the weekend, the Reddings took us to the Christian gathering, and Ethan acted like nothing had happened.

"By the way," he said, after we were back in my house before he left for Riyadh, "I won the Rivkin award."

"The—how could you not tell me before now? All this time."

"I forgot."

The Rivkin award is an honor given to a mid-level officer whose dissent cable is judged the best dissent cable of the year.

"For the cable your father suggested you write?"

"Of course. How many dissent cables do you think I write?"

"I'm proud of you. I bet your parents are, too."

"Oh, sure. I've won an award, but I'm not sure anybody has paid attention to my arguments."

"Is it bothering you so much? You seem as melancholy as I've ever seen you."

His expression struck some deep place within me like an arrow hitting its mark. "Sorry, Squirt. I'm trying to work out some things that I—that I'll tell you about later. Okay?"

"Sure." I was too scared to probe. I didn't want to hear him talking about Allison.

* * *

After Labor Day the visa load dropped off, and I was granted leave for a long weekend in Paris.

"I feel like school is out," I told Ethan as our plane left Jeddah. "You're right. I needed this."

We stayed in adjoining rooms in a small hotel within walking distance of the Seine River and its famous Left Bank.

Evidence of Western civilization's march through history surrounded us: soaring cathedrals, bridges and streets trod on for centuries by pedestrians, and the smells of soup and fresh bread wafting through cozy, ancient neighborhoods. Easy to put aside our everyday concerns and talk about whatever floated into our minds.

While we ate in an outdoor café, he told me about a conversation he had with a Saudi businessman.

Once in a while Ethan practices fasting. It's a discipline Chopra taught him in prep school when they had a particular problem or question to mull over and wanted God's special guidance.

"Not an attempt to manipulate God," he explained, "just an exercise to focus ourselves on discerning the direction God wants us to go."

Ethan was fasting one day in his Riyadh office. I think it was when he was trying to decide which post would be his top bid on his next assignment. He had picked a day when he didn't have any appointments, but the businessman called unexpectedly and asked Ethan to see him, so Ethan did.

As custom dictated, the Saudi gentleman, an older, courteous man, had his secretary serve them tea.

Ethan begged the man's pardon but explained his pledge to fast that day. The man understood the tradition and was intrigued that his guest, presumably a normal American, would practice it. Ethan explained that he was a Christian and fasting was one of the Christian disciplines.

In the discussion that followed, the man asked, "Do you think Christianity is necessary for democracy?"

How did we get into this? Ethan told me he wondered as he grabbed at thoughts to answer the man. "Well, I don't see that any nation could pass as democratic before the eighteenth century. So, obviously, Christianity didn't make nations democratic for the first millennium and a half of its existence. I do think, though, that some of the teachings of Christianity aid in the formation of democracy after they've had a chance to percolate through a society for a long time."

"And those teachings?"

"More than anything else, the idea of servanthood. You can't have a long-lasting democracy without a significant numbers of those who govern believing that their purpose is to serve their people, not be served by their position."

They tossed around ideas for a while, Ethan told me, enjoyed an interesting discussion, and parted in a friendship that reached across cultures.

That day I had my first inkling of Ethan as a reconciler, as a negotiator that both sides on an issue would trust, someone as called to his vocation as any contemplative is called to the meditative life. I knew he feared he carried too much of Joshua's arrogance, but I saw a touch of humility foreign to his father, born, I think, of needs and doubts that the older man never had.

After finishing the story, Ethan ate the last of his French baguette sandwich, then wiped his hands on the cloth napkin. "So many new democracies struggle to make it. To make a go of democracy, the country has to have a tradition of working for the common good, not just the good of one's family or tribe or personal wealth. That's hard for a lot of countries."

I leaned forward. "You know, everybody except the loser likes being liberated—the ones liberated, the victors, the people back home who read the newspapers and see the cheering crowds. They don't realize how hard it is to make things work after the shouting's over with."

Ethan frowned before he spoke. "This job's discouraging sometimes. I keep wondering if humans have the discipline to handle freedom for very long. All too soon, we're back working on the same problems all over again. We so seldom know how to make the peace or the freedom or the liberation work."

A sober assessment from a diplomat, I thought. Did he talk to anybody else the way he talked to me? What an inward person he was, lonely in his inwardness.

"So where does hope come from? What makes you keep on in your job?" I said.

"Because I'm called to be there in case we have opportunities to make things better."

"Like now, after the end of the Soviet Union?"

"If we don't withdraw into our own materialistic cocoon." He tossed down his napkin. "Come on, let's walk a bit."

We stopped to admire a soaring cathedral. Once again, Ethan pricked me with his cynicism. "Wonder how many people worship there now?"

"Well, anyway, I'm blessed by its beauty."

"Ever hear of the Aga Sophia mosque in Istanbul?"

"Can't say I have."

"What about St. Sophia, one of the most beautiful churches ever built? Constructed when Istanbul was Constantinople at the height of the eastern Roman Empire. Soaring arches. Breathtaking. We'll have to go there someday. Only it isn't a church anymore. It's the Aga Sophia mosque I just asked you about."

I pondered. "You think Western Christianity's in danger of disappearing?"

"Possibly. Not because of conquest. Because too many Western Christians aren't concerned with the things Christ was concerned about. The life of the Spirit, for example." He glanced at me. "Sorry. Now I've succeeded in dragging you to my level. Actually, it's a wonderful day, and we're in Paris. Let's enjoy what we have right now."

We found our way to Luxembourg Garden, as beloved by Parisians as Central Park is to New Yorkers. We watched them meander the walks and gesticulate through waves of French that rose and fell like the breeze that tossed still-green leaves and hinted of coming fall.

Seated on a chair across from me, Ethan said he had placed his top bid on the Department job. I had expected he would but turned my head so he wouldn't see my disappointment.

He said, "You know if you're in Europe or North Africa, it's not going to be that difficult for us to get together."

"No, of course not." *But what if you marry again?* That hit me harder than the thought of not seeing him every month or so. Ethan seemed oblivious to the frank stares the Parisian young women slid his way, but I wasn't.

A young couple strolled by. The man's arm surrounded the woman's waist, and their soft nonsense floated in the air like drifting bubbles.

I blinked and turned my gaze away in a fruitless effort to halt longing that my subconscious could no longer contain.

The water in front of us was a pond for children's boats in the French park, but I saw Saratoga Passage, from which Ethan had plucked me when I was nine, then later comforted me with awkward compassion.

The feeling I had for him that day seized me now, in adult form.

39

I raced through arrivals at SeaTac and rushed into Matilda's arms. "Tildy, you look marvelous. It's been so long."

She pulled me back and searched my face. "Too long. Come on, now, look who I've brought with me." She turned me toward the group approaching from the side.

I stared. "Ethan? I thought you weren't coming until Christmas Eve." Beyond him were Joshua and Eleanor. "All of you? This is great."

Joshua said, "We had to do something to honor your first trip back from your beginning post."

He drove us to the Island in their comfortable Lincoln with Eleanor beside him and me between Matilda and Ethan in the back.

"How's Hong Kong?" I asked the two in front.

"Getting exciting now that the British will be handing the colony back to the Chinese in a few years." We discussed the coming change to Hong Kong's status until we drove onto the ferry.

I stood with Ethan on the outside front deck, oblivious to the frizzing of my hair by the wind, straight out of Canadian snow fields. "I love it. I love it."

He put his arm on my shoulder a moment before withdrawing it and turning to stare at the frigid water.

The Island's winter green tranquility soothed me as we slowed, cocooned for a season from the rushing world.

We cooked in a leisurely fashion, and all of us did something toward the Christmas meal, even the men.

I couldn't believe Joshua, cavorting around in one of Matilda's aprons, acting silly while he followed his sister's oral instructions for turkey dressing. Ethan and Eleanor took charge of pumpkin pies and the table setting, working seamlessly together. They had such an easy love for each other, those two. Joshua showed not the slightest jealousy of their relationship. Perhaps he loved Ethan vicariously through Eleanor.

I knew where Ethan got the sweetness he tried to hide, and the forgiving spirit.

I made Christmas cookies and a salad and handled dishwasher duties. Matilda took care of the rest.

After we sat at the table, Matilda asked Joshua to lead in prayer.

"Lord, Father, we thank you for more blessings than we can possibly enumerate. But we especially thank you for the safe return of our children after a time of war, for the plenty we are privileged to enjoy, and for our Savior, your son."

I had never heard Joshua pray before. I didn't even know he could.

After dinner, we played the usual games, this time not interrupted by phone calls. The TV stayed off.

The next day I visited Cindy and Les and returned by way of the post office. A letter threatened to ice my cheerfulness. It was addressed to Ethan, and the return address was Riyadh's pouch address under Allison's name.

Why had he given her his address on the Island? He wasn't going to be here more than a couple of weeks. Couldn't he stand to be without her?

I considered ripping up the letter and tossing the pieces in the trash can by Sam's Place. Then I considered opening it first to read it before I tossed it.

I did neither, of course, just passed it to Ethan with no comment and laid the rest of the mail for Matilda, who was out with Joshua and Eleanor.

While Ethan sprawled on the couch and read his letter, I pretended to study the *Seattle Post-Intelligencer*, daring a glance at him from time to time. He frowned, and his eyes kept moving as he read the letter. And reread it, obviously.

At least he didn't turn goofy. He folded the letter, put it in the envelope, and placed it on the table, then lay back and stared at the ceiling.

I hoped he'd leave so I could grab the letter and check it out, but after a few minutes, he got up and took the letter with him up to the study, a kind of second guest room, where he slept on a futon.

Matilda, Joshua, and Eleanor came in from a drive to the state park north of Madrona Harbor. "The front's moving up from the south. Going to be damp tonight," Matilda said. "Time to crank up the gas logs."

That reminded me of how unhappy I was that she had replaced the wood stove with a gas fireplace. Which reminded me of my other unhappiness. Ethan had been up in the study quite a while. I imagined him writing a letter.

Dear Allison, can't wait until I return.
Darling Allison, I am thinking of returning early.
Dearest and only one, can stand it no longer, will you marry me?

I groaned. Matilda lowered *Good Housekeeping*. "Are you feeling okay? You've been looking a little peaked."

"I'm fine."

"Would you like to go to the movie tonight? Joshua and Eleanor and I decided to see *Hook*. Robin Williams and Dustin Hoffman. Supposed to be funny, for the family, not one of those where everybody goes to bed together the first time they see each other."

"I think I'd rather stay home and read one of the books I got for Christmas."

"Sure you're feeling all right?"

"I feel fine. Please don't worry about me."

Ethan also declined to accompany them to the movie. "Things to think about." Joshua looked at him but didn't ask him to elaborate.

"We'd better hurry, or we're going to be late," Matilda said after supper. "Kaitlin, dear, could you and Ethan handle the dishes?"

"Sure."

After the others had left, we sat across the table from each other, the remains of Matilda's Good-bye Turkey casserole congealing and smelling the way food does when you're sick of it.

Ethan sat with his chin on his clasped hands and appeared fascinated by a leftover morsel of pumpkin pie. He raised his head, put his hands in his lap, and glanced my way, but not at me, more like the Saudi men who don't want to look you in the eye. "We're going to have to get married."

In the silence, I heard the *whish* of the gas logs. I dashed a wave of hope that threatened to engulf me. Marriage? Us? Have to? What did he mean by that? Oh, of course. Allison had turned him down, and I was the consolation prize.

I damped down my anger. Or tried to. "Do you think you could explain that?" I wished he would stop sidling his gaze toward me.

"I mean it would make my seeing you a lot easier instead of rushing over with a visitor's visa to wherever you are. And besides—"

"Rush over—" I crossed my arms. "I didn't realize I was such a bother. Why don't you go back to your career, and I'll try never to call on you again."

"Kaitlin, I—"

I rose with such volatility that my chair fell over. I picked it up and slammed it in place. Then I clenched a knobbed end on the chair's back.

Ethan scrambled up, dashed around the table to the chair, and held the other end as though he feared I would pick it up and brain him with it. He twisted his hand around the chair knob. Back and forth. At least he turned his eyes toward me. "Look. I know I'm damaged goods. If you can't accept that I love you, just say so."

I stared. "Love me? What about Allison?"

He released the chair and stood with his arms hanging at his sides. "Allison?"

"You got a letter from her, remember?"

His face looked like the clearing Island sky after a Pacific storm. He even laughed. Laughed so hard he had to sit down in the chair. He pulled me onto his lap. I fought to hold my anger, which threatened to evaporate under the heat of our closeness.

His words tumbled out as he nuzzled my hair with his chin. "I've never been in the least attracted to Allison. She's brilliant, but she's also about as shallow emotionally as Didi was. Stop squirming. Do you know how long I've wanted to hold you like this?"

"But you gave Allison this address."

"I'm hopeful. You seem to care if another woman writes me."

I straightened up, but I couldn't force myself to leave his lap. "You are so arrogant."

"I gave Allison my address so she could write me about her wedding plans."

"Wedding plans?"

"She's planning to marry an Italian diplomat she met when she was stationed in Rome. It rather complicates her status as an American Foreign Service officer. Anyway, she wrote to tell me they've decided to marry this summer. Before I left for Christmas, she told me they planned to run off somewhere and marry over the holidays. I advised caution, to follow the rules, don't mess up both their careers, that sort of thing. She wrote to tell me she thinks I'm right. They're going to take a few months to work things out."

"Oh."

"Well?"

"Well?"

In one swift motion, he put me on my feet and stood beside me. "Look, I love you. Are you going to marry me or not?"

"How long have you loved me?"

"What does it matter? I don't know how long. I guess I realized it when you wrote me about Michael."

"So why'd you wait so long to tell me?"

"You were just a kid. It didn't seem fair to shackle you when you were so young. I wanted you to—know more about yourself first."

"Oh."

"Well?"

I whirled away from him. "Tell you on the beach." I grabbed my jacket from the entry hall, flung open the door, and raced down the path. His steps pounded behind me.

The tide was going out, and sea lettuce odor oozed from the sand. The lights on the island across from us twinkled across the Passage through shreds of fog. The breeze from the south meant rain, probably before morning, and the air hung balmy like it does before a front moves through.

I loved it, the wildness, the water, the trees. And Ethan.

"Yes!"

He grabbed me, and we danced closer to the tide.

Then my Ethan, esteemed political officer from the U.S. Embassy in Riyadh, whirled into the shallow water with me, and we splashed around in ripples lapping from the Sound and ignored the chill and our sopping shoes. Taking my hands, he circled with me in a glad dance.

* * *

"Do you suppose," Ethan said after we deposited our dripping shoes and socks in the foyer, and flopped on the couch with our bare feet toward the gas fire, "that we should do something about the dishes before they get back?"

I snuggled under his arm. "No. Warm me up."

"Pleasure."

Then he released me and sat up. "I almost forgot."

"Forgot?"

He pulled a small box from his pocket. "Your ring, silly."

"Oh, that's right. I'm supposed to have a ring."

"Dear Squirt."

I oohed and aahed as he slipped a diamond and sapphire circle on my finger. I have never been big on jewelry, but Ethan was mine, and the ring was our symbol.

He coughed like he was embarrassed, this man who had supported our President before foreign potentates. "Do you suppose we could be married before we go back to Saudi?"

Interesting that his question didn't surprise me, nor was it unpleasant to consider.

He looked ashamed. "I'm sorry. I suppose you want to have a big wedding and all that."

"Actually, I'd like a small wedding, right here in this house with just the family and a few close friends. And I've known you practically all my life. I don't need a long engagement. What've we got, a couple weeks before we go back?"

We didn't hear the family until the door in the foyer clicked open.

"What's happened?" Matilda asked, coming in with her coat still on. The other two filed after her. I suppose our wet shoes and socks in the foyer puzzled them. One does not often go wading in the Sound in winter.

"Ethan?" Eleanor said, but Joshua's lips turned upward, as much as he allows, like a movie in slow motion.

We stood, and I extended my left hand toward them.

After Matilda emitted a joyous shriek, she and Eleanor alternated in hugging me. As soon as he could make his way between them, Joshua kissed my cheek, then studied me. "About time. I congratulate my son on his superb taste."

"He told you?"

"No. It's just so obvious he's in love with you."

I shook my head. He wasn't as emotionally challenged as people thought.

We had barely sat down, Ethan and I on the sofa, Joshua and Eleanor in the love seat, and Matilda in the big chair, when the "adults" (I still thought of them that way) began planning our wedding for us.

"Early June," Eleanor said. "It doesn't give us a lot of time for planning, but we'll make it."

"You have that church in Washington, don't you?" asked Joshua. "Washington's the best place for it. We've got so many friends there."

"We need to begin on the guest list. And think about the reception." This from Matilda.

Ethan stood and faced his parents. "Kaitlin and I are getting married before we go back. Here. On the Island."

Eleanor's eyes widened, and Joshua sat like he was in some negotiating session and couldn't risk showing his thoughts. Only Matilda studied us with the beginning of a smile.

I really did want to get married as soon as possible, but I hoped to start on the right footing with my in-laws. Besides, I liked them. "Perhaps we could talk—"

Ethan swiveled and glared at me, then crossed his arms and faced his parents again, specifically his father. He enunciated every word. "Dad, with all due respect—and I think you will agree that I've respected you all of my life—Kaitlin and I have made the decision. We're marrying here before we leave."

Joshua leaned forward, and I could sense the quiet anger that he had bequeathed to his son. "There's no reason to rush, is there?"

Matilda spoke before Ethan, his back tensing, could reply. "Joshua."

I turned to her, relieved that Ethan was saved from whatever he was going to reply, words that might have torn familial ties.

"Kaitlin and Ethan have known each other all their adult lives. They've endured an assignment to a country at war. They've grown in faith together. Neither you and Eleanor nor Ray and I had as much to recommend marriage to each other as they do. Now will you please stop trying to make Ethan in your image? Their decision blesses us. Can we please just claim the blessing and let them marry as they wish?"

She got up and hugged Ethan, then sat and embraced me.

The sound I heard was like nothing I could identify until I undid myself from Matilda's grasp and realized Joshua was laughing. Really, I had never heard him go all out like that.

* * *

Something old, something new, something borrowed, something blue.

Matilda insisted on the old adage. She had a dressmaker create a white velvet dress trimmed in blue for my wedding outfit. For the old, she arranged on my hair the wedding veil she had worn to be married to Ray. Cindy lent me a blue bracelet to go with the trim on my dress.

Ethan and I were married in the living room of Matilda's house by the sainted Brother Gunderson. Cindy and her mother made and served the cake and punch afterward. The house teemed with our family, Matilda's friends and a few of mine still on the Island, and dear Chopra, flying in from Illinois before he returned to India to practice medicine.

Later we sent announcements to our Foreign Service friends, scattered in various parts of the world.

That was after our honeymoon in a little ski lodge in the Cascades, where I became Ethan's wife and he became my husband. I have never regretted it, and I don't think he has either.

Even if our careers challenged us from the beginning.

40

Our plane landed in gray weather, unusual for Jeddah, but it happens sometimes in winter. Once it even rained that year, causing people to marvel, the way they do when it snows in the deep South in the U.S.

Ethan grasped my hand in the back of the van as Mohand drove us home from the airport.

Home? We spent one night together in the little compound house under the gnarled trees before he returned to Riyadh.

"I don't like it any more than you do, sweet darling," he said. We had awakened before the alarm rang, even though it was set ridiculously early. I had to return to work and Ethan to the airport.

I nestled in his arms, tickled by the mass of his chest hair while I listened to the early prayer call. "Pretty soon, it'll be worse," I said. "You won't even be in Riyadh."

"When I finish there, you'll have less than half a year. Then you get home leave. With me."

I almost sobbed. "But after that I'll be in Algiers, and you'll still be in Washington. To think, I could have bid on Montreal."

"You'd never think about resigning and being a Foreign Service spouse, I don't suppose."

"How come my career's expendable and yours isn't?"

"I make more money than you do."

"Ethan, really." I started to roll away, but he grabbed me back, as I knew he would.

"Sorry, Squirt. Your career's as important to you as mine is to me. Obviously, we're going to have to plan our next bids carefully. We've chosen rather challenging work for a two-career couple."

"Ethan, about children."

His hold loosened. "I thought we'd decided on that. I've gone along with you about not having them right away. Let's not go too long, please. I don't want to wait until I'm Dad's age to have them."

"Look, let me get my career on track, get tenured, and settled in for another tour."

The alarm rang.

* * *

Ethan and I tried to make a holiday of his leaving Riyadh the next June. I traveled with him to Rome and we spent a couple of days there before he left for the States and his new Washington assignment, and I returned to Jeddah. I left first from Leonardo da Vinci airport, and he saw me off.

I returned to the house on the Jeddah compound. In all probability, we would never again enjoy it together. It smelled of mustiness and being too long shut up, already belonging to the past.

The last months in Jeddah dripped by like cold molasses, as my mother used to say. Would they never end? My only regret was leaving friends behind. Lynne and Charles Redding had already left for an assignment in Washington, and Susan shopped in catalogs for winter clothes for her next assignment in Switzerland.

"I don't care how cold it is. I'll be able to drive," she said.

At least I might see the FSOs again on other assignments or in Washington. I hated leaving Lavali and Ramelon and Farid. Whatever success I'd had on the job came in part from them.

They, of course, were used to their bosses leaving. I invited them over to my place for a final gathering and almost cried, but they joked and made me feel better.

When I watched Jeddah receding from my airplane window, only the seat belt restrained me from dancing in the aisle.

Ethan met me in London. We shopped and dodged sudden rain showers, and he surprised me with a proper British tea at Harrod's. After a hop across the Atlantic pond, we returned in triumph to the house in Arlington. I giggled when he grabbed me and carried me over the threshold.

Ethan went to work every day, but I had two weeks of home leave. After that, the Department had scheduled me for several weeks of training and consultations with the Economic Bureau and the North African desk officer. How deceptively long our time together stretched ahead when I first arrived, so lost was I in the renewal of our conjugal closeness.

I played housewife, cooked exotic dishes that even Matilda would have praised, and replaced pictures in the master bedroom with impressionist reproductions that I bought in the gift shop of the National Gallery of Art.

Ethan studied the master bedroom after I'd made it into a cozy enclave. "This is going to seem pretty lonely after you leave."

"I'll have to do something with our Algiers house, too. That's a hint for you to come over a lot. You get more leave than I do."

His gaze caught mine. "Believe me, I'll come as often as I can. I'm going to work in as much leave as possible with all the traveling I'll be doing in the fall."

We entertained Anson and Betsy, who'd gotten married and looked as love-struck as we did. Anson was headed out to his new assignment in Guayaquil, Ecuador, but Betsy was in Washington for Spanish language training before she took her posting there.

"I'm cramming," Betsy said. "Going to learn it as soon as I can and go out early."

She probably would, I thought, and envied her language ability. She already knew French and German, though I had an idea neither she nor Anson would need those languages in their careers. Maybe Portuguese for assignments in Brazil.

"One of the few places I've never been, South America," she said. "I can't wait. I've read about the Incas all my life. Now I'm going to see all those magnificent ruins."

Over the dinner table where we'd spent so many hours together an age ago, Anson leaned forward. "I've got opportunities like I never had before. My last year in Bogotá, I lay-pastored a little mission church on weekends." He glanced at Ethan. "And to think, I once thought my life was over."

Ethan put his hand on top of mine. "A bit stupid, weren't we?"

We ate out with Patrick Holtzman and his wife, Celia, at a Lebanese restaurant in Georgetown. Patrick was finishing a Washington assignment before the couple left for Germany. His wife's presence, I suppose, contributed to Patrick's less reserved manner, though I sensed tension between them. He loved her, I decided, but an undercurrent hummed beneath their relationship.

Celia talked of her Maryland family, one with lines back to colonial times. *Who did she remind me of?* I asked myself, and searched until my mind clicked on the memory. Didi, of course. Didi breathed new California power while Celia's background was old Maryland money, yet I caught a scent of the same disdain for foreign living.

Was Patrick and Celia's marriage destined for the ruined heap of Foreign Service divorces, unable to weather challenges of life abroad, of constant change? Like Ethan and Didi's?

And he and I? Separated by our careers after short weeks of togetherness? Toward the end of my time in Washington, the thought of the days ahead without him sent an ache through me as I woke each morning.

"Please," I said when he brought up the subject of children again, "I just—well, I need to get my career on track."

I didn't have the words to tell him the other reason, because it hovered in a vague mist, hidden from me. It had something to do with fear, fear of what could happen to your babies. The odd feeling nagged, like dull pain that one ignores, its presence just below the surface.

We renewed old acquaintances at the Falls Church gathering, including Charles and Lynne Redding, and we visited Joe and Robin Harlan in their home. Robin was too weak to go out, and a nurse attended her during the day. Joe spent every minute of his spare time with her, but they still laughed together. I hurt, thinking of Joe when that laughter would be stilled.

Maybe Robin's impending death colored the last days of my time in Washington. I never can enjoy good things for long before sadness overtakes me, a dreadful understanding of life's surging and retreating, like tides on the Island.

* * *

"Basically, the Algerian people have grown sick of the old politicos, the ones who engineered the struggle for independence but now are slimy with corruption," one of the speakers in our area studies said. He was explaining recent Algerian elections. An Islamist party, the FIS, had won against the party that had been in power since Algeria's independence.

"Well, the old guys haven't given up power. They dissolved the legislative assembly, canceled the next round of elections, and set up a high council to carry out their wishes. In addition, they took control of FIS offices and pronounced the FIS no longer a political party. They've begun arresting its members."

Like its neighbors, Morocco and Tunisia, Algeria was imprinted with French culture. France had begun the conquest of Algeria in the 1830s. French farmers and businessmen poured in, taking land for farms and eventually sending representatives to the French national assembly. The native Muslim population, however, remained outside the governing European community.

The struggle by native Algerians for independence in the 1950s and '60s was stained with blood. Both sides committed unspeakable atrocities, as Ethan had alluded to when I contemplated bidding on Algiers.

Now, after a few decades of some prosperity, based mostly on oil resources, and growing national pride, Algerians were again spilling blood, this time among themselves. Algeria had been a leader of nonaligned nations during the Cold War when the world was neatly divided into Communist, non-Communist, and nonaligned, including the so-called "Third World."

Algeria played a part in the release of American hostages from Iran in 1981, being the nation to which the hostages were released before they came home to the United States.

"Algeria looks to follow the path a lot of former colonies do," the desk officer for Algeria told me during my consultations with him. "You know, the guys responsible for the liberation can't relinquish power themselves."

The party in power had followed the Soviet model in the development of the economy. The desk officer thought Algeria more cursed than blessed by its oil resources. "Big oil fostered corruption," he said. "Plus their economy became one-sided, too tied to oil."

Thus, by the 1990s, the country was beset by bloated state bureaucracies, corruption, an economy tied to heavy industry, and the neglect of its agricultural sector. High unemployment was endemic, fed by one of the highest birth rates in the world. Young men wandered around with nothing to do and no hope for tomorrow.

Ethan pointed out what happens in too many newly independent states. After the first few years when the anticipated good life doesn't materialize and the economy skids and selfish tyrants grab power, hopelessness feeds a belief in revolutionary change, the quick fix. Because Algeria is an Islamic state, it took the form of Islamic fundamentalism, at first in political form. Algerians voted overwhelmingly to rid themselves of the old party, which they viewed as corrupt and unresponsive to their needs. They voted in the FIS.

Faced with what the older leaders perceived as their extinction, the ruling elite turned their back on the democratic process. Many Islamists were jailed, and others fled. Splintering of the party followed. Moderates lost ground to extremists.

This was the country from which I would shortly be sending back reports to the State Department.

* * *

The last days were choked with tasks. We shipped the car Ethan picked out for me, a four-wheel-drive Jeep Cherokee. "Four wheel for climbing those steep Algiers hills and safer for the mad traffic you'll be in. Not as bad as Cairo, I've heard, but still pretty awful," he said.

We shipped my consumables, things like toothpaste and bathroom tissue and peanut butter, as my parents used to do. Jeddah, with its modern shopping, was not a consumables post, but Algiers was. Both Algiers and Jeddah were furnished posts, meaning my quarters would have the necessary furniture. My minimal household goods for such a post, things like dishes and linens, had been shipped from Jeddah to Algiers. I crossed my fingers that they arrived before I did.

One evening Ethan brought home an unclassified cable sent in just as he was leaving the office. He stood with hands in his pockets, the lines between his eyebrows deepening while I read it.

Boudiaf, the Algerian president, brought in by the ruling party's high council, had been assassinated. In deference to unstable conditions and possible additional violence, the State Department was ordering the evacuation from Algeria of minor dependents of U.S. government employees.

"You sure know how to pick assignments. You bid on Jeddah, and a war starts. You bid on Algiers and the place implodes. Well, next time we're bidding together for sure. At least I'll be with you."

He stared out the window. The bright colors of autumn were deepening into darker colors, gold into amber, scarlet into faded burgundy, the browner leaves dropping to reveal bare limbs. "The FIS have done it. The Islamist movement's gone violent. It's not going to be over for a long time."

I shrugged. "I'll be reporting on economic issues, not political ones."

"Kaitlin, everything is going to be affected by this." After a pause, he said, "I wish you'd consider resigning."

"Are you out of your mind? You traveled to Dhahran all during the Gulf War, and you expect me to turn tail and run?"

He ran his hands through his dark hair. "I thought you'd say something like that."

When I told Ethan I didn't want him taking me to Dulles for my flight out, he bristled at me like I was one of his junior officers. "I'm going with you. Help you with your luggage and make sure it's ticketed straight through. All that."

At the airport, we sat a few minutes and held hands.

"Go out as quickly as you can through the arrivals area when you get there. You're not as safe after you leave—"

"Ethan, I know that. I've had the security seminar, remember?"

He touched my cheek with his free hand. "Call me as soon as you can after you get there, okay?"

He watched me exit through the checks into the departure lounges. They no longer allowed non-passengers beyond that, or I'm sure he would have stayed with me until the plane left.

I did not look back and wondered how long he stayed after I walked down stranger-teeming passageways.

41

I didn't spend time in Paris, just waited a couple hours in Charles de Gaulle airport for the flight to Algiers on Air France. I didn't want to be reminded of the last time I had been there with Ethan.

The plane, an Airbus, not the familiar Boeing, climbed through patches of clouds to clear sky. The view from my window allowed glimpses of the Eiffel Tower, then the vast Parisian megalopolis before we crossed southern France and hovered over the gray-blue Mediterranean. The ancient Romans called that sea *Mare Nostrum*, "our sea," an apt description since Rome had conquered all the lands around it. At that time the area to be known as Algeria was part of a North African province that supplied Rome with wheat, olives, and grapes.

A haze appeared on the far horizon and took focus as the Algerian coast. I shifted in my seat to gain a better view of my assigned country and reviewed its bloody history. Over millennia, Roman, Vandal, Arab, Turk, and French had conquered Algeria, each playing their role in turn. Known in early Christian history by the church fathers, Algeria was the birth place of one of the most famous, Augustine. He died there, as barbarian Vandals besieged his city of Hippo, a sign of the world to come after the Roman Empire crumbled.

At the other end, I suppose, of the theological spectrum, Albert Camus, the modern novelist, was born in Algeria of a French settler family. He based his novel *The Plague* in the Algerian city of Oran.

Algiers slid into view, clumps of urbanism sprouting from dry brown. Bruce Roberts, who was to be my boss, told me later that he had seen it first on the car ferry from Marseilles and that it was much more impressive, with the old Medina rising on a hill from the sea, newer buildings and villas surrounding it, gracing steep hills.

We circled, then landed and taxied in. Bright sun glared from a cloudless sky, the land dry, but a different dry from Saudi Arabia, where the aridity belongs to the land, not like this overdone baked crust. Algeria had suffered drought for several years, no longer the land of fertile farms it had been in earlier times.

I had seen busier airports. A Saudia plane took off after we landed, probably to Jeddah, and an Air Algerie touched down afterward. Most of the planes on the ground were Air Algerie. Algeria is a huge country, over three times the size of Texas, and much of it is the Sahara Desert. Air travel is the preferred way to traverse it.

The expediter, Ferhat, met me on arrival. Unlike the missions in Saudi Arabia, the local employees of the U.S. Embassy in Algiers are almost all citizens of the country. Some are Arabs, and others are descended from older Berber stock, a people there before the Arabs arrived with the Muslim conquest. Many continue to speak their ancient Berber language.

Adele, the American information officer and my sponsor, was with Slimane, the driver. She was about my age, and her matter-of-fact acceptance of me reminded me of Cindy.

I searched the new milieu as our van raced into the city on a superhighway, then darted off into a maze of side streets. People—so many people. I did not see extreme poverty, just lots of small, down-at-the-heels shops. Tall tenements rose skyward beside large villas, evidence of the government's struggle to deal with the explosion of population growth that perplexes many developing nations. We went up and down hills on little lanes, across ravines, then up again, squeezing past traffic snarls.

"Funny," I said to Adele. "In Jeddah I couldn't wait to get to a country where I could drive a car, but this is terrifying." I gaped at the small spaces between cars, the seemingly erratic lines of dirty vehicles merging and stopping and crossing like an ant colony gone berserk.

Adele laughed. "I came from Cairo, and I know it's hard to believe, but the traffic's much worse there."

I watched a car merge into the tiny space in front of us. "It is hard to believe."

"Oh, everybody's more careful than it seems at first. That's because automobile parts are hard to find if your car gets zonked."

We turned and ascended a steep hill, past a bakery and a fruit stand, then down a narrow lane flanked by large houses within walls, a neglected air hanging on them, on the whole neighborhood.

The driver stopped in front of one that seemed too large for me.

"This is it," Adele announced. Perhaps the cheeriness in her voice was supposed to allay any anxiety I might have.

I stared at the three-story monstrosity behind the concrete walls and iron gate. "Looks like an apartment building."

"Actually, I think it was a three-flat thing before the owners offered to lease it to the Embassy. We pay our bills, you see. Got it cheap, I would imagine. A lot of the well-off folks have fled to France."

She used a key to unlock a chain around the gate posts, and we opened the gate for the driver to pull the van into the short driveway. Her Jeep Wrangler was pulled off to the side.

I felt like Alice leaving the rabbit hole rather than entering it. Outside was the higgledy-piggledy world of lanes and people and shops. Inside, the quiet fell strangely around us.

The middle floor was the living area with the usual rooms, large ones except for a tiny kitchen with a water distiller, since the Embassy considered the tap water unsafe. The foodstuffs and supplies were adequate, but less diverse than in Jeddah: cornflakes, no pop tarts or oatmeal; evaporated milk rather than dry; nothing frozen.

"We're expecting a shipment before long at the Embassy commissary," Adele said. "Right at the moment, it's a bit bare. I did manage to scrounge several rolls of toilet paper. The type you get here isn't exactly petal soft—that is, if you can find it."

We wandered into the living area. Most of the windows were covered by mechanical shutters.

"They all work," Adele informed me, "except for the living room big window. I'd just leave it down since it looks over the street. I asked the GSO about repairing it, but he says they don't have parts at the moment."

We passed a bathroom, large, but with a slight odor. "The bathrooms work upstairs. This one, though, you might want to be careful with the toilet. There's a bucket there to flush it if it seems a little slow."

Upstairs were three bedrooms, two bathrooms, and a laundry room with a washer and dryer. The master bedroom had a balcony overlooking a ravine and facing a tall tenement on the other side.

The driver left once we took in my suitcases. After we had explored the house, Adele said, "I've got my car, and I could take you around, but you might feel like chilling out after your trip. Anyway, we can't stay out too long because of the curfew. Nobody's supposed to be out after nine at night. I try to be home sooner. Tomorrow might be better to tour the place."

I thought of returning to this mausoleum after dark. "I am a bit tired. Tomorrow's the beginning of the weekend, right?" I had to get used to Thursday/Friday weekends again. "I think I'd rather fall into bed early tonight."

We made arrangements for the next day, and I secured the gate with the chain after she left. I took one look around the small yard. In the back were rows of citrus trees, a garden that looked like somebody at one time had carefully tended. It would be a pleasant place, with its fruity scents, if the windowed tenement didn't overlook it.

Who had lived here before, I wondered. A French family? Perhaps they had a small farm when the population of Algiers was more modest.

I noticed a movement on one of the tenement small balconies. I couldn't tell if the young man was looking at me or not, but I left the back yard and entered by the front door, taking a while to figure out the locks and keys.

My steps echoed as I closed shutters and turned on lights in strategic places. The furniture was the normal government issue and allowed me a tiny sense of familiarity. Not much.

After I unpacked everything in the bedroom, I made another round of the house, checking all doors and shutters. Then I gathered my courage and took a shower, being sure to lock the bathroom door.

The shower released my anxieties along with the travel grime. I didn't even try to read, just bolted the bedroom door and crawled into bed, falling into instant sleep.

In the middle of the night, I jerked up. What had awakened me? I listened for noises in the house, sounds of intrusion.

I thought of the tree in the front yard, growing over the wall. Could someone reach the limbs and use them to scale the wall? Sensing emptiness, I opened the door, and the huge darkness terrified, as did the silence.

A windowed door in the hallway led onto a balcony. I crept to it and stared through the glass, which had no shutters, to the neighborhood below my house. In the distance I heard the noise that had awakened me. Gunfire. Someone shouted, and a dog barked.

I returned to the bedroom and listened for the dial tone of my phone. If someone broke in and I called the Marine on duty at Post One, would he be able to send anyone to me? No one was supposed to be out at night except the police.

I gave up on sleep and grabbed my clothes. When Adele called several hours later, I startled awake from the couch in the living room, the remains of my breakfast cold on the coffee table.

* * *

"They're called 'wall-holders,'" Adele said as we crawled through the neighborhoods of Algiers in her car. I had remarked on the young men who stood around, seemingly with nothing to do.

"I knew the unemployment rate was high," I said, "but I guess I didn't know it had affected the youth that much."

"The official unemployment rate is about 20 percent, but we think it's more like half the population of those between eighteen and twenty-five."

She drove with ease through winding, traffic-clogged lanes, but I had no idea where we were most of the time. Directionless, I wondered how I would function without getting lost once my car arrived.

Graffiti-defaced walls, most of it praising the FIS, the Islamist group now suspected of murdering the Algerian president.

"This neighborhood seems to be pretty sympathetic to the FIS," I said.

"The poorer neighborhoods tend to be."

She gunned the car around a slower, rusty Peugeot and up another of the innumerable hills. "I'm going to show you a church."

"A church?"

"Do remember Algeria was French for over a century. Some churches and even monastic orders are still here."

After Adele parked, we entered the Catholic sanctuary. "I'm amazed it's open," I said, "given the environment of the city."

An older man worked on papers in one of the rooms off the foyer. He favored us with a glance and continued shuffling through his papers.

"Aren't they scared?" I asked when we returned to the car.

Adele shrugged. "Probably. But it's what they believe in, I suppose. I don't know how much longer they can last here."

We passed the Embassy on the way to her house for lunch. "It's actually not such a bad place to work, except that it's so old. It was a former villa of some expatriate. British, I think. A lot of Brits used to come here for the Med climate."

"George MacDonald."

"Pardon?"

"A writer back in the late 1800s. He mentioned coming to Algiers in his journal."

"Don't think I've heard of him."

"Is there any kind of church close to my place?"

"Let me think about it. Here's my house."

She lived a short distance from the Embassy in a smaller house that lacked the gloom of mine. I discovered one disadvantage, however.

A small furry animal scurried across the living room when we entered, and I squealed. "What is it, a mouse?"

Adele appeared unruffled. "Probably a rat. I need to get some more traps, I guess. First one I've seen in a while."

I tried not to keep looking down at my feet as we ate tuna sandwiches and fruit salad. "This bread is delicious."

"Good bread is one thing you can get because the government subsidizes the flour."

"You were going to tell me about churches."

"I think there's an Anglican one not too far from where you live. There are still British doing various things in the country, plus English-speaking west Africans who've landed here for one reason or another."

Her tone indicated a lack of interest in religious topics.

Later that night I managed to get through to Ethan.

"What took you so long?"

"I wasn't awake long enough last night to call you."

"Sure is lonely here."

"You should see this place. Gigantic. I liked my little place in Jeddah."

"I may soon be seeing it for myself."

My heart leaped. "You mean you're transferring?"

He laughed. "No, Squirt, sorry if I got your hopes up. I'm going to be taking some trips, though, closer to where you are. I'm going to make sure I have a visa for hopping in if I get the chance."

I guessed it had something to do with shuttle diplomacy in the Middle East, now in vogue. The Secretary of State was always traveling to the Middle East to take advantage of our recent victory in the Iraq war and encourage peace in a region little known for it. "Are you—" I tried to phrase my question in some innocuous fashion. "This is a good opportunity, I mean, for your career and all?"

"Very good. Only thing is, I can't let you know when I might hop in. That okay?"

"I'll need to tell my current boyfriend to call me before he comes over."

"Very funny."

That evening I wandered through the house feeling like I was caught in some science-fiction alternate universe. If I weren't careful, I'd scare myself with the notion that I could never escape.

* * *

The security briefing was as thorough as any we'd had in Jeddah. The security officer, Nate, an ex-Marine, gave me a radio and a stand to charge it on. I chose "Island Diva" for my call sign.

"We have radio check each Wednesday morning at 0700. Listen for your call sign. Listen for everyone's call, because some of the houses are hard to reach, and you may need to tell us that you hear them respond."

I didn't ask him if my house was one of the hard to reach.

"Be sure you're home before curfew. A Russian diplomat got killed a month or so ago, out after curfew. Word is he was drunk and didn't respond soon enough when the police asked him for his identity. Maybe talked a bit rudely to them. Who knows? Anyway, they shot him. Don't take chances. Don't depend on your dip ID to get you out of a tight spot."

After a few other cautions about watching my surroundings whenever I was out and driving defensively, he released me with my new radio.

I lugged it back to the desk in my office, a damp hole in the basement across from the Marines' restroom. The other facility was two flights up. I got lots of exercise.

The shelves were crammed with papers. Adele told me that my predecessor was a slob. "I mean, his work was all right, but I don't think he ever threw anything away. Got at least one warning for leaving out classified material. Better go through his papers and make sure he didn't stuff away something classified."

I attempted to do this, carrying massive amounts of useless material to the shredder, located in the main pol/econ section, light years from where I worked. On one of my trips there, Lil, the office manager, told me Bruce, my boss, was back from a morning meeting and would like to set up my incoming interview after lunch.

I had just enough time to check the GSO's office about my car and household effects before a quick lunch.

Ferhat answered my questions. "Your HHE is in today. Abdulaziz is there now, getting it through customs. We can deliver it tomorrow if you like. You car should be here in the next few days."

We arranged for the HHE delivery the next morning. I wasn't sure I'd be as happy to see my car.

42

Bruce and I spent the first minutes talking about mutual acquaintances, including Joe Harlan and Christine Armbruster. He relaxed in a chair across from me in an office made less spartan by pictures of his family and colorful Navaho rugs hung from the walls. He was, I learned later, part Navaho. His family was back in Phoenix.

"Nelda, my wife, could have stayed, of course, but not the children, so she went out with them. We're more fortunate than most. Our house isn't rented out, and our folks live nearby." He leaned forward. "The ambassador's planning a trip to western Algeria. Show the flag at one of our oil camps near Oran and visit our English language school there. He'll make a visit to a couple of the governors. We'd like you to accompany him as note taker."

"That's wonderful." I finally had a reporting job like my father.

Embassies and consulates make plans each year for issues they wish to research and report on back to Washington. We discussed the goals for Algiers economic reporting and decided I would begin researching population issues and the implications for population growth on Algeria's future.

Schools were jammed, and no one knew where jobs could be found for the children when they reached adulthood. Already, recruits from Algeria's jobless swelled the ranks of the FIS. How would U.S. policy be affected by the huge numbers of aimless youth? Would Algeria become a hostile Islamic state like Iran?

The two FSNs of the political/economic section greeted me, Gabir and Basem. Gabir apologized for his inability to suppress a yawn. "Sorry. I did not sleep well last night. Too much gunfire in my neighborhood." He spoke as matter-of-factly as if he were talking about a neighbor's loud radio.

My meeting with Ambassador Tim Caldwell went well, much better than my first meeting with Margaret McPherson in Jeddah. He was Texas tall and lanky, surprising given his Irish name. He had the facility, like George Lannigan, of putting people at ease, even a second tour junior officer. I left the meeting glad I'd like the man I'd be spending several days with on a busy trip.

And so the days went. My car arrived, and I discovered driving in Algiers was not so difficult and began to take the crowded streets with ease. I learned to plot exactly where I wanted to go before I left.

Soon I was venturing off the main road to and from work to find alternate routes, which we were encouraged to do to throw potential terrorists off track by changing routine. I learned to walk to the bakery for bread and pastries and to the fruit vendor for fresh fruit, ignoring the stares of ordinary Algerians, which became a part of the life I had to tolerate.

I located the Anglican church in an ancient building hallowed by past visits of English royalty, and I attended most weekends. Despite the different tradition than what I was used to, the time with other Christians, many of them sub-Saharan Africans, blessed me.

A shipment of American goods arrived at the Embassy commissary, and I managed to buy peanut butter and toilet paper before they were sold out, as well as other assorted goods. My consumables would arrive "soon" I was told.

Bruce came in one morning while I was scanning the morning's French and Arab newspapers for stories of interest to the U.S. government, one of my jobs. He showed me a piece of paper, printed in Arabic. "Gabir brought this in. Seems the FIS is circulating it throughout Algiers."

I read it. "They want all foreigners out of Algeria within 30 days or they're vowing to—the word is *exterminate*, I believe—exterminate the foreigners, I mean."

I handed it back. "I presume they're particularly interested in the oil company workers."

"They'd like to shut down the oil industry here. Oil is the main revenue source for the government they hope to topple."

"And set up an Islamist government on the model of Iran, I suppose."

In my faxes to Ethan, I did not mention the warning. My fax machine arrived with the rest of my HHE, and I set it up immediately. The connection wasn't all that great; faxes crept from the machine like slow-moving mud, but at least Ethan and I were able to communicate without using snail mail.

Mail was especially slow for the Embassy because we could only use the diplomatic pouch, which appeared to follow a haphazard delivery schedule. We had no military APO like I had taken for granted in Jeddah.

> Dear Ethan: Isn't it wonderful, being able to get each other's letters when we write them? Even though sometimes I have to send my faxes several times before they finally go through, it sure beats the pouch mail. I still haven't received the package you said you sent me.
>
> I'm so excited about my trip to Oran with the ambassador. I'm finally doing what I want to do.

Dearest Squirt: Perhaps you'll receive two packages at once. I've already mailed you a second. Not to worry. Neither one will spoil.

You will, of course, be extra vigilant when you're traveling with the ambassador?

* * *

The ministry official in charge of population issues preferred French to Arabic. He resembled Gabir in appearance—both, I decided, of Berber ancestry. He shook my hand after Gabir had introduced us and waved us to chairs across from him. After the introductory civilities, I asked if Algerians still preferred large families.

"I myself have eight brothers and sisters," he said, "and my family was considered small by the standards of that day."

"And now?"

"Our studies show that younger Algerians prefer family sizes of perhaps three or four children. However, they often end up with five or six."

"I read pamphlets that some of your Islamic scholars have written. The pamphlets say that Islam does not prohibit birth control. It forbids abortion, of course, as does my own Christian religion."

He nodded. "Our lack has nothing to do with our beliefs. It has to do with supply. We do not have a steady supply, for example, of birth control pills, as we do not of many goods and services."

A frank admission, I thought.

He continued, "We are trying to develop a facility on our own soil that will produce the pills, but as yet we cannot obtain the necessary investment."

Later as I wrote my notes into a cable, I discussed reasons why investors might be reluctant to fund a factory that produced birth control pills.

> The Islamic militants would probably be as eager to destroy such a facility as they are to destroy Algeria's oil industry. Though moderate Islamic scholars do not condemn birth control methods, so long as they are used only by married couples, militants consider them a curse of the decadent West.

I paused. Yes, the extremists wanted to get the woman pregnant and keep her that way, her only reason for existence. In college I had briefly flirted with women's lib but soon abandoned it, turned off by what seemed to me an extremism, a hatred of family. I concluded that God blessed marriage and family, but judging by Christ's actions, he condemned those who took advantage of women in a male-dominated society.

In the West, a woman had freedom now, as I did, to use all my God-given talents. Yet that very freedom, welcome as it was to me, presented me with a dilemma. I wanted children, but how would they affect my career?

* * *

I picked up my ringing office phone, expecting Lil to tell me that Bruce had cleared my cable on population issues.

"Hi, Squirt."

"Ethan! Where are you?"

"Right now, I'm looking at the Air Algerie taking off to go back to where I just came from. En route from somewhere else I've been. I thought I'd take the slow way home, spend a couple of days in Algiers."

Bruce let me go early. "The cable's not urgent. I'll get the DCM to clear and have it for you tomorrow. We can take a couple of days to get it out."

Ethan waited for me in front of the terminal. He jumped in and leaned over to kiss me. The car behind had to beep before I remembered to move on.

I studied Ethan as I dodged and wove through traffic. "You look beat. Going to tell me where you've been?"

"With the Secretary at the peace talks. Interesting, if exhausting. We're going home to Washington, but I have permission to spend a couple of days here on my way."

"I'm sorry it's not the weekend."

"I'll sleep most of the time you're at work. You know, you handle the driving very well. I've only cringed a couple of times."

The two days together were like a nibble of rich chocolate. You want more, but even a couple of bites are luscious. He had a driver from the Embassy take him back, even though he wasn't an official visitor. "Just leave me here and go to work. It's better that way."

I agreed, but I dreaded coming home to the empty house.

As soon as I opened the door after work, I saw the note. It led me to a gold necklace and another note. Ethan had laid out a treasure hunt with chocolates and jewelry and love notes. I fingered them, thinking of his other presents that had finally arrived, a book of T.S. Eliot's poetry, which I had expressed a wish for, and a care package of M&M's and other comfort food.

If he had called me then and asked me to resign so I could be with him in Washington, I might have done it.

* * *

"What do you mean, the pouch is delayed?" I almost shouted. *Careful. Don't become an ugly American.* I forced a smile, a benign one, I hoped. "It's just that I'm looking for an important package."

Ferhat, bless him, checked once more, though both of us knew it was hopeless.

He sighed. "I'm sorry, Ms. Kaitlin. They say the pouch from Washington didn't arrive in Paris in time to make it here on the flight. At least, that is their excuse this time."

Ethan came the next weekend, not so tired as before and excited about the work he was a part of. Those trips raised hopes that were not fulfilled. Suicide attacks and civilian casualties on both sides eventually ended the talks, but he was optimistic when he came that weekend.

"You know," he said, "sometimes I'm frustrated, but I'm never bored in this job. I always feel like I'm working on something worthwhile." He pulled me close to him on the couch. "So you've landed a reporting job. Like it as much as you thought you would?"

"It's—fine."

"Not quite so rewarding as helping a distraught American citizen, though, is it?"

"Of course it is." I did not admit how my mind wandered sometimes when I had to read all those newspapers or try to outline what I would say to some official in a meeting.

Instead I talked about the trip Ambassador Caldwell and I planned in a couple of weeks. "I can't wait. If we have time on the way back, we might visit one of the World War II allied landing sites."

Ethan grunted. "A security officer going with you?"

"Of course not. We'll have the driver, though."

He rubbed his chin against my hair. We didn't talk anymore about the trip. I forgot to tell him about the pouch not coming.

43

I stared in fascination at the countryside from Algiers to Oran and a day later from Oran to Tlemcen, as Slimane drove us. It reminded me of eastern Washington's Palouse, with its rounded brown hills. History haunted the small towns, set around public squares like quaint French villages, but inhabited now by Algerians. I saw an abandoned church in one of the towns and wondered what it had seen. When had the last service been held?

Some of the large farmhouses lay empty as well. Had they once been the estates of French settlers, those tragic *Pied-Noirs*, "black feet," as they were called when they were exiled to France after the Algerian war? Like the French Acadians of Longfellow's *Evangeline*, they wandered, forever bereft of their homeland. This world has many exiles.

We met with American workers at an oil-processing facility close to Oran. They gave us hard hats to walk around the plant and told us they felt safe enough, that they trusted the Algerians to guard them from the beginnings of terrorism. After all, the Algerians had to have the oil. Unlike neighboring Tunisia, oil was Algeria's main source of revenue. The country had neglected its agriculture for decades in pursuit of the black gold that the world so craved.

My mind wandered in the meetings with officials from Sonatrach, Algeria's state-owned oil company. I kept having to pull my thoughts into listening mode, for I would write the cables to Washington detailing the talks. They gave us a huge luncheon, delicious, but I felt a little queasy when faced with what looked like a large crayfish and barely picked at it.

Afterward, on the way to Tlemcen, a seat of ancient Islamic schools where we would meet with the governor of the area, I scribbled everything I could remember from the talks while Ambassador Caldwell dozed.

After he roused, we discussed highlights of the meetings, and I wrote other suggestions for my cables. Then I dozed myself, to be jerked awake by a tone in the ambassador's voice as he talked to Slimane. "It's okay. There's a policeman with them."

The policeman walked to the car from the group of armed men clustered at the checkpoint. Before I could gather my wits enough to be frightened, the policeman politely informed us that the governor had sent us an escort.

Later I was to read of another Algerian governor and his bodyguards ambushed and massacred, but this was not that time yet. We were safely escorted into Tlemcen to the Ziadnid Hotel, which had seen better days. Nevertheless, I went to my room glad for a chance to freshen up. The rest areas on the trip had consisted of small stores with pit bathrooms, filthy and vile smelling. I welcomed the water to wash my face and looked forward to a good shower later, though the bathroom could do with some cleaning. I did not drink water from the tap, of course.

We ate in the hotel's dining room, and I picked at some cooked items, scared to touch the raw vegetables or fruit. Slimane ate with us, and he talked of his family. He was divorced but had a young son whom he appeared to love dearly. The boy lived with Slimane's former wife in the Berber region of Kabyle. This was not Saudi Arabia. Men talked about their families here.

I took an unopened bottle of water back to my room to drink and brush my teeth. Unfortunately, the tap water had been cut off, and I could not shower.

The next day I forgot my discomfort when a friend of the ambassador's, an Algerian doctor with a penchant for reciting haunted Arabic poetry showed us around Tlemcen. The armed escort accompanied us everywhere we went, getting out first and standing with what I presumed were Uzis, though I don't know much about guns. The guards looked as fierce as the guns, like I imagined Al Capone's men during the gangster wars of the twenties, but they seemed friendly enough, smiling at us through broken teeth.

The doctor took us to a ruined fort and recited poetry as we stood in light drizzle. I did not catch all of it but got the gist of a tragedy where the fort's defenders and their families had gradually starved to death in some long-ago bloodletting.

We visited an ancient mosque as well. The friendly imam showed us around, seemingly not bothered by our infidel status. We took off our shoes to view the mosque's lovely interior. Then the imam showed us the well whose water the faithful used to wash themselves before prayers. Ropes attached to the well's bucket had worn deep cuts in its stone sides over the centuries. I suspect that it graced the site of some water goddess worshiped in Roman times, and probably before that, too.

That excursion marked the last quiet of the trip. In the afternoon we met with the governor, and I dutifully took notes as he and the ambassador discussed the state of the country and western Algeria in particular. The governor was upbeat about Algeria's future. "We have our problems, but we will solve them."

We had one more night in the hotel, and I managed a quick dip in the tub before supper. The buffet, a bit scanty, included sardines, which I like most of the time, but that night they seemed slimy. I nibbled on a little pasta.

We did not linger the next morning at breakfast.

"Nate called me an hour ago," the ambassador said. "Seems some incident happened in one of the Algiers markets, and he thinks it best if we get back as soon as possible today. Sorry, but we'll have to forget about any tourist stops."

He didn't elaborate further, but the governor's escort was going all the way to Algiers with us. We now rated two cars, one in front and one in back.

Algiers was a long way, but I never doubted we'd reach it by nightfall, given the speed we traveled. Poor Slimane exercised all the skills he'd learned as the ambassador's driver to keep up with the lead car.

We hurtled through the countryside, our journey a combination of a fast pilgrimage by a Russian imperial czar and a Bonnie and Clyde getaway. Each time we overtook a car, the guards hung out the window and pointed their guns at the hapless driver until he pulled over and allowed us to pass.

When Slimane dropped me off at my house after taking the ambassador home, I was so weak I could hardly undo the gate chains. Once inside, I could have kissed the floor of the place, a haven after what I'd experienced.

Before morning, I'd thrown up twice and was suffering diarrhea. I called in, and Bruce told me to take it easy at home for a day or two. The cables didn't have to go out right away.

I limped in the next day, having written the first cable in longhand at home from my notes in my more lucid moments. I no longer had diarrhea but any thought of food turned my stomach. Once I had written and cleared the cables, Bruce ordered me back home. "Don't come back until you're well. You do know we're to keep a low profile because of the Russian woman?"

I nodded, having read the two memos to all officers that came from the DCM while we were gone. Terrorists had grabbed a couple of French diplomats. Several days later they released them with a note, saying the kidnapping was a warning. The next foreigners the group seized would be killed. Apparently, according to the next memo, the extremists intended to carry out their threat against foreigners remaining in Algeria. A Russian woman in Algiers, married many years to an Algerian, was murdered by a gunman as she came to the market to shop for her family.

A new terror was beginning. Murder or the taking of hostages by Arab terrorists had rarely included outrages against women. The murder of the Russian woman was the first instance I knew of the deliberate harming of a woman for political purposes. Unfortunately, it was to grow worse.

44

My fax to Ethan went through on the third try.

I'm researching for my meeting with the ministry on the high unemployment of Algerian youth. I don't know why I can't get more excited about it. I've had a short bout of dysentery; maybe that's why. A bug I picked up on the trip.

I'm sorry the killing of the Russian woman has upset you. We're taking precautions but are still allowed to go shopping as long as we go in our cars and vary our routes. No more walking around.

The other news would wait until I saw him in person.

I also didn't mention the young man who came up to me as I was untying the chain around my house gates the day before. The young man offered money for my gas coupons, indicating he knew I was a diplomat. We received gas coupons from the Embassy, insuring us a supply of gas for our cars.

He spoke in halting English and seemed surprised when I refused him flatly in Arabic: *La!*

What he wanted me to do was illegal, of course, but I was concerned that he might be feeling me out, trying to set up a hostage taking.

Another time when I came home, neighborhood children clustered around my gate. They wanted their ball, please, that had gone over the wall. I undid the gate but told them as politely as I could in Arabic that they must wait outside, and they obeyed.

After I found the ball and tossed it back to them, it occurred to me that the ball could have had an explosive device attached to it.

I hated the fear that ruled my life, that said I must trust no one. I hated being set apart, unable even to be friendly with children.

Ethan's reply to my fax came the next day:

Kaitlin, watch everything and everyone. Don't go out if you don't absolutely have to.

* * *

Even terror abates when nothing happens for a while. Terrorism had begun in the rural areas, where the FIS began attacking small villages, but Algiers remained quiet. The past event assumed dreamlike qualities. Despite Ethan's faxed instruction, I decided one weekend to lift my spirits with a trip to a shopping mall not far from the house. It was not the type of mall we think of as such back home and would have a minimum of things to buy, but I had a desire to do something frivolous and relieve the constant tension. I wondered if they might have a few women's clothes from France, something with which to surprise Ethan next time he came.

I never found out what kind of clothes they had.

After scanning the street that weekend morning, unlocking the clanging chain and gate, and driving the Cherokee through, I parked and got out to close the gate and rewind the chain. Rather futile, because anyone who wanted to grab me could wait half a block away in his car in the alley until he heard the chain, then race toward me before I had time to react.

Once out of the dust-choked back streets, I merged into a line of vehicles reminiscent of a demolition derby, meshed together on the road like a swarm of worn-out locusts.

The sparkle of the Mediterranean belied the tragedy of an Algiers jammed with desperate humanity. Rural Algerians streamed from the drought-cursed countryside, now fleeing terror as well. They crowded in tenements, crowded on buses, crowded against walls to stare at me as I passed. Even before the Embassy prohibition against walking, I had stopped my daily strolls, sick of the envy that followed me, palpable as the gas-laden heat waves, envy of the American, not locked forever in misery as they were.

I flung off the guilt that haunted me for my accident of birth and pulled into the parking lot of the mall. True, the mass of concrete reminded me of Soviet style architecture rather than a monument to consumerism, but guards patrolled it.

I hesitated after parking, attached to the perceived safety of the Cherokee, then picked up one foot to move away.

A clap like a thunder of retribution ripped the air and passed in a wave. Someone screamed—me—but the scream stayed mostly within, as though I had muted a TV. Did the force of the explosion propel me flat against the metallic surface of my vehicle? Or did my automatic gesture of protection push me there? I blinked, checked faculties, decided I survived intact, except for ringing in my ears.

I shook my head to clear it. Flames devoured the remains of the vehicle that had exploded in the mall parking lot, thankfully many rows over from mine. Crowded against my car, I clutched my belly as I smelled the stench of burning vinyl and oil and rubber. Burning. The odor that had clogged my nose and throat once before.

Not this time, please God. Not this baby.

My life in Algiers halted as in a movie frame. Memory's time folded years into moments. Then the elusive shred yanked free of subconscious tendrils and drifted to the surface, the one that haunted me in half-dreaming moments, yet never emerged in full form.

The final memory forced itself on me. A desert picnic with my parents.

"We have something to tell you," my mother said that last weekend, putting down *The Hobbit* that she had been reading to my father and me. She smiled at my father, spread across from us on the heavy blanket we used for picnics, and he smiled back. They had some secret between them, I knew, something wonderful.

"You're going to have a little brother or sister in a few months," she said and put her arm around me.

"Oh, Mama, really?" Then, impatient but proud of my knowledge about babies," Do we have to wait a long time? Like Thérèse did for her baby brother?"

"Oh, about six months. We waited to tell you until we were sure."

I hugged my mother. "I hope it's a girl. What'll we name her?"

My parents smiled at each other, that wonderful, shared smile. "We haven't decided yet, but you can help us think of names. Perhaps we should have a boy's name, too, just in case."

My father sat up and moved closer. "The baby will take some of your mother's time."

"Of course," I said. Did they think I didn't know about tiny babies? "I know babies don't come ready to play or anything. You have to feed them a lot at first."

My father continued. "You'll be pleased to know your mother's going to stop working."

"She'll be at home all the time, even during the summer?"

"That's right."

I turned to my mother. "You really don't want to work anymore?"

"I really don't. Not for a few years. I'd rather be home with you and Daddy and the baby. We'll do things together."

"You have to cry to heal," Matilda said. If so, my healing should be

complete with the owning of sorrow for my little brother or sister, murdered before my parents or I ever held it. So awful that I had repressed the knowledge for years, unable to face it.

I struggled back into the terrible world of now. I had to protect the other baby. Dimly remembered lessons from the security seminar surfaced. Might there be another explosion? Sometimes terrorists planted a small bomb, the instructor said, then when the gaping crowd gathered, set off a more horrendous one.

I entered the driver's side from where I had emerged minutes ago and prayed for the trembling to stop.

Breathe. I did so, several times, and managed to turn the ignition. I heard the car start. My hearing was returning.

The calmness that took hold of me cannot be explained. *Peace that passes understanding.*

I backed out the car and drove slowly through a milling throng of shouting, gesticulating pedestrians. I seemed to be the only one driving in this place. No one paid the slightest bit of attention to me until I reached the street. A grim policeman stopped me, then waved me though when I showed him my ID.

My next clear memory is the way the rough couch felt in the living room of my house as I ran my hand over it. I tasted the salt of my tears and let the images wash over me.

My parents. Their joy at another life.

Dear God, please don't let those people win.

I ran to the bathroom and examined myself, was delighted I seemed intact and was not bleeding.

Please, God, let this baby make it, Mama and Daddy's grandchild.

45

No one knew I had been close to the explosion, and I did not tell anyone. I should have told them, reported it in a cable, but I was too close to falling apart and did not want to relive my experience.

An explosive device had been placed under a car, the ambassador said after the weekend in the Embassy meeting of all employees, and the car driven to the parking lot and left there, then detonated from a remote location.

I almost laughed when he said the device was "not a large one." No one close to it would think it small. Fortunately, nobody in that crowded place was close enough to be seriously injured, physically, at least. My nightmares returned for a couple of nights. I accepted them, did not try to fight them, simply got up and read, and they vanished.

Ethan called a few hours after it happened. The connection was bad. Apparently he was back in the Middle East with the negotiating team. "Kaitlin, thank the Lord. I wasn't able to get through for the longest time."

"I'm fine. Hunkered down at home. We're supposed to stay put for the rest of the weekend." I pretended irritation. "I was going to shop for clothes."

"Stay inside like they tell you to do. Next time we're in the States together, I'll buy you all the clothes you want."

He came the next weekend. I waited until we were at the house before I collapsed into his arms, but I didn't tell him where I had been the weekend before or about that last memory of my parents.

Later at the table, I stared at the macaroni my fork had snagged, then ran retching to the bathroom.

When I returned, Ethan was sitting on the couch. He motioned for me to sit by him. "Do you still have that bug you picked up on the trip?"

I played with a button on his shirt. "No, just a little nausea once in a while."

"Kaitlin, I want you to see the nurse at the Embassy. I know you don't like taking things, but this has gone on long enough. It's not healthy."

"It's quite healthy. Women often are nauseous the first few weeks."

"First few weeks?"

"Of pregnancy."

"Pregnancy?"

"We're going to have a baby."

"Baby?"

"B-A-B-Y. Baby."

Ethan's jaw actually went slack. Then his lips curved up into a silly grin, like he had tasted a strange food and discovered he liked it. "That's wonderful. But I thought you didn't want children for a few years."

"I ran out of pills, and the pouch was late. Actually, my new prescription accidentally got in the pouch to Ulan Bator. By the time it was rerouted here—well, it didn't come until after that weekend."

"You didn't tell me."

I played with his shirt button again. "We were having such a wonderful time together, I never got around to saying anything about it. Would it have made any difference, do you think?"

His look softened my insides. "No. I don't think it would have. A baby. Our baby. We've got to tell the folks, tell everybody."

"Let's wait a little while. Until we're absolutely sure."

"You're not sure?"

It all came out, how near I was to the explosion, what I remembered about my mother's pregnancy.

He squeezed me to him and said nothing for a long time while I listened to his beating heart. When he spoke, it sounded like he had a cold. "Kaitlin, I want you out of here. Take a leave of absence. Whatever. I don't want you staying here. You need to be back in the States and seeing a doctor."

I tried to twist out of his embrace. "You go places all the time that are dangerous. Don't you think I worry about it? About all the fanatics who'd like to throw bombs at those meetings? After what happened to my parents, don't you think it terrifies me?" When I started crying, he let me up to look at him.

I swallowed more tears so I could speak. "I can't let those murderers win. I have to keep working, finish what they tried to stop my parents from doing."

After I saw the look that swam across his fathomless eyes, I guessed I'd have to do whatever he wanted, but I was torn in two.

He stroked my cheek. "Well, we'll see. For now, I want you to curl up on the couch. I'm going to reheat supper and bring it in here. We'll eat stretched out together on the couch. As cozy as we can manage in this cavernous place."

As it turned out, Ethan got his way without having to do a thing.

* * *

The call came early the next morning, Thursday, the beginning of the weekend. I struggled upward from sleep, dislodged myself from Ethan's arm that he had thrown around me while we slept, and answered the phone.

"Meeting," I told Ethan, now sitting up, when I hung up the phone. "Three o'clock this afternoon in the chancery. Everybody's ordered to be there. More security measures, I guess. I hope nothing else has happened."

We spent a leisurely morning, and Ethan did not once mention what we'd talked about the night before. I ate toast for breakfast, skipping the canned pineapple juice I knew I wouldn't be able to keep down. We went to the Embassy an hour or so before the meeting because I wanted to catch up.

"You've straightened the place," Ethan said when we reached my office.

"I still can't figure out a good filing system for the newspaper clippings."

"Care if I look at them?"

"Be my guest."

He threw away half the clippings, saying they were outdated, and labeled folders in his neat handwriting before filing the rest of the clippings.

"This is wonderful. How do you do it?"

"Practice. Someday your successor will have a head start."

"My successor?"

"You know what this meeting is about, don't you?"

"Stricter security measures. We probably won't be able to shop at all. I'll have to order everything out of the catalog, and it takes an age before things get here."

"I think they've decided to draw down the Embassy."

I squelched a rising hope. I was supposed to enjoy my job. "I'm a reporting officer. They won't send me back."

"Want to bet? You're a junior econ officer, not a consular officer. You'll be ordered out."

"You don't have to seem so happy about it."

He had the grace not to look at me when the ambassador announced just what he'd predicted.

* * *

Kaitlin, dear one, I'm so thankful you're finally back. I was worried about you in that place. Even if Ethan is gone a lot, I feel much better about you in Arlington.

I appreciate your invitation to spend Christmas with you, but I've decided to stay on the Island. I would rather come later in the spring when the weather's better. I'm also in the midst, finally, of cleaning out from the accumulation of a lifetime. Perhaps it's a stage one reaches as one matures. I realize I must order my possessions and not leave them for others when I'm gone. So many of them have meaning only to me.

I understand, what with Ethan's traveling, and you just back from such a dangerous place, that you prefer not to travel to the Island for Christmas. We'll get together later. I am so, so thankful you're safe.

How nice that you're taking a little time off. I think you need it after what you've been though....

I read Matilda's first letter since our return to the Arlington house. Her happiness had surged over the telephone when I called her after we arrived. I saw no reason to mention the explosion that led to the evacuation of most of the Embassy staff, much less my nearness to it. I said the State Department had concerns about the state of affairs in Algeria. I doubted if the explosion in a country little-known to average Americans had even been reported.

"When can we announce the baby?" Ethan asked during one of his rare moments in Washington. "Now that the doctor says you and our child are fine." Ethan acted like he'd like to hand out cigars—yellow ones?—right then. I could hardly hold him down with my explanation that I wanted to find another assignment before I told anybody about the baby.

"So what happens when this little guy/gal puts a few pounds on you?"

"Don't worry about it," I snapped.

I wouldn't even let him tell the Falls Church group. Robin Harlan had died while I was in Algiers. I told myself it wasn't right to share our happiness beside Joe's grief. That wasn't it, of course—Joe would have rejoiced with us—but the baby represented a dilemma to me that I couldn't articulate.

Back in A-100, one of the speakers had talked about evacuations and what they could do to an officer's career. You had the assignment you wanted, then it vanished in the evacuation, probably in an off cycle for new positions.

I worked with my career development officer on finding another vacant place, but most assignments change in summer, and mid-December was indeed off cycle. Several positions were available for junior consular officers in countries whose language I already spoke, and my CDO would have been delighted for me to fill one in Yemen.

"I'd rather wait for a political assignment."

"There's one in Romania, but it's language designated."

I sighed. Even if I could talk them into giving me six months of Romanian, I'd be about to deliver the baby when I finished language training.

Finally I took a leave of absence, like Ethan wanted, to think and decide how to get my career back on track. I struggled not to be jealous of his career, which zoomed into the stratosphere. When he bid next summer on overseas assignments, he had a good chance on a second-in-command at an Embassy, deputy chief of mission, or as a consul general, heading a consulate.

Where was I going to be then? What about the baby?

I visited my CDO one Friday afternoon.

"I have news," he said, "a cable for you."

Surely he meant he had an assignment for me? If he'd handed me the cable without the preliminaries, I wouldn't have felt like I'd been thrown from a cliff on reading it. I congratulated myself on my ability to murmur inanities to the CDO, saying I would be contacting him later, and made it home without dissolving into hysterics.

I saved the hysterics for my call to Ethan, halfway around the world in crucial negotiations. It didn't occur to me to wonder if the time were appropriate for challenging him with personal problems. I reached him in his hotel room.

"Kaitlin, what is it? Are you all right?"

I sobbed a moment before I could go on. "I got a cable about my coning. They've made me a consular officer, not a political officer. But I don't want to be a consular officer. I think I'll resign."

"Kaitlin, really, we just got—"

I could hear somebody knocking on his door. Ethan said, "Come in." Something creaked, probably Ethan's chair, and I imagined him rising to his feet. "Hello, sir."

To me: "I have to go. Don't resign." He hung up.

A lot he cared. I cried myself to sleep.

I spent the next day, Saturday, moping around the Balston Common mall. Back home, two days of dirty dishes accused me from the sink.

The doorbell rang, and I checked the peephole.

"Ethan, what are you doing here," I said, swinging open the door as I seemed always to be doing. "I thought you were saving the free world."

"Not just me. It's a team effort." Sometimes Ethan displays such subtle humor, you're not sure he's joking. "They needed somebody to carry a message to Washington, and I volunteered."

"You don't have secure lines over there?"

"Some things have to be done face to face." He looked at his watch. "I've got fifteen minutes. The taxi's waiting. You haven't resigned yet, have you?"

"It's the weekend, Ethan."

"Oh, I forgot. The days run together. I need to use the bathroom."

When he returned, I said, "So nice that the house is available for your pit stop before you rush off to the Seventh Floor of the Department."

"Actually, it's not the State Department; it's the White House. Give me a break. I just got off a military flight, I'm jet-lagged, and within minutes I've got to wax erudite before the National Security Advisor."

His exhaustion drew me out of myself. What had I been thinking?

I led him to the couch, and he collapsed like he hadn't slept in days. He had to be very tired or he would have avoided the hint of apprehension in his voice. I understood. He hadn't wanted to make this presentation. Ethan takes risks, but he prefers calculated risks. He knows his limitations, doesn't take on something he perceives is beyond his capabilities. But he had come anyway.

He opened his eyes. "You'd make a lousy political officer. You'd do much better at consular work. You're not cold and calculating like me. People take to you. They know you care for them. You're passionate and dramatic."

I practically screamed, "I'm not dramatic."

The smile that lurked on his lips thwarted my anger. I giggled and allowed him to pull me beside him on the couch.

"I wanted to be a political officer like my father."

"You're a daughter of both your parents. One was a consular officer."

"She never was one, except for a junior officer tour."

"She chose to be a wife and mother. She was called to that, too." I clasped my hands in my lap and stared at them while he continued. "I certainly wouldn't stop you from resigning if it's for a good reason, but this isn't. You've got to stop trying to live your parents' calling and find your own. In the meantime, stick with consular."

He shifted. I knew he wanted to check his watch but restrained himself.

"Okay," I said, "maybe you've just won a diplomatic victory. Convinced me to stay in as a consular officer."

He did check his watch then. "If I have time, I'll call you before I go back." The kiss he gave me before striding out convinced me I was not the only passionate one.

* * *

Ethan called from Andrews Air Force Base before his military flight left. We couldn't talk about his meeting, of course, but I could tell he wasn't happy about it. Later he sent me a fax.

The presentation went well in one sense. They liked me personally; it will probably win me brownie points.

But frankly I could care less about that at the moment. They listened fairly, bought into a minor portion of it but nixed the main proposal I presented. I can't go into specifics, but the proposal actually began with an idea I had that the ambassador liked. Too bad, but it never got off the ground. "Very creative, Mr. Coverwood, but a bit too bold," they said.

It occurred to me that I'm never going to rise any higher than Dad did, probably won't even make it that far. You're right. Part of what drives me is the desire to vindicate his fall. And yes, I do love him.

But now, having discovered that, I find I can't let vindication be the deciding factor in my career. If I'm going to be true to what I'm called to do, I'll always be a maverick, a gadfly, here to remind them of principles and that sort of thing. In one sense, I suppose, I'm my father's son. I have to tell it like I see it.

I replied.

You know what? I love you. And I'm not in Algiers. I'll be here when you come back. We'll hold each other and kiss away the hurts.

And he faxed back.

Darling Squirt, you make it all worthwhile.

Within a week of receiving that infamous cable announcing my future as a consular officer, I carried out two tasks. Ethan and I announced my pregnancy to the world. I also decided to continue leave without pay until after the baby was born. If I was going to work 24/7 in a consular capacity, I figured I'd better rest while I had the opportunity.

Consular was my calling, wasn't it?

Actually, God wasn't through surprising.

46

Our baby was born the next summer. We named her Victoria Eleanor after the grandmothers and called her Tori.

I wasn't prepared for the way Ethan held his daughter, looked at her, and stroked her head. He didn't even balk at changing her diapers. Would he continue to do that? To be a loving father? Perhaps with a daughter, but what if we had sons? Would he be like Joshua had been with him?

He thought she looked like me, and so it turned out, except, I was thankful to note as she grew over the years, she had fewer freckles than I did, more like my mother. Nevertheless, in temperament she was Ethan's baby. She followed a schedule from the moment she was born. A slight crankiness signaled her desire for food. Not crying. She rarely worked herself into a good cry. Too undignified, I suppose. After nursing, she slept, waking up perfectly content to watch and grunt and pummel her little arms and legs for an hour or so until another feeding and later to explore the mobile Ethan placed above her bed. She never woke us in the night, sleeping until five or six in the morning from the beginning.

All in all, a fascinating if controlled little creature. Her father's daughter.

Matilda changed her mind as soon as we told her we were expecting and came that Christmas and again for Tori's birth. Joshua and Eleanor came too, for a couple of weeks. They surprised us with news of their planned return to Washington.

"I've given notice to the company," Joshua said. "Told them I'd stay on a couple more months. I don't belong in business. I'm taking a position with the Council of Foreign Affairs, Washington office."

Eleanor smiled more often, as she did now. "We're checking out condos while we're here. We want to buy one in the District."

Later over a meal, Joshua alluded to his previous fall from power. "It was a long time ago, and it's over. I don't want to waste the rest of my life doing things I'm not really interested in."

When we were with the family, I got to feed Tori and that's about all. Ethan practically fought with them to hold her himself. Joshua became her slave. Eleanor and Matilda handled practical considerations, like bathing her and spending hours buying clothes for her. I think each of the three saw themselves reborn in her, as I suppose happens with each new generation. No wonder God chose to come to us as a helpless, tiny baby.

In the months before Tori's birth, I returned to something I hadn't done since college. In the extra time, I wrote two articles. Both were published, one in *State Department Magazine* about my evacuation experience and one in a religious journal about how I'd come closer to God as a result of living in countries where Christians were in the minority. I thought I'd be bored at home by myself so much, especially with Ethan's globetrotting, but found I wasn't. I jotted down ideas I had for other articles.

As soon as I was rested after Tori's birth, Ethan took off a couple of weeks, and we flew to the Island. As I expected, Tori was a perfect traveler.

The slow Island days charmed us into a grateful laziness, tuned us to nature's schedule of tides and ripe fruits and vegetables and glorious sunsets.

Early one evening, when Matilda was at a church meeting, Ethan checked on the sleeping Tori in her basinet, then joined me on the porch to watch the departing sun's rays paint the waters a shocking fuchsia below the house. A flicker pecked dully against an aging tree, and we inhaled forest serenity along with the earthy smell of decaying tree stumps and leaves.

"It's okay, not being a political officer," I said. "You were right. I'm not cut out for it. But, except for American citizens service, I'm not sure I'm cut out for consular work either."

"So specialize in ACS work."

"It's the hours, the being on call 24/7."

"You're not on call quite so much with visa work."

"I hate it. I feel so sorry for the people I refuse."

He was silent, and I thought I'd lost him to a meditation on the rippling water until he turned to me. "Write an article about it."

"About what?"

"What we were talking about."

"I don't follow you."

"You have this concern for the underdogs of the world. Why don't you become an expert on migration, the desire of people for countries not their own, something like that? Write articles about it. Being in the Foreign Service, you've got a perfect window on the issue. And it's something you could do on and off as you have the time."

I settled one elbow on the arm of the glider and rested my chin in my hand. His words cascaded into such possibilities that they jolted me as though I'd touched a live electrical wire. "Okay, I'll think about it."

* * *

A few days before we were to leave, Ethan and I and Tori returned to the house after a walk to Madrona Harbor via the beach. We had one of those backpack baby holders that Ethan carried Tori in.

I spoke to Matilda, sitting in a chair on the porch looking at a card of some sort, before I turned to help Tori out of the back pack. She had gone to sleep and barely stirred when Ethan took her to put her in the bassinet.

I scrutinized Matilda. "Tildy, are you all right?"

"I—well, I found this card. You know, I've been going through things. It was a Christmas card from your mother."

I sat in the porch swing next to her chair, leaned forward, and waited.

"It was—the last thing I got from them, but you didn't seem to know anything about it, and I saw no reason to make things worse for you. I forgot about it, what with everything that happened. I had buried the card with the others that year."

We both stared at it, graced by a picture on the front of the Madonna and child.

Matilda held it out. "Here, why don't you read it?"

I took it and devoured the few paragraphs.

> We wish we could be with you this Christmas, dear Matilda. I know it must be hard to endure the first Christmas without Ray.
>
> Perhaps some good news will cheer you. We're expecting! Yes, after all these years, another child. We are delighted beyond measure. John and I go around hugging each other.
>
> Kaitlin has been such a blessing to us. We wanted more children, and it's finally happened. Isn't it wonderful?
>
> Strange how God works. I was determined to keep my hand in consular work, figured someday they'd drop that silly thing about having to resign when you get married. And now they have.
>
> But guess what? After all my ranting about injustices to the female sex (I still think I was right to protest, because if I hadn't fought against the box that society tried to put me in, I'd never have had the wonderful experiences I've had), now I find I don't want that right now. At the moment I want to take care of John and my children in this wonderful but uprooted life we lead.
>
> I've worked it out of my system, the bitterness I felt over being forced to resign. It's not that I wasn't called to that job. I was, and I

should have able to continue. It's that I'm called to something else now, and I've fallen in love with it.

Funny how God works. You just can't put God in a box. He's always surprising you.

Love from us both at this time of celebration of the Savior's birth:

Vicki and John

I put the letter on the table so my tears wouldn't soak it.

Matilda got up and hugged me to her and stroked my hair, like so often when I was growing up. She didn't sit down, though, just slipped into the house after that.

A few moments later Ethan sat beside me. "Mind if I read it?"

I nodded.

It seemed a long time before he returned my mother's card to the table. I think he read it several times.

When I could talk, I said, "You know, I've been so concerned that Mama and Daddy's work got carried on, that their killers didn't win."

"I know. Since we first got to know each other. Right here."

I leaned into him as he put his arm around me. "I guess it doesn't have to be carried out in only one way."

"No."

"I do so wish they could be here with their grandchild right now."

"So do I. And with their son-in-law, too."

His unexpected words surprised me, and I laughed, and the laughter seemed good, like God had created it.

Ethan kept us rocking, gently, while I got it all out. "I'm pretty sure what delayed my parents from leaving the townhouse that day. I bet my mother suffered a touch of morning sickness, and my father stayed with her. If he hadn't, he wouldn't have been there to hold her in those last moments. It would have devastated him. Better that he give his life with her, I think."

"Ah."

"And there's another thing, too. In a way, I'll be able to fulfill the decision she never got to carry out. She's living through me again."

I went to check on Tori. She was awake. I changed her, wrapped her in a blanket, and brought her to sit in my lap on the swing while Ethan's arm kept me warm.

Tori was starting to gurgle sounds, but this evening, she stayed silent, just moved her head from time to time and seemed fascinated by the gentle swing of the glider and the darkness that crept down.

I spoke into the silence. "You know, I doubt my mother was thinking much about her career in those last moments. If she had any time to think—and I hope she had very little—I expect she was thinking of those she loved."

"Knowing your mother, I expect so."

An owl hooted from a tree on the other side of the house. Ethan's chest rippled with his quiet breaths against my head while Tori made little movements within my arm.

"Women in my mother's time felt guilty for working," I said. "Now they feel weird for not working. Kind of a freak, out of the mainstream. Of course, most mothers have to work whether they want to or not because of money needs."

"Except we can manage it financially if you choose to stay home."

"Yes, but I could have a professional career. Should I feel guilty because I'm not interested in breaking a glass ceiling?"

"Darling, I'm a man. A white, Anglo-Saxon, Protestant one, at that. I can't answer for you. We agreed once not to put God's calling in a box. Didn't Jesus call people to different things? He told Peter not to get wrapped up in John's calling, didn't he? Or what about different callings at different times? I don't think you should let society dictate what you do any more than your mother did."

"Maybe I'll write an article about it."

Darkness blackened the water, but lights on the island across from us peeked around trees, thrusting through the night.

I knew what I would do.

47

Ethan barged in the door, dropped his briefcase to the floor, and threw his coat on the couch. "We've got it."

I looked up from a tower of blocks Tori and I were building. Or, rather, I was building. Tori, at ten months, was not into blocks. She preferred to drag her worn stuffed doll into the kitchen and play with the cans, pots, wastebasket, and other goodies she found in the kitchen cupboards.

To an onlooker, I might be the child, and she the mother, babbling comments now and then to spur me on. The blocks were a lovely colored set from Eleanor and Joshua, and I hated to see them unused.

Tori jerked around to all fours, the better to crawl to her father, her diapered bottom grazing the tower and toppling it to the floor with soft clacks. She paid no attention to it. Daddy was home.

"The job we wanted? Damascus?"

"Ye-es. DCM in Damascus."

"That's great."

I watched the love affair between father and daughter as Ethan picked up Tori and whirled her in the air while she chortled and giggled.

He stopped and held her up. "Do you realize this child is a second-generation Foreign Service brat? Probably talk Arabic before she talks English."

He sat on the couch and put her on his lap facing him.

Tori had developed a baby language that seemed to entrance her as she played with sounds, none of which were intelligible to us. "Glop da wop bop," she crooned, staring into Ethan's face and twisting his tie around her fists as though for emphasis.

Gently removing the tie from her grasp and tossing it over his shoulder, he said, "Why, yes, Madam Ambassador, I agree we should sign the trade treaty with the Lilliputians as soon as possible."

"Buup."

I left father and daughter to their diplomatic tête-à-tête and finished putting supper on the table. By putting my mind to it, I managed decent meals now. Some of my dishes were a bit different. I didn't always follow the recipe if it seemed too much trouble. After all, overseas one had to improvise.

Ethan munched on the French toast at the end of supper. "I thought French toast was a breakfast dish."

"Of course it can be. But I thought it could be dessert as well. It's good and healthy, too, if I make it with whole wheat bread and egg substitutes. You don't like it?"

"Of course I like it. Healthy and good. Can't beat that."

After eating, we cleaned the kitchen, bathed Tori, and put her down for the night. Ethan retreated to the study to work on papers he had brought home. I settled at my desk in an alcove of the breakfast area to begin an article I planned to send to the *Foreign Service Journal*.

I had resigned my commission as an FSO with no regrets, though I held on to the notion of reinstating myself in the future if writing and housewifery palled. So far they hadn't, although tonight I had difficulty concentrating.

After a while I gave up and moved to the living room couch to stare into space.

I realized Ethan had come into the room only after the couch cushions moved as he sat beside me. "Darling, what is it? Don't you want to go to Damascus?"

I moved closer to him, coldness receding as he put his arm around me. "Every once in a while, I just—get a little scared, that's all. I have to learn to go on anyway."

"My brave Squirt. You and Tori could stay here, you know, and I could go unaccompanied."

I stiffened. "Ethan Coverwood, do not even suggest such a thing. Of course we're going with you. While we still can, before something happens and families are ordered out."

He brushed his lips against my cheek before answering. "Something is always going to happen, isn't it? Back when I first picked the Middle East, I told Dad I was choosing it because it's never dull there. Something, I remember saying, is always happening. Looking back, I guess those were the words of a very brash young man, someone who wasn't given to thinking how it might affect his family."

I looked him in the face. "It's dangerous in lots of places. Look at Columbia. Look at Liberia. You chose the Middle East because you feel called there."

"Yes, but do you?"

How could I explain it to him? "Just because I'm scared sometimes doesn't mean I don't feel called, too. Lots of times Christians are scared. Even Jesus was. So was Esther."

"Technically, Esther wasn't a Christian."

I poked him in the ribs, harder than I meant to. He winced. "Trying to keep to the facts, ma'am."

"What I mean is that I think both of us are here for such a time as this, like you said once. Like Esther."

"You and your father. You told me he said we were never safer than when we were in the middle of God's will."

"We don't have a choice but to go on then, do we?"

"I guess we don't."

"I just remembered something. My parents talked of going to Damascus but decided to go to Washington instead. Now I'm finally going there. To Damascus, I mean."

"One of the oldest cities in the world," Ethan said. "We can see the street called Straight, where the apostle Paul walked. Museums, mosques, churches, remnants of the old Hejaz railroad that went to Saudi Arabia—"

"The one Lawrence of Arabia attacked?"

"Right."

"Hmm. I think I feel some articles coming on. Maybe a story, too."

"Do you?"

"I think I've found my calling."

ANN GAYLIA O`BARR

Life in the "enchanted kingdom" is nothing like she thought.

Recent grad Kate McCormack, saddled with college debt, has limited options…until she accepts an offer to teach English in Saudi Arabia. Plunged into a foreign world, she's homesick and lonely, stuck in a gilded prison where women aren't even allowed to walk around the block by themselves. The future stretches before her like a leaden sky.

Journalist Philip Tangvald, on the trail of a story about illegal immigration routes through the Middle East and North Africa, is intrigued by the feisty Kate, but wonders if he deserves to find love again. Too much loss and betrayal has burdened his life. First, his father, when he was eleven. And, a year ago, his wife. Now he's free of everything—except the guilt from his past—and wants to stay that way.

Two worlds, two hearts in exile, are about to collide. And when they do, might they find a new song to sing…in Babylon?

www.AnnGayliaOBarr.com
www.oaktara.com

ANN GAYLIA O'BARR

What really happened the night
Dr. Byron White disappeared?

Todd Edwards, the much-loved son of a minister, and Byron White, who suffered from an abusive father, grew up together under the tutelage of Todd's father in the changing culture following the Second World War.

Both settle into professorships at Adair University, but Byron's actions cause resentment and jealousy among several faculty members. Then, one evening, Dr. White disappears…and is never seen again. Todd fears that his harsh accusation against Byron for a heinous wrongdoing may have contributed to what happened. The unfinished business haunts Professor Edwards like a bad dream.

When Kim Frazier, Todd's student, stumbles on the mystery, she's convinced one of her professors is responsible and won't stop until she finds the perpetrator.

Only one person knows the startling truth.

*An on-the-edge-of-your-seat mystery
with a twist of betrayal and romance*

www.AnnGayliaOBarr.com
www.oaktara.com

searching for home

ANN GAYLIA O'BARR

He told her he'd kiss every freckle
when he came back from Haiti.
But he never returned.

Two years have passed since Hannah Forbes' fiancé left for an ill-timed trip to Haiti. A blanket of nothingness has covered her like asphalt ever since. But as she visits a friend on the Mediterranean island of Cyprus, excitement stirs for the first time since Vance's murder.

When she meets the handsome, ambitious U.S. diplomat Patrick Holtzman, her drive to go back to the "safe" computer programming job in Nashville fades and the artistic calling she thought she'd left behind emerges.

But Patrick has secrets of his own…and when they're revealed, in the midst of tumultuous world events, both must decide just how much they are willing to risk to find their hearts' home.

*An intriguing romance-mystery
set in the exotic but dangerous Middle East*

www.AnnGayliaOBarr.com
www.oaktara.com

ANN GAYLIA O'BARR

A chance encounter...
or their chance for love?

Single mother Brooke Rohmer takes a cross-country train trip when her only child leaves for the Army and possible combat duty in Afghanistan. Bitterly she remembers her former husband's abandonment of her and her son. Though she longs for a change in her life, her choices, in middle age, seem limited.

Neal Hudson, a U.S. diplomat, still mourns his wife's death in an accident in the Middle East. He can't rest until his questions are answered. Did their argument lead to her death? And why was she in Beirut that morning anyway? Then, as his train streaks westward from the nation's capitol to the fjord-studded Pacific Northwest, he discovers a devastating secret.

To risk love, Brooke and Neal must first overcome the past fear and anger that could destroy their future...together.

Experience love the second time around
with a twist of mystery

www.AnnGayliaOBarr.com
www.oaktara.com

About the Author

ANN GAYLIA O'BARR was a Foreign Service Officer in the United States Department of State from 1990 to 2004. Assignments included tours in U.S. embassies and consulates in Jeddah, Saudi Arabia; Algiers, Algeria; Montreal, Quebec, Canada; Tunis, Tunisia; and Dhahran, Saudi Arabia. Washington, D.C. tours included assignments in the Bureau of Population, Refugees, and Migration and in the Bureau of Intelligence and Research.

Ann is the author of five novels, *Singing in Babylon, Quiet Deception, Searching for Home* (a finalist in the 2008 Pacific Northwest Writers Association Literary Contest), *Distant Thunder,* and *A Sense of Mission* (all OakTara). Ann's published articles include: "French Diary," published in *State Department Magazine* (December, 1996); "Bringing In The Kingdom With 51 Percent," published in *Liberty Magazine* (November, 2005); and "Jeddah and the 1991 Gulf War" appeared on the *American Diplomacy* website (March, 2006).

"*A Sense of Mission* may be my favorite of all the stories I've written," Ann says. "Kaitlin, especially, is close to me and is the only character, so far, whose story has come to me in first person. I think *A Sense of Mission* is an answer to the many tragic events in the world today in which innocent people are harmed. Kaitlin became the fictional story of one lone person, far from perfect, who overcame and even redeemed such a tragedy. All the main characters suffered hurts, but they were loved by the families around them. Love redeemed a potential life of fear to a life where, one of them says, they can have faith 'to trust the good times.' As a letter from the beloved apostle states: 'Perfect love casts out fear.'"

Ann lives in Washington State. To email her:
IslandFiction@hotmail.com

www.AnnGayliaOBarr.com
www.oaktara.com